Family Medicine
Natasha Jeneen Thomas

Paperback ISBN: 978-1-7374143-0-8
Hardcover ISBN: 978-1-7374143-1-5

Published by Newham Wilcott

Follow the author at www.natashajeneenthomas.com

Cover Design: Robin Locke Monda
Author Photo: Tammy McGarity

FAMILY MEDICINE

NATASHA JENEEN THOMAS

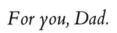

For you, Dad.

"The longest distance between two places is time."

- Tennessee Williams, *The Glass Menagerie*

PROLOGUE

I THINK IT ALL SOUNDS THE SAME. Being underwater. No matter how deep. No matter if you're dressed for swimming or drowning. I went beyond the red bricks and the white lights. I slipped. They say if you're upset, you should try to feel the earth beneath your feet—that it can ground you. They say if you're grounded, you can catch your breath—you can withstand anything. I'm not sure. Inside, a flash of lights turned my whole world green. I ran outside. I took off my heels. I felt the cool bricks beneath my feet. My breath still outpaced me. My toes reached for the edge of the walkway.

Okay, I can admit it. No one's ever on that side of the building, so I jumped. And then I remembered I wouldn't be able to catch my breath underwater, either.

Water fills the building next door. He asks me if I want a ride. Sir, you sleep in the park across from Mercy Hospital. Thank you for the offer, but you cannot give me a ride. The water was black and thick. But I see more water ahead. It's blue. It has crisp waves. It makes a light on the side of a building. It's not too far away. I could swim there, but that would probably get me arrested. I'm going to walk. I know the building. It's the Aquarium. I've had good moments there.

My head throbs. I'm in a soaking wet dress. He put me back on the red brick walkway without my permission.

Who goes to celebrate and ends up drowning? Well, I guess a lot of people. But hands pulled me up and out. I didn't want to gasp in his face, but I did. I

1

want to know how he even saw me. I'm wearing all black tonight. Even my toenails are painted black. I look at my toe rings as he pulls me to stand. My grandmother told me respectable girls don't wear jewelry on their feet. And maybe that's why I'm in this very predicament. Maybe I'm not a respectable girl.

He wants answers. So do I. He wants to know why I was floating on my face. I want to know who he is and why he stinks. I've already forgotten where I am. If he could remind me, that would be particularly helpful.

I know the other man's voice. The man who didn't see me. He's big. His voice is, too. I want to know why he's comforting her and why they're standing there—together.

I

THIRTY-FIVE MINUTES PASSED. Phoebe couldn't take the noise anymore. She shuffled to stand in Therese's wood-framed doorway.

"Therese! Your alarm. Again." She rubbed her eyes and pulled her fingers through her loose blonde ponytail. Her hand came to rest on the deep curve of her hip. "Therese!" Still nothing. Phoebe leaned into the side of the bed and nudged it with her knee, startling her roommate. Therese bolted straight up, sable brown hair cascading over her eyes.

"Did you hear that bird singing, Phoebs?"

"It's not a bird, hun; it's your alarm clock. It's been going off since six, which was about forty minutes ago."

"Ugh, no! Nooo!" Therese groaned. Six months. She had waited six months to audition again for Leigh Liliane. Her last shot. Now, she was about to miss it. "Why didn't you wake me up?!" she asked, looking at Phoebe.

She kicked both legs from underneath her white comforter. Her white-and-blue Coca-Cola halter top barely covered the bottoms of her breasts. She ripped off her red shorts and stood on them as they hit the floor inside out.

"I'm sorry, T." Phoebe shook her head and left the room.

By the time Therese made it to the station, she had missed the 7:15 A.M. train into Fiesta Heights. The thought of missing auditions made bile

3

surge in the back of her throat. She thought she might vomit. Instead, she sprinted from her silver Camry through the parking deck.

She rushed to her usual spot on the platform but not before bumping into a toddler's petite body. The tiny girl had been holding her father's leg. Her green-and-yellow sippy cup dropped from her chubby hand, and her father lunged for the cup. The toddler did, too.

"Oh, my goodness, I'm so sorry." Therese touched the man's back with her fingertips. He stared into her eyes, and then dropped his gaze to the floor. So did his daughter. Neither of them spoke a word. Neither responded to Therese's apology. Her stomach dropped. She walked to her spot, looking at the duo from the corner of her eye. A passing ache gripped Therese's ankle. She'd almost twisted it while trying not to fall on the little girl.

Therese would have to wait ten minutes before her chariot arrived. She hoped that would leave at least a five-minute window within which she could still audition. Her white, split-sole Balera shoes squeezed all the blood from her ankles. Even though she would not dance in them, she had made them tight. Tight enough to hold her together if the day fell apart.

As the blue, white, and green train came screeching to a loud stop, Therese pretended not to see her. She pulled her bag close to her chest. From the corners of her eyes, Therese scanned for a seat. One that allowed her to put her back against the wall. The woman approached and sat across from Therese, staring.

Stop looking at me, Therese thought. She glanced at her phone, wondering how her timing could be wrong every day. In six months, she had never been able to shake this woman. The first few encounters, the woman's messages doused Therese in confusion. She had walked up to Therese with a strange grin and missing eyebrows and said, "'Member me?" Therese had shaken her head "no," apologized, and looked for a corner seat.

Soon, the messages developed into brazen, unnerving verbal assaults. They had replaced the memory of her choreography and sabotaged

Therese's spring audition for Liliane's production of *Pain on a Random Wednesday*. Today, Therese fought off a childish urge to burst out laughing at the woman—at the absurdity of it all.

"Hey!" the woman began.

Therese looked up. The woman was missing more teeth today and had dyed her hair the color of red velvet cake. Layers of patchwork blue and purple fabric flowed over her petite body. Evil-eye jewelry on thin silver chains draped her neck, wrists, and ankles.

"Yes?" Therese replied.

"Not gonna say 'hi?' You know, your mother has totally blown this whole thing out of proportion. What happened is not my fault. Plus, your grandpa's got *All-Timers*, and I'm the only one who figured out the whole thing was manmade."

Therese gazed at her phone. *I don't want to be rude. Please go away.*

The woman's nostrils flared.

"Really, Summer?! Wow! The entire family is against me now. And that's fine. But you, Summer? C'mon! Is your mother telling you to do this? Don't be like her. She's vindictive, and all she does is lie."

The woman's stories of scandalous dementia and Therese's mother unsettled her because she couldn't remember the last time they'd spoken. Therese knew her mom's love had not faded. It just needed time and space. What's more, she knew her mother loved her family. And everyone in it. She brought kindness to the world. Her life lived on the opposite side of the road from scandalous and vindictive.

Suddenly, Crazy Train Lady (as Therese thought of her) stood. It wasn't her usual stop, but she stood. She scrambled to gather her things: a tattered denim sling-purse, folders, gallon Ziploc bags full of dirt, and a stuffed, dusty sienna pillowcase.

"Tuh-rez," Therese responded at last. The woman stared. "My name isn't Summer. It's pronounced Tuh-rez."

"Oh God, you've gone batshit crazy!" The woman scoffed and rubbed her eyebrows for a hair to pull. "See you later, Summer. Oh, and this is my train, by the way. If you don't like it, tough!"

Pretending to read on her phone, Therese kept her head bowed. She left it that way so long she almost missed her own stop. When she realized she had arrived, her heart sank. She had not marked or rehearsed any of her routine. She needed to practice. Especially today. There would be no mirror. There would be no reflective companion pulling her from one move, posture, or point to the next.

Evan wouldn't be auditioning with her, either. After nearly ten months with him as her partner, she floundered in routines without his guiding holds and tosses. She had been shocked when he announced he had chosen a better partner. She had wanted to beg him to reconsider, but she couldn't get rejected twice. She didn't think she would survive it. Instead, she tried to forget the warmth of his arms. The strength of them. She just wanted simple love. In naivety, she had tried to squeeze it out of their dance holds. Of course, she had failed.

"Therese Hughes-Baldwin! A beautiful name. Distinguished, in fact." Therese scrambled into the studio where some classmates and other competitors sat silently around the perimeter of the floor, gloating. Ballet bars hovered over their heads, and the room waited. "Shame to see it burdened by such an overwhelmingly mediocre, predictable woman like you, dear."

"Madam, I truly apologize."

"Please! Latecomers have one, no two, fatal flaws: lack of discipline and selfishness. And how could a dancer ever be selfish, Therese? Dance is about giving—giving interpretation to life! This very well may be your last performance in my studio. Begin!" Madam Liliane stood in the middle of the studio, dressed in black velvet and black dancer's shoes. She placed her folded hands on her left hip.

Therese turned to the nearest wall as tears threatened the last shreds of her dignity. She removed her sweats in the haste of humiliation and clumsily knocked her bun back and down to the nape of her neck. A sob began to squeeze and burn the insides of her throat. Since she'd first found herself in Boca Raton a year ago, dancing for Leigh Liliane had been her sole reason for being. She was there taking her chance on the biggest dream she could muster. Stripped down to her leotard and tights, she dropped to the floor to put on her ballet shoes. Then, she straightened her back and stood in the center of the room. Therese swiped her thumb against a silver ring on her forefinger.

"EXCUSE ME, MA'AM. Would you like to support the South Daytona Dance Troupe?" Therese had arrived one August day last year in downtown Daytona Beach, Florida. Between two sets of lampposts, twelve middle school-aged girls in teal and black clustered together, wiping bangs and sweat from their faces. They held posters and stood behind rented folding tables.

"Uh, sure," Therese had responded. She pulled her wallet from her backpack. "How much?"

"Well, you can get a real silver ring for just ten dollars," a little girl with strawberry blonde hair answered. "It's real silver. If we sell enough, we can go to the 2006 nationals."

"Aw, that's awesome!"

"Yep," the little girl replied. "I want to be a dancer when I grow up."

Therese smiled and handed her a bill. "Me too."

"Ma'am, which ring do you want?" a girl with a dark brown ponytail and teal bow asked.

"Uh, how about you choose?" Therese waited, smiling.

"How 'bout this one?" The girl tried the ring on each of Therese's fingers. It was too loose until she reached Therese's right forefinger. "Perfect! This is going to be your good luck charm!" she exclaimed.

"I hope so!" Therese's eyes sparkled. "Thank you! And good luck at nationals, guys!" she said as she drifted down the sidewalk.

Daytona's bustling Harley-Davidson bike shop livened what it could of downtown. A defunct nightclub towered over the neighboring post office. Two beach bums and a bike with rope in the spokes sat on the white steps. Therese looked around, frustrated with herself. She wondered how she would make it three hours from the little town limits of Daytona to the full-on glitz of Boca Raton.

Three dollars and thirty-eight cents remained in her wallet. Her gas needle pointed to the last quarter of her car's tank. In true Therese fashion, she had lost her driver's license. Her cell phone was down to six percent of its battery life, and the car charging port seemed to have blown a fuse.

Hunger twisted her belly as seafood smells warmed her nose. She followed the scent of fried shrimp until she arrived at Dot's Seafood. The bell tied to the door announced her entrance. She stood smelling grease, fries, and catfish while she tried to catch the eye of the man hustling back and forth from the kitchen to the counter. His name badge read "Jimmy."

"What can I get ya, hon?"

"Um." She looked down and into the cloth wallet in her hand, then to the plastic-covered menu taped to the counter.

"Wanna shrimp basket? It's $3.99." Jimmy looked impatient. He tapped on the counter and stuck his blue Bic behind his ear, glaring into the kitchen. He breathed like a bull.

"Well, I've never been here before."

"Look, baby girl, we have shrimp baskets on Friday. Today's Friday. You want one? It's $3.99. If that's too much, give me a dollar. Dot's in the back. She won't notice."

"Sure." Therese pulled out a dollar, and the glint of her silver forefinger ring caught the waiter's eye.

"Damn, you're pretty." Jimmy looked up. Her green eyes set against brown skin, shielded by a massive head of curly hair. "You're not from Daytona. Where you visitin' from?"

Therese raised her eyebrows and sighed. "I've been riding so long I can't even remember."

"You know what, baby girl?" Jimmy whispered. "Put your money away."

Therese found herself walking out of Dot's Seafood with a free shrimp basket and two extra hush puppies. The heat of cooked food warmed its red-and-white carton, burning the palm of her right hand. The dollar she'd wanted to give Jimmy stuck to the greasy paper bag. Therese's mind swirled, not quite sure what happened. She'd heard of Southern hospitality and small-town charm, but she'd never received anything free. She hadn't even had to flirt with ole Jimmy.

"WILL SOMEONE, PLEASE, for the love of all that is holy, play the song?!" Madam Liliane spoke up and into the air of the studio ceiling. "Sophia dear, you have no idea what you're doing. Sit down."

Therese had been standing in the middle of the room, waiting for her music to begin. Sophia, a member of the dance company, was fidgeting with the CD player. While Therese waited, the sound of that singing bird from the morning came back to her mind. It fell as a soft and distant enchanting call. She seemed to remember black branches against a silver sky. They had swayed in rhythm to the sound of rushing water in her ears. She still couldn't be sure if she'd been dreaming.

The birdsong sounded identical to Therese's alarm clock. But it also mimicked the beginning of Nikiya's entrance in Liliane's urban interpretation of *La Bayadere*. By the time the song was noticeable in her daydream, her competition was set in a chorus of lilting giggles.

"Dance!" Madam Liliane yelled. Therese's eyes stretched, and her mouth fell open in shock. She had missed the opening of the song.

In perfect lines, though, Therese's arms lifted overhead as her chiseled body narrowed to the point of her toes. She moved from the daydream of the birdsong to the daydream of mesmerizing her ballet lover, Solor. She executed each move with control. The glory of being beautiful and perfect in her dance burst on display. Girls in the studio scowled and shifted on their thin behinds as they watched Madam Liliane's eyes brighten from black holes to lagoons of admiration. She loved Therese's dancing as much as she hated Therese's apparent shiftlessness. Therese reached the end of her piece with what appeared to be no exertion at all. By the end of the routine, she had claimed her place as the most graceful and gifted in the room.

Seven hours later, though, Therese's talents would mean nothing. She out-danced all who came for auditions this August day. But she had not danced away Madam Liliane's contempt for her tardiness and excuses. Therese had not been selected. She had not earned the honor of dancing as Nikiya.

She limped out of the studio breathless, her ego suffering a sucker punch to the gut. She called Phoebe.

"So?" Phoebe's bubbly voice answered the phone on the first ring. "I've been waiting all freakin' day!"

"Order sushi," Therese replied. She hung up and slid back into her sweats.

Standing at an abandoned bus stop just outside the studio, Therese noticed the sky's topaz beauty. She pulled her sunglasses out of her dance bag and placed them on her head. What was left of her bun unraveled as Therese rummaged through her bag for her headphones. She realized she had left them on her dresser in her rush to leave home. Now, she had no device to drown out the insults she would hear from the woman on the way back home.

"Welp, you look like crap now, Summer!" Crazy Train Lady shook her head. She no longer had the pillowcase. She fished around in her new CVS bags. She pulled out lotions, African black soap, and insect repellent. "Here!" She reached toward Therese and laughed. "Want a nail clipper?"

Therese pulled her sunglasses down from her head and over her eyes, fighting to stifle her bitter, salty tears.

2

"LET ME GO. I gotta go after her!" Victor placed his thick fingers on the insides of Mair's thighs. He let his square nails dig into her ivory white flesh.

Mair sat tensed with her legs in the shape of a four around Victor's waist. She had perched herself on a mahogany plank before him. Her head floated inches from the burgundy walls.

"What?!" Mair exclaimed. "You're going to go *after* her?!" She slid back and away from his groin, pushing his chest back and closing her legs at the same time. "I swear, Victor. You do that, and I'll drive your car into the Harbor."

Victor stood back. He zipped up his gray slacks. Looking down, he calmly pressed the heated wrinkles from his shirt. He searched for a mirror. Disgraced, Victor didn't want to also appear savage. That would be easier without his mistress's lipstick smudged across his mouth. He found a small pewter-framed mirror sitting just above the first coat rack. At five foot six, he could only see down to the bridge of his large, sharp nose without standing on his toes. Victor's silky black hair had been cut and coiffed into a helmet-shaped pompadour. The front swooped up and to the right. The blackness and smallness of his eyes looked not quite human. He didn't find any makeup on his face or neck but found the tiniest pimple between his bottom lip and the border of his goatee. "Hmm," he said. The sight of it disgusted him. His olive skin never blemished.

"Hmm?" Mair still sat on the mahogany coat-check counter. Moisture from the heat of her behind and the friction of their foreplay clung to the surface beneath her. "What are you saying that for?"

Victor's thoughts battled against a rushing wind in his head. The clamor of a bustling restaurant seemed to recede into a black hole the second his almost-fiancée had walked through the swinging coatroom door. She'd gasped deep enough to inhale the whole world around them. She had screamed and stumbled as she turned on her heels to leave, slamming her head into the mahogany door threshold. A framed picture of a black horse had stared her in the face. Cameras had flashed. A passing waiter resembled a spinning jewelry-box ballerina. All in black, he'd stood up on his toes, and his round serving tray floated above the melee on his outstretched hand, parallel to the floor and the chaos below.

"Jesus! Now I'll have to go find her." Victor rolled his eyes as he repeated his sentiments. He grabbed his light gray jacket from the top of a nearby rack, patted his thighs and backside for his keys and wallet, and pushed his left hand against the coatroom door.

"Wait!" Mair released a futile yell. He'd already determined to leave and still couldn't hear anything but wind. Victor's shoes created a *tip-tap-tip-tap* as he sprinted past the onlookers. He knew some of them would be yelling his name. It had been Victor, after all, who had called them to the Inner Harbor's best seafood restaurant for a surprise proposal to his girlfriend of two years.

He had made this other girlfriend aware, too. Except instead of an engagement party invitation, Mair had received notice their four-year relationship would end as soon as his nuptials were complete. She had not agreed nor conceded. Instead, under advice, she had shown up to the party, instructed to use whatever powers necessary to sway him. She had been fine with being second place. Having no place, though, would not do. Still, her wiles had failed. Victor left her amidst strangers' abandoned jackets and scarves in a restaurant where seafood allergies meant she could not even eat the food.

Mair's silk magenta spaghetti-strap dress clung to her thighs and hips. Despite the fact that it revealed the crease of her behind from the rear, she hadn't bothered to wear panties. She hopped down, cursing to herself, and wiped the counter with her left hand.

"Hate him!" she said, pulling off the ruby promise ring he'd given her just three months before. She slid the ring in her unusual dress pocket, telling herself she didn't need him. Mair looked around the room. Mahogany lined and framed everything. The walls sported forest green and burgundy with stripes in some places. The room's shadows suggested the fragrance of cigar smoke. Instead, the antiseptic smell of Victor's breath and body lingered. He smelled of medical cleaning solutions and the alcohol of a stringent mouthwash. It sickened her at times.

Mair grabbed her clutch from the floor, where it lay in a silver sequined heap. Beside it lay her wrap and black, strappy heels. "Mair, what are you doing?" she asked herself and sighed. So that she could see herself in the round mirror, she pulled a chair up and stood on it barefoot. She peered at her face. "Really?" she said laughing, though her appearance embarrassed her more than it humored her. Purple eyeshadow and black liner meant to accent her deep-set brown eyes were smeared down the left side of her face, sitting on her cheek like a bruise. Her lip gloss had been kissed away. Only a few small flecks of its glitter remained right at the crest of her top lip. She grinned and noticed harsh laugh lines polluting her face.

"Okay, Dr. Victor Jacobs, I want a refund. You were at least supposed to Botox away these wrinkles."

Mair licked her fingers to wipe the displaced makeup from her face, pressed her wavy, auburn hair behind her ears, and rubbed her lips with the back of her right hand. She held a taupe tube between her forefinger and thumb and squeezed it. Gloss bubbled to the opening. She bent down in the mirror and puckered her lips. A deep bang came suddenly from the right side of the room. Her head snapped around to look.

"Where is she?" a creamy-skinned, hourglass-shaped woman demanded. She wore a floor-length, green dress, her hair gathered back into an elaborate bun. Her words sounded as if she were speaking Spanish. "Where is she?!" she yelled again. Her arched eyebrows touched as she scowled. The woman's presence stunned Mair into silence. The woman pivoted on her golden high heels and left the room before the door swung closed, calling Mair "dee-sgust-eeng" on the way out. The word disgusting had never stung so much.

Mair stretched her long, thin legs down from the chair, left then right. She trembled inside. No lie she told herself would assuage the shame of being a man's caught mistress. Never, ever. She gathered her belongings and slipped her toes back into her shoes. Her heels pressed down on the back straps. She sat on the chair and didn't move until a crowd started pouring in an hour later. Mair wondered why so many people carried coats in August. She also wondered where her rival had gone. She slithered along the walls and out of the room. Mair held her head down as she passed the hostess station. She stepped outside and faded into the Baltimore summer night.

3

"Phoebs, I'm heading out." Therese stood in the hallway by Phoebe's bedroom door, awaiting a response. *She's waiting for my feet to disappear,* she thought. "Phoebe, okay, I'm sorry," Therese spoke out into the quiet again. She walked to the front door and put on her black Keds. Though she lingered for it, the sound of an open door or a "see ya later" never came. Nothing bade her adieu but silence.

Sushi night had ended with raised voices and thrown food. Phoebe had asked too much.

"T," she'd said, "are you going back to the studio?" And "T," she'd asked, "are you sure you didn't make it?" Then "T, what did Liliane or Leigh—what's her name again?—what did she say?" Her grand finale found itself in the suggestion that Therese had intended to sabotage her audition because Evan ditched her.

"Like, wouldn't it be kind of a betrayal to do *La Bayadere* without him? Like maybe subconsciously you wanted to blow it or something?" Phoebe had suggested.

Therese had punted the last of her edamame and fried rice across the living room. She wiped her mouth on the inside of her sweat-scented leotard and said, "See ya in the morning, Phoebs." She left grains of sesame-oiled rice stuck to the carpet. Dressed in a dance bra and tights, she'd walked to her bedroom and slammed the door. A cry stifled since early

15

morning flowed out in low wails. She lay on her back and pulled down sections of hair to braid. Norah Jones sang "Come Away with Me" as tears slid backward into Therese's ears. But in an hour, when her anger had passed, Therese wanted to clean the floor, then share popcorn and laughs with her roommate and best friend. Phoebe always soothed Therese with her tiny blonde presence.

"Phoebs!" she had yelled from behind her closed door. "I'm gonna make popcorn."

Heading to the kitchen, Therese's heart had lifted, thinking she heard laughter. But standing just outside her door, she'd heard Phoebe speaking in hushed tones. Therese stood in the dark, arched hallway between their rooms for a few seconds, dipping her head to listen. Phoebe spoke low and in a cadence Therese hadn't recognized. But after the day she'd had, she didn't have the energy to try to make out the conversation.

The next morning, Therese knocked and Phoebe still didn't answer her door. Therese worried a tad. But time, the lack of it, pushed her out the door before making amends. Back to work. Back to the platform. Back to the Fiesta Heights train. Back to the woman.

She'd prepared by looping her headphones around her neck. They'd be a distraction for her. She hoped they would be a deterrent for her metro assailant, too.

An odd quiet filled the Saturday morning train. Therese looked out the windows to the left. Boca Raton, as Florida's crown jewel, sparkled with unrivaled allure. Looking out the windows of the train, Therese watched tiny-chested women jogging with the *swish-swash* of ponytails moving side to side, running in place at intersections. Men in their convertibles tried to look casual despite the insecurity of wind-vulnerable hairpieces.

Selfies were being taken outside the Kendra Scott store in The Shops at Arian's because why not? Therese laughed to herself. *How can everything look so perfect?* Life moved in sun and slow motion like one of those "Come to Jamaica and feel alright" commercials. It didn't reflect Therese's life, though. She couldn't afford a purchase anywhere inside The Shops at Arian's, except maybe at Justice or some other kids' store. And in a town of nearly one hundred thousand people, Therese was one of only forty-four black women. People never guessed her ancestry at first. It was the green eyes.

She turned to look back into the train, then over her shoulder, and back in front of her. *Where is she?* she wondered, ready to slap on head-phones in a heartbeat. The Crazy Train Lady didn't show for the first time in six months, and Therese worried she'd pop up from under her seat. Awful as they were, she'd come to expect her twice daily assault sessions. Today she'd made it to work without seeing her.

The almost-school-season filled the bookstore with buzzing middle-aged moms and kids in flip-flops and shorts sets. The café's line trailed halfway to the north book section, which annoyed Therese. She rushed to clock in, but not before being poked on the left arm. "Hey there, gor-geous!"

"Dara! Oh, my goodness, so good to see you!" Therese beamed, see-ing her favorite patron with the generous tipping hand.

"Same here! I've been traveling a ton. Just finished running one of my workshops in Delaware." Dara's crystal blue eyes hid behind glasses that aged her by at least twenty years. She tucked her red bob behind her ears and dug into her purse. "But I brought you something!"

She wore square-topped French manicure nails from the drugstore, no less than seven charm bracelets, and a red, long-sleeved blouse, despite the weather. She had tucked it into a floor-length cotton skirt patterned with a design that resembled peacock feathers. Dara looked like a model from a Chico's ad. An enormous aquamarine engagement ring adorned her right hand. Therese had complimented her on that piece of jewelry the first time they'd met. Dara had explained it had been given to her by her first husband. The ring was a showstopper—almost her trademark. From her bag, she pulled a thin, silver charm bracelet with one charm, ballet shoes, dangling from a link.

"I've been dying to know about your auditions!"

Therese's gut dropped as she offered her wrist for Dara to fasten the bracelet. She'd forgotten she'd even mentioned the auditions to her.

"Oh wow, thanks, Dara. You certainly didn't have to do that! You gonna be here a little while today? Gotta catch up!"

"What time are you getting off?" Dara asked, smiling. "I'm running another workshop not far from here this afternoon. If you can make it, I'd love for you to stop by and see a little bit of what I do."

"Uh…" Therese squinted and looked away.

"Oh," Dara interrupted, lifting her hand. "If it's weird to hang out with a customer outside work, I totally get it. No pressure."

Of course, now there's pressure, Therese thought.

"I have nothing to do after work tonight. Of course, I can," Therese responded. "But let me go get clocked in and get started, so I won't have to hear his mouth." She looked over her shoulder and motioned to the café manager, Forrest, then rolled her eyes and laughed.

"Here." Dara rushed to pull a flyer from her purse. "Here's tonight's information. It's not really open to the public, but I figured you may find it interesting. Remember, no pressure." She placed a gentle touch on Therese's arm and tilted her head.

Therese folded the flyer into the back pocket of her black pants and trotted behind the café counter to clock in. "Who's next?" she asked as she ran by.

4

VICTOR PANTED THROUGH HIS SPRINT from the restaurant. He opened his car door. Inside, the coolness of the charcoal, leather Audi seats helped settle the raging humiliation in his gut. It had been his goal to keep these worlds separate. Forever. His tiny black eyes searched his face in the rear-view mirror. Splotches of red speckled his neck and cheeks. His brow furrowed. Readjusting the mirror and putting the car in reverse, he backed out of his spot and his tires squealed through the parking lot. He never noticed the gathering crowd watching him from the restaurant entrance walkway. Women folded their arms across their chests and clung together in groups shaking their heads. Some had their mouths open in protracted gasps.

He reached to turn on the air conditioner but instead decided to roll down his windows. The smell of fish thickened the air around him. Victor whipped his head left, right. He tried to imagine where his girlfriend might have gone. He tried to remember why he wanted her.

Theirs was an empty, loveless relationship, full only of the promise of clout. Victor had overlaid his long affair with Mair with this more strategic one because of where it could land him. An oral surgeon, he had education but no connections in a city that thrived on them more than most. Short, slight, and average-looking, pretty-people power would not open any doors for him. He hailed from nowhere important. His name rang no bells. Victor knew these things doomed him to nine-to-five office hours, an upper-middle-class salary, and weeklong vacations sufficient to post photos of online. But he wanted dominance—and this woman, though disappointing, was the easiest way to claim it.

Her looks placed her in the painfully mediocre box in his eyes. He preferred Asian women of all sorts. But he thought it would be impossible to break into their upper echelon's iron-clad inner circle. That hadn't stopped him from trying, though. He had moved to Ellicott City, the area with the highest density of Koreans in Maryland, to scout a wife. That effort left him frustrated and empty-handed.

Though love would have been a good hobby for him, it was power that seduced and secured him. Victor aspired for the dean's seat at the university's dental school. He had matriculated there but passed by the thinnest margin. He deemed himself special. With his hands there stood no doubt. He carried a gift. However, his skill never endeared him to a single professor. The girl—she held the right keys to the right doors just by virtue of her presence and pedigree. Her flippancy about her access to the highest of influential circles made Victor fantasize about choking her. She lived as Baltimore-medicine royalty. But when she met with uncle so-and-so from this university or that board, she saw it simply as a time for wearing sundresses and brunching. Victor had to find her now despite the banality of their relationship façade.

"Come on!" he yelled, chuckling at the red light at the intersection of President Street and Eastern Avenue. Flashing his brights, he continued to laugh, embroiled in frustration and ridiculousness. "She thinks she's gonna run my entire life," he said, punching the steering wheel. "Come ON!!!" he yelled again, challenging the traffic light as if he thought he could fight it. Traffic accumulated across from him, triggering the light to shine green.

Victor turned left and rode in silence, his beady eyes scanning the street. "She's not gonna be over here, it's way too close," he said as he sucked his teeth and sped up. "Ugh!"

The emptiness and wetness of Baltimore weeknight streets amazed him. Police parked beside closed buildings every few blocks. Victor didn't bother to slow down, though. He decided to turn left on Baltimore Street. His girlfriend worked at the hospital. He drove to the Greene Street entrance, parked, then reversed in confused haste.

He looped throughout downtown Baltimore for an hour before abandoning his car and walking to the Westminster Hall and Burying Ground. Though he frequented various cemeteries, Victor could clear his mind most in this place.

He pressed his face against the wrought-iron fence. His eyes closed, and his warm breath collided with the night's humid air. The red brick of Westminster appeared muddy in the streetlight. Victor looked at the mortar. Insignificant in composition, but mighty and necessary in role. He imagined the mortar turning from white to golden over its two-hundred-year tenure there. This plot of old Presbyterian land was the resting place of Maryland's once most powerful. It shouted to the Charm City, "Take up the torch!" There lay statesmen and founding fathers. It boasted Maryland-born American heroes. It paid tribute to national-anthem writers whose faces were immortalized in bronze along its walls. And, of course, it held Poe. Victor had never been intrigued or spooked by his writings, but Poe's personal story drew him. They were both motherless men of identical hair color, frame, and height. Victor's black eyes and narrow forehead were his only differences, at least in his mind. No, he wasn't a writer. But he was a master at creating mystery.

"How did you even get here?" Victor spoke out to the darkness, hoping his words would float to the poet's ears. He remembered the story. Edgar Allan Poe was discovered in a stupor at a pub in Baltimore hours from his home in Virginia. He had worn another man's clothes. Unable to command any words to explain how he came to be in such a state, Poe lay ill and dying in as macabre a way as his stories lived. And he had inspired Victor. What type of character possesses enough oddity for his name to be burned into the consciousness of every generation since he'd lived, even inspiring jocks and the name of an NFL football team?

Victor turned himself to look toward the sky, took a deep breath, and pushed himself from the bracing of the iron fence. His shoes clicked on the moist road as he walked slowly back to his car. Victor decided to drive home just as his cell phone rang. His heart dropped, then lifted and raced in his chest. It was his father.

"Victor!" His father didn't even wait for a hello. "Son, what the heck is going on?! Where are you? And who was that woman?"

"Dad…"

"No, Victor, I'm so sick of the stuff you pull. You can never just live life and do the right thing, can you? There's always a con, a trick, always some secret behind the scenes with you. What is wrong with you?!"

"Dad…" Victor tried again to interject, but his father continued to demand answers.

"Where are you? I'm coming to help. Have you found her? Did you try the hospital? Her house, maybe?!"

"Dad, I went to the cemetery awhile. Now I'm just going to go home."

Victor heard a second of silence. Then his father shrieked. Victor pulled the phone from his ear and gazed at it, smiling. "Are you insane?!" he could hear his father yelling. "You went to a cemetery to do what?! You're just going to go home? And you have no idea the whereabouts of the woman you brought fifty of your closest family and friends here to propose to?"

"Dad!"

"Shut up, Victor!" his father cried. "Son, I don't know where she is, but I know there is something seriously wrong with you. How could I have raised a son like this?! Do you know you ran right past her parents when you left the restaurant? Do you?!" Victor could hear a woman's voice in the background trying to calm Victor's father as he dissolved into heaving sobs.

Victor sat in silence, deep-burning guilt roasting his gut. He'd always known his father hated the man he'd become, but he'd never heard it until now. Though he'd managed to see success, Victor's ethics in life always scared his father. His striving for recognition left no tactic off-limits. Because of this, he'd had various brushes with the legal world. He had been a defendant in several theft cases and faced two charges of stalking academic competitors in high school. Caught, Victor had explained the stalking away as a joke—that he'd planned to just egg their homes or something harmless, even fun, in its juvenility. After the second complaint, though, a permanent restraining order had been enacted. It was something he had never disclosed on his college or dental school applications. It never showed up in background checks, either.

Guilt quickly turned to rage. Victor hung up on his father and continued driving. When he pulled into the first of the four full garages at his Columbia home, his phone vibrated. Before leaving the car, he sat with the door open, checking his cell phone's call log. He'd tuned out the sound of six missed calls, only one from his father. The remaining five were from Mair, and the phone vibrated in his right hand now. "Phoebe?" he chuckled, looking down at the caller ID. "Hell no."

He powered off the phone, grabbed his jacket, and stepped out of the car, reaching his arms straight up to the sky and arching his back. He pushed the top corner of the car door to shut it, reveling in the solid, deep, and smooth sound of it closing. "Nothing like luxury." He patted the top of the car as one would a puppy's head and turned to go into the house.

This was Tuesday night. Regardless of the shocking display of failure he'd put on this evening, tomorrow, during a regular day in the office, he'd be hailed as Ellicott City's best oral surgeon by patients and assistants. None of them had been there to see the evening. In the morning, his life of feigned normalcy could proceed, completely unencumbered by the repulsiveness of his truth.

VICTOR WOKE UP WEDNESDAY to the glaring sun coming through his windows. He'd always enjoyed the way its rays looked like a spotlight shining on the walls of his home, every surface turned a shade of orange, even the backsplash in the kitchen. That one looked more muted orange, though, as it had been tiled and not painted. He had purchased this home at the beginning of his second year in private practice. Victor saw his multimillion-dollar home as an investment. Not the property itself, but the look of wealth it communicated to the people in his world. His father, though, thought it idiotic.

Victor's thick toes looked almost identical to his fingers. He spread them on his carpeted floor. As he rose from bed, he folded himself forward to stretch. The black rectangular face of his cell phone caught his eye and made his stomach turn. Instead of powering it back on for an onslaught of calls and texts about what level jerk he'd achieved, he decided to turn on the television instead. News reports on every single station focused on the devastation left in the wake of Hurricane Katrina.

Victor stared in disbelief at Tuesday's footage of the floodwaters and rooftop-stranded Louisianans. His mouth hung open, and he backed up to the foot of his bed, lowering himself to sit on the edge. Between his preparing, plotting, and the pursuit that became his Tuesday, he'd missed news of the destroyed levees—and lives. Victor had lived through his share of tropical storms during his oral surgery residency in Miami. He remembered, now, how grateful he had been to have missed both hurricanes Charley and Frances. He'd never been closer than a television screen to anything like this. His heart dropped as he imagined himself in that predicament. Tears began to well in his eyes, but the news anchor's time announcement jolted him. He couldn't be late.

Steam billowed over the top of the shower door. Hot water rolled down Victor's face before scorching his back as he turned. Though his nails were already perfect, he spent five whole minutes cleaning them with a clear, plastic brush. Victor didn't think of a shower as a shower—it was a sterilization. Finally stepping out of the shower, his feet met a spongy mat.

He wrapped his waist in a stark white towel, then stepped to stand at his vanity. He was not a muscular man. His small brown nipples looked sad on his concave chest. Hurriedly, he stuffed his arms into the sleeves of a black terry cloth robe to hide his physical inadequacy from his own eyes. Throughout the grooming process, Victor did not apply typical colognes or deodorants. Instead, he used Medi-Pak and any other medical brand of grooming tools or creams his girlfriend would bring from the hospital. He aimed for a scent reminiscent of a strong, bleach-based bathroom cleaner.

Before leaving home, he decided to power his phone on. Ding after ding rolled in. He glanced at the log again, seeing calls had come in from the expected. The one missed call he was looking for had not, though.

"She must really be pissed," he said. He stood in his kitchen staring, biting his bottom lip, squinting, and tapping two fingers on the counter-top as he thought. He didn't know how he'd be able to correct this situation. His stomach sank. Losing her would be catastrophic—and he didn't know how to stop it.

But Victor loved his drive to work. Ellicott City had the cleanest streets. Pretty parks. Full foliage trees all year. As he started for his office, he hoped the drive would ease his mind.

"Good morning, Doctor!" Kelly smiled wide, revealing perfectly straight, overly whitened teeth. Leaning on her elbows, she shifted her weight onto the front desk sign-in counter. She was blonde, petite, and just over twenty-two years old. She also fought a serious infatuation with Victor. Kelly wore pink scrubs and white socks with pink heel patches that peeked out from her clogs. Her hair, just as bleached as her teeth, was pulled back into a low ponytail. She'd told the other women in the office she coordinated her Victoria Secret bra and panty sets to match her scrubs, just in case. And even though her bras were filled with more padding and wire than breasts, she always found a reason to jut them out or push them together when in Dr. Jacobs's presence.

Victor noticed the flirtation from Kelly and a few others among his office staff. He deserved the admiration, or so he thought. He pretended not to understand the power of the white coat. Had he been his average-looking self on the average street during an average day, no heads would turn for him, and he knew it. He wished his "girls" noticed his brand of genius. Victor doubted any of them paid much attention to the giftedness of his hands. He could remove wisdom teeth, create bone grafts for later implanting, or repair a facial laceration with uncanny precision, even in an outpatient setting. During his oral maxillofacial surgery residency rotations, his hands made him shine. Mair had been impressed, he remembered, watching him create a seamless suture repair of a scalp laceration. She'd stood as his assistant at the trauma center that night, pocket full of foil suture packets. She placed one foot atop the other, her eyes fixed on Victor's hands as he replaced a scalp that had been lifted by a sharp blow to the head. Their patient had been standing on a small boat intoxicated and hadn't noticed how low the bridge hovered until it peeled his scalp backward like a tin can lid.

"'Morning, Kelly." He entered the scheduling office, picked up his mail from the previous day, sifted through his faxes, and checked the sample closet. Kelly stood so close he could feel the hairs on her arm stand.

"Could you please call the rep? We need a few things," he said and looked directly into her face. She appeared to blush, but he couldn't quite tell over her pink explosion of an outfit. "Are you bright enough?" he quipped and jostled his left elbow into her side. "Stick with navy or forest green, maybe even purple scrubs." Victor hated bright colors, except for the orange walls of his home.

"Sorry." Kelly looked down. The earlier perkiness in her voice vanished. "I'll call them right away."

Victor walked back to his office, placing his bag and mail down in the hallway to free his hands and open the locked door. The cell phone vibrated again in his bag against the wall. He felt no urgency to answer even though he knew it could be important. He wished a hospital would call to tell him his father was dead.

Once in his office, he smirked. Oral surgery he could take or leave.

But hunting for victims made him tingle with satisfaction. He sat down, opened his laptop, logged into his electronic medical record, and stared at the beige-and-blue screen listing his patients for the day. Each patient had a chart of photos. The first, a simple profile picture of their face. Their charts also held digital files of flawless Gendex panoramic dental X-rays and Kavo CT scans—top of the line technology. He had been scheduled for four major procedures—one more than he typically wanted to perform on any given day. But it would be worth it. It would give him more money to stack, or spend, in another prestige-seeking endeavor. Between the major appointments would be a few quick follow-ups. Then he'd see the kid whose wisdom tooth extraction had been botched by another surgeon.

"What was that kid's name again?" Victor searched the schedule. "Chae… Joseph. Here it is." Victor scanned his demographic information and the tabs of the electronic medical record looking for a parent's identification. He found a home address, a Humana dental card identification number, phone numbers, and an email. "Come on, where is it, Joey?" He continued to look, clicking through each tab until he located the photo ID of Joseph's mother. Victor grinned, leaning back in his oversized black leather office chair with a deep, near-moaning sigh. His fingers wrapped around themselves in a tight clasp as he took in her picture. Leslie Chae. Forty-five years old. Maybe forty in the driver's license picture. Even in a black-and-white copied image, her stunning beauty shone. They would be in at 3:00 P.M., Victor's last appointment for the day. He pressed his top teeth into the pink of his bottom lip. "Perfect."

He scanned his schedule. No one else intrigued him quite as much. There were a few other possibilities, but some were too fat. Others had no children, therefore disqualifying them from his unwitting collection of porcelain-faced beauties.

"Let's get started," he announced to the room. Victor pushed his hands onto his comically large desk, lifting himself suddenly. He exchanged his white, starched coat he insisted on driving in for the other coat that lived in his office. The room held three mirrors, and Victor walked to each, his hands clasped behind his back. He leaned in, peering into his own eyes, finally posing in the middle of the room where he could be captured in them all. He was the light of interest in this room. He slid each hand back into its cool pressed pocket, gazing with his chin elevated just over his left shoulder.

5

INSIDE THE LOBBY of the Embassy Suites hotel, Therese stood gripping her folded café apron. She wrapped it over her arm, then folded it as small as possible and tucked it beside her elbow, holding it against her body.

"Ma'am, may I help you?" A concierge in a silk suit came smiling with folded hands, inches from her face. Therese frowned and took two steps back.

"Uh, yeah, I'm looking for a class. Um…" She pulled the folded flyer from her back pocket. "Um, led by Dr. Dara Clemens."

"Can I take a look?" The concierge leaned even closer. He read the flyer aloud, "Join us for the 150th Annual Costivak Workshop, hosted by psychiatrist and psychoanalyst, Dr. Dara Clemens." He smiled at Therese and placed his hands on his breastbone. "Oh, that sounds intriguing! I'd be afraid they would make me spill all my secrets, though!" he chuckled. "Looks like it's on the third floor. Room 300. Let me take you."

"Oh no, that's okay." Therese shook her head. "I can find it. Which way are the elevators?"

"To your right, ma'am." The concierge extended his arm in their direction.

"Thanks," she replied. For a few seconds, she watched dripping-wet kids in bathing suits run to the elevator, pushing the up button no less than five times a second.

The maroon-and-white spotted carpet of the banquet hall had a golden shield-shaped design in the middle of the floor. All thirty heads turned to Therese at the door, which slammed closed with a loud, deep boom.

She grimaced and dipped her head. "Sorry."

"Oh, Therese, so glad you could make it." Dara sat barefoot on the floor. "Please join us. Everyone, please say hi to my friend Therese. Can you open a space for her in the circle?" Therese pulled her apron in front of her chest and walked toward them as if on a four-inch balance beam. Once near the circle, she kneeled beside a very tan man with a beard and a glowing white smile.

"I'm Bob." He offered his hand to shake.

"Uh-uh! Bob! No introductions yet," Dara said. Therese looked around the circle as everyone laughed.

"Therese, we are going around the circle listing five things about us. Any five things." Dara pushed her hair behind her ears. "You're the last to go. Ready?"

"Uh, sure, I guess." Therese felt the beam of all sixty eyes in the room looking at her mouth. She licked her lips, shrugged, and smiled. "Uh, my name's Therese, which you've heard."

"No explanations, just a description," Dara interrupted. "For instance, when it was my turn, I said, 'My name is Dara Clemens. I'm from Winter Park, Florida. I've been married to a guy named Manny for twenty-eight years. We have one child. And I love croissants.' Understand?" Therese nodded. "Go ahead, try again."

The strict introduction protocol pulled a frown onto Therese's face. She never thought herself shy until this moment.

"Okay." Therese cleared her throat. A girl across the circle from her in a green sweater giggled. "Um, I'm Therese. I'm twenty-six. I love to dance. And I have weird dreams."

"One more," spoke a man with a small head and glasses.

"And, um," Therese continued, "I'm single."

The girl in green laughed again. This time, Therese squinted at her.

"Excellent, Therese." Dara nodded. "Please, everyone, move to our breakout session room, number 302." Therese remained seated on the floor for a moment, confused.

"Come on." The man named Bob reached down to lift her to stand. She stared. Her mouth hung open.

"What kind of workshop is this?" Therese whispered to Bob.

"Ah, you'll see. The next session is going to be really fun." He winked. The group of participants shuffled excitedly, like a tribe of hyper goats. Therese looked behind her for a sign of Dara, but she had gone.

"You'll see her in the next class," Bob said with a hand on Therese's shoulder.

Room number 302 held no décor except chairs arranged in circles. One big circle embraced smaller and smaller rings of rolling black chairs. Participants eyed each other, and then selected seats. Some sat with their fingertips under their thighs. Some men crossed an ankle over a kneecap and slouched. Some leaned forward. Therese folded her feet up in the chair when she realized they hung down in an awkward position.

Dara walked in the room with two others who hadn't been there before. She did not make eye contact with anyone, even though Therese tried with a small wave. She sat. The two following her sat. Silence.

"Some people here are obviously desperate," the girl in the green sweater announced to the anxious group. She laughed. No one responded. Therese looked at her from the left corner of her eye. *What?* she thought. More silence.

Dara looked at her legs and said, "If you want to create it, you can." Therese looked to Dara, then the girl in green, and wondered if they were in on a secret or a joke. Stillness shrouded the room for seven full minutes before someone burst out laughing.

"This isn't real, you know," the laughing participant said.

"How can you participate in a process that isn't real?" the man with the glasses responded.

"Maybe you hope it isn't real." The girl in green joined in. "Because

31

you're a liar."

The laughing participant shook his head. "No, I had to. It was a residency program requirement."

"Bullshit," a man in a brown sweater and acid-washed jeans interjected.

"He's a liar?" Bob turned his attention to green-sweater girl. "Are you pathologizing him?"

Therese's face became contorted. *What in God's name is going on in here?*

"I love children," Dara stated, then stood. The two others that followed her into the room stood, too. They walked out in silence and did not return. After a few moments of tense air, participants began to stand and look at each other. One girl across the circle from Therese crumpled in tears.

"I'm leaving," she told a woman who stood with her arm draped over her shoulders. "I'm not going to spend my weekend like this."

Everyone else filed back into the main meeting room, and Therese followed, unsure what to make of the worried feeling that nestled into her belly.

Food had been placed in the back of the main meeting room on long buffet tables. Creamy chicken Marsala, mushrooms, and mashed potatoes were piled on red plates on one end. Steak with arugula salad and tomatoes sat on white plates at the other. Therese looked at both meals, unable to make a choice.

"Hey, Therese." Dara had come to stand behind her. "You okay?"

"So, that was, um, something." Therese turned and realized she'd just taken her first deep breath since she'd walked into the hotel.

"It can get intense," Dara responded.

"And confusing," Therese said.

"Yes. But it really helps young psychiatrists understand the subconscious mind," Dara replied, nodding.

"Is this something you do with patients?" Therese asked.

"This experiment? Oh God, no. It's instructional only. Shall we?" Dara motioned to select a meal. "Let's eat. We have another workshop in half an hour. I don't need too much. I already feel as big as a cow from the snacks they gave us earlier." Dara carried a briefcase and a book she'd purchased earlier in the day from the bookstore, *Love's Executioner and Other Tales of Psychotherapy*.

"How long have you been doing this?" Therese asked. She moved toward the steak.

"Psych? Oh, man, feels like forever now. I started med school in '76. Met my hubby there. Then started my psych residency around 1980 in Baltimore. So now I've been in practice over twenty years." She lifted her shoulders to her dangling green earrings and dropped them again. "Got kinda bored just doing therapy and meds, so I started teaching around the country. Well, mostly the East Coast."

"And why'd you get into psych?" Therese pulled out a chair at the table beside Dara.

"Betrayal," she responded, laughing. "Isn't that the driving force behind every woman?"

Therese nodded, laughing, too. They shared no words as they tasted the first bites of their meals. Dara took a sip of her iced tea.

"But, if I can, I wanted to ask you something," Dara said as she wiped her mouth.

"Yeah. What's up?" Therese asked.

"I'm flying out again tomorrow night. You know we've got this beach house about forty minutes from here—in Riviera Oaks. For the life of me, I cannot figure out how to get there this month to make sure it's okay. I thought maybe you and a few friends may want to stay there for a couple days. A week? I'd need you to do a few 'round the house things. I'm sure it could stand to be dusted and freshened up—little things." Therese listened intently. "It's a gorgeous place," Dara continued, "up on the only hill we have in Florida." She laughed. "Secluded with a private nightclub, bike trail, and park."

Therese had declined three previous invitations to visit Dara's home for dinner parties or cookouts. She thought them polite more than sincere.

With this invitation, though, she thought of her failed audition, the woman on the train, and Evan.

"I could actually use a break like that, Dara. Thanks a ton." Therese leaned over and gave Dara a hug. She would get a week away in a doctor's beach home with nothing but the sun and her best friend. *Well, I hope Phoebe's still my friend*, she thought.

"What's your number? I'll text you the address and the gate instructions. If anyone asks you, the house is registered to Dr. Dara Clemens. Can you go next week?" Dara stopped. She flapped both hands toward her face. "Are you warm? I feel like a heat wave just swept over me." She pulled a small, motorized fan out of her bag and winked. "Probably menopause." The fan hummed.

"Yep, it shouldn't be a problem to get a few days off," Therese responded, laughing at Dara. She mindlessly slipped her apron back over her neck without reason.

"Are you going to wear that into the next workshop?" Dara grinned.

"Uh, sure." Therese looked down. "Why the heck not?"

"Great. Come on, let's head back in."

Therese took a bite of a dinner roll she'd slathered in butter and stood.

The participants filed back into the room. Green-sweater girl sat with her back to the group. Therese aimed for her previous seat. A girl in a pink baby doll dress rushed to take it.

"Okay." Therese frowned and shook her head as she moved to the next seat.

"Hey, why are you wearing that apron?" The guy in the acid-washed jeans leaned forward to talk to Therese.

"Oh, I work at…" Therese stopped as Dara returned. The same two people trailed her. Everyone fell silent.

The girl in green kept her back to the group. Every few minutes, snickering giggles floated from her seat. Most people sat swinging side to side in their rolling chairs, folding their lips in to avoid being the first to speak. Suddenly, the door to meeting room number 302 swung open. It was the man with the glasses. He was flushed.

"Can I join late?" he asked Dara. She didn't respond. He went to take a seat. Therese glued her eyes on him.

"Why are you late?" Therese started the conversation.

"What?" he responded.

Another woman behind her repeated the question and added, "And where are your shoes?" The entire room looked at his feet to spy white-and-gray socks. They read "Hanes" across the toes. He pulled his feet back and under the chair.

"I had to go to the bathroom," he replied. He avoided making eye contact with anyone. The door opened again. Two more people came in laughing. Therese looked at them and then back at the man.

"Were you with them?" she asked. The latecomers dissolved into raucous laughter.

"Justice is the correction of wrongs," Dara said. She looked at her fingernails this time, then crossed her legs.

"I had nothing to do with them," the man continued.

"Yeah, right!" Therese responded, surprising herself.

"Secrets are meant to be exposed," one of Dara's flunkies said.

The man with the glasses stuck both his middle fingers up at Therese. The entire room looked at her to read her reaction. Her heart galloped in her chest as she tried to make sense of his response.

Bob interjected. "Whoa! Calm down, bro. She's new here."

Glasses shoved his chair out of the circle and stood red-faced, throwing up obscene hand gestures in rapid sequence like gang signs. He pushed the silver bar on the door to exit and tripped on his own foot while trying to slam it. Green-sweater girl turned around and laughed so hard her face glistened in tears.

Dara did not respond to his outburst. Instead, she stood and left. The silent two followed. Therese sat in her chair, shaking. The room sat in silence another fifteen minutes until one of Dara's proctors returned to signal the exercise had ended.

"We're done for tonight," Bob said to Therese in muted tones. "Isn't this workshop fascinating?" Therese could not understand what just happened or why. "Oh, you're a little overwhelmed. Don't worry; you'll be fine." He attempted to reassure her. He pulled his phone from his back pocket and said, "I have to call my wife now." He held up a photograph of his wife standing on a mountain landing and shrugged. "She's not very pretty, but she's loyal. Are you staying at this hotel tonight?"

Therese's face remained frozen. She looked to the back of the room for another exit. When the room emptied and Bob walked away in his corduroys, she slunk out the second door.

6

"HELLO, HELLO!" VICTOR CALLED OUT to his office hallway. He encountered two patients. Each trailed behind an assistant clad in blue scrubs
and plastic, whitened smiles. A short woman with white curls wore a
fuchsia cotton top and beige capri pants. Her purse pressed into the second
roll of her matronly belly. She shuffled in tiny steps with her shoulders
raised to her ears. Trepidation beamed through her clouded gray eyes.
Victor encountered this look at least once a day. "Don't worry, it's going
to go great," he said just above a whisper. He placed a gentle hand on her
shoulder. "You're Jan, right?" She nodded.

"I remember you from the consultation last week. Jan, we have per-
fected this procedure, and it goes very, very well." He nodded his head as
he spoke. Victor knew well how to cast the air of concern and confidence.
Jan drew a deep breath and smiled, revealing the problem teeth. "You're a
little early, but you can go ahead and hang out in the back lobby. There's
a TV. We'll come get you when we're ready to start." Victor said as he
turned to walk to the next surgical suite.

"Danny Montcliffe!" he exclaimed, seeing his high school buddy-
turned-patient. Victor's black eyes danced from the brightness of the dental
light mounted in the ceiling. "My Ravens are looking good this year."

"Not as good as those Steelers, though, Doc!" the men laughed and
shook hands as the assistant, Christy, shuffled into the corner of the room.

She smiled with her hands folded in front of her. A hand-picked Filipina, Victor had selected her to be the newest surgical assistant. She filled the space with looks, not talent. And he had regretted the choice every day since. Behind his mask of casualness, Victor was livid. He turned to look at Christy.

"We're ready to begin," he said through clenched teeth. He turned back to Danny, laughing. Christy flushed and turned her back to the men. Her fingers fluttered like a flock of seagulls startled on the beach's shore. She had not prepared his surgical trays. Victor placed his behind on the black stool at Danny's side while Christy scrambled to unwrap the sterile trays packaged in light green transparent plastic. Her dark hair swung wildly in her haste. She grabbed her head, then pulled open a drawer, searching for a cap and tucking her tresses inside. She turned to look at the patient. His pulse oximeter dangled from the chair instead of gripping his finger. Christy's face faded from rose to pale white.

"Relax, you're going to make our patient nervous." Victor pretended to be joking and punched Danny in the shoulder. Danny grabbed his arm, bunching up the plaid cotton of his shirt. "I'm gonna sue, Vic, I'm gonna sue."

"Well, if you do that, I won't be able to afford your 2005 Super Bowl ticket to see Baltimore kick whoever's ass." The two erupted into laughter again and traded football stats as Christy finalized her preparations.

"Alright, buddy, remember what we said we were gonna do today?" Victor began. "You still want sedation, right?"

"Yeah, Doc. As tempting as it is to stare into your beautiful eyes, I'm gonna knock out for this one."

"Aw, c'mon," Victor replied. "You're scared? I thought cops were supposed to be tough guys."

BY THE TIME the front clock read 2:50 P.M., Victor had completed the foundational work for three bone grafts and finished Danny's extraction. Even still, his stomach rippled with anticipation and bubbling energy. Had he not been wearing Medi-Pak antiperspirant, the pits of his white coat would have been damp. He paced the back office's wooden floors, peering through the sleek glass leading to the lobby. Victor's tongue struck the backs of his teeth. To distract himself from his nervousness, he teased his curly-haired assistant, Bonnie, walking backward in front of her every time she tried to pass.

"Bonnie!" Victor's voice rang through the office. "How's everything? You didn't work with me at all today. You're not avoiding me, right?" Bonnie flushed, highlighting the yellowish-green hazel of her eyes.

"Dr. Jacobs!" she replied with a hollow laugh. "Of course not!" She stepped forward on her right then shuffled back on her left. She held a manila folder to her chest and grinned only with her mouth. The rest of her face read annoyance.

"No, seriously, sweetie, how are things going? Anything you need from us?" Victor asked, referring to himself and his practice partner. As he spoke, his head drifted to his left. His eyes blurred then cleared. Afternoon light poured in a diagonal as the front door opened. A petite foot in snakeskin sandals sliced through the light. It was her.

"We're pretty good," Bonnie said, "but we could use some more gloves."

Victor turned to Bonnie, hugging her low around the waist with a quick pulsing squeeze.

"Okay, my three's here." He pushed past her, trotting to the reception desk. A stunning Asian woman and her son were in the waiting room. The woman wore oversized, black sunglasses. She stood with her hands overlapping on the thick strap of the bag hanging before her. Dr. Leslie Chae was shrouded in black, except for her sandals. Maroon glitter encrusted the wedge heel. Highlights of auburn waved like river streams in her dark hair, which had been tied in a sleek topknot.

"Joey!" Victor slowed his trot, thrusting forward his right hand. "How's it going, buddy?" Joseph's broad, defined chest and longer-than-usual arms hinted at his expected growth. Already six feet tall, he hovered over the heads of his mother and oral surgeon. Light blue fitted shorts highlighted the chiseled legs and golden complexion soccer had given him over the past two seasons. He wore a backward cap of similar blue that pushed dark brown bangs just over his eyebrows. Unassuming beauty—the loveliest kind.

He pursed his lips as if on the brink of laughter. "Hi," he whispered. "It's going good."

"Don't be shy!" Dr. Chae leaned forward to Victor, tapping his forearm. "Hello!" she said as their hands embraced. Butterflies tickled Victor to nausea. He released his grip, looked at the floor, then back at Joseph.

"Joey, how old are you now?"

"Seventeen. I just graduated."

"High school? You did? Wow, congrats! Well, I was thinking you had one more year. Where are you headed for college?" Victor asked.

Dr. Chae answered for her son. "He's leaving for Stanford a week from today, believe it or not. We've got to get these teeth pulled, and he has a soccer tournament, and then he's out of here."

"I hope your dermatology practice has been going well, Leslie," Victor attempted to make more small talk. "Everyone wants to live the life of a dermatologist."

"Indeed," she said with a laugh. "I told this one," pointing to Joseph, "it's incredibly competitive these days. I hardly got into my training program. People still hate me for stealing the last spot in the class." Her chuckle floated like a chime in his ears.

"Well, let's go ahead and get started! Christy will get you set up, and then I'll see what questions you have, et cetera." Christy posed at the corner of the reception desk. She blinked three times.

"Follow me, please," she said. No warmth exuded from her eyes.

Victor boiled inside, angry at himself and his assistant. He wondered why she had to be awkward and incompetent and why he had hired her. He also wondered why he had let himself appear flustered in front of Leslie.

In the surgical suite, the aroma of antiseptics calmed Victor's disdain.

"Dr. Jacobs…" Joseph whispered again, "…how long is it going to take me to feel better? I don't want to miss the tournament this weekend." The rapid rise and fall of his breath heaved his blue shirt up and down.

"Well, your X-rays look great, Joey." Victor reassured him. "You have mild impaction. You're young, with no other dental issues. Most times, people like you recover from getting their wisdom teeth out in a few days. Take it easy at the tournament, and you should be okay." Victor stood in his white coat and scrubs, his blue-gloved hands folded at the base of his sternum. He stepped backward, looking over his shoulder. He pointed to Christy to begin IV set up for Joseph's sedation.

"Joey, bud, have you had anything to eat or drink since one this afternoon?" Victor relaxed his voice to calm his patient.

"Uh, no," he replied.

"Christy, what food can he eat today, after this?"

Christy replied, "Soft foods." She was unsure of her response.

"Are you asking me or telling me?" Victor sucked his teeth. "Joey, when you leave, get your mom to get you some Ben and Jerry's. You like ice cream, right?" Victor laughed again. "Eat soft food the first few days, like yogurt or mac and cheese."

Leslie chimed in, "Joey, that doesn't sound so bad. Maybe I can be on this diet, too." She winked at Victor.

"Christy, what's the most important thing for him not to eat in the first few days?" Victor's heart pattered in his chest. He tried to distract himself from Leslie's glances, pretending to be aloof and unfazed.

"Um, no acidic foods, and also no seeds or popcorn," she replied.

"Right," Victor said, placing a gloved left index finger gently into the right corner of Joseph's mouth. Christy puffed out air in relief of getting the correct response.

"I'm just going to take a quick look." Victor did the reassurance thing again. "I know last time, at the other place, things went really poorly. We're going to make sure you don't feel a thing. You'll get a little sleepy, a little silly, and when you fully wake up, we'll be done. Mom, I'm gonna have you sit in the back office waiting area once we get started." Leslie winked again. Victor allowed himself to look at her. Heart-shaped lips balanced just above her petite, graceful chin. Her skin mimicked shining white glass. Her face held large, baby doll, almond-shaped eyes.

"Absolutely!" She stood. "Joey, do you have any other questions for Dr. Jacobs? I'm going to step out now."

He shook his head "no," and she nodded once. The bergamot fragrance of her Clive Christian No. 1 lingered after her departure. Victor felt faint. His hearing muted.

"Dr. Jacobs?" Christy asked tentatively. She stood with glistening steel dental tools flat against her covered palm. Victor looked at her, unsure of how long he'd been daydreaming. Joseph's face eased as he slept.

"Go ahead and get suction," Victor commanded, hoping he had not done or said anything in those moments that would signal weakness. "I'll take the cheek retractor and elevator. Joey, can you feel this?" Victor was prodding tooth number one with the blade of his elevator. When Joey did not respond or flinch, he began.

Together, Christy and Victor worked in near silence. For each tooth that Victor extracted, Christy aimed the light-teal suction device diagonally across Joseph's tongue, striving to keep Victor's work field clear. As if having a meal with a fork and knife, Victor held the retractor in his left hand and used the elevator to easily push and prod Joseph's teeth out of their spaces. Unlike the previous oral surgeon, Victor made sure his technique left no broken tooth fragments—and that his sedation and anesthetics would last throughout the procedure. The first tooth fell into the pocket beside Joey's cheek. Christy used her suction device to retrieve it.

"Hmm, divergent roots," Victor commented. He plucked the tooth from the suction and examined it underneath their overhead lamp. He handed it to Christy and prepared to continue. "We're going to make a small incision at thirty-two," he noted. Christy swapped his elevator for a scalpel and then swapped it again. "If I can do this without creating a flap, it'll be a good day," he commented. Christy's eyes melted behind her mask and eye shield. In her initial interview, she had told Victor his reputation for surgical precision was the reason she wanted to work for him. Joseph's impacted teeth were no match for Victor's skill. His hands were smoother than butter.

"Wow, that was beautiful, Dr. Jacobs," Christy cooed. She turned to face him with her eyebrows raised.

A rush of warmth filled his chest. He was terminally susceptible to flattery. If not strategic, Christy's comment was opportune. It saved her from certain criticism for a full day of mediocrity. The two ended the procedure. Victor instructed Christy to sit with Joseph until he could answer a few simple questions.

"Bring him to the lobby and have him sit on the couches once he's cleared up," Victor said.

Leslie stood at the front desk receiving aftercare instructions. For any other case, Victor would have come out to reassure the patient that everything had gone well. He then would have disappeared into his office to dictate notes. Instead, after Joseph's procedure, he speed-walked to his office bathroom, checked his face in just one mirror, and blasted two sprays of Listerine into the soft palate of his mouth. He smoothed his eyebrows and lifted his lip to examine his teeth. He jogged back to the front counter.

"Leslie, it went great. He was a champ," Victor said. He leaned on the counter. "Tooth fragments are all gone. He slept like a baby all the way through. Did Christy go over aftercare with you?"

"Indeed, she did, Doctor." Leslie offered the slightest bow. Victor mimicked her. "Perfect. Kelly, I'll get them all set up."

"Huh?" she replied. "I mean, excuse me?" Kelly questioned. Her bright pink scrubs appeared even more ridiculous to Victor than they had in the morning.

"I will get Joey checked out," Victor repeated, nudging her out of her seat behind the desk with his knee.

"But do you know how to?" Kelly responded.

"Thanks, Kelly." He laughed. "Geez, I guess they don't trust me with the computers around this place." Victor shook his head, smirked, and rolled his eyes. "Leslie, do you still live at 8473 Wandering Lane?"

"We do," she said.

"Is that in Ellicott City? 21043?"

"Yep." Her eyes looked at his, then down at her "Wisdom Teeth Extraction: What to Expect After Surgery" pamphlet.

"Okay, perfect. Everything went as we planned today. You're all set. You are welcome to wait here with him as long as you need to."

Dr. Chae nodded and turned to gather her son, who had been sitting on a couch laughing at nothing. She waved thank you and bye, her giant baby in tow. Victor watched as she opened the door to a white Land Rover for Joseph.

"Dr. J, you know you didn't collect from her?" Concern rumpled Kelly's young face. "I can draw up an invoice." She caressed her damaged blonde ponytail.

"Yeah, we'll take care of it later. Don't mail an invoice." Victor pushed away from the desk. He attempted to conceal a growing erection with a file folder and his white coat. Even though he'd worked a full, busy day and had had a disastrous night before, the Chaes had invigorated him. Proximity to the type of woman who filled his nightly fantasies loaded him with surging blood. He couldn't wait to get home for his favorite activity. He'd go home and write in his logs about today's luck. For him, it was an activity that transcended all eroticism. Victor pressed his lips together to keep from bursting into maniacal laughter.

SQUINTING IN THE PARKING LOT from the blinding sun, he started to whistle. He stepped down from the entrance sidewalk and onto the freshly paved and painted lot. His car was stationed below his "Dr. Victor Jacobs" sign.

"Victor!"

Victor's brow dropped and his lips protruded. He looked in front of him, then over his shoulder around the parking lot.

"Victor!" Victor's father stood silhouetted by the sunlight, just three parking spaces behind him.

"No, Dad." Victor's pace accelerated, and he gripped his bag until his fingers burned, pressing the trunk key on the fob in his pocket. He tossed his bag in, shut the trunk, and reached for the driver's side door.

"Son, I've been calling you for twelve hours. This is unacceptable."

"We're not doing this here," Victor warned.

"Then where? Let's go to Red Robin and grab dinner," his father replied.

"No, Dad." Victor wouldn't face his father but tried to scan the parking lot to make sure neither his staff nor Leslie witnessed this exchange.

"Son, get your butt in that car and to the restaurant. I'm not asking."

"Fine, I'll meet you." Victor's top lip did not move as he growled at his father. He had no desire to discuss his love life over salmon burgers and cold steak fries. He ducked into his Audi and nearly backed into his father's knees. Victor drove two blocks to the restaurant, muttering under his breath the entire way. Inside, his father attempted to make conversation while they waited to be seated. Victor did not respond. Instead, he busied himself drawing on the large chalkboard beside the hostess's station.

AT HOME THAT NIGHT, Victor reached into the closet beside his bedroom's TV. In the dark, his hands fingered the spiral of his journal. Stark white. No marking on either cover. Gold binding wrapped the spine.

He'd attached a pen from the office to the front flap. His breath quickened as he reached for the drawing pencils nestled beside his notebook. He took one and walked backward to his bed.

He would spend the rest of the evening making sketches of Leslie Chae's face. He jotted her address in the upper right corner of the page, tracing over it twice.

"8473 Wandering Lane," he muttered. Dinner with his father had been as much of a pain as he'd anticipated. Of course, there were no updates on where his girlfriend ran off. And the family was humiliated. And, sure, Victor's future endeavors were in jeopardy. But none of that could dampen his satisfaction at this moment. Once he'd drawn a sketch to his liking, he held it in front of his face and kissed the lips he'd created. "I love you, Dr. Leslie Chae. You're perfect." His mouth curled. Pencil graphite dusted his lips.

7

A GOLDEN GRAVEL DRIVEWAY greeted Phoebe and Therese as they pulled into 111 Crystal Cove.

"Whoa," Therese said. She leaned forward and gazed upward to see if the height of the walls stopped before they ran into the clouds. Sunlight glared down through the windshield, making her wince.

Fresh flagstone surrounded the Clemens's home. It led to an ivy-bordered path and ended at an oversized wrought-iron and wood door. As she stepped from block to block, Therese fumbled for the house key in the hip crevice of her denim cutoff shorts. Two days later and the exercise with Dara still disturbed her. Phoebe noticed her hands trembling and laughed.

"You're not still weirded out about that class, are you? Relax, T. It's just an empty house. There's no boogeyman inside!"

"Shut up." Therese laughed and placed the key flat against the keyhole, rubbing it up and down.

"Would you come on? It's freakin' five thousand degrees out here!" Phoebe groaned.

Therese continued to struggle with the key until Phoebe finally dropped her bags, snatched it, and turned her wrist left with a quick glare as the door unlocked. "Honestly, Therese."

Though the home remained vacant for months prior, the air was crisp and cool in the foyer. No beachside mugginess. No dust. Not even the smell of salt. The girls stood on the marble floor with their mouths open, taking in the elaborate décor.

"It's a bit over the top for a beach house, right, T?" Phoebe laughed and walked down the hallway slowly, gazing from side to side as if in a museum. Creams and whites drenched the living room to the right. In its center stood an elegant glass coffee table that disappeared in her peripheral vision. Eight loveseat-sized chairs waited for visitors. Hints of gold accented the room. Coral plaques stood displayed on the marble end tables. A bust lived in the niche leading to the kitchen.

Therese slid off her flip-flops and tiptoed through the living room. She made sure not to let her legs rub the furniture as she passed. She rounded a corner leading to a full chef's kitchen on the left. Vertical pantries at either side of the kitchen flanked the cream, glass-doored cabinetry. Copper pans floated over a custom butcher's block and sink.

"How many sinks does one family need?" Phoebe allowed her fingers to glide over the arched silver faucet of the third sink she'd spotted. Ceiling-to-floor glass created the east wall of Dara's cooking space. The windows gave a clear view of descending beach hills and a bridge leading to the dunes.

Since they'd entered the home, Therese had not spoken a single word, but her lips remained parted, barely breathing. The house swallowed them, dwarfing them both. It made her feel small, not only physically. Aside from driving through the part of town where people "had money," had she ever seen a home's exterior and *imagined* this is what existed inside.

The two ventured upstairs, peeking into the massive bedrooms arranged at either side of the staircase. A third-floor loft sat atop the second set of stairs. The girls wandered, mere specks in the space.

"T, which room do you want? I really don't mind." Phoebe peeked in each doorway, whispering "wow" in each.

"I don't know, Phoebs. These rooms are so huge. Wanna share one?"

"Are you still scared, T?"

Therese's eyebrows rose to her forehead. She dragged her fingertips across them.

"Not really…" she laughed, then paused, "…okay, kind of. That workshop was weird, and this house is huge. I'm not scared now, but I probably will be tonight. Don't laugh!" She began to giggle.

"No biggie," Phoebe responded with a shrug and smile. "You know I love sleepovers." She winked at Therese. "Let's stay in this one."

The room they chose looked out over the ocean. Phoebe sat on the mauve, curved window bench in the fishbowl. She could have slept in that space comfortably—it was larger than a full-sized bed.

"What is it this lady does again?" she asked Therese.

"Doctor. But she's a psychiatrist. Didn't know they made this kind of money," Therese gazed around the bedroom at accent walls and lighting fixtures.

"They don't. What's her husband do?"

"Not sure. I think they're both doctors, though." Therese placed her bag in the middle of the room.

"Can you imagine this is their *spare* home?!" Phoebe shook her head. "Honestly, this kind of house is embarrassing. How can you even enjoy it when you know there's homeless people probably five minutes from here?"

"Guess you just don't let yourself think about it." Therese was taking off her traveling clothes, revealing a white bikini underneath. She pulled a cover-up and comb from her bag then wandered to the room's daylit bathroom mirror. She parted her hair down the middle to place it in French braids. Phoebe turned on the light behind her. Therese winced again.

"Oh my God, Phoebs!" Therese exclaimed. "We don't need that light!"

"What?" Phoebe looked up and down at the wall.

"Why are you turning on that bright light?!" Therese's voice nearly lifted into a shout.

"Seriously, T? What's the matter? It's not like Dara can't afford her electricity bill," Phoebe said.

"Not the point!" Therese said. She grabbed her comb off the counter and turned to leave the bathroom. A rushing wave inside her head knocked her off balance. Her weight shifted as if the floor had opened beneath her. When her head stopped pulsing, she looked over her shoulder at Phoebe, frustrated. "Want to go down to the beach?" she asked, pretending the dizziness hadn't frightened her.

Phoebe frowned. She put her hands on her hips. "Uh, yep," she replied, "let's head out. Car or no car?"

"No car. Let's just go see what the beach is like," Therese responded in a strained voice.

The girls walked out the back of the home. They passed the sitting room leading to an expansive porch. It spanned the full width of the home, sprinkled with high-backed rocking chairs. Therese jogged down the three steps leading to the yard and kept going, not necessarily waiting for nor leaving Phoebe.

A three-foot fence guarded the small bridge over a babbling, mosquito-filled creek. Therese kept walking. She felt her feet speed underneath her and thought her knees would buckle a few times. It was as if a magnet to the ocean had been placed in her belly. Once she got to a place where her flip-flops disappeared in the sand, she took a huge breath. She looked left and right and upward at the dream-like sky. Looking down at her hands, she noticed they were pink, hot, and shaking. She became so entranced by them that she didn't notice Phoebe standing beside her, frowning again.

"Therese, are you okay? Seriously."

Therese looked back into her friend's eyes. They weren't as blue as she'd thought. In fact, everything appeared drained of color. Phoebe looked almost gray, her blonde highlights white, and her skin ashen under the overcast sky.

"I think I'm getting another migraine or something." Therese turned and walked parallel with the ocean. "And I forgot my sunglasses."

Phoebe pulled her shades off her tank top and handed them to her friend, then reached for her hand. "Maybe you need a neuro appointment soon, T. But let's have fun this week. This is, like, a once in a lifetime…" she trailed off, not sure what to say next.

"I know, sorry. Maybe I'm just still upset about auditions." Tears burned the backs of Therese's eyes, and she dropped Phoebe's hand to put on the sunglasses. "Maybe I'm just crabby."

Phoebe snorted with laughter. "Crabby 'cause you're on the beach? Or crabby 'cause of what you do in the sheets?"

"You're corny, Phoebs." Therese's face eased, and she shook her head. Phoebe giggled as she stepped over a series of tiny shells.

"No, but seriously," Phoebe said as she reached for Therese's hand again. "We haven't been spending as much time together. I miss you. You're like, my person, you know?" Phoebe wrapped her free hand around Therese's arm. Therese remained silent, wiping tears from beneath her borrowed sunglasses. She squeezed Phoebe's hand as if she'd never let go.

The pair walked until they happened upon a small but bustling beachside bar. It welcomed the girls with multicolor flashing lights. The beats of a fake tin drum pounded overhead, and a long, brown, grass skirt wrapped around the bar. Phoebe took a seat, and Therese stood behind her. She tried to measure if her head would be able to tolerate all the noise.

"Get my friend a drink!" Phoebe shouted at the bartender. His skin was hot pink from either the sun or the cheap lighting.

"I got you, beautiful." He turned to the bar, shaking and mixing to the rhythm of UB40's "Can't Help Falling in Love."

"I hate this song." Therese leaned into Phoebe's ear, yelling.

Phoebe turned around, hopped from the barstool, and grabbed Therese by the waist. She wound her body down to the floor.

"I love it!" Phoebe mouthed. The bartender slid the girls two drinks floating obligatory paper umbrellas and cherries.

"On the house for the first one, girls," he shouted over the music.

They each took sips, and Therese's tense brow released. She took a spot at the bar and twirled the wispy edges of her hair around her index finger. Easily the youngest and prettiest in the place, Therese and Phoebe lost hours drinking, laughing, and theorizing on various nonsensical drunken topics.

During one drinking break, Therese glanced over her shoulder and noticed a young man wearing medical scrubs, clogs, and glasses. He sat alone at a far table against the wall. She watched him cross his legs, take a sip from a black-lidded paper cup, and continue to read the magazine in his hand. He wore his dark brown hair gelled out of his face. His hand rested on the back of his neck.

"I'm gonna go talk to him," Therese announced. She swung her legs around to the back of her stool and hopped to the floor, focusing on him. He did not look up. At his table, she pulled out a chair and sat down. Her breasts bounced once in her white bikini top.

"Hi!" she said.

"Hi," he responded, looking up from his magazine and smiling.

"I'm Therese."

"Nice to meet you, Therese."

"Not gonna tell me your name?" she asked. She shifted to reveal the left side of her face. She thought it her best angle.

"Oh, my apologies. I'm Tomas."

Therese smiled and began unbraiding her hair.

"Toe-maz, what's up with the outfit? Are you a doctor or something?" she asked. He nodded. "And what's a doctor doing at a bar in the middle of the afternoon?"

Tomas sat back in his chair and stretched one leg out toward Therese, revealing white socks. He smiled at her but didn't say anything. She could see a gold chain peeking from under his scrubs. He looked down, then back at her eyes, and took a deep breath.

"I'm really not sure, to be honest." Tomas's words were touched with a hint of Spanglish accenting—like someone who was not a native Spanish speaker but whose parents were. He waited for Therese's next question without looking away.

"Well, I'm on vacation here for a week," she told him without being prompted.

"That's good."

"Yep, that's good. Are you going to be here for a while?"

"I'm not on vacation. My parents come up here sometimes. I'm visiting them today."

"So, that's a 'yes,' then?" Therese concluded.

"That's a 'not really.'" He propped his hand under his chin.

Therese looked around the table for a cocktail napkin. She didn't find one but did see that Tomas had four pens in the pocket of his scrubs. She took one and wrote her phone number on her own left palm. Tomas smiled.

"Is that for me?" he asked, pointing to her ink-covered palm. She giggled as he picked up her palm and pressed it into his. The number transferred backwards on his hand.

"Thank you, Therese." He grinned.

He stood and folded his magazine around his paper cup. Then, leaning forward, he pushed up his glasses and kissed Therese right at the part of her now-loose hair. "See you."

LATER THAT EVENING, the girls stumbled back through the beach sand and up to the house. After the bar, they'd made friends with the waiters at the club's karaoke set, staked out the jacuzzi with its adjoining wave pool, and even found a little green park with bicyclers and white wicker benches. It looked like a scene out of *Anne of Green Gables*. They deemed Dara's whole fancy beachside getaway perfect and joked about how they could con her into letting them live there.

Inside, the air conditioning chilled the place colder than a refrigerator.

"Oh my God! Buzzkill!" Phoebe laughed and ran to find the thermostat.

Therese walked back and forth in the kitchen, running her hands, covered in Hawaiian Tropic and sand, along the glistening counter.

"You know what's weird about this house, Phoebs? There's no pictures. Of anyone. I saw this in a movie once—about kidnappers." She laughed and leaned forward on the counter, putting her forehead on top of her folded hands. "Do you think Dara is a kidnapper?"

"Yes. I'm pretty sure John Walsh is on her trail right now," Phoebe said as she looped her finger into Therese's back pocket and pulled her toward the stairs. "Let's go to bed, weirdo."

8

VICTOR GAVE HIMSELF FOUR DAYS to kill Joseph Chae. He would need to be dead by Monday. Tuesday could be too close. Wednesday would be too late. He was leaving for college on Wednesday. Pressing into cobra pose from the fluffy whiteness of his sheets, Victor lifted his chest, swung his chin from side to side, and yawned, reaching for his alarm. His mouth pulled into a full "O" while his eyes shut of their own accord. In one move, he rolled to his back, then swung his feet off the side of his bed. He sat facing the floor-length wall of windows overlooking his rolling, flawless yard. He'd accessorized it with lighting, a fire pit, a figure eight-shaped patio, and an adjacent, small turquoise pool. No sun shone today to spotlight the orange bedroom walls.

He glanced to his left. At the foot of his bed lay his sketch of Leslie Chae's face. He thought it looked as if she, too, was well rested. "Hi baby," Victor said, yawning through his sleepy-eyed good morning. He rubbed her cheek passionately, as if feeling her youthful flesh rise to meet him. He closed the notebook only after telling her to enjoy the day. He wiped graphite residue from his thumb.

"You can make yourself at home. I've got eggs and coffee downstairs if you're hungry," he said, standing and stretching. "Or I can run and get you an iced coffee from McDonald's."

Opening the book to look down at her face one last time for the morning, he thought he saw the slightest change in expression that said, "It's okay, I'll make myself something."

Victor recalled the first day he met her. She was wearing a white lace baby doll top and tapered Bermuda shorts. The ribbons of her Champagne-colored silk wedges crisscrossed her legs and tied in perfect bows midway up her shins. She leaned in the direction of her oversized purse holding a large, iced coffee in her left hand, just below her small breasts. One finger prominently displayed a yellow diamond ring that had to be at least three carats. A jade bracelet adorned her delicate wrist. That day, she had said she was one of the few Chinese women in the area happily married into a Korean family. Ignoring the ring, Victor asked about the bracelet. She'd explained it had been given to her by her parents to symbolize their love and offer her protection. She'd also explained the controversy her transcultural love affair created in the family at first. It had been resolved, though, and Victor assumed it had been settled by the surety of a beneficial financial arrangement for the in-laws.

He didn't want to leave her alone in his 7,500-square-foot home today, but it was imperative for both their sakes. Today's first task would ensure that, soon, Leslie Chae would be held tight in Victor's embrace.

Before dawn, the thinning veil of darkness still covered Ellicott City's streets. The sunniness of Wednesday gave way to summertime clouds at 6:00 A.M. Thursday morning. In the low light, the green of elm trees appeared indistinguishable from the purple-leaved prunus lining the roads. Driving his silver 2000 Camry, Victor was again accompanied by nothing but the sound of the summer's moist heat on the streets. His morning journey took him past Howard County General Hospital, over a train track, and around a Giant grocery store. He ended in a sprawling community, haunting in its sparseness.

"8473 Wandering Lane," Victor said, turning right under the direction of his GPS. His car's headlights gleamed over the subdivision's sign on the entryway façade—black lettering mounted on white and cream stones. As the headlights' beam predicted the car's direction and fell on the asphalt,

Victor contemplated turning them off to help him move through the neighborhood without fear of detection. It didn't hurt to drive a neutral-colored, early 2000s Toyota Camry—one of over four hundred thousand in the nation. The car would be hard for police to identify. Victor placed "lost tag" or "tag applied for" signs in the rear of his automobile specifically for times like this. To date, he'd made over sixty, never duplicating their subtle differences once. This car lived parked all year in his fourth garage except when it was needed for anonymity.

The subdivision consisted of three parallel streets, with a fourth that veered off to the right into a cul-de-sac. "Oh God, the whole neighborhood is Wandering Lane?" he asked himself, suppressing frustration. The clubhouse near the entrance was understated to the point that it read wealth. It, too, had a façade of whites and creams.

"Where are you?" he whispered, driving at ten miles per hour, his chest hovering inches from the steering wheel, eyes peering. He gambled on the cul-de-sac first, circling through, hoping to find Leslie's white Land Rover. "Eighty-four, seventy-three," he sang to himself.

As he rounded the circle, an early morning walker startled him. The legs of an elderly white man in a navy nylon sweatsuit—complete with a silver reflective strip down the sleeves and pants—interrupted the head-lights' beam. Waiting for Victor to pass, he walked in place, his left hand atop a rickety walking stick and his right holding earphones in place. Victor's stomach collapsed into a soup of nerves. Pretending not to notice the walker, he picked up his speed only by the slightest nudge. The neighbor gave him the ubiquitous suburban test of belonging: brief eye contact and a wave. Victor failed. He did not respond. When he looked in the rear-view mirror as he drove past, Victor spied the old man standing still, staring at the back of the car.

Victor rounded the first corner.

"Come on," he said, the back of his throat tight and dry. There would be no way he could continue lurking through the neighborhood with the early walker out and about. Besides, there may have been more of them.

Maybe they all met in nylon sweats and walked in lockstep in the low dawn light. Maybe their exercise plan was part American Heart Association mandate, part neighborhood watch. If Victor did not find house 8473 on the next street, he would have to leave and come back, maybe mid-afternoon, on another day, and with another made-up tag.

Victor realized each street ended in a cul-de-sac, which at least allowed for a second pass without a second drive around. The corner lot home's mailbox resembled a chest tomb and read 8460. And there, at the top of the cul-de-sac, on an elevated plot, sat the Chae house: white, stately, and unexpected with its towering columns and coned lights, the house numbers listed vertically on the front door. Their neighbors must have been the unwitting peasants of Wandering Lane. To the right of the hill, a wrap-around stone driveway split into three and ended at black garage doors. Victor thought that behind the house, the hill might descend to water—a man-made lake or a creek. He couldn't be sure. Outside the garages sat a forest green Jeep Wrangler, parked at an angle as if on a showroom floor. Its tan soft-top favored velvet in the home's outdoor lighting. Victor stopped driving and glanced in each mirror. He scanned the street for passersby and window watchers.

This place probably has cameras everywhere. He felt nauseous as the thought occurred to him for the first time. On the bottom of the Jeep's driver-side window, Victor noticed a shield-shaped decal. Royal blue, the sticker had three golden crosses over the top and read "CSA" across the body. Victor noted the symbol and decided to leave Wandering Lane. Twenty-five minutes remained until the sun would be rising from its slumber.

"Well, this is great." Victor slowed. He lifted the fingers of his left hand off the leather of his steering wheel. He tried the *I'm-not-a-threat* wave. The elderly man in navy strode across the street to Victor's car, walking stick and walking partner at his side. In two quick moves, he signaled Victor to stop and roll down his window.

"Can I help you find something, son?" The man placed his left hand over Victor's window and leaned in, looking into the passenger and back seats.

"Ah, no, I'm just looking."

"Yeah, I know. But looking for what?" He smelled of coffee and Icy Hot.

"Um," Victor began, "just new to the area. My wife and I just moved to DC. Hill jobs for us both."

"You're pretty far from Capitol Hill, aren't you?" The old man squinted. His walking partner stood with his hands behind his back, yawning. "Listen, this neighborhood…" he began.

"Is beautiful," Victor interjected. "We've been eyeing it for weeks now. The wife wasn't too happy to be moving here from California. The Hill job, that's my dream. She just wants to live somewhere peaceful and spacious and a good long distance from the craziness. This place, well, it's perfect. Hard to meet up with a realtor with our work schedules and…" Victor paused as the old man opened his mouth again.

"Seems a man smart enough to land a job serving our nation's capital would have noticed there's not a single house for sale out here." He pushed off the car, lifting the walking stick. "I tend to believe you don't have any business in this neighborhood—none current, none future." He shifted the stick overhead, holding each end in a hand. "You know how wives can be, right? Sorry, son, didn't catch your name."

"Sam," Victor replied. He leaned back, made strong eye contact, and offered a hand to shake.

"Sam, you do have a wife, right?" The old man ignored the hand.

"Yes, sir."

"Ah, the sir's not necessary. You looked me square in the face and lied three times already; no need to be respectful now." He noticed a penny on the ground, stooped to pick it up, and groaned as he stood again. "You don't have a wife, do you, Sam? Nothing about you says, 'married.' You don't even have one of those rubber rings guys your age wear these days. And you're looking at homes without the decision-maker?" The old man chuckled, placing the stick between his feet. "Not sure I believe that one."

The man continued, "A married man would know that an old dude like me is outside all day long. Women, they give us errands and assignments, right, son?"

Victor remained silent.

"Your mom doesn't do that to your pop? Lucky man."

Victor looked down at his thighs. He blinked slowly as a flash of his mother's graveside funeral dropped into his mind as if on a screen. Victor saw himself at six years old in a gray suit and black tie selected by his grandmother. His father sat lost in a row of white chairs, talking in low whispers to people Victor did not know. Victor's mother lay in a gray-and-white casket that dripped with white freesia and shockingly bright lavender peonies. It was waiting to be lowered into the ground. The cool metal of a Hot Wheels toy truck met Victor's tiny fingers in his sagging pocket. He pulled it out, pretending to himself it could take him to see his mom. And when it did, she would let him have two cookies from her bakery shelf out front. But really, as a big boy of six, he knew he would never see his mother again.

Just as he had every night since his mother had died, Victor's father doubled over in loud sobs. At home, Victor had heard him wailing alone and wished he had died with his mother. At the funeral, though, a woman stooped in front of his weeping father's chair. She pulled his hands away from his face and began speaking to him. Victor sat at a distance with his grandparents. He couldn't hear what she said. But for the first time since his mother's death, Victor saw his father wipe away his tears and smile. This woman held some sort of power in the pleats of her yellow-belted dress. *Or maybe*, he thought, *it's in her hands.* Victor knew right then he wanted to be able to bring that same kind of rescue to others drowning in sadness. A few weeks later, through the cracked door to his father's bedroom, he saw the woman lift his father's hand to her bare breast. Victor's ears had burned. He looked for his Hot Wheels car again. The cool metal in his palm soothed him.

"And Sam, you may be too young to know"—the old man's words jerked Victor out of his time capsule of grief—"but the older we get, the more our wives hate us." He placed a hand in his jogging suit pocket. "The more we clash with their furniture and Hallmark movies. So, they give us garbage to do, all day long, so they don't have to look at us." Victor stared at the old man, confused.

"Got any idea what that all boils down to, Sam? Don't disappoint me now."

The old man glared at Victor. Victor dropped his chin to his chest and looked up, as if over a pair of spectacles. "Uh, I'm not sure."

"Yeah, figured that." He shook his head and sighed. "It means that if you ever come back to this neighborhood, I'll see you. I'll see you on my way to Costco or the post office. I'll see you on the way to take my wife to meet her friend Gladys for lunch or on my way to get my damn prostate checked." The old man continued. "And I'll definitely see you on one of my three walks a day."

"It means if you're anywhere around this neighborhood again, chances are good that I'll see you. I don't forget faces, I won't forget this car that you and every other cheap shmuck in this state likes to drive, and I'll be making sure you made it to the DMV to get your tag." He tapped the rear windshield with the walking stick. "It also means I'll have your scrawny ass locked up for trespassing." He handed Victor a business card from his left pocket.

Victor had been looking down as if trying to see his own nose. He reluctantly accepted the card.

"Understood." Victor pressed his teeth into the flesh of his lip. He sighed deep into his belly, then smiled. "You'll never see me or this car anywhere around here again."

"Good, son. That's exactly what I wanted to hear." The old man slapped his palm on the top of the car once and turned to resume his stroll. His partner stood behind him, nearly asleep.

9

"PHOEBE, IT'S TOO HOT IN HERE." Therese waited for a response. Her eyes remained shut. "Phoebs." She flopped to the right to face the pillow where her friend had been. She'd always been most comfortable sharing a bed with her whenever they traveled to new places. She stared into the blue blackness and saw nothing at first. She blinked for several seconds. Therese reached out to Phoebe's spot in the bed. Cotton sheets and empty coolness met her hand. Once her eyes cleared, they confirmed Phoebe was gone.

"Ugh, come on!" Therese slid out of bed and walked through the dark, hands out in front of her. "Phoebe!" She patted the hallway wall, hoping to find a light. "Phoebe!" she whispered and then stood still. She didn't have her footing and the backs of her knees tingled in worry. She stood at the top of the curved staircase.

Therese heard a man's voice rumbling through the A/C vent above her. *I know that voice*, she thought. Her heart quickened. She didn't know who he was or if he'd done something to her friend. She listened again, unable to make out any words. Distracted, she didn't notice a shadow bounding up the stairs until it nearly knocked her over.

"Oh my God, T! Why are you standing in the hallway?" Phoebe whispered.

"I heard a guy talking. Where were you? Is everything okay?" Therese whispered in return.

"What?" Phoebe leaned toward Therese's face.

"There's a man in here somewhere, Phoebe. Listen. *Shhh!*"

The two stood huddled in the hallway for a few seconds... and nothing.

"No, seriously, Phoebs, I heard something."

"Hello?" a voice came from Phoebe's hand.

"Are you on the phone, Phoebe? In the middle of the night?" Therese demanded.

"Yeah, sorry. But I wasn't talking to a guy."

"So, who were you talking to then?"

"No, I was just... I couldn't... I was, um, was checking voicemail from earlier."

"So, your voicemail says, 'hello' now?" Therese stared as Phoebe fumbled with the phone. "Whatever. It's hot in here. Could you please adjust the air? I'd do it myself; I just don't know where the controls are."

Therese turned and walked back toward the bed. Her eyes had begun to adjust to the darkness. Phoebe shuffled behind her, offering apologies. Therese reached the edge of the bed and lifted the sheets. She lay facing away from Phoebe. Her back prickled with uneasiness. She scooted to the edge of the bed as if to distance herself from her friend's shady behavior while grappling with the certainty she'd heard someone else in the house. But with Phoebe claiming she had been listening to voicemail, she figured it must have just been noise from the phone. *Who's she talking to at 4:00 A.M.?* Therese asked herself.

She tried to fall back into a dream of loving Tomas on a scorching Portuguese beach. She wanted to conjure him up by thinking of his hair and the confident way he looked her in the eye at the bar. But her stomach tied itself in a knot, her heart pounded in the base of her throat, and muscles in her forehead spasmed. An hour later, she found herself inside a much different dream.

The beach house at 111 Crystal Cove sat above a basement. Therese didn't know how she ended up in the basement, but she knew Florida beach homes never had them. She stood at the basement doors and saw an expanse of rooms

*unfolding before her. Blue and green walls filled the space. The furniture looked
as if it had been taken from an orphanage.*

*Each room had two sets of bunk beds. The central great room held sagging
living room furniture in florals and tweeds. Therese walked down the hall and
came to a wooden alcove, abutted by what looked like barn doors. As she came
closer, she realized it was a horse stall. She placed her hands on the top of the
door when, with a whoosh of wind, she found herself flying horizontally, floating,
holding on to the door desperately. Moaning sounds began to creak out of the
wood and the surrounding bedrooms. The living room furniture multiplied. The
basement became bigger and deeper. She waved in the wind like a half-mast flag.*

She heard a voice ask, "Why are you here?"

The dream went black.

MONDAY MORNING, Therese opened her eyes to the sound of her Black-
berry vibrating. She grabbed it from the nightstand to keep it from
waking Phoebe, whose mouth hung open in her slumber. Therese rolled
her eyes. *I'm sure you're tired today, nightwalker!* She had never before
caught Phoebe in a lie, and it disturbed her. Their friendship had become
a sisterhood—at least that's what Therese thought.

Free-spirited and unashamed, if Phoebe called someone for a late-
night romp, she typically would have just said so. Besides, Therese did not
see her talk to anyone at the bar.

"I can't worry about that right now," she mouthed to herself and
typed "0815" into her phone's lock screen. She'd just received three texts.
She hoped they were from Tomas. Sitting on the side of the bed, she began scrolling through:

Good morning. I hope this doesn't
wake you. I'm pretty good at reading
backwards, but let me know if this
number DOES NOT belong to the
gorgeous woman named Therese I
met at Margaritaville yesterday.

I get off early today.

Tonight, I'm having a few friends over
to my parents place in the Gables.
Would love to have you come by.

Therese started to type a response and deleted it three times. The fourth time, she accidentally sent part of a message that read, I just sa… A muted laugh tickled her nervous belly. She figured she needed to commit to the message.

I just saw this message.
Yes, of course, I'd love to! Is
it cool if I bring my roomie?

She'd hoped to deliver something clever and coy. But the message had been sent, so she waited. When Tomas responded, he welcomed Phoebe, too. Skepticism filled her mind. Her relationship with Phoebe was inexplicably growing tense. Maybe a day apart would be good. But then again, the car didn't belong to Therese, she needed a ride, and she had only just met this man.

Five hours later, the girls sat in the summer heat of Phoebe's red Jetta. They figured driving south in the afternoon would be easy, but in true South Florida fashion, traffic slowed to a near stop at regular intervals both ways on 95. Driving south into Miami felt like Russian roulette. At any point, someone could come flying between lanes, or a mattress might sail from the divider clear across to an exit ramp. It took heart, necessity, and a little insanity to drive there.

Despite the danger and rife opportunities for laughter, only silent tension between friends filled the car. She looked at Phoebe from the corner of her eye.

"What, T? I see you looking at me," Phoebe said. She turned both hands upward, slapped them on the steering wheel, and pulled all her hair over her left shoulder.

"Guilty conscience," Therese said, without changing her expression. She looked forward, clenching her teeth.

"No, you're acting like a stalker and staring at me. Just say what's on your mind."

"Why don't you say what's on your mind, Phoebe?" Therese felt her heart begin to gallop in her chest. "No, how about you explain why you seem to always be sneaking around with your phone—like I'm your mom or something! You're being shady, and you know it. Who were you on the phone with last night? Evan?!" Therese's voice ratcheted.

"What?! Evan? God, no. He was *your* horrible mistake. And when was I sneaking around?!" Phoebe squinted and looked to her right.

"Last week!" Therese exclaimed. "I walked by your room on Friday night, and you were whispering then. Do you not trust me anymore or something?" Therese asked.

"Oh, you mean Friday night when you threw a bunch of fried rice at me?" Phoebe shook her head. "Sorry if I wasn't in the mood to hang out with you after that."

"It's fine," Therese replied in frustration, "let's just forget it." Therese aimed the car's air condition vents at her underarms and turned the air to full blast to stamp out nervous sweats. "We're almost there. Do I look okay?" Therese asked.

Therese wore a yellow sundress that highlighted her hair, skin, and the glint in her eyes. She donned sandals of perfect summer gold, with thin straps and small rhinestones just over her toes.

"You look pretty, of course. He likes you," Phoebe said with a sigh, "you don't have to worry about that."

A quaint peach-and-white home on Mariposa Court met the girls at the end of their journey. Many of Miami's wealthy lived in sprawling Spanish-style homes. Tomas's leaned away from arches and iron, though. He opened the door as Therese and Phoebe reached out to ring the doorbell. His brown eyes sparkled through his glasses even as he tried to remain reserved in his excitement.

"Ladies, you made it! Please come in," he said between cheek kisses. "I'm so sorry you had to drive this far, but I really wanted you to come tonight. My friends are here, and I want you to meet everyone."

The girls walked onto the back patio.

"I just started making steaks. Are you hungry? Please tell me you're hungry." He smiled again. "Girls, you remember Luca, right?" Phoebe produced a smile that looked more like a grimace.

Therese responded, "I'm not too sure we've met. Hi, Luca." She leaned in for an obligatory Miami cheek kiss. "Nice to meet you."

"Likewise," Luca said, then he looked at Tomas and said something in Spanish that left both girls standing there with a "what'd you just say about me?" grin. Tomas thanked him and turned nervous attention to his newest guests. He shifted and fiddled with hands, in and out of his pockets, fluttering like a bird. First, Tomas wanted the girls to have food, then drinks—but what drinks? Then he wanted them to sit comfortably with a group at one table but decided to move them to another group where people were not playing cards.

"Do you girls want to see my house?" he finally asked. "Luca, keep an eye on the meat."

Therese stood, aware of herself. It seemed everyone on the patio turned to watch. Not that she wasn't used to it, but she was the only black woman there. And though she'd been in plenty of similar situations, she felt like she was under a microscope. The room could read Tomas's attraction to her, and the room didn't like it. Everyone donned painted-on, tight-lipped smirks as she and Phoebe lined up for their tour. Dressed in name brands Therese barely recognized, they all looked like sweaty, rich, twenty-something mannequins, and it made Therese's nape hairs rise. *Why do these types always act like they've never seen a black person before?* she asked herself as she stepped back into the cool air of Tomas's home.

Tomas's sincerity refreshed Therese—especially after Evan. He led her to each room, at times placing his hand on the small of her back, wanting her to see every inch of his home. Family portraits. Exercise bikes. His little brother's elementary school artwork—everything. It was clear Tomas's parents valued family and entertaining. Besides the enormous outdoor patio, full kitchen, and pool, they'd also invested in features like a full wine cellar.

"Tomas, you look exactly like your dad!" Therese looked at the portraits, then back at him.

"I do, just with a little more hair," he joked. He put his arm around her shoulders and leaned close to her ear. "You look gorgeous," he said.

After the tour, Therese made a stop in the bathroom to check the mirror and make sure her skin shone, and her face and teeth did, too. She beamed at herself. Happiness had become a foreign emotion. For months, she battled anxiety about dance. Part of that battle was self-loathing no one else could truly see. Despite her love for Phoebe, sometimes being around her flooded Therese with jealousy. At work, she battled restlessness. Boredom dogged her at home. But tonight, standing in Tomas's bathroom, happiness glowed from deep within her belly and radiated out of her chest. She realized it floated up and filled the room, too.

"Okay, calm down, T," she said to herself. "You don't want to look desperate when you go out there."

She left the bathroom, looking over her shoulder before she switched off the light to make sure she'd left it tidy. She tiptoed through the house, not quite sure she remembered the way back to the patio. She passed the room with the exercise bikes and elementary school artwork again. Once she stood at the patio threshold, she looked around, noticing some of the guests had already departed. *That little tour must have been longer than I thought.*

The party had taken on a more intimate tone. Those remaining were sitting together at one table and sharing deep conversation she couldn't quite make out. The guests were all of Cuban-American descent, and they sprinkled Spanish over many of the English phrases they found insufficient to express their points and positions. Therese noticed neither Tomas, Phoebe, nor Luca had joined the other guests at the table. She walked a little further to search for the trio, passing a man tending sizzling *churrasco* on the grill.

She followed the curved patio wall until she found them in conversation, standing uncomfortably close together. Phoebe's face was flushed and her brow furrowed. Wrongness replaced the happiness Therese had welcomed in the lavatory mirror moments before. Their voices mumbled, and Tomas appeared flustered, explaining himself to Phoebe. Finally, he placed both hands on her shoulders as Luca looked on. He tilted his head to the side as pity traversed his face.

"It'll be okay," Tomas said, loud enough for Therese to hear.

"Everything good, guys?" Therese asked as she approached, pretending she hadn't seen their exchange.

Tomas jumped, then rushed over to Therese, smiling.

"Of course, are you hungry? I'm still cooking," he asked. She had been, right up until she ran into their secret meeting.

"Yes," she lied. "And can I have a drink, please?" Tomas's countenance lifted and brightened. He'd become a bird again, fluttering at speed to make her a plate of grilled skirt steak and get her a glass of cherry brandy.

Luca grinned. He pointed in the direction of the main patio and walked away with no explanation.

"Phoebe," Therese sighed, placing her hands behind her back and tilting her head, "what is going on?" Her words had become staccato and sharp.

"We were just talking," Phoebe replied.

"Clearly. But about what?" Therese pressed.

"Something that was said while you were in the bathroom."

"Which was?" A pit formed in Therese's stomach.

"I'll tell you on the way home. Don't worry about it," Phoebe said, sliding her hand through the opening created by the bend in Therese's arm. "This boy wants to feed you! Let's go eat... again." she smiled.

Despite the awkward way it began, the night ended with lots of "let's all get together again" and phone number exchanges as guests started to leave and say goodbye to Tomas, sitting by Therese's side. It was just the social thing to do. Therese didn't expect to ever see these people again unless it was coordinated by Tomas. There were kisses and Spanish-laced farewells.

"Therese, don't worry, we'll teach you some Spanish. It's easy," a girl named Carla said, holding Therese's hands and smiling. Her black hair was pulled back into a classy chignon. The humidity of the night revealed the deep wave in her flat-ironed hair. "¡*Besos*!" she exclaimed over her shoulder, blowing kisses as she left the last few revelers.

Therese and Phoebe left almost immediately after. Of course, Tomas escorted them to the front door. Therese wondered where his family had gone and when they'd come back. As if reading her mind, Tomas announced, "I wanted you to meet my family. Next time." He leaned down to kiss her on both cheeks, pulled her close for a hug, then held her at a distance to take a last look. "I'll call you soon," he said.

Therese climbed into the car, lifted the lever that reclined her seat, and pushed back. In one day, she'd been angry, paranoid, and elated. Now, the residue of these emotions overwhelmed her into exhaustion. Tomas stood in his bricked driveway, waving happily at the girls. Unlike any guy she'd ever known, Tomas had no interest in appearing cool. He liked her and wanted it to show.

Phoebe backed out of the driveway, looking over her shoulder. The street's bustle had settled.

"Phoebs, on the patio," Therese asked sleepily, "what were you guys talking about?"

10

BEEFY RED HANDPRINTS SPLATTERED across Victor's abdomen. He stood seething in the steamed mirror of his bathroom. His scrubs for the day were loosely tied and settled low on his hips. He breathed as if he had been running. The worst words flew through his mind—one self-deprecating thought after another.

Slap. Slap. Slap. Slap. Victor alternated hands as he hit his flexed abdomen with open palms. It had to be as hard as he could muster. He deserved it.

Slap! Slap! Slap! Slap! Victor screamed a deep roar at the top of his voice, his head thrown back like a wolf howling into the night. He could not believe that his excitement about finding the Chae home made him lose his form. It had never happened before. He wanted to be imperceptible. A true ghost. A never-there entity. But instead, he ended up having a full-fledged conversation with a retiree from the Maryland Bureau of Investigations.

Victor ripped his scrub bottoms off and with one smooth, startling motion, sliced a four-inch laceration just below his left testicle with a razor blade. His scrotum recoiled in shock and protest. He sat on the edge of his tub with a string of small blood droplets clinging to his skin. Victor's abdomen rose and fell quickly as the drops expanded, rolling into one. Victor leaned his elbows into his thighs and formed a halo around his head with his hands, squeezing his temples as he cried. "Moron!"

He stood, wiping the tears from his face with his arm. He marched downstairs to the kitchen, where he'd tossed the card from retired Agent Marvin Cline. Victor's heart raced so quickly in his chest it generated its own radiating heat. He moved to the center of his orange-tiled kitchen and squeezed all ten fingers into his head as if trying to burst it. Cheeks full of air tensed and flattened as he forcefully exhaled through pursed lips. Victor had to figure out what to do. The morning's drive was meant to be phase one of a carefully executed plan. He'd let down Leslie. He didn't want her to feel thwarted. How could he explain his failure to her sketched face upstairs? He stood in the kitchen puffing and squeezing and bleeding, pressing his fingers behind the angle of his jaw into his carotid artery. Finally, he could feel his heart slow to a manageable pace.

"Victor! Think!" he shouted. He turned and looked at his reflection in the microwave door. *Calm down, think.* Victor had seen one valuable piece of evidence while at Wandering Lane: The blue shield. It must mean something. Something important enough for a teenager to put on his own car. It must have meant something he loved—a team, a sport, a club. Something.

Searching Google Images for a blue-and-gold shield in Maryland brought up at least twenty-eight shields—all except the one he needed. Flat, shiny, some 3-D. Of course, the state's crest appeared repeatedly, though it had no blue. Victor went back to the search bar and deleted "blue and gold shield CSA Maryland" and rapped his fingers on the laptop's black-and-silver keyboard. He bit his bottom lip as he entered a simplified search: "CSA Maryland." Leather purses filled the screen, some adorned with pearls and others gold buckles. Victor kept scrolling, even passed an auburn spider. He couldn't fathom how that was relevant to his search. At the left bottom of the page, though, he found a photo of teenage boys in royal blue soccer uniforms. "CSA Cup 2005" filled the caption line.

"Soccer! God, of course!" Victor recalled that Joseph had asked about getting back to soccer as soon as possible after his wisdom teeth were removed. Victor also recalled he wore a royal blue shirt with gold stripes down the sides. "I bet that was a soccer jersey." His voice lifted in excitement.

What's YouTube? Victor asked himself, clicking on the icon of the soccer players. It took him to a new landing page he'd never seen before. A list of video icons littered the right margin of the screen. A larger video sat to the left.

"Christian Soccer Athletes, First Blue." Victor nodded and pressed play. He watched twenty-eight minutes before he realized his first patient would be in the office before he could even get there. He had been sitting naked on his leather tan couch under vaulted ceilings.

Victor enthusiastically closed his laptop. Though he still had a driving urge to return to Wandering Lane, he'd do so in a different manner the next time. He sprinted up his staircase. In the bathroom, he reached into the back pocket of his discarded scrubs. His fingers found a crinkling flat foil packet. It had a black arch on the white and orange wrapping. Sutures. They brought even more relief. He'd stitch one or two into his cut. Though not needed, he saw placing sutures as a way to practice a small amount of self-forgiveness. He grabbed a scrub top from his closet, not even caring that the hanger protruded at an angle over the one beside it. He also didn't bother with his white coat and decided to wear one he had at the office. He did make sure to use his Medi-Pak dental products before leaving. No matter what, he wanted to smell as close to a packet of anti-septic wipes as he could.

"DR. JACOBS…" Kelly said, "…um… Mrs. Evensohn is pretty upset about her wait today," Kelly whispered to Victor as soon as he entered the front office to collect his mail. She was dressed in black scrubs, and her hair was pulled into a French braid. Her face was so close to his he could smell Juicy Fruit gum on her breath.

"Well, that's totally my fault. I'll make it up to her somehow." Despite how he'd spent his morning, Victor remained dedicated to his image as a caring oral surgeon. "Would you please apologize profusely to her? I mean really, really apologize." Victor looked over his shoulder at his glaring client. "She loves cats. Tell her my kitty was sick this morning, and I had to run her to the vet."

"You have a cat, Dr. Jacobs?" Kelly asked. Victor took a deep breath. "Oh, never mind. Sure, I'll take care of it." Kelly said, smiling broadly, ready for the opportunity to gain good office girl points. "Mrs. Evensohn?" Kelly leaned on the counter. Mrs. Evensohn rushed to the front with a file folder of dental records under her arm.

"Well, I certainly hope he's ready now." she said. She looked into the front office.

"He's gone to his office, and he'll be ready in just a moment." Kelly leaned in and whispered sadly, "His kitty got sick this morning, and he had to run her to the vet. He works such long days. He didn't want her to be home alone suffering all day, you know?"

Ms. Evensohn put her folder down on the counter and placed both her wrinkled, jeweled hands over her heart. "I should have known something came up!" she said, shaking her head. "Oh, I feel terrible. Listen, honey, I'm going to go sit down in the waiting room. Please tell the doctor to take his time. I'm in no hurry."

"Thank you so much for understanding, Mrs. Evensohn." Kelly pressed her eyebrows up and together. She closed the window, sat behind the desk, and called Victor.

"Dr. Jacobs? Don't worry about it; she's totally fine."

"I'M GOING TO HEAD OUT at three today, girls," Victor announced to his back-office staff. No one paid attention except Ann.

"Okay, how come, Dr. J?" Ann, a veteran surgical assistant, was preparing for a final procedure with Victor's partner. "Are you feeling alright?"

"Well, I've seen everyone on the schedule. I'm gonna do my charting at home tonight. Want to get some sun, maybe even a run," Victor replied as if asking permission.

"Okay, cool, Doc. Hope you have a nice night." Ann moved from the office to the hallway, laden with materials for the procedure. "We have a kid coming in for a frenectomy, like, right now."

"Oh, yeah, how old?" Victor asked. Ann shifted from her right foot to her left and repositioned her materials.

"Uh, I think fourteen?"

"Fourteen! Has he been able to close his teeth?" Victor continued the conversation, intentionally ignoring Ann's body language.

"*She's* actually got a large lingual frenum to remove, Doc." Ann turned to walk down the hallway. Victor looked through the glass and into the lobby. It was still empty.

"You guys are doing a tongue-tie release? We never do those." Victor followed.

"I think a community dentist wanted to send their patient here for it." She placed her materials on the surgical suite counter. "Just a favor."

"Well, I hope it works out." Victor moved his bag across his chest. "Poor kid's probably getting teased to death at school."

"Exactly," said Dr. Brent Michaels, Victor's partner. He stood in the doorway. "Haven't seen you all day. Busy?"

The men shook hands, and Victor stepped aside so that Dr. Michaels could access his supply counter.

"Yeah, pretty much. Heading out now. Gonna catch a run. Maybe go do notes at the park or something. I think I've spent less than thirty minutes outside this entire summer. When it gets cold, I'm gonna regret it." Victor's eyes focused on his colleague's face for disapproval or suspicion.

"Exactly, dude. The kids have me outside every single weekend with something. Cheerleading camp. Track practice. Swim. Soccer camp." Dr. Michaels towered at six foot three. He was deeply tanned with golden-blond hair. Sitting on his examination stool made him about Victor's height, and Victor wanted to hate him. Of course, he'd have the perfect wife and kids and life and outdoor summer activities. Victor didn't hate him, though, because his life sounded exceedingly boring.

"Three kids and five thousand clubs, dude." Dr. Michaels laughed. "The wife and her mom sign them up for every possible thing."

"I forgot they were getting into soccer these days." Victor's mind began to race. "How old are they now?"

"Dude. Twelve, ten, and seven already." He shook his head. "It's crazy."

"Well, time flies, man." Victor turned to walk out of the suite, and Ann rolled her eyes. She wanted to get started so she could leave work soon, too.

"Oh, hey, buddy," Victor paused. "Where do the kids play this summer? Might check 'em out on the weekend."

"Totally. Can't believe I forgot to invite you. The wife would tell me I have horrible manners." He laughed. "Dude, every Saturday. The little one is playing at Snellen Elementary this weekend. Big ones are so stoked. They're letting them play at Centennial, where the high schoolers normally practice. 9:00 A.M." He looked at Ann. "We're pretty much ready, right?" She nodded.

"Well, I'll probably stop by," Victor said as he tapped the glass door frame, thinking about Joseph and Leslie. Victor's partner hadn't mentioned if his kids played for CSA, but Victor couldn't ask. When he executed the plan, he didn't want anyone to know he had anything to do with it.

"9:00 A.M. on a Saturday for kids that aren't even yours..." Brent teased. "That's dedication, Uncle Vic."

Victor laughed, too. "Alright, buddy, take it easy."

He decided to stop at home first. The afternoon scent of cleaning solutions greeted him at the front door. His maid had been there. The house never dirtied. But she came like clockwork every Thursday at noon. The idea of an immaculate home intoxicated Victor. He easily became consumed by its perfection. Though he found no evidence of the maid's presence, Victor walked through each inch of the home. He wanted to be alone as he prepared.

"Alright," he spoke aloud, "I'm gonna change real quick." He headed up the stairs again, not as briskly as in the morning. "I should probably go to the fields first." He coached himself. "In and out, Victor. In and out."

His original plan included tracking Joseph through his daily routine, but summer break complicated things. Who knows—this kid could've slept all day. Maybe soccer practice happened early in the morning, maybe late in the evening. Maybe he had a summer job. Maybe he didn't. Victor's ability to find out had been compromised by the morning's events at Wandering Lane. Now, if he didn't find that truck at the Centennial soccer field, he'd have to stop by the other spots. The spots where teenagers cool and rich enough to have brand new Jeeps hung out with their friends.

He took off his scrubs, folded them into a square, and placed them in the bottom of his hamper. He continued speaking to himself.

"Remember, Victor; you're not looking for the kid. You're looking for the kid's car." He stood biting his lip with his arms folded. He spoke again. "Wait, okay. If you see the car, then what?" Victor pulled a nude push-up bra out of the top bureau drawer in his closet. He looked behind the bras for the pad inserts. He placed one strap over his shoulder, then the next, expertly closing the hooks behind him. He continued talking aloud, easing his head into one of his favorite stalking disguises.

"Okay, think. If you see the car, then try to park somewhere out of the way and keep your eye on it?" he asked himself. He stepped into the matching panties. "No, that'll make it so much easier to get seen." He tied the baby pink halter dress around his neck. The lace fell to the tops of his feet. On the far-right wall inside the closet, a hanging board held a dozen long necklaces for summer, fall, or whenever. He selected one in gold with baby pink beads. *I really don't feel like wearing earrings—clip-ons hurt.* Victor opted for a fuller black bob wig than others that might reveal his ears. This one had adorable bangs and an angled bob, long at the jawline and layered and stacked in the back. He slid it over his hair and tugged to secure it to the back of his head, pushing the bangs out of his eyes with the tips of his fingers.

He picked taupe Michael Kors oversized shades and placed them in his wig while he continued getting ready. He needed a few bracelets and a little rose lip shimmer, all lying on top of the drawer in an '80s-style mini Caboodle. His maid always complimented him on how tidy his girlfriend kept her things. He never corrected her.

Victor walked on his toes in his summer dress into his bathroom. The perfect lighting complemented him. His skin looked flawless. He didn't have to shave. Nonetheless, he still dabbed MAC NW20 concealer under his eyes. And over his top lip. And around his chin. He put on the sunglasses. With them on, he could be taken for a twenty-five-year-old Asian woman. To complete his look, Victor added a thin jade bangle, one he'd bought three weeks ago in honor of Leslie Chae.

The Audi would suffice for this part of the plan. Changing cars was low yield the last time he searched for the Chaes. In fact, Victor realized, if he'd driven the Audi and looked like he belonged in that neighborhood, retired Agent Marvin Cline may not have paid attention to him at all.

Right before heading to the car, Victor pulled a pearlized, pink, crossbody purse from the hall closet next to the garage. He kept his shoes in a mudroom by the door and never wore any in the home. He slipped his feet into wedges, wriggling his toes right up to the front.

"Perfect." Victor nodded at his flawless feet. "This is going to go perfect."

II

TUESDAY MORNING, Therese received a text from Tomas:

I want to take you to Lincoln Road
for gelato.

She rubbed her eyes and slid upright against the headboard, waking herself to respond. In her usual post-heartbreak mode, she would have played things slow. The freedom of a week away from her rejections added momentum to her feelings, though. She forgot she had met Tomas just two days before. She had also forgotten that Phoebe had never explained the patio encounter.

Therese knew the pulse of falling in love. It happened rapidly, maybe even dangerously so. It was necessary and unstoppable. She thought it might be happening now. So she let it make her put plans in place. Therese had asked to borrow Phoebe's car. Before she had pulled out of the driveway, Therese searched for riding music, for fantasies of romance. In the console, she stumbled across a Dave Matthews Band cassette tape.

"Yes! 'Crash!'" she shouted.

Phoebe had watched from the living room window. She stood with one hand on her hip and waved with the other, grateful Therese couldn't tell she was crying.

Therese sung, "*I say my hell is the closet I'm stuck inside—I can't see the light*," as she backed out of the driveway. She stuck out her tongue, then blew Phoebe a kiss. *Phoebe's petrified*, Therese thought, laughing to herself. She tried to keep a straight face. She knew Phoebe had good reason to worry. Therese had no driver's license, nor insurance, nor a sufficient attention span. Driving down to Miami, she sang, and daydreamed, and almost ran into at least one mattress. But she felt free and grateful for the city's beauty.

At Seaside 46, she entered the most breathtakingly beautiful lobby she'd ever seen. The room boasted marble floors, mahogany, gold, and an entrance window view of the ocean. The concierge station sat prominently to the left of the room. An elderly Latino man sat behind the raised station. He watched the door, straightened his tie, and tidied his space.

"*Buenas noches, señora*," he nodded, grinning with a mustache that covered his lips.

Therese had lived in and around Florida long enough to understand a great deal of Spanish. However, she'd rebelled at taking Spanish classes in school and was embarrassed to attempt it as an adult because she didn't know the grammar rules. The concierge bowed his head, realizing she was one of the unfortunate souls who could not converse in his mother tongue. He walked over to her, guiding the elbow of her left arm, and led her to the elevators.

"*Gracias*," she replied. Therese's few Spanish words always caught people by surprise. She pronounced them with the speed, rhythm, and accent of native speakers. Combined with what people deemed a racially ambiguous look and the rainbow of complexions and textures of the Latino world, many people thought she was only pretending to be an exclusively English-speaking beauty.

She had stepped in the elevator, pushed thirty-three, then found herself catapulted from the lobby to her destination in an instant. She disembarked with a "Wow," stepping out and looking back at the elevator like she'd been on a spaceship.

"Come in!" Tomas's voice boomed. Therese's finger had lingered at the doorbell. She tried to buy time before she entered to hide her nervousness.

"¡*Buenas*! You made it!" Tomas walked to the foyer to greet Therese with his arms wide open. His simple, white button-down shirt accented the hint of golden brown in his skin. He wore contacts instead of glasses. His hair hadn't been gelled. It fell feathered in a soft, dark brown mane around his face. She thought his whole look reminiscent of a young Andy Garcia. Beautiful.

Tomas could never greet her without a hug. And this time, he cupped her face with his right hand and placed his lips gently on her cheekbone. She found her fingers lingering at his back much longer than could be considered casual or even polite in some circles. He stepped back, beaming.

"You look pretty. I made you a drink," Tomas spoke. She wanted to compliment him or say thank you. She managed, though, just to look down at her feet.

"Let her get in the door first." Luca was there. He'd come from another room, somewhere out of sight. Therese hadn't realized he was Tomas's roommate. Tomas laughed and stepped back, allowing Luca his turn at cheek kisses and other greetings. Transported from Haiti and Cuba, the ultimately up-close hybrid culture of Miami still threw Therese at times. Just an hour north in Boca Raton, much less warmth existed. There, one could be made to feel invisible. Miami soothed her heart. She knew she'd never go long in *this* town without a congenial touch.

"Luca! Good to see you again."

"Likewise, likewise," he said, "You kids enjoy yourself tonight." He waved on his way out the front door.

"Are you hungry?" Tomas seemed to scramble to the kitchen, pointing out the sofa as he ran past the living room. From the kitchen, Therese heard rumbling and clanking dishes. She took a seat and looked around the apartment. White marble and glass. Everywhere. *These people have so much money,* she thought, realizing this was at least the third property Tomas and his family owned.

When Tomas placed a cherry brandy before her and exclaimed, "Try it! I made this from my own recipe!" Therese obliged and drank it all. Her chest burned. "See," Tomas said as he grasped his hands behind his back, "it's not strong is it?! Basically juice!"

Heat rose through Therese's nostrils, and her eyes wavered as if they might cross. Tomas stared at her. Silence. She pushed her lips together and looked at the floor. He was still staring when she looked back up.

"You okay?" he asked.

"Yes," her response escaped her lips in a hoarse whisper.

Tomas laughed. "You sure? I promise I'll feed you but come outside first." Tomas reassured her.

Therese stepped out into the salty, blue breeze of the Atlantic. Even as high up as the thirty-third floor, its intoxicating fragrance added to her infatuation with it. It made her feel beautiful and alive. It made her feel loved, protected even. As long as the waves came in, keeping the surest of universal laws, Therese knew that ultimately, things would be okay.

Together Tomas and Therese took in the water beneath them, blue as the Caribbean.

"What did you think of the party last night?" Tomas asked. "Everyone thought you were absolutely stunning."

"Aw, thanks," she replied. "I wasn't sure."

"Yeah. They loved you," Tomas responded. "I thought Phoebe would have told you. She heard them while you were in the bathroom. They told me you were out of my league." Tomas shook his head and tossed back more brandy. "How is Phoebe anyway? Bored?"

"Oh no, I just spoke with her. She's fine on the beach."

"Are you sure?"

"Yep," she laughed. "Wanna call her to check?"

"Yeah! Let's call her." Therese didn't love the idea of contacting Phoebe in the middle of their breezy turquoise paradise, but she complied. "Let me go get my phone."

Therese turned to walk back through the glass door leading to the living room and her purse. As she turned, she could see Tomas in the glass reflection watching her backside. She could pretend to be offended, but she was flattered. Besides, she knew her behind in jeans was a force, a superpower, even though Madam Liliane always hated its inability to go unnoticed.

"Phoebe, what's up?" Tomas spoke into Therese's cell phone.

"Hello! What are you guys doing?!" She sounded more excited than Therese expected she would.

"Here, let me put you on speakerphone." Tomas adjusted the call and continued, "I'm about to take your beautiful roommate out to dinner." Tomas looked into Therese's eyes, then winked and pulled her in for a forehead kiss.

"Oh, that's nice." Phoebe's enthusiasm waned.

"We just wanted to check on you," Tomas said. A smile came through in his voice.

"Thanks. You guys have fun," Phoebe responded. The call dropped.

"Bye, Phoebs." Therese chimed in too late. She felt a twinge of guilt. Maybe it *was* a little selfish to spend her girls' week with Tomas, but his allure was magnetic. She needed a place to feel new and special.

In the car, Therese's halter-topped, bare back clung to the leather. Her hands never could find a comfortable resting place, so she decided to sit on them. She'd been to Lincoln Road a few times before, but the visits were spaced enough that each one was a rediscovery. A paved carmine path beyond the crosswalk led to a long corridor of glass-fronted shops, divided by palm trees. The couple had found the perfect time to hit Sushi Samba, which would become overrun by the dinner crowd within the hour.

"Can we sit outside?" she asked the host. "If that's okay?" She looked at Tomas.

He nodded. "After you!"

Facing the breezeway, Tomas and Therese watched passing patrons as the evening began to take form. Unlike all the others, their table was missing an orange umbrella. Therese preferred it that way. She always feared faulty patio furniture, as silly as she knew that seemed. Besides, she loved the way her own skin tingled with the heat of an evening in Miami's summer sun. Tomas watched her as she got comfortable in her seat and smoothed her hair up and out of her face. Her skin glistened as if encrusted by a trillion tiny, brilliant diamonds. Tomas ran his hand over her left forearm and sighed.

A feast was spread over their round silver table. Nerves led to a few clumsy false starts with dropped napkins and chopsticks. Over a shared plate of tempura shrimp and vegetables, they settled into a conversation. And once there, they locked into each other, rendering the entire world around them silent and obsolete.

"I was recently married." Tomas began to share. "It was something I never should have done. I wasn't even in love." The marriage was as doomed as it was rushed, he said. Its inception at the courthouse was one of thousands of red flags. Loving his family as passionately as Tomas did, nuptials in the absence of his parents and brother felt empty, but it was what the woman wanted. They split just eighteen months later.

Relationship experts would have condemned Therese and Tomas's conversation—it wasn't first-date light and airy. But it was as real as the food sitting on their plates. It had texture. It had depth and temperature, even. It fed the soul. Therese had been in dire need of this type of presence and the proper audience for emotional nudity. Tomas was up for the job.

"Well, since we're sharing," Therese took a napkin and dabbed her mouth, "I recently dated this guy from my dance studio. We met like a year ago and practiced together a lot for this one audition last spring." Therese gauged Tomas's face for disapproval. His face looked open, his eyes accepting. She continued, "Something happened earlier the day of the audition that threw me off, and I blew it." Therese considered stopping. The bad taste of Evan's antics soured her food. "Anyway, we were supposed to audition again for another role. He told me he picked someone else as his partner and just stopped talking to me three weeks ago. I haven't seen him since. I should have known this was coming; he wasn't the nicest. Kind of stupid of me, right?" Therese took a sip of her coconut *leite*.

What she didn't want to say was that she allowed Evan to treat her as if she were deserving only of love under the cover of darkness. Out of sight... always and most importantly out of sight. She remembered the disgust his friends showed when one night, he had driven them all to a Dolphins football game. She rode in the front seat of his father's big-body Benz. He told his friends to sit in the back. He made a point to stay by her side all night. He kissed her on the cheek for the Jumbotron. He played and danced with her in the parking lot afterward. His friends stood by smelling the threat of interracial, intercultural, interclass love. They despised it. She had gotten out of her place. A few days later, Evan's tone had changed. He had informed her that she should become comfortable in the shadows. And for some time, she had convinced herself she should, too.

Tomas drank sake in between puffs of a cigarette.

"I don't judge people, Therese," he said as he reached for her hand, "on anything besides how they treat others." She didn't know how to place her body or hands after recounting the details of the disappearing act that was Evan. "Who am I to judge anyway? Look at my life." Tomas blew his smoke away from her, then leaned over and put loose hairs behind her ear. "Want to order dessert?"

She laughed. "Um, I thought we were getting gelato."

"We can have both! C'mon get both. We can have whatever we want." He raised his hand to get the waiter's attention. "*¿Puedo tener un menú?*" he asked. The waiter brought back a menu already flipped to the desserts.

"Speaking Spanish at a Japanese restaurant, Tomas?" Therese teased. "Very Miami of you."

"I can't speak Japanese." He winked, then flipped to the front of the menu and read, "Sushi Samba serves up Brazilian-Peruvian-Japanese cuisine! See, it's fusion! Basically, all languages are welcome!" They laughed and decided on a chocolate banana cake for dessert. She let him feed her the first bite.

"So, what happened that threw you off?" Tomas asked, caressing the silver ring on her forefinger.

"What do you mean?" Therese sipped her drink again.

"Remember, you said with your auditions... something happened?"

"Oh Lord, that's a crazy story you may not want to hear!" She giggled, looking down at the table and shaking her head.

That day, she told him, she'd been standing on the train platform waiting and marking her routine with tiny hand and foot movements to stave off nervous thoughts. Just as she'd completed a miniature *rond de jambe*, a pitter-pat to her derriere in rhythm to the words, "Uh huh, uh huh, uh huh," surprised her. She explained how it was her worst encounter with the Crazy Train Lady but decided against that particular term in case it made her sound mean.

"I turned around, and, literally, she was dressed from head to toe in super old denim and evil eye jewelry, humping the air behind me. Her lips were puckered like she was about to kiss someone. And she was doing this weird thing with her nose—trying to make it look like a bull, I think."

Tomas nearly spat his drink out on the table. He leaned away from Therese and let out a hearty laugh. "What?!" he cackled. He held a black cloth napkin to his face, turning pink.

"Seriously, she literally assaults me twice a day!"

"Wait, who is she?!" Tomas continued to laugh.

"I have no idea! She calls me Summer and talks about my mom all the time." Therese continued laughing, but Tomas looked at her with a fading smile.

"How'd she come up with the name Summer?" he asked, but Therese was already shaking her head.

"No clue!"

"Hmmm, that's weird. Be careful with this lady—this crazy train lady!"

Therese looked down and grinned. "Yep, that's what I call her. But only in my mind."

THE TIME FOR A WALK AND GELATO wound its way into their night. They somehow tuned out the world long enough to miss the dinnertime throng, now spilling out the restaurant's door from the hostess station. As if they'd been together for years, Tomas reached for Therese's hand as they left the patio.

Therese struggled to keep her tummy tucked in, but she could find room for raspberry gelato any day. They sat on a bench outside the closing shop, her in his lap, trading tastes. By the time they'd finished their second dessert, the sun had hidden behind the trees then wrapped itself in the ocean. The breeze caressed the night and their new love.

It had to be close to eleven when they returned to the condo and the couple went to the balcony. The tone and mood had settled from the hyper frenzy of a day on the beach. Tomas put his forearms on the balcony and leaned forward, looking off into the distance. Therese wanted to look at the night ocean with its white-topped wave crests. But the wave of hair over Tomas's eyes captured her. She lifted her hand to touch it. It was as soft as she thought it would be.

"I'm really not sure what I'm doing with my life, Therese," Tomas said. She listened and let her mind bounce around to find meaning for his sentiment. Finding none, she remained silent and waited. "I'm totally lost sometimes with what I want to do."

"Oh, I thought you delivered babies. Right?" She looked up and into his face.

"*Si, pero…*" Tomas remembered her language, "…yeah, but that's not really what I want to do. It's what I'm training to do because it's what my father does. His practice is mine to have one day." She listened and waited again. "If I had my choice, I'd leave Miami. I'm ready to see more of the world."

From preschool through his specialty residency, Tomas had gone to private schools in the same fifteen-mile radius. He'd never lived anywhere but Miami, ever.

"What would happen if you did? If you left to experience more of the world?" Therese asked.

"I can't leave my family. That's not how it is. It's different for me—especially being the firstborn," he explained.

"I see," said Therese, wishing she had family to whom she felt so connected or even shackled. Tomas looked at her, cupping her dewy face in his hands. He leaned down with lips parted to kiss her but stopped short and looked back out at the water, dropping his hands.

"I shouldn't be doing this," he suddenly whispered.

What do you mean? Therese thought over and over. She searched his face and listened intently for an explanation to her silent thoughts. The crash of ocean waves below her filled the space. Tense stillness grew like a wall between them.

"What's the matter?" Therese asked.

"Let's go watch TV," Tomas responded. "What kind of shows do you like?" He turned around and slid the glass door to the living room open.

"I'm trying not to be awkward," Therese said as she stepped across the threshold, "but you're acting a little, um," she stopped. "Is everything okay?" she finally asked.

"Yeah, everything's fine," Tomas replied. "Do you like reality shows?" He sat on the couch and turned the TV to E! Entertainment.

After watching an episode of *Dr. 90210*, Therese accepted there would be no kiss. She had fallen into a withdrawn silence. Despite this, Tomas asked if he could see her the next day for a dinner with friends. For professionals that were well beyond school age, Tomas and his friends partied often.

"I'll call in the morning and come get you at five if that's okay—we're going to dinner in Riviera near the beach house."

On the late-night drive back to Dara's beach home, Therese replayed the end of the evening. Until the last hour, it had been perfect. Tomas endeared her to himself by refusing to capitalize on her obvious attraction to him. He had been as open as possible—so had she. She wasn't sure what she'd missed, but she wanted to know why he felt something they were doing was wrong. Her heart had plummeted on the balcony and sat low in her belly. A deep wave of disappointment washed over her and accompanied her on the ride back to Riviera.

12

NEITHER JOSEPH NOR HIS JEEP were visible at the Centennial soccer fields. He wasn't at Chipotle on Little Patuxent. He wasn't at the mall's food court. He wasn't even at one of the fast-food spots on Snowden. Before leaving one lot, Victor decided to buy a large fry in a drive-through. The heat of the fry grease and the polyester of Victor's pink dress made the backs of his thighs sweat. *This is so gross*, he thought, pulling out and driving across three lanes to turn left onto Waterloo Road. Victor opened his white paper bag for napkins, wiping salt and oil off his fingers and the steering wheel.

He looked in the mirror to check his gloss. From the corner of his eye, he saw red brake lights suddenly appear. He stopped, and his square fingers pressed the horn. He yelled at the windshield, watching the driver complete their unplanned right turn.

"Dumbass," he said, then wiped his mouth. Three seconds later, though, he held a different sentiment. "Oh God," he laughed, shaking his head up at the roof of his car. "Thank you!"

The car in front of him had turned into the Cold Stone Creamery off Waterloo. Visible from the street, Joseph leaned on the back of his Jeep, facing the main road. Alone, except for his waffle cone.

"Well, Joey, you got the ice cream!" Victor kept driving, nodding and giggling. "But you're not supposed to eat the waffle!" He shook his head, cackling again.

Victor pulled into the entrance of Ashton Woods Apartments just a few blocks down and waited. He took a gamble. Joseph could finish his ice cream and head anywhere. But Victor knew he would have to pass those apartments, loop on the roundabout, and exit left if he wanted to go home.

Victor waited. He ate his fries with deliberate intention, sucking the salt off the ends. *I'm going to follow you and kill you, and you'll never see it coming, Joey. You'll never see it coming.* His thoughts rumbled like a corral of horses. A circular track. *You'll never see it coming.* The idea of surprise allured him. The idea of control overwhelmed him. The knowledge that he could, and would, determine how many more days Joseph lived intoxicated him.

Joseph drove by, holding his mouth open for the last bite of his waffle cone. Victor rolled his car to the stop sign of the complex and let a black Lexus pass in front of him. *Up the hill. To the yield sign. Yield to traffic in the circle. Go in. Pass one exit. Pass two exits. Leave on the left exit. We're back by the Giant grocery store.*

Two cars sat between Joseph's Jeep and Victor. He pulled down the sun visor, comforted by the added layer to his disguise. *Well, where are you headed, Joey?* Joseph passed the grocery store and turned left into a bricked strip mall beside it. Victor tried to hang back, but several cars piled behind him. He drove to the end of the parking lot, looking in the rearview and side mirrors at the Jeep. The animal hospital parking lot held a space right at the front. Victor parked and watched. Joseph had stopped at the first store, a restaurant, and sat on the front of his truck. The parking lot was full. Summer sun glared off every hood. A Latina walked up and stood between Joseph's knees. She stood about five feet tall. From a distance, she looked like a pole in her black jeans and Hunan Legend T-shirt.

"Joey, you've got a girlfriend?" Victor found something else to make him cackle. "A Mexican one?!" Victor shook his head. "Mommy and Daddy definitely must not know. A Mexican!" Victor clapped his forehead. "Yuck!"

He wondered how Joseph could have foregone the perfect beauty of his Korean classmates. Victor's face warmed with rage. *Looks like someone deserves to get killed.* Victor watched the couple from behind his designer shades. They climbed into the truck and talked. Joseph had removed the Jeep top and doors. Victor could see his hand on his girlfriend's thighs and his soccer bag in a back floor compartment. Joseph reached behind her seat and lifted a large, green Gatorade bottle. He took a long gulp. *The ice cream must have made him thirsty*, Victor thought as he watched.

Joseph tossed the bottle over his shoulder, and it landed with a bounce on the floor. Fifteen minutes of break time ended with a long, sloppy kiss and tickling. The Latina disappeared back into Hunan's. Joseph adjusted his shorts, waved, and motioned he would call her later. He reversed his truck and started to leave. Victor backed out, too.

You need to stop and turn around, Victor told himself, then he ignored his own warning. Instead of going home, he turned right into Wandering Lane. He was returning in under twelve hours. There were no cars between him and Joseph. It was 5:49 P.M. The old man could be walking again. Victor had two thoughts. He could go to the clubhouse and pretend he was there for whatever event was responsible for the cars in the parking lot. Or he could stay directly behind Joey. *I'm going crazy*, he thought, as he decided to follow Joseph so close it would be impossible for Joey not to notice. Once they turned by the house with the chest tomb mailbox, Victor slowed down to a crawl. He wanted to see what Joseph would do with the things on the back floor of the truck. Meanwhile, the old man came to stand at the subdivision's entrance, talking to two walking buddies.

Joseph stood in the driveway with the back of his Jeep open. A boy of about twelve came out of the house and tried to wrestle with him. Though they looked almost identical to his, his brother's bigger legs and arms dominated the middle-schooler. They laughed as Joseph held him in submission on the ground. Then he got up and lifted his blue bag from the Jeep. Victor was one house over. As he rounded the cul-de-sac, he looked carefully at Joseph's hands. *He must leave that water bottle in the car all the time*, Victor thought, as he sped up and left the street. Joseph and his brother didn't notice they'd been surveilled and went through an open garage door pretending to fight.

The old man waved as Victor rolled to a stop before leaving the Wandering Lane neighborhood exit. Though nerves bubbled his bowels, Victor managed a quick flitter of his fingers in a polite wave. He attempted a demure smile and small bow. Retired Agent Cline nodded and raised his walking stick. Victor took a quick left out of the subdivision, relieved.

THE THICKEST WET BLANKET of summertime humidity met Victor at the soccer fields on Saturday. Friday had been almost unbearable. Even though he had watched Joseph again during the 5:30 break at Hunan's with the Latina and the Gatorade bottle, Victor wouldn't allow himself to go back to Wandering Lane. The wait almost killed him. So did his father's repeat voicemails. Mr. Jacobs wanted to announce that he found it very odd that Victor had not mentioned or searched for his almost fiancée in three days. *Maybe I killed her,* Victor joked in his own mind during one call. He would have to address the girlfriend situation, but the lure of Joseph's death claimed every inch in the landscape of his mind.

Centennial soccer fields were clamoring. Moms in cellulite-squeezing yoga pants rushed past carrying team snacks. They yelled to Matts and Joshes, "Come on, get your stuff," and chastised them with, "It's too late now; if you don't have the right cleats, you'll have to sit out."

Dads stood around with their hands in their pockets or folded arms resting on their bellies. They talked about team records and strategies. Coaches paced. Even at six years old, the children in the junior tournament bore the seriousness of these competitions. The weight of their parents' egos rested squarely on their tiny backs.

Joseph's Jeep was parked in the far-right lot. There was one empty space three cars down from it. Victor took the space and flipped his longer black wig over the shoulder of his royal blue maxi dress as he descended from the car. Casual gold flip flops and a gold bag accented a series of thin, gold necklaces and a large, braided ring. It was still morning cool. He draped a mustard yellow silk wrap over his shoulders and scanned the parking lot. At least five overdressed Asian moms in blue and gold disembarked cars and flipped their hair over their shoulders. He would blend in.

Victor turned to his trunk and lifted a crate of large, green Gatorade bottles. Nineteen bottles in rows of six. Except for the middle row. It held seven. Victor carried the bottles through the emptying parking lot. Families scrambled to fields holding lawn chairs and babies. Victor stooped behind Joseph's Jeep. He placed the crate on the ground, then stood and leaned to look into the back of the truck. He lifted the middle bottle from the middle row in his crate. Victor had filled it with Halcion and water in his orange-walled kitchen that morning. Six Halcion, in fact—the Jeffrey Dahmer sedative of choice. Victor pulled Joseph's bottle from the trunk and tossed his sleeping solution-filled replacement to the truck's floor. *I should replace the top with the old one. This one looks too new,* Victor thought. For fear of looking suspicious, though, he left it. He bent to lift the crate and took a few more steps until he heard a voice behind him.

"Ma'am."

Victor kept walking.

"Ma'am!" a middle-aged man called again. Victor looked over his shoulder, then turned to stop. "Here, let me grab this for you." The man took the bottles. "What field?" Victor pointed to where the juniors played and was careful not to speak, satisfied that his shades covered the majority of his face. He attempted a traditional Korean mom bow. Joseph's original bottle sat on the bumper and Victor shuffled over to stand in front of it. "You're Sung's mom, right? I've seen you at a few of these things. Good luck! Go Blue!"

The soccer dad propped the crate up on his shoulder and walked toward the field, his cargo shorts resting above his calves. Victor hoped Sung's mom was not at the field. He hurried back to his car and left the

94

games. He hoped he would hear a breaking news report of a shutdown highway somewhere near the fields. Maybe helicopter reports. Maybe even an explosion.

JOSEPH AND HIS TEAMMATES posed for formal pictures and fun ones. They were the summer tournament champs. The team wanted Joseph to have the game ball. They told him to put it on a dorm shelf at Stanford. He made great saves that day. He was their starting goalie and the oldest on the team. His parents patted him on the back and let him celebrate with his teammates.

"Hey, Joe!" A sweaty teammate shouted across the parking lot. "See you at lunch, right?"

"Yeah!" Joseph replied. "I'm going to call my girlfriend and see if she can come. I'll meet you guys!" The team had decided to celebrate with a meal at the mall—The Cheesecake Factory, of course.

"Hello, thank you for calling Hunan's," the Latina answered the phone at her summer job.

"Hello, may I speak to Ariana?" Joseph replied.

"Hey! It's me."

"I know; I just try to sound professional." His voice tremored with enthusiasm. "We won! Wanna go get lunch with us at Cheesecake?"

"Oh my God, yes! Congrats!" Ariana's voice lifted through the restaurant. "Oh, I have to ask if I can take lunch now. You're going now, right?" Ariana asked.

"Yeah, I'm gonna come get you," he replied. Joseph heard his girlfriend put down the phone and could hear the distant conversation. The restaurant was still empty.

"Okay!" She returned to the phone. "He said I can have extra time. Come get me!"

"I'll be there," Joseph said. He was looking over his shoulder for his water bottle as he spoke. He grabbed it from the floor and squirted water into his mouth. "I'll be there in about ten minutes. I love you." Joseph was already putting his truck in reverse and taking another drink from the bottle.

"Love you, too!" Ariana hung up.

Two miles away from the restaurant, Joseph became drowsy and swerved up the hill on Waterloo Road. Horns beeped and blared as he raged forward, somehow thinking going faster would blast him out of the sleepy fog descending on his vision.

Up the hill. To the yield sign. Yield to traffic in the circle. Go in. Joseph, sedated, couldn't remember what he was supposed to do once inside the circle. Instead of following the curve to the left, his head bobbed as he pushed the Jeep's brush bar into the first guard rail. Grinding metal screeched as his truck hopped the barrier. Joseph, in his topless Jeep, dropped forty-five feet to the quiet Saturday morning highway.

13

THERESE WAITED UNTIL NINE at night and then, standing naked in the middle of the bedroom, found herself pushing the telephone icon on Tomas's contact screen again.

"You've reached 305…" a robotic operator answered. Therese swung her arm in the direction of the bed, hoping the phone would land on the mattress.

"Forget it," she groaned.

Four hours. He was supposed to have picked her up four hours ago. She had spent the entire morning waiting to get out of bed, hoping a text from him would come through. She spent the morning fending off the growing knot of rejection in her core. And Phoebe, being who she was, spent the morning giving her love and warnings.

"T, the other night at the party…" she had said as the two sat on the house's back-porch rocking chairs.

"Yeah?" she leaned forward and gnawed on the inside of her cheek. The balls of her feet pushed her back in her chair.

"I overheard someone asking Tomas why you were there." Phoebe had continued.

"Who?"

"I don't know, some guy." Phoebe piled her hair in a bun. "I think people forget that just 'cause we can't *speak* Spanish doesn't mean we can't *understand* some of it." She shook her head. "I pulled Tomas to the side to ask what the guy's problem was."

"And what did Tomas say?" Therese looked from Phoebe to the wooden planks of the porch floor and back again.

"Honestly, it was more what he didn't say."

"What do you mean, Phoebs?"

"I mean, he didn't say anything." Phoebe had explained. "He just looked at the guy and laughed it off. I pulled him to the side and was, like, 'You like my friend, right?' and he said 'of course' and all this other stuff, so I asked him why he wasn't standing up for you."

"And?" Therese's eyes had begun to burn.

"And that's pretty much when you walked up. He was just saying it wasn't that serious and I should relax." She wrinkled her forehead and pressed her lips together. "Honestly, Therese, I'd forget him. You don't really know him anyway."

Now it was night, and for the past hour, Therese had been naked and crying. She had cried in the shower, where the warm water made her head feel as if it was floating in a pool of blood. She had cried looking at her perfect, bronzed figure—her breasts and behind stood at opposite sides of her flat abdomen. She knew beauty was fully hers. She also knew in this world she was trying to live in, her beauty did not matter. Neither did her talent, nor the love she wanted to give. Therese's salty tears mingled with the warm shower water. And when she couldn't cry anymore, she had patted her body dry with a thick, lush pink towel and stood naked in the middle of the bedroom.

Her phone rang at 9:13.

"Therese!" It was Tomas. He sounded too happy for her liking.

"Yeah?"

"I'm so sorry; I left my phone in the car. I'm downstairs. Can I talk to you?"

"You're downstairs where?"

"At your house." His voice faltered.

"You left your phone in the car when?" Therese tried to avoid the bubbling craziness that would make her interrogate a man she'd known for just three days.

"All night," Tomas replied.

"So, did you see it ring a few minutes ago?"

"No, did I miss something?" Tomas's voice was just above a deep, low whisper.

"Um, how do you know which house we're in anyway?" Therese asked, looking for another angle.

Tomas was silent for a long pause. Finally, he said, "Uh, I just drove the neighborhood until I found your car."

Therese stopped to think before responding. The subdivision was large. Driving around to find their house seemed inefficient, at best. *Why didn't he just call?* she thought.

"I'm sorry." Tomas apologized. "I didn't think you'd mind."

"It's fine." Therese frowned. "Let me throw something on."

Downstairs, the front door creaked. Therese stepped onto the flagstone in thin white flip-flops. She'd tied a lavender halter at the nape of her neck. She'd piled her hair up and held it in place with a large brown clip that disappeared in her cascading curls. Dewy, her skin glowed from the heat of the shower and shine of shea butter. Johnson & Johnson gel made the rest of her glisten. Eyelet lavender lace laid flat against her skin, starting sharply at the undercurve of her breasts. Her belly was exposed all the way to the crest of her hips, where a soft, flowing, linen skirt in the same shade of purple flowed to the ground.

"Wow," Tomas mouthed, staring at her and running his tanned hand through his hair. He set his black-and-white paper coffee cup on the trunk of the car. He had been leaning there in linen of his own—a shirt in light blue, cuffed at the wrists and pushed to his elbows. He pushed his glasses up on the bridge of his nose.

"*Buenas noches,*" Tomas said, turning to lift three peach-colored tulips from the back of the car. He gently pressed them into her hands, then pulled her in to place soft kisses on her cheeks. She felt the warmth from his hands on her shoulders. Her heart fluttered, and she looked at the white leather straps on her feet and rings on her toes. No matter the time, he always had a five o'clock shadow that she could both see and feel. It was soft and masculine at the same time. Therese felt warmth at the meeting of her thighs.

"Hi," she said timidly.

"I apologize. I need to talk to you. I needed to see you." Therese squinted with concern as Tomas spoke. "I should have come for you hours ago."

"What happened?" she said. She watched a black ant tracking its way over the golden stone. "Is everything okay?" Therese looked up and Tomas removed his glasses. She knew his eyes were beautiful and sincere. She didn't know they were so piercing, though.

He stared at her, placing his hands on her waist. "Everything's okay. I just... I don't know. I feel more for you than I should, maybe. I don't want to go too far or make you feel scared."

Evan had used nearly identical words in his love confession to her a few months before—all sentiments that evaporated when she finally refused to be the jezebel he kept in his closet. His eyes had sparkled and pierced, too, but there was a difference. His eyes had danced with the thrill of the chase and the coming kill, not with the terror of an exposed heart. The difference was as subtle as it was cataclysmic.

"Well..." Therese shifted her weight and stood stiffly holding her flowers, "...what does that mean?"

"You know I just got divorced in February." He held her face as she began to nod. "Does that bother you?"

"Not if it doesn't bother you," she answered. "But are you worried you don't know what you feel? Is this just an impulsive thing, like getting married at the courthouse?"

Tomas dropped his hands from her face, leaned back against the car, and pulled a pack of cigarettes from his pocket. He flicked the box with his middle finger, and then stared at it. He knew it represented a surrogate for his emotions. Placing the box on the trunk, his loafered feet took two small steps to Therese, and he lifted her chin, deeply kissing her mouth.

"I'm not perfect, Therese, but I'm not a bad guy. I'm not a guy who takes. I probably give too much," Tomas said. He waited for her response.

Therese pulled the top of his shirt down and towards her, kissing him again. Neither of them realized Phoebe watched from the stairwell window on the second floor, fuming.

"Can you please come with me tonight?"

"Where?" Therese asked, knowing she'd go.

"Anywhere, *amor*."

Therese noticed the inky blackness of the sky. Stars danced with the musical accompaniment of ocean waves crashing in the distance. Wind sidled between the potentiality of these new lovers, carrying messages from the goddesses at the bottom of the sea. The moon hung overhead. Therese realized the rhythm she felt pulsing through her loins was coming from the fullness of her heartbeat. A cicada sang a swelling score of passion.

She floated into the house to let Phoebe know she'd spend the night with Tomas. Instead of giving an excited endorsement, Phoebe stood in the kitchen, her feet apart and her fingernails pushed pink by the pressure of her hands around her hips.

"So, let me get this straight, T…" Phoebe squealed.

"Phoebe, please…." Therese tried to interrupt.

"No! No, let's talk about this," she continued. "You've been crying to me over Evan using you for what, two, three, four months, a year? I don't know."

"You know it hasn't been a year." Therese crossed her arms over her bare waist.

"Really feels like it." Phoebe's wavy blonde locks began to look like a mane as her face reddened.

"Wow, Phoebs." Therese's eyebrows pushed toward her hairline as she replied. "I didn't know I was such a burden."

"I'm not saying that, and you know it." Phoebe's breath was short, and her body seemed to tremor. "I'm saying *why*? *Why* let guys just have you at their disposal? Why not make them work for something?! He literally stood you up today, and now you're running to go sleep with him."

"Okay, so now I'm easy?" Therese turned to walk out of the kitchen, looking at the now-familiar hallways in Dara's home. "I'm going to go pack some stuff."

Phoebe lunged forward and gripped Therese's right shoulder. A nail sliced her skin. "What the hell, Phoebe? What's wrong with you?!" Therese whipped around and glared down on her petite, seemingly rabid friend. She wondered if she would have to hit her.

"You know what? It's fine. It's totally fine, T. Go! Go with him wherever you want and let him break your heart by the time we leave this so-called girls' trip in forty-eight hours." Phoebe's voice cracked. She brought tremoring fingertips to her eyes.

Therese stopped. She looked at her friend and pulled her face into a frown. She shifted her weight to embrace Phoebe, but Phoebe stepped back abruptly, pushing her hands away with a scowl.

"Seriously, Phoebe?" Therese said, crestfallen. "I never thought I'd see the day. Never." Therese turned to the stairs and ran up crying, crushing her tulip stems in her hand.

She took a deep breath in the bedroom and scanned for her things amongst the mess of strewn beachwear. Her goal was simply to find something clean. The search was enough of a challenge that she had calmed by the time she came out of the room fifteen minutes later, descending the spiraling stairs with her bag over her shoulder.

"Honestly, it's pissing me off because he's not doing what we agreed." Therese stood at the third stair listening to Phoebe's angry voice rasping to another unknown phone mate. "We have a clear plan. It has to happen this week, right? Well, he's just doing whatever the hell he feels like. I'm sorry, excuse my language. But he is! There's only three days left!" Phoebe hadn't noticed Therese had walked up behind her as she stood in the arched and art-laden marble hallway.

"Who. Are you. Talking. To?" Therese's voice became staccato. It rumbled like far-off thunder. Ominous.

Phoebe slid the phone slowly from her face, ended the call with the click of a red phone icon, and keeping her back to her friend said, "Forrest."

"Forrest? You think I'm stupid? Why Forrest?" Therese breathed on Phoebe's neck.

Phoebe began to turn now, revealing a tear-streaked face.

"Because, Therese, there is a problem at the freakin' store, and he wants us to come back early. People who agreed to cover my shifts are flaking out. And now I am trying to take care of it, so I don't ruin date night for you and your new Latin lover. Okay?!"

"So that's why you said, 'excuse my language?' To Forrest, whose vacuous head is filled with nothing but air and four-letter words? Right."

Therese said nothing and pushed past Phoebe, though the hall was large enough to accommodate twenty people.

"Whatever," Therese snarled through her teeth as she yanked the front door. It was so heavy and statuesque itself that it seemed like more than a door. It seemed like the portal to an entirely different life.

OUTSIDE, THE CICADAS, moon, and ocean settled Therese at once. The car seat she'd nestled in for the first time the night before felt like a familiar embrace. She placed her purse between her feet and pressed a black tab button to open her window. Tomas rummaged through CDs in his console, finally sliding one out from the pile.

As he backed out of the driveway, the hushed crunch of gravel underneath his tires whooshed into the rhythm of tossing waves behind the house. A gripping guitar harmony plucked in trios filled the car. Dual soprano saxophone notes weaved in to match their cadence, lifting and dropping at once. The tones embraced. From underneath them, a singer breathed, "Spring sweet rhythm, dance in my head."

"Remember this?" Tomas smiled and squeezed Therese's left knee.

"It's familiar." Therese looked at him and back out the window. "Who is it?"

"Listen, you know this one." Tomas smiled. "Kiss me, won't you kiss me now and sleep I would inside your mouth," he sang in a startling clear-toned tenor.

"I don't know this I don't think." Therese turned her ear in the direction of the car's CD player, trying to tune her focus. "It's pretty, though."

"They had a concert here last summer," Tomas suggested.

"Oh, I didn't go to any concerts last summer. Definitely sounds like DMB. Who is it?" she asked the second time, her voice lifting sweetly.

"Dave Matthews, yeah! 'Member they were here last summer for two nights? Their Summer 2005 tour?" Tomas tried again.

Therese shook her head "no" and tucked her fingers into the space beside his thumb. "Sorry." She looked down, smiling at his hand.

He was staring at her and squeezed her knee. "It's okay. My friends and I love this song. It came out when we were in high school in '94." Tomas reminisced. "We all thought we were in love with someone whenever it came on."

Therese reclined in her seat. "I can see why," she replied, drifting into slumber. The day—its twists and upsets—had exhausted her. Dave's lyrics in "Lover Lay Down" and the warmth of Tomas's hand conspired to lull her into more security than she'd felt in months. Soon she was dreaming.

Therese saw herself as a little girl in a neighborhood shaded with lush trees. A wooden house, smaller than all the rest, sat on the corner. Robin Read Road sat in front of her. She stared at the stop sign. Turning right on her bicycle, she had the distinct feeling of being in a place fancier than she deserved. She came to another stop sign. Just across the intersection was a sparkling crystal-blue lake. The colors of everything were supernaturally vibrant. It could have been Heaven.

Each home had character. Balconies, and lofts, and high, high, high, roofs— floating-in-the-sky roofs. Black ones. They were all black. She looped around the same block twice. The tallest tree was covered in layers of vines. It looked like it could come to life. And tell her it was God.

Back at Robin Read Road, she dropped her bike into the grass right outside the home's chalk-white sidewalk. The home was full inside. A meeting. An angry one. Adults looked at her as she walked in. She was told to go and find her father. Ride up Robin Read Road and find your father. Therese was not sure which way to turn at the corner. But she decided to go right again. And then straight, until the pretty neighborhood disappeared when she looked over her shoulder. Instead, she was on a rough, busy road.

An industrial-looking place. Rough. Cement walls with holes—that rough. Train tracks and cloudy skies rough. People blaring their horns. "Get out of the street!" rough. She rode past brown buildings. Dingy gray buildings. A raggedy old gas station and raggedy old men were to her left. They felt close enough to grab her. She could not pedal hard enough to get up the hill so they wouldn't grab her. Was she on the wrong side of the street, anyway? "Hey, kid, are you lost?" someone shouted, laughing, driving right on by. Therese was lost. She turned to go back toward the beautiful neighborhood. If I just keep going straight it will come back. *But the pretty neighborhood never came. She went straight and it never came back. Just the rough neighborhood—block after block after block. She never could get out. It kept going forever.*

An old man, homeless. Urine-stained and black. Teeth jagged. Kind. He asked, "What are you doing here?" Therese told him, "Watching them."

"What'd you say, sweetie?" Tomas was still holding Therese's knee. He moved his face back and forth from her to the street as he drove.

"Huh?" she replied.

"I thought I heard you say something about watching someone. Aw, are you talking in your sleep?" Tomas smiled.

"Oh no!" Therese giggled and pulled her seat upright again. "I'm sorry. My day was so long."

"Why, *amor?*"

"Why?!" Therese laughed and tugged hair on his arm. "Because I was tormented wondering what happened to you."

"Ah. *Lo siento*. I'm sorry. Truly," Tomas said, "for everything I've done. I hope you'll forgive me."

14

VICTOR'S PHONE RANG. He rifled through his purse and lifted it to his ear. *Mair*. Their relationship resembled a cage. It hadn't happened naturally. It was a backroom deal. Like any powerful industry, medicine has its backrooms, too. Sometimes the connections are clear. Sometimes they are muddled or messy. If you are not supposed to ask questions, you do not. Mair was a questionless arrangement.

Victor had been standing on a balcony at a beach condo. It belonged to one of the anesthesiologists. He was hosting a party. Everyone was there. Very big wigs included. The man they all called "Doc" was the biggest of them all and visiting from out of state. He shook Victor's hand. Said he'd heard "good things." Doc asked for everyone to clear the balcony. Doc was one of the nation's top chiefs of neurosurgery. When he asked for the balcony, he was given the balcony. People scurried. Victor thought he should scurry too, but he was told to wait. He was also told that Mair Kent, a third-year medical student, would be assigned to rotate with him and that he should lend "special attention to her inside and outside of the hospital." There was another handshake, a firmer, scarier, *maybe he'll toss me off the balcony* handshake. Victor understood and agreed—though his consent was not required.

"Hello!" Victor's voice sounded bright.

"Hello?" Mair responded. "You sound happy."

"What's up?" Victor said.

"Uh, yeah. You haven't called or answered my calls," she replied. "Things were crazy the last time I saw you."

"Yeah." Victor waited.

"Okay, well. Um, I was calling 'cause…'"

"You're still here?" Victor received this call at least once a quarter. She would come to Baltimore, plan to leave on a certain date, and somehow extend her trip through the weekend. He almost wondered why the ER where she worked hadn't fired her, but he knew why.

"Um, yeah," she answered.

"Are you calling 'cause you want to get together? We can get together if you want." Victor rubbed Joseph's old water bottle in the seat beside him.

"Well, yeah, do you want to?" She played coy, but they both knew she hoped for a Victor-sponsored visit to the Bombay Club on DC's Connecticut Avenue. It was her favorite Indian restaurant in the country. Victor hated the place, found it mediocre. But if she wanted it, she would have it.

"I honestly don't care. If you want to get together, we can. If not, it's fine." Victor turned on the radio. "Just tell me what you want to do." He continued, yelling over an American Red Cross commercial and Hurricane Katrina donation plea.

"Right, okay, well, um…" Mair fumbled words. "Yeah, let's go."

"Come to my house. I'll drive to the restaurant, but I'm not coming to get you," Victor warned.

"Oh yeah, that's totally fine," she replied, then sighed. "What time?"

She rang the doorbell at 4:16 P.M. and found herself in Victor's bed by 4:27. Obligatory intimacy surrounded by orange walls and white sheets held the potential for awkwardness. It was not, though, because Victor was as detached as Mair was delusional.

"I knew you'd want to get caught up with me," she giggled. In reality, Victor just didn't want to eat Indian cuisine. Or miss the evening news.

"So, are you and your little girlfriend still," Mair flipped her hands to the ceiling, "a thing or what? I really don't see how you guys were ever a fit. I mean, is she even your type?"

Victor pulled his white duvet up to his waist and reached for his TV remote.

"Neither one of you is my type," he said. "You know I like Asian girls."

Mair gathered her hair into a tail and threw it over her right shoulder. She ignored the comment on his preferences momentarily, then replied, "You know it's gross to fetishize groups of people, right? Anyway, can you get me a drink?"

Victor did not respond. He searched for news. Channel 2. Channel 11. Channel 13. Nothing. He looked at Mair, laughing. "What?" He turned his attention back to the TV. "What time is it?"

"Victor, can you get me some water, please?" Mair amplified the intensity of her request. He knew she'd pretend near-death if he didn't comply. Victor whipped the covers from his body and turned to stand in front of his nightstand. It was 4:45 P.M.

"Howard County police report a vehicle has plummeted onto US Route 29, resulting in three fatalities," a black news anchor in a gray jacket and yellow tie reported. "More details tonight at six."

Victor was exuberant. He had killed Joseph. As he wanted to. And with two days to spare. He turned suddenly to face Mair. "Let's shower and go eat at seven." Mair was delighted. He planned to watch the six o'clock news to hear the full report. And he'd take her to eat. He'd celebrate with a mango lassi.

"You're the best, Vic," she said and blew him a kiss. For how the day was shaping up, he thought so, too.

NEWS REPORTS ANNOUNCED the location of Joseph's wake a week after the accident, though there could be no viewing. People whispered that Joseph's remains could not be fashioned into anything less than a horror. There was a gathering, though, mainly for Joseph's high school friends. Victor never got out of the car at the wake but followed the Chaes when they left.

In the scorching late summer sun, Victor pulled up to a parking space at CVS. Cracked asphalt and wavy white lines separated his car from Leslie Chae's. A man sat in the driver's seat of her white Land Rover. As a grieving mother, she looked ethereal. Thin. Dressed in white silk. Her hair had been fashioned in small loops just above her neck. She walked through the automatic doors. The bottom of her dress blew between her ankles.

Victor held his head down and walked into the store behind her. His pace gave her the opportunity to get to the pharmacy in the back before he walked up the side aisle of Maybelline makeup. He waited at the intersection of the beauty and first aid sections, watching her in a dome circle mirror lodged against the ceiling. She spoke to the pharmacist. Victor could not make out the words, but sadness oozed out to the world around her. It changed the way she moved. Her confidence and friendliness were broken by the loss of her firstborn.

For a moment, Victor thought he would dissolve into tears. A gripping remorse wrapped around his abdomen, and he thought he'd need to find a bathroom. But Leslie was finishing up at the pharmacy. She had a small, white bag. It was on the counter. She peeked in as the pharmacist explained that her new medicine "shouldn't be combined with other sedatives."

Victor kept watch. A woman behind him asked him to move; he was blocking the ankle wraps. Startled, he stepped aside. He stopped staring at the mirror and instead closed his eyes and listened for Leslie's steps. After eight of them, he stepped into the aisle in front of her.

"Leslie?" He stopped. She stopped, too. She frowned as if she recognized his face but couldn't place him.

"Victor Jacobs?" he floated his name to see if her mind was gone in the grief.

"Ah, yes, Dr. Jacobs," she bowed slightly. "Please forgive me." She stood there in silence. He did, too, watching her.

"Uh…" she began, "I'm not sure if you heard about Joseph."

Victor frowned and put his hands in his pockets, shifting his weight in concern. "No, is he alright?" Victor's stomach dropped, and his heart raced. She began to turn the palest of pinks.

"Did you hear about that huge crash on 29? A car fell off the overpass at the Waterloo Road roundabout?" She blinked away tears. Victor brought his hand to his lips.

"That was Joey," she said as her head dropped. She placed her white pharmacy bag at her chest as she tried to hold herself upright. Tears dropped on the bag and the backs of her hands. Victor stepped forward and gently placed his arms around her, pulling her into his starched yellow shirt. He offered no words at first. Leslie Chae let her head rest on his shoulder.

I knew she would eventually love me, he thought, as the warmth of arousal filled his pants. He lifted his right hand to cup the back of her head. She lifted herself before he could, though, and apologized.

"I'm so sorry," she tried to wipe tears away. Victor opened a plastic pack of tissues from the aisle and handed three to her.

"Oh God, please don't apologize. Joey was a special kid. You should be so proud of what he accomplished. I know there's not much I can do, but if my office can help in any way…" he trailed off, pretending it was natural.

She nodded and rushed out of the store. Victor watched as he stroked her tears into his shirt. The woman from the aisle behind him noticed him standing, smiling, and stroking his chest. She turned and walked down another aisle.

At the checkout counter, Victor handed the opened pack of tissues to the clerk.

"Is that all for you today?" she asked.

"Yep. You never know when you'll need a few." Victor's face brightened. He squeezed his packet of trophy tissues with pride.

15

AT NIGHT, THE SEASIDE 46 LOBBY WAS FULL. Not of people, but of golden light, and marble, and the ease of wealth. Therese hadn't noticed so much last time. Leaving Tomas's home then, confusion over the almost-kiss filled her mind. Tonight, life promised her another open door, with love standing just inside. The valets lifted her from the passenger side of Tomas's Mercedes and placed her on the ground as if on a cloud. By the time she landed, Tomas was standing there, offering her his blue linen-clad arm.

"Thank you," Therese smiled.

He kissed her on the cheek and replied, "*Vamos*," as they went.

The elevator sped to the sky. As it did, she determined some things. She would love him. He would love her. And she would let him have her. His home waited—silent and fully lit.

"Is Luca here?" Therese asked. She sauntered into Tomas's white-and-glass bedroom, looking for a place to set down her purse.

Tomas noticed. "You can put that anywhere, *amor*. Please make yourself at home here." She placed it on a chair in a corner of the room. She stood with her arms behind her and her ankles crossed.

"I promise I won't bite you," he laughed. So did she. "I don't think Luca's here right now. He was out with everyone tonight. They're probably at a club or something. Why?"

Therese didn't want to say why. She'd hoped he understood the question. "Oh, no reason," she replied.

"Come," Tomas invited her to the bed. He sat on it, fully dressed. He leaned back against his pillows. She sat on the very edge of the bed and moved closer and closer to him as he watched her. She reached to kiss him. He removed his glasses again and held the back of her head. Her hair fell from its clip. Therese pulled her dress up on her left leg and began to lift her body to lie on him, but he gently pushed her back into the bed and gazed into her eyes. Her freesia-scented hair fell around her face. Tomas lay beside her, held her hand, and looked at the ceiling. Like Monet's *Water Lilies*, they were a swirl of purples and blues and whites and waves. They would remain that way all night. Talking until the first hints of sunrise.

By the time she decided she had to leave, a whole day and a half had passed. Wednesday night turned into late Friday morning.

"I really need to head back, babe." Therese had settled into pet names over twenty-four hours, and there was no reason, in her mind, to hold back.

"*Lo se*. I understand. You guys are leaving tomorrow, no? It's your last night at the beach house?" They were in the kitchen, and Tomas was holding her waist while he tended steak and scrambled eggs.

"*Si*," Therese said. She winked.

"You're so adorable." He shook his head. Therese saw genuine appreciation for her in his eyes. It was a heart-swelling first. "Let's do this: Let me take you home. I'll send you and your friend to get your nails and toes done?" Therese smiled and nodded. "*Bueno*. Then, tonight, around seven, eight, we all come up, and we eat at my parents' place. What do you think?"

"If Phoebe's not still pissed at me, I'm totally down for it." Therese hugged him, placing her cheek onto his chest. He kissed the top of her head.

On the ride back to Riviera Oaks, Therese didn't sleep. Instead, she and Tomas settled into another conversation. Therese couldn't remember ever feeling so easily synched with any other man. She asked him to tell her about his family, his friends.

"I once had a very good girlfriend," Tomas began. "We could literally talk about anything."

"Was she your girlfriend, girlfriend?" Therese's heart dropped slightly.

"Oh no, sweetie. She was beautiful and brilliant, but we were always platonic," Tomas replied. "I did have feelings for her, *pero* she didn't feel the same." He looked at Therese, who looked at him.

"How come she *used* to be your friend? You're saying that like you're not friends anymore." Therese continued watching his face.

"Oh, I'll always have a special place in my heart for her. But she moved away, and some dynamics changed. I think her boyfriend wasn't a fan of mine." He chuckled. "And I'm definitely not a fan of his."

"Uh-oh!" Therese joked. "Is it like a love triangle? Are you one day going to fight to the death for her?"

Tomas laughed heartily. "I've done many things in my life, sweetie, but fighting's not one of them." He continued laughing. "Hopefully, it never will be."

"What do you think she'd say about me? About you having a—" Therese stopped.

Tomas laughed again. "Don't stop now! You're about to call yourself my girlfriend? *¿Mi novia?*" Tomas was giddy and squeezing Therese's bare knee. She'd exchanged her lavender outfit for white shorts and a fitted green tank top.

Oh my God, she thought, *he's going to think I'm a possessive freak.* "No, no! I'm not saying that!" Therese's stomach folded in on itself.

"*Amor,* listen," Tomas stopped laughing. "It would be my honor. I clearly like you. It seems like you're interested in me. You've accepted the things I've told you about my ex-wife. At least I think you have?" he asked.

She nodded.

"What else has to happen for us to say we're going to, uh..." he shrugged, "...date?"

"We live an hour apart," Therese's mouth was drying, and a prickling heat spread across her scalp. She pretended distance was a concern but securing love was everything to her. Sixty minutes certainly wouldn't deter her.

"Honestly, I feel like everything in Miami is an hour apart once you add traffic. Boca's basically right up the street to me. If you want to make it work, if you want to say, 'let's be together,' then let's be together."

Therese could respond with nothing more than, "Okay," and a happy flutter of her eyelids.

An hour later, they drove past the shimmering blue lake for which the area was named. "I love that lake," Therese said, gazing past Tomas as they passed it, sparkling alive with reflected light and magic. The couple pulled back into the gravel driveway of 111 Crystal Cove and Therese stared at the house door.

"Wish me luck!" Therese grinned. The prickling heat on her scalp returned.

"Do you want me to hang around a bit?" Tomas asked. "I can." He pushed his glasses up. "I can just hang around outside."

"Oh no, it's totally fine. Go enjoy your day, and I'll look forward to dinner tonight." Therese leaned over, pulled his chin toward her face, and placed her lips softly on his. She sat back, looked at him, and winked.

Tomas's brows were converging.

"What's the matter?" Therese thought he looked worried.

"Ah, *nada*. I'm a little concerned but..." Tomas replied.

"Concerned about what?" Therese had gotten out of the car and leaned down to the window.

"You and your friend." He nodded toward the door.

Therese shook her head. "Oh, don't worry, we'll be fine. What time is it now?"

Tomas looked at the car clock in the dash. "One-thirty."

Therese nodded. "Stand by for a call from the nail shop, *papi*." She tried to keep a straight face but burst out laughing. She turned to go through the heavy wooden front door.

THE HOUSE WAS FREEZING. The cool white of the living room glowed almost fluorescent. The sun was shining through the front windows but offered no warmth. *Why is it freezing in here? Where is she?* Therese contemplated yelling out for Phoebe but decided against it. They weren't on I-can-yell-your-name-from-anywhere-and-you'll-come terms.

She dropped her bag in the hallway and stood in the living room. The brightness of the sun on the white furniture irritated her eyes. An arched, silver-framed floor mirror leaned on the wall in front of her. In the reflection, she saw Phoebe standing behind her.

"Oh my gosh, Phoebs. I didn't hear you." Therese jumped and turned to face her friend. Phoebe didn't reply. Instead, she walked up the three steps into the living room, staring at Therese.

"Phoebe?" Therese asked. She walked backward toward the mirror and then back into the hallway, dodging the glass table in the middle of the room. Phoebe stared.

"You leaving again? You walking out on me already, T?" Phoebe's face, which had looked washed-out in the harsh whiteness of the room began to flush. Her eyes spilled one tear each.

"Phoebs, oh no! Why are you crying?" Therese rounded the table and stood face-to-face with Phoebe, reaching to hold her hands.

"Because, T, I really needed this girls' week with you. This was the only thing I have even looked forward to since my mom died last year. Now it's basically over. And you left me here for days." She began to sob. "Alone! I would have never done something like that to you. No matter what." Therese dropped her face and gulped. She felt as if she might cry, too.

"Oh my gosh, I'm so sorry, Phoebs." Therese reached down and hugged Phoebe. Phoebe returned the embrace, holding on tightly. Therese remembered how difficult life had been for her best friend since her mother's bizarre vulvar cancer diagnosis, rapid decline, and death. At work, Phoebe would sometimes have flashbacks. Certain perfumes would bring her to tears or make her run out of the café.

"You are. You are sorry, T." Phoebe held her. "A sorry whore."

Therese stood sharply. "What did you say, Phoebe?"

Phoebe wiped each drying tear with the backs of her forefingers. "You're a whore. I've always thought so."

Therese dropped her head to the side and squinted. "Are you actually going to look me in the face and call me that, Phoebe? What the hell?!"

Phoebe nodded. "I am. I'm also going to tell you this friendship is over. You can move out of my apartment when we get back to Boca."

"Your apartment?" Therese asked as Phoebe placed her hands on her hips.

"Yep," Phoebe nodded again. "My apartment. The one I found. The one that has my name on the lease. Yeah, that one."

Therese's mind throbbed. "We found the apartment together, Phoebe. What are you talking about?"

"Did we?" Phoebe frowned and walked right up to Therese's face. "How did we meet again, T?"

Therese had begun to pant, and she couldn't find her thoughts. She knew she'd landed in Daytona then drove to Boca Raton in her car the summer before. "At work!" Therese responded, baffled.

"Right, Therese. Weren't you living in your car at the bookstore when we met?"

Therese began to cry. "Phoebe, stop!" she shouted.

"Right? Didn't I tap on the window and tell you to roll your windows down 'cause you could die sleeping in a closed-up car on a Florida summer day?" Therese began to feel nauseous. Phoebe shoved her.

"Phoebe, seriously. Stop! You're making me feel like I'm gonna be sick."

"I'm making you what?" Phoebe taunted her. She shoved her again, then stepped forward and shoved her once more. Therese pushed her with her full force, and Phoebe went tumbling to the floor, barely missing the coffee table. She rebounded and grabbed Therese's tank top between her breasts.

"Phoebe! Chill out! What are you doing?!"

Phoebe reached for her neck with her free hand and dug her nails into Therese's flawless skin.

"Let go of me!" Therese shouted.

"Or what?" Phoebe asked, squeezing Therese's neck. Therese tried to pry Phoebe's fingers off, but Phoebe was floridly enraged and would not let go.

"Phoebe! Stop it!" Therese managed to lean over and grab the coral sculpture on the end table. Phoebe let go and backed up to the mirror.

"You gonna hit me with that?" she yelped before charging Therese. Therese flung the sculpture in her direction, hoping it would not hurt her. It was heavy and difficult to throw. The coral went crashing into the mirror. Phoebe stopped, turned to look at the shattered glass, then pushed past Therese into the hallway and ran out the front door.

Oh my God! Therese stood shaking in the middle of the room, staring at the front door and the trail of craziness that got her friend to it. She pushed her curls up into a mushroom-shaped crown. Her neck throbbed from Phoebe's scratches and her tank top sagged at the breasts. She pulled it down a few inches and saw more scratches and small beads of blood. Therese looked up and into the shattered mirror. *Oh my God. Dara is gonna kills us.* Tears streamed down her face. She placed large pieces of glass on the coffee table. She bent before the right corner of the mirror to pick up smaller pieces, stopping to pull her hair out of her face. As she lifted her head to put her hair into a haphazard braid, she realized there was something behind the mirror. She placed her hand through the gaping hole. She realized she was not touching a wall, but the threshold of a door.

She stood and walked to the left side of the mirror. The weight of it made it difficult for her to reach the doorknob behind it. She inched it out until there was a foot of space and slid her right hand and arm behind the mirror, which rested on her shoulder. Therese turned the doorknob, expecting it to be locked. Instead, with the slightest turn, it flew open to another living room—identical in style but filled with photos in silver picture frames.

She slid her entire body behind the mirror. The hidden living room boasted a crystal floor-to-ceiling bookshelf that spread from wall to wall, with at least twelve drawers at the bottom. In the middle of a lower shelf sat a picture of five '80s-era children at SeaWorld. Four of them sat in a row along a stone fountain, legs crisscrossed in front of them. A little boy with a brown bowl cut and glasses sat in the middle. Two girls sat to his right and one to his left. His arms hid behind their bodies with bunny ear fingers lifting behind their thick heads of hair, one glossy black, one curly brown. Therese lifted the picture and frowned. The only one who stood was a tiny little girl with wavy blonde hair. She had her hands on her hips and was laughing.

The room spun, and Therese stooped and vomited on the closest crystal shelf. She placed the photo face down in it. With splattered emesis on her feet, she stumbled back toward the room's door and pressed her chest against the mirror to gently lift it again. She stumbled into the main living room and into the kitchen, leaning over the butcher's block sink to wash her face with cool water. *I need to go lay down.* She gripped the stair rail tightly enough to whiten her knuckles. As she turned to go into the bedroom, she looked up at the next staircase, leading to the loft upstairs. Heartbeats rattled in her ears, and she vomited again, soiling her stretched tank top. Looking down at the remnants of Tomas's steak and egg breakfast, Therese began to feel disoriented. Her surroundings waved in and out of her consciousness as if she were inside one of her dreams.

Her hand trembled as she reached for the knob to the loft door. It, too, swung open, revealing a bedroom in gray and brown. It was not carpeted but had pictures hanging on the walls. Nearly every wall. The bed in the middle of the room had no headboard. Whoever had been sleeping there hadn't bothered to make the bed, but they had showered. In the bathroom to the left, a light and extractor fan were still on, and a faucet dripped. Therese looked at the floor. Wet footprints, too large to be Phoebe's and too thin to be a man's, tracked a path through the room.

"Hello?" she called. The blowing fan and dripping water answered.

Therese walked in further, not noticing a security camera at the left corner of the ceiling. She scanned the first picture—a graduation. At the very bottom of the photo was Dara, beaming. She sat at a table with her hands folded under her chin. To the right of her stood Phoebe and Tomas, linked arm-in-arm in black-and-green graduation robes, doctor's hoods, and their matching caps and tassels. To the left stood a black-haired beauty and stunning tall redhead with dimples wearing the same regalia as Tomas and Phoebe. A dark-haired man stood in the rear of the picture. His jaw was perfectly square. He had deep set, dark brown eyes and towered over all the others. His thick hands rested on the shoulders of another graduate who stood in front of him, just behind Dara. Therese's hands came to her mouth as she realized that the last student in the photo was her.

OUTSIDE THE HOUSE, the glare of the sun oppressed Therese's vision, squeezing her head into the vice grip of a migraine. *I gotta get out of here*, she thought. She walked into the front yard and through the gravel. Her feet burned. They looked foreign. She wondered why they were bare outside on Florida's baking asphalt. She decided she would need to leave the house and get back somewhere. She wasn't quite sure where. She had left her bags and the house keys in the hallway. She lurched forward, walking as if she might collapse to her knees, catching herself before falling each time. Therese rounded a circle that she thought might lead to the subdivision's exit.

"Therese!" Therese did not turn to look but could hear a car driving along her left side. "Therese!" a voice repeated. She stopped walking as the car pulled up closer. She turned to her left. A man in a charcoal gray Mercedes said her name with a Spanish accent. She had been squinting in the glowing white sun. Her face relaxed as her eyes fell on the gold chain he was wearing.

"Eighth-grade graduation," Therese replied, standing and swaying as if intoxicated.

"*Amor*, what are you doing in the street?" It was Tomas. "And what happened? Are you sick?" he said, looking at her shirt.

"I gave you that chain at eighth-grade graduation. Epiphany. 1993." Therese stood staring at the chain, not noticing Tomas's eyes widening. She turned and started again down the street. Tomas parked the car and got out.

"Therese, get in the car," he yelled. She ignored him. "Therese!" She walked as if in a trance.

"Summer!!!" Tomas's breathing quickened, and a vein running down his forehead became visible. Therese stopped, turning her head slowly to look at him. "Get in the car." Tomas's voice softened as he closed his eyes. Her mouth opened, and her eyes darted from side to side. She frowned as she walked back to the car. Therese climbed inside and pressed her head on the passenger-side window.

16

LUXURY VEHICLES PARKED IN ANGLES on the gravel driveway of the Clemens's beach house. Tomas and Therese parked on the street in front.

"Don't move," Tomas said, "I'll help you get out."

Therese shifted her soiled body off the door. A moist ring of sweat remained where her head had lain. The interior of the car waved in her vision. Tomas walked around to the trunk for one of his beach towels and a bottle of water, then stood at Therese's door. He offered her his hand. Blank green eyes stared beyond him. Therese did not respond to any of his questions, suggestions, or touch.

"Sweetie, I'm going to help you get out, okay? I'm going to move your legs," he said, bending to pull her feet to the side of the car. The movement animated Therese. She tried to lift herself off the seat as he held her arms just above the elbows. "Watch your head." Tomas saw her arms tremoring.

"I'm sorry," Therese said. She didn't know why.

"Don't worry." Tomas placed his body between Therese and the windows at the front of the house. He took off his shirt and draped it on the top of the car, straightening his undershirt against his chest. Without a word, he pulled the loosened straps of Therese's tank off her shoulders and down to her ankles. She made robotic stepping motions in place as the shirt hit the gravel beneath her feet.

"Take off your shorts," he said, nodding. Therese watched the movement of his lips. "*Lo siento.* It's going to be a little cold," he added. Tomas poured water on the towel and wrung it out. He patted and wiped all of Therese's exposed skin and put her in his shirt. It hung just above her knees like a nightgown. He removed a leather bracelet from his wrist and stood behind her, gathering her hair into a ponytail.

Tomas wrapped Therese's soiled clothes and water bottle in the towel and left them in a bundle on the ground. "There." He looked at Therese and smiled. "It's okay. Everything's okay. Come on," he said, and took her hand.

Four people sat in the kitchen. The last notes of spoken words hung in a hush over the room. Therese gripped Tomas's hand as they stood in the hallway. Phoebe sat on a barstool crying. Dara, who had been standing with her arms wrapped around Phoebe's shoulders, looked up and smiled. A man stood with his back to the rest of the group, his hands resting on a countertop as if pleading a case in a courtroom. The girl who wore her hair in a bun at Tomas's party was there. Therese couldn't remember her name.

"*Buenas*, everyone," Tomas said, subdued.

"Oh, my goodness." The girl with the bun hopped off a barstool and kissed Tomas on both cheeks.

"Hi, Carla." Tomas hugged her and began to weep. She nodded and pulled his head into her shoulder. Therese didn't understand his tears.

"Therese," Carla asked, "do you remember me?" Therese nodded. *Yeah, from the party the other day. You wear your hair in the best chignons.* Therese heard her thoughts in her head, but nothing came out of her mouth. Carla touched her hands to her heart. Therese also realized she knew everyone in the room except the man at the counter. She released Tomas's hand and put her arm around his waist.

"Who's that?" she asked and motioned as if pointing with her mouth.

Dara had been watching with her pointer finger over her puffy pink lips. She spoke. "Therese," she began, "how are you feeling? Why don't you guys come sit down?"

"Dara, I'm really sorry about the mirror," Therese responded, looking out of the corner of her eye at Phoebe. "I'm so sorry you had to come down here to deal with this." Therese assumed Phoebe had called her into town from Delaware, not realizing only an hour had passed since their fight.

As Tomas and Therese found seats, the man at the counter spoke.

"I don't think we need to do this today, Dara." He clenched his jaw.

"Manny," Dara responded, exasperated, "we're out of time. It's been a whole year. There's a possibility we'll never get her back if we let this keep going." Dara looked at Phoebe and lifted her chin. "You did the right thing. Both of you did," she said walking over and pushing Tomas's hair off his wet face. "Tomas, look at me." Dara focused on him. "You did the right thing." He sighed and folded his arms.

Carla began turning off the lights in the kitchen. The sun sat over the home and the windows in the back gave minimal light. The room darkened and Carla pulled a small, white penlight from her blouse pocket. She walked up to Therese, who pulled her chin backward into her neck. Carla caressed the side of her arm.

"*Relajarte*," Carla said soothingly. She swung the light from the white tube into Therese's eyes. "*¿Therese, puedo mirarte a los ojos?*" Carla asked. "Can I look in your eyes?"

"*Ya me estas mirando a los ojos,*" Therese responded. *You're already looking at my eyes.* Her words slurred.

"Oh my God," Carla exclaimed, excited to hear Therese's response in Spanish. Therese fell backward, grabbing for Carla's wrists. Tomas and Carla braced her fall. She collapsed on the kitchen floor with her eyes closed. Tomas held her as Dara and Carla turned on the room's lights.

"*¿Me entiendes?*" Tomas asked.

"Of course, I understand you, *Bebo*," Therese continued in slurred Spanish. "What kind of question is that?"

Tomas gasped hearing his nickname. The heat of his emotions fogged his glasses.

Dara drew a quick breath and squatted in front of Therese. Phoebe's methods may have been aggressive, but they had worked. Therese scooted back on the floor to focus on the features of Dara's face. She squinted and lifted her chin.

"Mom?" Therese looked at Dara's crystal blue eyes, then down at the floor. Carla, she realized, wasn't just the girl with pretty hair from Tomas's backyard party. Therese grasped at the stool to stand.

"Summer?" the tall man spoke. Therese turned to his booming voice. The man's dimples and brown eyes suddenly seemed to emerge from his face like a sculpture from stone.

"Hi, Daddy," Therese said casually. "I feel really sick." She looked around the room, from his chiseled jaw to everyone else's faces. She hugged her father. He held her longer than she thought necessary.

"What's wrong?" she looked around the room. "You guys are freaking me out. When did we come down to the beach house?" Therese stood in the middle of the kitchen, gripping her head and abdomen.

Carla began praying as the rest of the room cried. Therese frowned and shook her head at the scene. Dara finally spoke.

"Summer," she sighed, "do you need to sit down?"

"No," Therese replied. "What's going on, though?"

Dara grasped her hands and exhaled. "Do you remember moving back to Florida last summer?" Therese looked up, thinking. "Do you remember that you moved to Boca? You lived with Phoebe and worked at a bookstore café?" Dara paused as Therese laughed.

"Mom, I dropped out of a psych residency to work at a café? Okay." Therese shook her head.

"Summer, you started going by the name 'Therese.' Do you remember that? Any of it?" Dara stopped talking and removed her glasses.

Summer looked at Phoebe. She would have laughed, but her friend was still crumpled in a pile of tears.

"I changed my name to Therese?" Summer scoffed, "why would I do that?!" She looked at Tomas, Phoebe, and Carla—friends she'd known her entire life. "Guys? Why would I do that?"

They had done everything together since the womb. They were doctors' kids—doctors who met as students themselves at the medical school in the 1970s. Once the time came for them to enter the world of medicine, Summer studied psychiatry and Phoebe, pediatrics. Carla was born to be a neurologist and knew that from her first day of medical school. Tomas was preparing to take over his dad's obstetrics and gynecology practice in North Miami.

Summer began to feel dizzy and reached to sit again. "What are you talking about, Mom?"

"Okay, baby girl," Dara pushed her red hair behind her ears and pulled ChapStick out of her pocket, rubbing it back and forth over her lips.

"Dara, please," Summer's father said. Dara ignored him.

"Summer, tell me, what's the last thing you remember doing?"

"Why? You guys were all there," Summer responded in a blur of Spanish and English. "My head hurts. Why are you guys acting like this? Weren't we all at the restaurant?" Summer tapped her forehead. "Oh gosh, what's the name of it? Tomas, what's it called again, the place with all the fish and that random horse picture?" Tomas did not reply but only sat cross-legged, stifling tears. She continued.

"Anyway, it's dark inside, but it has all the really good seafood. The one in the Harbor." Summer paused, frustrated. "Well, anyway, I remember we just got to the restaurant. We parked. Carla was waiting at the front door. Right, Carla? She was wearing—you were wearing a super fancy green dress, right? It was so crowded. You guys were all acting weird. I went to check my jacket then—"

She stopped.

She had been staring straight out, recounting the events on her fingers. But when she stopped, her gaze fell. She pushed her tongue into the soft flesh below her bottom teeth. Her nose began to run. Tears rolled from the corners of her eyes. She turned to look at Phoebe and asked, "Where's Victor?"

17

"UGH, WHAT?!" Victor grabbed his dinging cell phone from his nightstand. A text message notification from his father flashed. Victor had been ignoring him for longer than he ever had. It had been a full year since the dinner party that never was—since Joseph Chae ceased to be. He didn't want to see him. But he also hadn't gone grocery shopping and knew his dad would buy him food.

I'm coming over.

Why Dad?

We need to talk. Order Chinese.

Fine. What time?

Sometime after 530.

Ok.

Looking down at his father that evening, Victor had a thought that warmed his heart. *I could stab him at the base of his skull, and he'd be dead in an instant.* Victor's father knelt beside Victor's Camry tire. The stretched and faded orange T-shirt he wore was slack around his aging neck.

"Victor," he said, "even though this car is older, if you take care of it, you can sell it." He looked up at his son, winded just from kneeling. "Camrys last forever."

"I know, Dad."

"Oh, you know, huh?" He wrapped his fingers, the same thick fingers as Victor, around another tire cap to screw it into place. "What else do you know? Do you know why you haven't called me in nearly a year?"

"The phone works both ways, Dad."

"Of course, it does, Victor. But it doesn't work very well if the person you're calling never answers."

Victor's father pushed himself to a kneel, then stood. His faded jeans sagged over his backside. The same height as Victor, he appeared to be shrinking—sinking into the ground with age and stress. "Anything else need to be done around here?" He looked around the garage. Besides an oversized toolbox, it stood empty. There was not a single blemish to the walls or floor.

A black sedan pulled into the driveway beside the station wagon Victor's father had driven to the house. A teenager stepped out carrying a large, folded brown bag.

"Oh!" Victor's father reached for his wallet. "I've got it. How much?" He unfolded dollar bills. Victor stood with his arms crossed. He walked in the house, leaving his father fumbling with the bag and searching his pockets for change.

"Sorry, keep the change." He smiled at the delivery guy. "I don't know why I was looking for coins." He turned around and realized Victor was gone. The door to the house stood open. "Victor, come grab the food!" he shouted as he tried to manage closing the garage door and taking off his boots before stepping inside. Even though it had been a year since he'd seen his son, it had been longer—since Victor had first purchased the home—that he'd actually been allowed to visit. He stepped in, placed his hands behind his back, and scanned the room from one wall to the next.

"Goodness," he said, looking up into the vaulted ceilings. "This place big enough?" He chuckled and shook his head. "You always were a bit extravagant." He walked to the sink to wash his hands. "And what's with all the orange?"

"Dad, why'd you decide to come over all of a sudden?"

"All of a sudden, son? I don't think so. I came over because you've been ignoring me for the past year." He gripped the sink frame. "Look, I know losing your girlfriend had to be hard."

"It was, Dad."

"I'm sure! Even though it's not the same, losing your mother was the most pain I've ever felt in my entire life."

"How's it not the same?" Victor grimaced at his father in disgust.

"Well, she was my wife for seventeen years," he replied, shocked that Victor needed him to explain the contrast.

"So?" Victor opened his eyes wide.

"Son, come on—she was my wife and your mother. We'd gone through getting married and buying a home and having you—and dealing with her accident. Not to compare ill fates, but you'd only been with your girlfriend for two years, and she's not dead."

Victor shrugged. "I don't know that."

"Anyway, Victor, I'm sorry that you lost her. I know you've probably been lonely and maybe even a little depressed." Victor's dad searched his face for some emotion. He found none. "Anyway," he sighed, "did you hear they're reopening your mom's bakery? Right down by the hospital! Right down where it used to be!"

Victor had placed a small portion of food in a bowl.

"They didn't bring any chopsticks!" he shouted, rummaging to the bottom of the food bag.

"I know you heard me, Victor."

"Idiots. I hate eating Chinese with a fork."

"Losing your mother was the greatest loss you will ever experience, Victor."

Victor mouthed, "Not really," out of his father's view.

"But this loss hurts, too. Don't pretend it doesn't. Besides, I can't help but think—" he stopped.

"Think what?" Victor stopped rummaging.

"Nothing, son. Let's eat."

Victor had already turned his back to his father and was flipping through TV channels for news.

"High school seniors in Howard County are looking forward to beginning the 2006 school year this Tuesday." Victor's favorite news anchor reported. "But reports of a staff member's drug use have some parents worried..."

"Victor." His father sat, stewing, growing more agitated with each passing news story. "Can you shut that off? I came over to talk." He wiped his mouth with a napkin.

"Want a drink?" Victor responded.

"I'll get something in a second. Listen," his father continued, "I'm worried about you. How do you spend your time? I mean, besides work. Are you alone all the time?"

"I see Mair on occasion."

"Who's that?" his father asked.

"The redhead that got me into this mess." Victor smirked and rolled into a full-throated laugh.

His father watched his son's Adam's apple bobbing in his neck. "Victor, do you think maybe it would be good to see a counselor? To talk to someone?"

"I'll be right back." Victor suddenly disappeared back into his garage.

"Victor!" His father listened but heard no rustling. There was no sound other than the television singing, "Red Robin! Yummmm." He walked to where Victor had disappeared around the corner. The garage was dark.

"Vic?" he asked into the echoing space. "What are you doing?" He squinted, trying to force his eyes to adjust to the lack of light. "Victor?" He stepped back into the hallway, frowning, looking over his shoulder. "Where are you?"

He skimmed his hand around the right side of the garage wall, just next to the door. *Where are the lights?* His middle finger caught the switch tip and flipped it on. Victor's feet were planted far apart on the garage floor. He held a small, folded greeting card covered with pink and white flowers. His father jumped.

"Son," his dad laughed, "why are you standing in the dark like that? You scared me. I thought maybe you came out here for a soda or something." Victor did not speak. He covered his left ear.

His father walked closer. "What's the matter, son?"

Victor held up the card to his father's face.

"Dad, what's this?"

"What?" his father asked.

"What's this?!" Victor yelled and shoved the card so close to his father's face it touched the tip of his nose. His dad leaned back and frowned to focus his eyes. His heart fell.

"Son, where'd you get that?" he pulled his wallet from his back pocket and opened it. He realized he'd dropped it when he paid for the Chinese food.

"Give it to me, Victor."

"Who is this woman?"

"No one, so hand it to me."

"Are you sleeping with someone, Dad?"

"No, Victor. She was a friend of your mom's. Give it to me."

"Right, so now you stay in touch so you guys can comfort each other?!" Victor stood inches from his father's face. "Huh?!!" His breathing had become shallow. His father tried to step backward. Victor grabbed him at the chest of his orange shirt.

"She's a nice lady. She's actually helped me out with several things concerning you, son. Her generosity has benefited you a great deal."

"I don't need some stranger's help!" Victor pushed his father to the floor with little effort. His father scrambled to get up, pushing back with his stocking feet toward the wall. He slipped and turned over to his hands and knees. Victor's kick to his father's ribs lifted him slightly from the floor.

"Ugh!" his father groaned to his back. "Victor, stop." His father, though only twenty-five years his son's senior, had become weak in grief, having lost his hope for having a happy family decades ago.

"It's not about her," Victor growled. "It's about you." He kneeled by his father's side, shoving the paper between his teeth.

"You swallow it! Swallow it!" Victor squalled. He leaned into his father's ear, squeezed his hands around his throat and hissed, "Swallow it!" His father's face became dusky red as he choked, coughing and trying to pry away his son's fingers. He blinked once with slow, heavy lids. Victor let go and waited, standing up by his father's side. His father began to pull wet paper from the roof of his mouth, tears ran out of the corners of his eyes, and he trembled. Once he began to catch his breath, Victor jumped with both feet onto his father's abdomen. The sound of gurgling fluids emanated from his throat.

Victor walked to the garage door and pulled it down with his hands. Like a flipped caterpillar, Victor's father writhed on the floor. He blinked again, trying to stay alert. The fluids in the back of his throat accumulated rapidly. As he struggled to get air into his lungs, Victor scurried to the kitchen for his keys. He pressed the remote start button. Palpitations flicked his ribs with excitement. He closed the door to the inside of the house and returned to watch the rest of the news. A volume of twelve was enough to drown out his father's pleas.

Once silence and darkness fell, Victor released the carbon monoxide through the large steel garage door. He lifted his father's dead body from the floor and placed it, strapped upright, in the passenger seat of the wagon. Victor reclined the seat so that his father's drooping head would not be noticed by nosy drivers on the road. He lifted his father's thigh for his keys in his back pocket, backed out of the driveway, and once he entered the highway ramp, let out a scream. He drove twenty minutes into Baltimore, stopping in an area of condemned buildings near a grove of established oak trees. He dragged his father from the car and placed his body at the base of a tree. He drove the car up and over his father's groin and chest to his sternum.

Victor left the car running. "I wish they would have brought me chopsticks," he said aloud. He turned to face the blackness of the night. *Body-more, Murderland,* Victor thought of Baltimore's violence earned nickname, *your blue safety streetlights fail again.* He chuckled.

18

THE IMAGE OF VICTOR leaning between the legs of Summer's childhood friend flew into her mind's eye like a 3-D movie. Mair. Mair, the daughter of her mother's absolute best friend. The redhead everyone thought was Dara's child. The one who'd destroyed Summer's dream. Summer wanted to be a wife, a mother. She wanted a family with babies that she bore and birthed, not ones that had to be adopted. Not ones that had to be rescued from a Cuban slum like her. They would be loved and worthy of love. They would not be like their mother.

Summer remembered seeing Mair seduce her man in the hot pink dress she'd lent her during one of her visits from Tennessee. She remembered the flashing lights of cameras and the noise of the restaurant. Summer brought her hand to the side of her head, again feeling the pain where she'd hit her temple on the coatroom door's threshold.

"Where is Victor?!" Summer demanded, looking around the room.

"This is exactly what I knew was gonna happen!" Summer's father yelled in the direction of his wife. "It's just going to retraumatize her to go through all this crap again."

"Manny, yelling isn't going to help either." Dara stood by her husband's side, stroking his arm.

"Dara," he said, lifting his elbow away from her, "you always think you know everything, don't you?" He turned and stormed up the stairs to the loft.

Phoebe tilted her head as she watched him, then spun around to ask Dara, "Have you guys been here the whole time? Where were your cars?!"

Dara folded her arms over her red suede vest and pink cotton dress. "The cars were down the street at a neighbor's. And yes, unfortunately, we had to be here, Phoebe, precisely for this reason." She waved her arms at the scene in the kitchen and began to cry. "But at least I was able to see what happened today on the cameras upstairs. And be here once you girls needed me." She turned her back to her daughter and her friends, who made a huddle of their chairs. Dara remembered them as toddlers. She remembered how they'd always seemed more like siblings than friends.

"Oh, my goodness, T, that's the voice you heard the other night!" Phoebe looked at Summer, hoping the explanation would reassure her.

"What?" Summer responded. "What voice?"

Phoebe sighed, staring at her hands. "Never mind."

"Summer," Dara said over her back, "we think you went into a fugue. It took a trauma to put you in the fugue, and it looks like it was the trauma of that fight today that brought you out. We think finding out about Mair and Victor," Dara sighed, "just put you over the edge, honey. You already were going through so much, between the move and work stress, and the miscarriage. It just got to be too much, and your mind shut down. That's why you didn't recognize any of us. Phoebe and I have been talking, trying to figure out how to get you out of it."

Phoebe looked at Summer apologetically. "Waiting wasn't working. So after your auditions didn't quite work out, T, we came up with the plan to bring you here," Phoebe added. "It was going okay, but it seems like bright lights, even sunlight, really impacted your mood while you were under that fugue. You were so irritable."

"This is crazy. I don't even know what you're talking about. And what auditions?" Summer replied. Dara pointed to the ballet slipper charm bracelet on Summer's wrist. "Ballet?! Funny, Mom. I'm a runner, not a dancer."

"Yes, ballet," Dara replied, then continued as Summer looked dumbfounded at the silver hanging from her wrist. "Tomas tried to help by taking you around all your friends."

Phoebe rolled her eyes. Even though she loved him like a brother, she thought Tomas's tactics were focused on his years-long crush on Summer, not her mental health crisis that made her think she was a woman named Therese.

"You've been gone an entire year, baby. A fugue can—"

Summer cut her off, humiliated. "Mom, I know what a fugue is."

Tomas stood and walked to the back patio. He needed to smoke. He needed to look out on the ocean and talk to it. He didn't want to know that Summer had become pregnant by Victor—a man he suspected had never loved her.

Even though he didn't focus on the brain in his studies, Tomas knew that a fugue was an extreme reaction to stress. It was strong enough to make you forget who you were. *Only because of amnesia would she give me a chance,* he laughed to himself, taking a long drag from his cigarette. In the six days since he saw Summer on the beach in her white bikini top, he'd been able to express feelings for her that he'd been forced to swallow for twenty years. Of course, he wanted Summer to realize she and Therese were the same woman. But he didn't want to lose those six days. He knew that since she had emerged from the fugue, all memories of their week together were gone. Permanently gone.

This week was the first time he'd seen Summer since the engagement party the previous year. He'd found her shoes beside the water on the brick walkway. They all thought she'd drowned in the Harbor. When they couldn't find her after a week, they called off the search, presuming she was dead. But Dara would not believe she drowned.

Instead, she had enlisted an investigator who easily found Summer heading to Florida in her Camry. When Agent Cline tried to introduce himself to her casually at a bar, she denied being, or knowing, anyone by the name of Summer. With a fugue state the only possible explanation for Summer's abrupt behavior, Dara thought it might overwhelm her for old family and friends to appear in her new world repeatedly or suddenly. It was the same reason she hid all the pictures in the beach house. And why she'd asked Tomas to stay away.

Tomas wondered if Phoebe would expose him. He didn't want Summer to know he'd finally been able to kiss her, hold her. He didn't want her to feel he had taken advantage of her. But what Summer pushed away and tried to ignore, Therese pursued. They had fallen in love. For six days, though. Just six days.

Tomas whispered to himself on the back porch. "I'm not going to let her go this time." He ran his fingers through his hair and blew smoke from his lips. "I'm not."

"Girls, I think we could all use some rest." Dara was swiping her lips with ChapStick and swinging her crossed, skinny legs from her barstool. "Summer, do you want to shower and get some sleep?"

Summer nodded and stood from her barstool onto the kitchen floor. Tomas glanced into the kitchen and saw her going to the stairs, holding his shirt tightly around her waist.

"What are you going to do about Victor?" Carla asked.

Summer turned before walking up the stairs. "I don't know. I think I've got to get back to Baltimore. I need to talk to him in person."

Carla shook her head. Phoebe shifted on her barstool.

"T, please don't. If you feel like you need to get revenge or go off on him, or whatever, let us handle it." Phoebe had been calling Summer "T" since they were three, when she couldn't pronounce Summer or Summer's surname, Martinez. She could pronounce the "T" from Martinez though, and she'd always stuck with that. When Summer started to call herself Therese, the "T" was not only convenient, but it was also a gift.

"Phoebe, it's not to get revenge," Summer's voice had softened. She looked at Phoebe with her head to the side. "I have to talk to him and see if we can salvage things."

"Salvage things? Salvage what things, Summer?! He's sleeping with one of your best friends! He doesn't love you!" Phoebe stood to go outside with Tomas as Dara hung her head and Carla sat with her hands folded in her lap.

"He does, Phoebe. You guys aren't seeing the whole picture. And you know how Mair can be. I'm not going to throw away the love we have—and my chance to have my own family. I can let things go and be alone forever, or I can go talk to him and see if we can save things. I need your support 'cause I can't do this on my own!" Summer's eyebrows met in a point on her forehead.

"Do what you want!" Phoebe shouted.

"*Shh, shh.*" Carla tried to calm her friend.

"No, Carla! No matter what we do, no matter how we turn our lives literally upside down for her, no matter if she's Therese or Summer, she'll never feel like anyone loves her." Phoebe looked at Dara with tears in her eyes. Dara tried not to move.

"You know the big loud guy in the loft? *He* loves you. See the guy sitting out on the porch in tears over you, T," Phoebe pointed outside, "*he* loves you. Your mom basically set up an entire world around you to help you come back to yourself after Victor crushed your heart. Crushed it! I spent the last year watching and protecting you every single day. Even when I felt like crap, missing my mom." Her voice cracked. "I was supposed to be taking care of myself this year. Myself!" Phoebe pointed at her chest, then tried to regain control of her voice and whispered, "You already have your 'own' family, T. It's right here, in this house."

19

"T, DO YOU WANT ME to come with you?" Phoebe watched Summer pack. "I can come for a little bit and leave on Sunday." She had calmed from her rant at the beach house. Back in their apartment, she'd been able to work her way back to her usual supportive stance.

"No, Phoebe." Summer opened a box and started to toss in cosmetics from her bathroom sink counter. "You need to get started with your rotations. You're already off-cycle," Summer puffed. "Plus, I took up all your bereavement leave. I feel really bad." She stopped and looked into Phoebe's blue eyes. Phoebe sat with her feet splayed on the blue bathroom tile. Her fingers gripped the toilet lid between her thighs as she watched her friend. Phoebe missed how Summer had taken to calling her "Phoebs" in her fugue state. *She must have been thinking about Friends,* she thought.

"I'm not sure another few days will matter, T," Phoebe offered again. She loved Summer through protecting her. She protected her through watching her. She watched and redirected as many choices as she could. Most of them were laced with the potential to destroy her self-esteem—especially when it came to guys. Especially now.

"You've been looking out for me my entire life," Summer responded. "I feel like a burden. Don't worry. I'm going to counseling when I get back anyway."

"That's good, T, but are you really ready to move back to Baltimore with Victor now? I mean, you're packing everything. Why don't you just go for the weekend, see him, come back, and think things over?"

"I agree, honey," Dara shouted from the living room. "I'd feel better if you were here with your friends—in case Daddy and I are working or traveling."

"Mom," Summer began, "I already told you guys I need to get back to my job. I'm twenty-six years old. And I don't want Victor thinking I don't want to work things out and start our family soon."

"I know, baby girl, but you also need to take it easy on yourself. We don't want you to end up breaking down again." Dara walked toward the bathroom and leaned on the door's threshold. "It's not worth it, Summer. You don't need the money. You don't even have to worry about going back to residency. And whenever you're ready, your father will call Uncle Mike. There's no need to worry or rush."

"I don't want Dad to call Uncle Mike, Mom." Summer shook her head. "Not everyone has a dad who is friends with all the program directors and department chiefs. It's not fair."

"Baby, Mike Aarons has been our friend for thirty years. And now, yes, he's the psych program director up there. I'm sorry, but you're not like every other resident." Dara leaned down and ran her fingers through her daughter's curly locks.

"And there's an empty apartment I'm guessing you and Dad spent, what, thirty-six thousand dollars on last year. And it just sat there?" Summer was shaking her head again. "Just because we have money doesn't mean we have to waste it."

"Summer," her mother replied, "we didn't know things were going to go on this long."

"When you were Therese," Phoebe started, the corners of her mouth pointed toward the ceiling, "you didn't care about wasting money," she teased, not noticing Summer's upturned lips. Two days out of the fugue hadn't given her perspective or humor.

"You guys, come on. It's not funny." Summer lifted her box of bathroom belongings, walked it into the living room, and came back with a garbage bag for the unwanted beauty products under her sink. "I'm planning to get back in my apartment, meet with Dr. Aarons, and also go to couple's counseling with Victor."

Dara blew a huge breath across the bathroom.

"What? You want me to never have my own kids? End up all alone?" Summer spun around on her toes to face her mom, her behind resting on her heels. Dara shook her head, looked at the floor, and took her Chap-Stick out of her pocket.

"We aren't making fun of you, Summer, and no one wants you to end up alone." Dara became serious, "Phoebe is trying to make you lighten up. For you, just one night has passed. For us, it's been a full year of watching everything you do and making sure you're okay. Do you think we want to see you put yourself right back in a bad situation? I mean, honey, Victor is sleeping with Mair. That's really bad." She looked up at the ceiling. "I'm not sure where Allie went wrong with her," Dara lamented about her best friend's parenting failures.

"Mom, that was a whole year ago." Summer rolled her eyes and crouched under the sink. From underneath it, she continued, "You have no idea what's going on with them now."

"Summer, he barely even looked for you when you disappeared," Dara retorted. "When the rest of us were working with police to find you, he was ignoring our calls for two, three, four days. Finally, Daddy just told me to stop calling. He's not a good guy for you, baby."

Phoebe sat silently on the toilet lid. Her mind drifted. *God, I'm so ready to be done with all of this. I just want to go back to the Gables and sit on my own bed and call my mom—or at least think of her.* Tears stung the backs of her eyes, and she wiped them away before they could be noticed. Phoebe knew if they saw her crying, she would become the center of their pity. The idea made her feel weak.

"Mom, I'm not like the rest of you." Summer stood and faced her mom. "The thing is, I'm not like Phoebe, or Carla, or you. I've already been thrown away once. I've already lost my first chance at family. They didn't want me."

"They couldn't afford you," Dara corrected.

Summer ignored her. "I love you and Daddy. I do. But I need a family for me. That comes from me."

"Oh my God…" Phoebe started.

"Phoebe, you don't understand. Your mother never abandoned you on a bench outside a grocery store. You had a mom that loved you literally," Summer pinched the air between her forefingers and thumbs, "until her dying breath!"

Phoebe stood and moved to the bathroom door. Tears filled her eyes. "I'm gonna go lie down until it's time to load up your car."

"Seriously?" Summer squinted at her friend. "Okay, Phoebe. Well, I'm trying to leave in the next hour or so."

Dara watched Phoebe close the door to her bedroom. She turned to Summer. "She's probably so sad to see you leave, and on these terms. She probably can't understand how you can feel so alone when we all love you so much."

"Or maybe she's glad, Mom. With Phoebe, you'll never know." Summer closed her garbage bag and looked around the bathroom. All traces of her were gone.

"HOWARD COUNTY POLICE ANNOUNCED in a press conference today they're reopening the investigation into the deadly 2005 car crash involving teenager Joseph Chae. His vehicle fell onto US Route 29 last summer from this roundabout, instantly killing him and two others." A reporter from WBAL-TV stood at the side of the road where Joseph's truck plowed through the guard rail. She wore an ill-fitting navy skirt suit and a messy brown bob haircut. It bounced as she moved her head for emphasis.

The grass at the roundabout came to her knees.

Victor stood third in line, watching the report with his mouth ajar. He was surrounded by powder blue and white walls at Athena's. Their television hung lopsided, just behind the ordering counter. A laminated menu was taped to the counter. Below sat a glass window display of baklava. He was meeting Summer and her mom for souvlakis.

"At the conclusion of the autopsy last year," a Howard County police spokesperson began, "it was determined that the first driver, Mr. Joseph Chae, had been intoxicated with a high dose of the sleeping aid, triazolam, also known as Halcion."

The Chaes stood on the stage, arms draped over each other's shoulders. There was a podium, a line of supporting officers and officials, the state and American flags, and a man in black translating the speaker's words into American Sign Language. The shot cut away to a one-on-one interview with the police chief from earlier in the afternoon.

"Thanks to a new tip, we were able to take a look at some evidence that just wasn't pursued initially," the chief reported, dabbing sweat off his forehead with a folded napkin. "And that included video surveillance of the hours just before Mr. Chae's death. Previously we looked at this accident as the result of driving under the influence. What we've seen changes things."

"Did surveillance show someone else may have been involved?" the reporter leaned in with her microphone inches from the chief's lips.

"Based on surveillance videos, we are fairly certain Mr. Chae did not intentionally overdose or intoxicate himself. We can't go into detail, but we do intend to begin questioning potential witnesses," the chief replied. Then he added, "As of yesterday, we have identified a person of interest."

The chief's suit was tight, and his face was summer-produced pink. He began to shift his weight back toward the cool of his building. The reporter continued, "Chief, just one more question: Will Howard County police be releasing the surveillance video to help the public identify your person of interest?"

"At this time, we do not have immediate plans to release the video, but that could change." The chief concluded the interview with, "That's all we have to report at this time," and rushed back inside through the precinct's glass doors.

A whole year had passed. Victor had been enjoying life. He had given talks at the dental school. He had Mair's body for play every few months. He'd gone to a Detroit-based Super Bowl. He'd traveled to Paris. Now, the sound in Victor's ears began to swirl. His stomach turned. He'd made a miscalculation. Police had never figured out a single homicide of his. They'd never linked the budding oral surgeon to missing-persons-turned-dead-bodies found in woods, or cabs, or apartments. The last words in the news report whirred into the sound of whooshing wind. Victor couldn't hear. Not the man at the counter asking if he could help. And not Summer, who had walked up behind him and said his name.

Summer wore a gray suit. Her hair was pulled back into a smooth bun, and she wore full interview-day makeup and pearls. She had met with Dr. Aarons at the psychiatry training office. Aarons had stood when she had appeared at his doorway and welcomed her with a hug—an uncharacteristic move for her very reserved family friend. His first words, "Welcome back," made her suspicious that her parents had already talked to him, despite her insistence that they not. Summer waited to be invited to sit, held her portfolio on her lap, and explained why she was ready to return to her rotations. She explained what had been explained to her— that she'd gone into a stress-induced fugue.

But now she was "back" and was working with a therapist. She insisted she could be trusted and was ready to resume the impossible work of understanding the human mind. Dr. Aarons made therapy her only stipulation and told her she could resume rotations in December. It was later than she'd hoped. She was not, though, going to display an ounce of disappointment. She stood, they shook hands, and she reached for a second hug.

"Dr. Clemens-Martinez," Dr. Aarons said before Summer left his office, "psychiatry is the most powerful medical specialty in the world, though people may not see it that way. You need to be healthy. Your mind must be clear. You must be trustworthy. There is enough controversy around our field—people worry that we're doctors you can't trust. You are one of the most gifted young psychiatrists I've ever worked with. You can really help people. Get well, okay? The field needs you."

Excitement levitated her as she had floated two blocks down West Pratt Street to Athena's.

"Victor?" Summer asked, smiling. When he didn't respond, she leaned forward into his face and waved. Summer touched Victor's shoulder with her fingertips, and his hypnotized gaze broke away from the TV above. Their eyes hadn't connected in a full year. There would be obvious topics spread on the table of conversation. There were also things Victor knew he'd never mention—including the fact that he'd poisoned a kid after a soccer tournament the year before for a reason he didn't fully understand. It was the reason he had killed before. It was the reason he planned to kill forever.

"Hello," Summer continued, "remember me?" She laughed and reached to hug him. He smiled, wondering when he'd feel the knife plunge into his back or the shank in his side. Summer's hair held the same freesia fragrance it had every day since he'd met her. It replaced his urge to vomit with the urge to cry. It always had that effect on him.

20

"LET'S GRAB A TABLE," Summer suggested.

She looked around Victor to her mom, who was whistling next to the hostess podium at Athena's restaurant. Dara wore a brown layered skirt set. She winked at her daughter like she knew a wistful secret. Worry, though, folded into each line of her face.

"Do you have anything by the front window?" Summer asked the hostess.

"Sure, ma'am, right this way."

Already set on the reddish-brown table were menus and glasses of water. Silverware sat tightly rolled in a single napkin at each place setting with more laminated menus that doubled as small trays. The table wobbled on its legs under the weight of their elbows and purses. Victor was silent as a stone.

"So, Summer," Dara asked, "what's good here?"

"Everything!" she responded. Her voice and face were bright. "I love the crab cakes, though."

"Crab cakes at a Greek restaurant?" Dara looked skeptical.

Their waiter confirmed, overhearing their conversation as he approached. "Yes, ma'am, they are incredible!"

"Well, I guess I'll need to try them." Dara handed her menu back to the waiter and took a sip from her condensation-covered glass.

"Excellent," the waiter replied. "And for you, ma'am?" He turned to Summer. "Wait. Hey! I haven't seen you in forever! Where've you been? You used to come here with your friends all the time."

"Yeah!" Summer's belly tumbled. She hadn't given much thought to the inevitability of people wanting to know where she'd been. She didn't know what to say. "I had to go out of state for a while. Just got back."

"I see. I know you studious types are always going away to do research or something like that." He laughed. "Didn't you used to get the crab cakes yourself?"

"Impressive memory, Dom!" Summer replied, refreshing her own memory with a glance at his name tag.

He nodded. "Two crab cakes. And for you, sir?" He looked at Victor, who had been trying to read the options. The letters danced over the menu, pushed to the perimeter by a vision of police arriving on his front porch.

"Uh. Hmmm. Well, what's your most popular dish?" Victor asked. His appetite had disintegrated as he'd watched Leslie Chae standing behind the police representative, being consoled by her husband. Etiquette, not Victor's stomach, demanded he order something anyway.

"Ah, the chicken souvlaki for sure!" The waiter's voice bubbled with enthusiasm, but his eyes revealed boredom.

"Okay," Victor announced, "I'll take that. Can you leave onions off, please?" The waiter nodded, stretched his wrist forward to take the remaining menus, and looked back at Summer.

"Welcome back, sweetie!" he said. "Good to see you back at your favorite table. Still has the picture you like." Everyone at the table looked up at a picture of a woman in a large vineyard surrounded by baskets of grapes she'd harvested. The picture was all greens, blues, and bright white.

"It always makes me feel like going somewhere," Summer nodded at the waiter. "To Greece I guess..." she drifted off. The waiter smiled.

Over the meal hung heavy anticipation. It threatened to fall—crashing onto their plates. Dara flaked crumb-sized pieces of crab into her mouth. She pretended that she was too occupied to speak or burst the seal of the moment. Victor faced the fork-and-knife or hand dilemma as he navigated his souvlaki. They ate with no words among them for ten minutes.

"Victor." Summer dabbed her thin white napkin at the corners of her round, pink lips. She leaned forward on her elbows, clasping her hands at her chin, and pulling his eyes into hers. "So, did you hear about all the stuff that happened? Apparently, I moved to Florida. I was a dancer. Not that kind; I mean a ballerina. I was living with Phoebe."

He nodded. "Yes, I knew that."

"Okay. So what do you think?" Summer continued to stare at him, dropping her forehead an inch.

He shook his head, wiped his mouth, and shrugged. "Well, I've never known that to happen to anyone."

"Did you speak to one of Summer's friends?" Dara's head tilted to the left, and she tried not to squint.

"No. Um, I haven't talked to any of them," Victor replied, looking down into his plate.

"Why?" Summer wanted to know. Victor seemed perturbed, and she found it satisfying.

"Well, Phoebe called me, but that was the night everything happened. I didn't—I couldn't answer the phone and deal with Phoebe. She already isn't too fond of me anyway."

The tension in Summer's face broke like an egg. She released a laugh that surprised her mother. It was true. None of her friends were Victor fans.

"Baby girl, I didn't realize you and Victor had already talked about everything." Dara's head was still tilted as she rotated it toward Summer.

"We haven't, Mom, that's why we're meeting today—although admittedly this isn't going very well." Summer giggled and caught a small square of feta in the back of her throat. She sipped her now-tepid water.

Like a claw had gripped the middle of her face, Dara looked pained. "I'm sorry. So, Victor, how did you know what happened?"

"What?" he replied.

"How did you know what happened to Summer if you haven't talked to her friends? I'm just wondering how you could have known." Dara placed her fork face down over her second crab cake.

"Uh," Victor's eyes searched the top of his skull for a response, "I, um, talked to my father. My dad told me." He took a deep breath. The waiter came before Victor had to create a follow-up statement.

"How we lookin', folks?" He removed Summer's shining plate. "I see you didn't enjoy that at all!" he laughed. "I'm glad wherever you went and whatever you studied didn't take away that appetite." Everyone nodded politely.

"It sure didn't! Can I have a slice of baklava? Anyone else?" Summer looked around the table with her eyebrows raised. Victor and Dara shook their heads "no." Dara watched Victor as he stared at his folded hands on the edge of the table.

"I'll be right back with that baklava for you, sweetie."

"Oh, sir," Dara said, "would you please bring the check?"

"Yep, no problem," the waiter replied. The porthole window in the swinging door to the kitchen flashed forward then backward with a glare.

"Mom," Summer frowned, "you ready to go? We haven't talked at all." Summer lifted her eyebrows.

"Yeah, baby girl, I'm a little tired. And I think this conversation might go better when it's just the two of you after all. Maybe you guys can meet up later."

Victor continued to stare at his knuckles overlapping each other. With praying mantis stillness, he did nothing but breathe in response to Dara's words.

Summer struggled to break the flaky layered crust of her baklava with her fork and finally picked it up and bit it as she looked out at the chaotic traffic on West Pratt. Honey dripped over her silver forefinger ring. Victor's head turned back toward the TV. Dara studied the picture above the table. A detail in the bottom right corner seemed to glow from the art. She couldn't believe it but hid her excitement. Instead, she casually pulled out her cell phone and snapped a picture of it. Summer scolded her mother as if she'd removed the picture from the wall and attempted to put it in her purse.

"Relax, baby, I'm just going to see if I can find it somewhere for you," Dara said, looking down and grinning, "since you like it so much."

The failed trio stood and began to shuffle toward the restaurant's front door. Dara walked behind Victor and Summer, who walked beside each other like strangers in a doctor's office, trying not to make eye contact. When the dark brown cactus carpet kissed the gold-framed linoleum tile in the foyer, Victor and Summer quickly sidestepped a group of raucous men entering the restaurant. One walked in backward, gesturing huge circles over his head with both hands. The men in his group laughed. One spun him forward and patted him on the back, laughing from his gut.

"Marvin?" Dara's voice was lemony bright. "Oh, my goodness!" The backward walker opened both arms to invite an embrace.

"Dara!" he replied. "So great to see you! Manny told me your good news!"

"Yes! Yes, here she is!" Dara's face was beaming as she waved Summer to her side. "Summer, this is Agent Marvin Cline! If it were not for him, we may not have ever found you!"

Victor pressed his back into the glass of the cigarette vending machine beside the front door.

"Young lady, because of you, I notice every single silver Camry that crosses my path!" He bellowed in laughter.

Dara hugged him again. "Summer, Mr. Cline used to spend a ton of time investigating people, until he retired. He came out of retirement a little just to help us find you!" Dara winked at him.

"Wow, Agent Cline, thank you. This is my fiancé," Summer reached back for Victor, who stayed plastered to the machine. "Come here!" Summer's social laugh lilted over their heads. Victor walked toe to heel as if magnetized to the floor. Summer turned back around to meet Agent Cline's lifted chin and narrowed eyes. Victor bit his lip and covered his left ear.

"Huh! Haven't we met, son?" Summer whipped her head to view Victor, smiling with her lips touching. Dara eyes opened like a morning flower. Agent Cline continued. "Yep, he, uh, was in my neighborhood looking for a house. For his wife," Victor began to nod.

"Oh yes, that was quite a while ago," Victor replied.

"Nah, not too long," Agent Cline stared at him with no expression. "Late summer. Last year. Coulda been around the time we were looking for this doll." He smiled at Summer then let the smile drop from his face. "I never forget faces, son. I never forget cars. I never forget stories. Some people like to tell stories, you know what I mean?"

Summer and Dara held their breath and let their eyes bounce between men.

"So sorry to interrupt." An elderly gentleman leaned into the circle of four. "Marvin, we're gonna be over there." The man pointed to a large corner table.

"Don't let us keep you," Summer smiled. "Can I give you a quick hug, though?" Marvin opened his arms again. "Agent Cline, thank you so much. Thanks to you, I can get back to my life!"

He handed Summer a card. "If you are ever at loose ends, you let me know, Summer. You're one of my VIPs." Agent Cline winked. "Dara, great to see you," he spoke into their third hug. He offered a handshake to Victor. "And Sam, small world, great running into you again."

Victor's eyes fluttered, and he nodded at the old man of Wandering Lane.

On the sidewalk outside, Baltimore's street sounds of horns, yelling conversation, and the release of air brakes blew through Summer's hair. "You're so silly, Victor. Why didn't you tell him your name?"

"Uh," Victor quickly glanced at Dara, then back at Summer, "you know, correcting someone is so awkward."

Summer agreed.

"I'll call you later, Victor," she began. "We really need to talk." Summer reached for his hand, but he didn't offer it. "Don't worry. I'm not going to ambush you. I know you love me and that whole thing was a mistake. I think we should see somebody for therapy, though."

Dara turned her back and walked a few feet down the sidewalk.

Had he known Athena's restaurant was a reckoning ground, Victor would have searched out neutral territory. Instead, the goddess disguised herself behind the mediocrity of a neighborhood ethnic restaurant and crushed him with boulders. Victor stood with his hands behind his back on the sidewalk, attempting to tear skin from the fleshy pad above his veiny wrist.

"LOOK, SUMMER," Dara laughed. "There's a Red Robin," she drove while pointing at the restaurant.

"Oh my gosh, Mom." Summer smiled and shook her head. "You don't have to point it out every time we see one. You should focus on the road, old woman." Summer chuckled. "You know driving's not your thing."

"Can you say it right yet, or do you still call it Robin Read Road?" Dara ignored her daughter's teasing. Summer had always confused the restaurant moniker for her estranged grandmother's street name.

"I'm surprised you're bringing her up." Summer shook her head and chuckled. "Have you talked to her recently? Nazi Nana?" Dara's face flushed with shame as she shook her head "no."

"So, you remembered the waiter's face? After a whole year? That's not like you, Summer!" Dara changed the subject, and her daughter laughed. "He was nice. But what did you think of Victor's behavior today?" she continued. Summer watched the charm of Baltimore slide by through the window. Red brick. Black iron. Cafés. Rich men. Poor men. White coats. Smokers. Shouters. More food. Water and red brick and glass and the Harbor. The cadence of the passing structures pulled Summer into a daydream.

"Summer?" Dara asked again. "You okay, baby girl?

Summer pulled herself back in and up to the comfort of her mother's car seats. "Oh, sorry, Mom. Yes, I'm okay!"

"Did you hear what I asked you?"

"No, I'm sorry. What did you say?" Summer looked at her mom. Her stomach dropped. Since her fugue cleared, she worried about slipping away from herself again. Dara squeezed her knee.

"It's okay," she said to her daughter. Summer felt a rising sensation at the top of her abdomen. It leaped into the center of her chest, accompanied by a flash of heat.

"Mom, why do you always do that?"

"Do what, baby?"

"Squeeze my knee and say, 'It's okay.' You did that one night in Miami," Summer flushed deep pink and rolled down the window.

"When, honey?" Dara frowned.

"That night. I can't remember where we were going."

Dara was grateful for a red light. She stopped and looked at her wide-eyed and pink child. It was the same scared look she'd seen in her four-year-old eyes when Manny brought her home from the adoption agency on Biscayne Boulevard in '84. She'd been born in his hometown of Havana. The day she was ready to come live with them, Dara was on an overnight call at the hospital. She'd met Summer for the first time on their front porch. Manny had always told Summer her first set of parents drowned on a raft journey to the States, coming ahead to build a better life for her. But when she was twelve, Dara admitted that Summer's mother had abandoned her at a grocery store. No one knew who her father was. Not her, not Dara and Manny, not her biological mother.

Summer loved to imagine she was carried to the sands of Miami's

154

largest bay by a teenage boy, Miguel—a boy magical enough to steer a crashing raft with both hands and still hold on to Cuba.

"Summer, baby, we haven't driven around at night in Miami since God knows when. Years and years." She was holding Summer's hand.

"Yes, Mom, when you came to get me. You asked if I remembered a song and when I said 'no,' you did the same thing. You squeezed my leg and said, 'It's okay.'" Summer's eyes welled.

"Okay." Dara reached into the purse at her feet for ChapStick. She sat up, applying cherry-flavored wax to her mouth. "You did great today," she said, maneuvering Summer away from her false memory. "I'm so proud of you. You're a brave woman, Summer. Do you want to let your seat back and take a nap?" Car napping in recline was a technique from Summer's childhood that always helped her battle overwhelm.

Summer's hand had already been positioned to push the motorized lever backward. She descended into slumber in less time than it took to get in the fast lane on the highway. As Dara drove to the rhythm of her sleeping child's breath, she tried to pull the pieces of the day together. She saw cracks in her daughter's veneer of politeness at lunch. Her enthusiasm unsettled Dara. Victor troubled her in his politeness, too. The doctor part of Dara believed him to be in a rage just under the surface, like Manny. But he was a Chihuahua-sized man. That made him safer—but in some ways scarier. He was smaller and able to get into all sorts of places where he didn't belong.

Dara stopped in her home's mile-long driveway. She turned to wake Summer, who lay staring at her in silence like a fresh corpse. She parted her lips and said, "I was at the Aquarium."

21

"WHAT'S ALL THIS STUFF?" Summer leaned her hips into the dining room table and tucked her hair behind her ears. Surrounded by orange walls and mirrors, her reflection read joy from every angle. On a large beechwood table sat a spread of boxes wrapped in shades of purple. Three large boxes made a pyramid in the center of the table. Two smaller ones sat on either side of a bouquet of three calla lilies secured with brown twine.

"Well, yeah, it's not a big deal or anything," Victor replied, leaning on one of the dining chairs, his free hand tucked knuckle-deep into his jeans pocket.

"Kind of looks like a big deal, though." Summer's racing heart pushed her to breathlessness. She remembered the early days of Victor's sweet gift-giving.

"Is today my birthday?" she joked.

"Uh, sure. Happy random September day." Victor did not smile, did not blink. Summer noticed his restrained expression. She also noticed the smallest box, a ring box, in front of the flowers.

"Where should I start?" Summer asked as she reached for the top of the pyramid. The box was large, square, and lighter than expected. She tucked her fingers into the gap left by the triangular paper fold on the side. She flipped the box upside down, avoiding her lilies. Cream and black lines hinted at Chanel.

"Oh, my goodness, Victor. What is this?!" Summer's fingers pulled off the lid and plunged into white tissue paper, revealing a large gold purse. "Oh, my God, this is gorgeous!" She skipped to the largest box on the bottom, hurriedly opening it as if it held all the world's happiness. Again, her fingers fluttered around white tissue paper. This gift required two hands to lift—not due to weight, but to texture.

"What's this, Vic?" She lifted the garment slowly. "A scarf? A dress? A dress?!" Summer lifted it and turned to the mirror behind her. Held at her shoulders, the royal blue cascaded to just above her perfect toes hidden in the plush white carpet. "Baby," she said, draping the dress over a chair, "thank you!" Summer placed her wrists on Victor's shoulders. Though they stood at the same height, Summer tried to shrink herself to feel delicate in his arms. Her head tilted and pressed lips into the cheek he offered. Returning to intimacy of any type was progressing in the slowest of steps, but she did not mind.

When she finished her box openings and surprised expressions, Summer gathered her spoils and changed into them. A gold ring, her gold bag, and the accompanying yellow wrap. The blue of the dress subdued the richness of her skin.

"All you need is sandals," Victor said, smiling as if to showcase every tooth. "I bought you some, then I realized they looked like someone already wore 'em."

"Musta been a return," Summer spun around in the middle of the living room, stopping to push her hips from side to side and cup her breasts for comical cleavage. "I probably already have shoes that go with this!"

"You look really good." Victor nodded, still smiling.

"I have a confession," Summer started. "I thought the ring box was going to be my engagement ring."

"Well, considering everything, I have a lot of surprises you're gonna get first." Victor's face became serious. "But I'd give you the ring today if things were where they're supposed to be."

"We're gonna get there, baby." Summer stopped spinning.

"You really think couples counseling is going to help you forgive me?" Victor folded his arms.

"Yep!" Summer replied. "People get over infidelity all the time. Not saying it's gonna be easy, though, especially since you're leaving soon. Why? What do you think?"

"I think I'm gonna mess up in some other way and you're gonna get totally preoccupied with that."

"And if I do," Summer pushed her lips out and swirled her hips, laughing, "I have plenty of time to work on my coping skills!"

Victor laughed. "Yeah, you're gonna need those."

"Can you believe Dr. Aarons won't let me come back until December?! What the heck?" Summer still laughed. "What am I gonna do with myself all that time?"

"Well, you never know what may come up. I'm sure you'll get yourself into something. Or catch up on *Grey's Anatomy*. What about today, though? What do you wanna do?"

"First, I'm gonna take off my fancy new outfit." Summer was spinning again, laughing and dancing. "Wanna watch?"

Victor's forced smile lifted through his eyes as he nodded, pretending he was going to chase her. She hopped in place, then turned to run, disappearing upstairs.

"SUMMER? HEY, IT'S MOM. I'm just calling to see how you're doing, baby. Please give me a call." Dara was in a near-panic every day after Summer's bizarre car behavior two weeks before when she was in recline. Staring. Not sleepily rousing from a confusing dream but robotically staring, words about the town's aquarium spilling from her lips.

The two had left the car and driveway. Linked by hearts and arms, they had walked into the cool aroma of dinner being prepared by their chef. The Clemens-Martinez family brought a piece of Spanish style into the area, with a home interior quite similar to Miami's most exquisite. Summer enjoyed the house, but it was not home to her. To correct for this, her parents insisted on adding the warmth and love of a home chef who was more of an *abuela*, a grandmother, than anything else. Summer had been raised in the cadence of Miami, which held a rhythm much different than Baltimore. Spanish flowed in her veins and home and conversation with friends, family, and strangers on the street eating guava pastries. Here, there was no steamy, Atlantic Ocean-generated mugginess or crop tops and Latin boys under palm trees and blazing blue skies. Dara knew speaking in front of the family's nurturing adopted *abuela* would disarm Summer. Summer loved *abuelas*, and she'd only ever had one.

"So, Summer, you were saying in the car that you were at the Aquarium?" Dara sat at their large round kitchen table. "When were you at the Aquarium? I know it's one of your favorite places to visit ever since Daddy and I moved up here."

"What do you mean, Mom?" Summer was already sitting at the table, resting her head on her palm.

"In the car, didn't you say something about the Aquarium? You woke up and said, 'I was at the Aquarium,' remember?" Dara noticed a dull ache sitting at the back of her skull and tension across the crest of her shoulders.

"No, I don't remember. I mean, yeah, I said that," Summer responded. "But I think I was still dreaming or something."

"What was it, *mamita*? What was the dream?" the chef asked.

Dara looked at Summer.

"I barely even remember. I was behind the Aquarium, touching the blue wave light on the building. I could see the Harbor's water from where I stood. Then somehow, I ended up on the front side, walking upstairs to the ticket booth. I dropped an earring. Well, I realized I was missing an earring. I looked on the floor and saw it. It was forest green and squiggly. When I went to pick it up, I woke up."

"Ah! ¡*Muy importante*! Somebody have big news for you. Or *ad-bice*.

Mira, you need to find them." The chef kept rolling *croquetas*. "Water, clear water, *es bueno. Espiritual*."

"Do you have earrings like that?" Dara asked.

"I'm not sure."

"Were they squiggly like a snake?" Dara continued, her feet up on the chair beside Summer.

"Hmm, yeah, I guess."

"Aha!" The surrogate grandmother interjected, pointing a wagging index finger at the ceiling. "See, aha! ¡*Mira*! You need to find out. Somebody know something."

Summer put her head down on the table, still sleepy from seeing Victor. The energy of her imitation enthusiasm was beginning to fail. She never knew wearing faux anything could be so expensive. Her mother wanted to tell her the name of the painting in Athena's, that it was called *Therese and the Late Summer Harvest*. Dara had researched the title and learned the name "Therese" derived from the Greek term meaning both "late summer" and "harvest." Summer's subconscious mind had picked it up well enough during all those lunch visits with friends to recall it in her early days of stupor. The layered meanings fascinated her psychiatrist mother, but Summer's weary head on their wooden table signaled it wasn't the right time to discuss.

That same night, Victor called. He apologized for his lunch demeanor. He'd been feeling overwhelmed, he said. His business was expanding into new territory across state lines. He knew he would need to leave for a while, scouting partners and places. He had asked if Summer would come and stay with him for the weeks before he left. She had agreed, as long as they could get in at least a few counseling sessions. As she had left the belly of warm love and family security at her parents' home that night, her father had stood at the front door with his feet miles apart. His arms were folded, and his face was so devoid of expression, he should have surrendered his features for disuse.

"He's the snake, but somehow he has you crawling back to him, *hija*,"

Manny had warned his daughter, then he stepped backward into the house and shut the door.

SUMMER NOTICED THE MISSED "MOM" CALL on her phone and decided to text once she was up for the day. She slept heavily most every night and could live with missed mornings. Beside her, Victor sat up in bed, watching the news with the closed captions running.

"You can turn it up," she told him, rolling back over and pulling one thigh out from under the covers.

Victor quickly turned up the volume.

"I know you've always liked the news, but you seem to really watch it a lot now." Summer lay facing the windows to the backyard. "You're a little obsessed, right?" she teased.

"You're right." Victor reached over and rubbed her nude back. "Let's get up and make the best of this weekend."

"I'm gonna miss you!"

"I know. But I'm just gonna be in, like, Philly and Delaware. I can easily come back, or you can come up to me."

"And counseling?" Summer was still facing the windows.

"Counseling would be better later, Summer. If we even need it at all." Victor stopped to listen to a report about a cafeteria worker spreading hepatitis.

"Vic, I walked in on you about to have sex with a girl who's basically a sister to me. Or used to be." She sighed. "Unfortunately, we do need counseling."

"You don't trust me, but alright," he responded, aloof.

"I'm trying," Summer replied.

"You should probably act like it then," Victor said, ice running through his words. Summer flipped over to check his face for sarcasm.

"You're joking, right?"

"Kind of?" He was still watching the news report. A middle-aged woman in a white apron and hairnet sat with bent wrists on her haunches.

"I want to take you out," Victor continued. Summer rolled her eyes and wiped away a tear. "When you get dressed today, put on something pretty."

"I'm gonna go shower. I need to get some tampons."

"Can you get those before we go out?" Victor slid down in the bed, his chin nearly squatting on his neck. "Otherwise, you'll complain all day about having to go to the bathroom."

"Yes, Victor, geez." Summer fought a full cry until she turned on the shower. Still, she could hear him shouting over the water.

"Hey, Summer! Summer!"

"What?!"

"When you go to the store, you can take the Audi!" Victor yelled at the closed door, and then he turned up the TV volume.

Summer dressed in the walk-in closet to the left of Victor's sprawling bathroom. Her jewelry, purses, shoes, and all types of clothes lived solely in that space. She never had reason to open the closet doors lined across the front of the bedroom—the ones that held Victor's jade bracelet and wigs and lip shimmer.

This closet was constructed of mirrors. Summer held her head down to avoid confronting her own eyes in them. She knew they'd ask her just what in the hell she was doing back with Victor. She struggled to recall one day of fully felt happiness with him. The year they first started dating was as inevitable as it was curious. She hadn't expected one of the residents to take interest in a med student who could not yet do medical tricks. But he had wanted to see her outside of the hospital. And wanted to pay for her to eat. And he let people see them together. Most of all, he encouraged her to dream about their future. This was their weekend ritual—after her first party at his place for fireworks on the Fourth.

"Hey!" he'd say, driving, with the background noises of the trauma center behind him, "I'm leaving the hospital now, want to go out?" And she would always, always reply with a "yes." They'd talk about when and where they'd meet, which would always, always be his house. He would drive her in an Audi. He'd drive fast, and the car absorbed errors and rough streets. And then a trendy restaurant would appear as if dropped there by date gods. It would be chic and full of Asian women selling sushi. It would always be his favorite. And she felt sure she would never be his favorite. Not in any way her blackness could cause or cure.

He'd told her she looked pretty once. That had to be a hundred times fewer than he mentioned the same about other women. They'd talk, and he'd seem interested in her thoughts, but more interested in his own. He studied film, he'd explained. Not movies, film. Silent, black-and-white, obscure, indie, French, or Sundance-y film. She howled at Morris Chestnut in *The Best Man* with her friends, or tried to watch *The Ring* with them when they were all feeling brave. He informed her that she was not into film.

But she was twenty-four and thought she needed to be engaged. And after you'd gone to at least one donor dance together (and they had), you were med-school official. She planned to marry him in her mother's dress. His insults and lukewarm love she'd tuck away in the bustled fabric of her wedding gown.

22

"IF YOU MISSED THE MAGIC 95.9 SUMMER JAM, you missed out!" A Rickey Smiley weekday show was being rebroadcast.

Summer backed out of the garage with ten and two hands around the Audi logo. Victor occupied the doorway, watching. And because he watched, she didn't place her shades on the bridge of her nose. She did not rummage in her new gold purse. She did not move the Gatorade bottle beside it to the drink holder in the console. Victor motioned to her to turn down the radio. Through rolled-up windows, bass drops threatened his façade of class on this early Saturday morning. Once she'd let the garage doors down, though, Summer rolled down the windows. She gathered the blue dress up and over her knees and slid her feet out of gold rhinestone flip-flops. Her head bopped in a one-two down the first street. She entertained the stop sign with mouthed words and winding shoulders in rhythm with R&B's poster child for surviving lost love.

"Would you lie? Make me cry?" Mary J. Blige asked. Summer sang, "No!" at each pause and made a right turn. Her phone was ringing.

"¡Dime!" She shouted her Cuban greeting, looking for the volume control in Victor's car but giving up and singing into the receiver.

"Well neither would I-I-I baby, my love is only your love!"

"Oh my God, *Prieta*," Tomas laughed as he used the nickname her brown skin had earned. "You still can't sing! I keep thinking you're gonna grow out of it!"

She laughed, tossing her head backward. "Hold on! Hold on!" She looked around the controls and made a quick pulse on the brakes. The Gatorade bottle tumbled to the floor. She picked it up, still laughing, moved it to the console, and frowned when she noticed it read "Joey" on a plastic seam.

"¡Bebo!" she said, rolling the volume button toward her. "¿Que bola, 'sere?" She looked out the window and rolled it up as she asked him in Spanish how he was doing. "Oh my God, this neighborhood is so freakin' quiet."

"¡Guajira!" Tomas laughed.

"¿Guajira? What the heck?! I'm not a country girl!" Summer's cheeks stung with laughter. "It's not my fault Victor lives in this suburban nightmare!"

"What are you doing? Where's the idiot?" Tomas chuckled. Summer ignored the second half of his question.

"I'm going to get tampons!" She knew Tomas would make a groaning noise as he'd done ever since fifth grade when the topic of menstruation was mentioned. Even as a gynecologist, he continued this habit with friends—to make them laugh.

"Why are you calling so early? Are you post-call?" Summer asked.

"Si." Tomas let a little tiredness show through. "The hospital sucked last night."

"Ah, sorry, Bebo! Go sleep!"

"Yeah, I'm going to. I miss you! Just wanted to say hello when I could catch you."

"Awww! You wanna hear me sing you a lullaby before you go?"

"No! Bye!"

"Wait, wait, wait! I wanna tell you something?"

"¿Que?" Tomas laughed.

Summer began to sing, "I love you. I honestly love youuuu."

"Oh my God, bye!"

Summer fell into laughter and realized she'd missed her U-turn into

Target. She looped around and noticed the whirl of blue lights in the rearview mirror.

"Oh snap, *Bebo*, hold on! I'm getting pulled over." She placed the phone in the passenger seat and yelled, "Don't hang up!" Summer frantically pushed the radio station search button on the control, hoping to land on a white station. The tan and red of Target's storefront watched.

"Hey, everybody, it's TJ, and you're listening to Z104.3. We got the latest from John Mayer up next." The first piano notes of "Waiting on the World to Change" danced from the speakers as a police officer's waist became visible in the driver's side window.

"Ma'am, can you roll your window down?" An officer stood with a pad and pen at his belly.

"What's the matter?" she shouted through the window. Fear rattled her voice.

The officer pointed his left forefinger and rotated his hand in backward circles. She rolled the window down four inches.

"Ma'am, roll it all the way down, please. Do you know why we're pulling you over?"

Summer had once been told to always respond "no" to that question, even if it was lie. "No, Officer. What's the matter?"

"We need to talk to you."

"About what?" Summer removed her sunglasses and shut off the radio entirely. The crackle of Tomas's call was audible. Summer's heart threatened to pound a dent into her back.

"Summer!" she heard Tomas shout. "Just do whatever he's asking you."

As she rolled down the window more, the officer draped his fingers over the glass. *Victor's gonna be pissed about fingerprints*, she thought.

"License and registration, please," the officer said, turning his hand upright.

"What do you need that for? What did I do?" Summer was nauseous and cramped low in her abdomen. "Officer, I really need to get in the store for some feminine products."

"License and registration," he repeated.

"This isn't my car."

"License and registration," he said, staring. Summer looked in the rearview and noticed another officer standing with his hand on the back right corner of the car. She sucked her teeth.

"I'm gonna get my wallet out, okay?" She looked at him. He didn't respond. "Here." Summer handed him her license, "This isn't my car; it's my fiancé's. I don't know where the registration is."

"Probably the glove box," the officer said, his eyes focused on her license.

"I don't feel comfortable opening the box." She sat barely breathing.

The officer walked to his car with the license. The other officer did not move. Tomas's call was still there.

"Tomas! Can you hear me?" Summer whispered.

"¡Sí! Seriously, Summer, do whatever they say, okay?"

"Okay!" she replied. The taste of salt surprised her tongue. She looked at herself in the mirror and realized she'd begun crying. A headache was emerging from her right temple.

"Ma'am, is this car registered to a Mr. Victor Jacobs?"

"Yeah."

"How do you know Mr. Jacobs?"

"He's my fiancé. Well, my boyfriend."

"Which is it?" The officer stared over his sunglasses.

"Technically, boyfriend," Summer replied.

"And how long has he been your technical boyfriend?"

"I don't know, two or three years." Summer was squinting. "Why?"

"Is it two or three?"

"Three, I guess." Summer sighed heavily. "Why are you asking me all these questions?"

"Where were you the morning of August 27th, 2005?"

"What?" Summer began to panic.

"Where were *you*," the officer pointed into her face, "on August 27th, 2005?"

Summer stared. She looked at the phone. Her breasts rose and fell with quick breaths.

"I don't know."

"Where was this Victor Jacobs?"

"I don't know, Officer," Summer felt a warm gush leave a wet puddle beneath her.

"This a hospital decal?" he tapped the sticker on her window. "Were you working on the morning of August 27th, 2005?"

"I don't know. I can't remember. I don't even know what day that was." Summer held her forefinger under her nose. "Officer, I need a tampon."

"It was a Saturday. Does that green bottle there belong to you or your boyfriend?" The officer pointed with a nod of his head.

Summer lifted the bottle. "I guess it's his, but it says 'Joey' on it."

"Ma'am, I need you to step out of the car."

"For what?" Summer asked, as he hooked his fingers on the door's latch.

"This will be a lot easier for everyone if you just do it." The officer swung open the door. She grabbed the door and shut it into her thigh.

"Get out. You're under arrest." He grabbed the door and lifted her left arm up by the elbow. "Let's go!" He pulled her from the car, smearing fresh blood along the seat.

"For what, Officer? Was I speeding?"

"Disorderly conduct. Obstructing an investigation. I don't care; take your pick."

"Oh my God, what?" Summer's voice went from trembling to screeching. "¡Bebo! Call Victor!" Summer's breasts were being pressed into the glass of the back window as her wrists were scraped into handcuffs.

"I'm under arrest?!" Summer shouted, swinging her head to plead with the second officer. His badge read Montcliffe.

"Ma'am, we want to talk to you about an investigation we think you may have some information on," the second officer said calmly.

"What investigation?!"

"You were caught on tape poisoning Joey Chae," the first officer responded. He pressed his thumb into the flesh of her arm as he trotted her to the patrol car.

"Who?!" Summer swung her head back to the first officer. "Tomas! Call Victor right now!" she shouted.

The sound of his response was stifled as the second officer shut the car door. He looked over his shoulder as Summer was pushed head-first into the patrol car. He pulled a small black cell phone from his pants pocket and turned his back. "Vic, we're all set. Meet us at the station."

23

"FORTY-EIGHT HOURS?!" Tomas exclaimed. "She didn't do anything! Why does she have to be there forty-eight hours?"

Dara sat in silence as she listened to the speakerphone conversation between her husband and Tomas.

"She went in this morning, on a Saturday," Manny replied, "Judge isn't back 'til Monday. Forty-eight hours."

"Can we visit?" Tomas asked.

"No. Inmates have to schedule on Mondays of each week for visitors. Plus, she's waiting on arraignment."

"So, what's gonna happen at court?" Tomas panted.

"I don't know. We'll have to see what the judge says. She's got no record, no previous offenses. He might set bail. He might not."

"He might not?!"

"Of course. Murder charges?" Manny replied, shaking his head at Dara. "It's entirely possible. And then she'll just have to stay there until her trial."

"I'm coming up there."

"No need to do that, *Bebo*. There's nothing you can do. Where are you now?"

"In the hospital parking garage. Sorry for all the noise. But for the case, aren't people allowed to come to the arraignment hearing? I think she'd appreciate it if I was there. She sounded terrified when the cops took her."

"I guess. I didn't ask the lawyer, but yeah, I think so." Manny covered the phone with the heel of his palm and whispered, "He's coming up here," to his wife.

She nodded. She'd been sitting in silence, just as she had been when the phone call came in. She was meditating on the sound of singing robins in her backyard. Beautiful songs to mark territory. Manny had softly said, "Summer's been arrested," into the robin song space. Dara sat. Silent. A flood of words slammed into the front of her brain. And none of them could make their way out.

"I'm going to be there for the arraignment, Uncle Manny. Is there anything else I can do now, from here?"

"When are you coming?"

"In the morning, probably. I want to be there in case she gets out early or something."

"It's going to cost you a fortune to get a trip on short notice like that. And we don't know that she's getting out."

"You know money doesn't even matter, *Tio*." Tomas turned on his car. "Can I stay with you guys?"

"Yeah, of course. Call us when you land." Manny said bye and hung up. Dara sat in silence for a few moments longer.

"He wants to come stay with us, Dara."

Dara nodded. She thought it would be helpful to have Tomas around. He was excitable but passionate about Summer. Listening to Manny's cold responses, she wondered if he even cared about their daughter.

"Victor's calling." Manny looked at the ringing phone in his hand. "Maybe I ought to ignore him now," he said, alluding to the previous year.

Dara sat silently.

"I'll be back, Dara. I'm going to make sure this conversation gets real ugly."

FORTY-EIGHT HOURS. *In this clear-walled cage. The guard told me to have a seat. That I get arraigned on Monday. That's a lifetime away right now. A lifetime. The linoleum is sticky. It smells like urine in here. And it's freezing. The funky pee and freezing air are making my throat hurt. But they said it's full. I can't get an individual cell. "You're not at the Four Seasons, Martinez." I know that. Trust me. I took a mug shot with period blood running down my legs.*

The black girl guard gave me a change of clothes. I couldn't shower. I folded a brown paper towel and stuck it under the water. I tried to wipe. I'm sure I missed spots. This maxi pad feels like a log. At least I have something. I have something besides just the cliché jumpsuit I'm in. I'm gonna keep sitting in this corner. Maybe I can get farther away from the pee smell. Maybe not.

"Martinez!"

Oh God, what are they calling me for now? Maybe they don't mean me.

"Martinez! Hey! Let's go."

They're looking at me and walking over. They mean me.

"Let's go, need to talk to you."

Why do they have to keep squeezing my arm so hard? I can walk on my own. Not gonna say anything, though. Long, narrow beige hallway. Linoleum floor. Brown doors. This place is ugly. I know it's not Disney World or anything. But does it have to be so ugly? I don't think so.

Montcliffe and the mean cop. I'm gonna have bruises all over 'cause of the mean one. He reminds me of that cop I see all over town in the TRAINEE vest. He's a lunatic. And I'm saying that as a psychiatrist. But this Montcliffe, he seems nice. He seems super familiar.

"Summer, so... you're under arrest for obstructing an investigation. That's how we put the charge down. Then there's this murder charge hanging out there. The problem is, we have this video."

Should I ask what video? No! I should be asking for a lawyer. I'm just gonna keep my mouth closed.

"Do you know what we might find if we look at a video from the morning of August 27th, 2005? At the Centennial soccer park?"

Just be quiet, Summer. You're the child of a shrink; you can sit in awkward silence for the rest of your life and not blink. I'm so freaking scared. I'm about to start crying again. No, if I cry now, they're gonna definitely say I'm guilty.

"See, we have a recording right here of you replacing a water bottle in the back of this kid's car. He drank whatever was in that bottle, tried to drive, and then drove off the highway. Right over off Waterloo. He was killed instantly, and he killed two other people."

"Oh my God." *That's horrible. I didn't do it, but that's horrible.* "Can I see the recording?"

"Now, we don't normally do this, Summer. But I'm going to make this exception for you, 'cause I want you to tell us we're not seeing what we think we are."

So do I. Let me see.

Okay, tops of cars. More cars coming in. People in a parking lot. More cars. I don't see anything else. What am I missing?

"Summer, watch this area here. That's the victim's car."

Alright, top of the screen. A Jeep. I still don't see anything. Just sitting there. People walking by. Um, okay a car just pulled in.

I shouldn't ask, but I'm going to. "What kind of car is that?"

"We can zoom in, Summer."

What's on the back of that car? What's that sticker? A decal from the med school. Oh my God, that's Victor's car.

Is that the bottom of a dress? Wait, this girl's got black hair. I thought it was gonna be Mair. Who the hell is this? When was this?

"Officer, when was this?"

"August 27th. Last year."

Who is this girl getting out of the car? My head is hurting. Wait, what is she wearing? Is she wearing the same… That's the outfit! That's my outfit! He gave me the same outfit he gave someone else?! This was in August? We were still together in August. That dinner party was supposed to be August twenty-second. It was the twenty-second!

"Can you zoom in more please?"

My purse, too? Oh my God. What is she doing? Look at this. Rummaging through someone's car in broad daylight?! Hello? Why are all these people just walking by? Okay. Okay, wait, this guy's gonna say something. Good. He's saying something… taking the bottles and walking away. He's just gonna walk away?! What? Come on!

"Summer, did you see the swap? I can rewind it."

Of course, I saw it. But that's not me.

"Officer Montcliffe, could you zoom in any more? That's not me. That girl has straight black hair. And she's light. That guy who comes up and takes the crate—did you talk to him? He could tell you I'm not the same person. I have curly brown hair. I'm black, Officer. That girl isn't even black."

Oh, wait. What is she doing? Is she waiting for someone? Signaling somebody? I don't see anyone. She's biting her lip and drumming her fingers like she's thinking about something, just like… Oh my God.

"You can stop it. That's not me. I know who that is, but it's not me."

"Summer. We picked you up in the same car. You have the bottle. It's got the kid's name on it. You were in the same clothes, for God's sake," the mean officer said.

"You're right. And I know that's weird. But that's not me."

"Well, who is it then, Summer?" Officer Montcliffe asked.

"It's Victor."

24

"MAIR, IT'S ME AGAIN. I need to talk to you. So call me back when you can, okay? It's important."

Tomas's plane sat in the glaring September sun at Fort Lauderdale's airport. He'd been on the tarmac for two hours, sweating in the failing air condition. He'd been trying to reach Mair for the past twenty-four hours. And he wasn't even sure he should be calling her. But he knew the things he knew—that she had always been obsessed with Victor, that nothing would make her give him up, and that if moving Summer out of the way was possible, Mair would capitalize on that with no hesitation. That meant she'd have details—gleefully obtained details—about Summer's arrest. Details Tomas didn't want to ask Dara or Manny.

The relationship between Mair and Summer had always been tense. Summer adored Mair, and Mair adored the adoration. But she also always felt contempt, envy, that no one in their group understood. Both girls were beautiful, though basically opposite in appearance. Both were brilliant. Mair's family life had its bumps, but so did Summer's.

Second place. Mair constantly spoke about having to accept "second place" to Summer.

"You can't possibly still be mad that she beat you out for captain on the elementary cheerleading team, Mair," Phoebe or Carla would say, teasing her about the outcome of Epiphany's 1990 cheerleading tryouts.

"No, I'm not saying that," she'd respond. "I'm just saying she always gets the attention. I honestly think it's 'cause she's not like us. She doesn't look like us. And it's different when your parents get to choose you."

The group would always end the conversation there. Talking about Summer's adoption, the tone of the skin she was wrapped in, or her textured hair—it all felt like a nasty betrayal. Mair acted like a hostage friend, like her companionship to Summer was forced. And she loved the group more than any one person in it. It did afford her benefits upon privileges upon prestige. Summer never saw the betrayal, though they'd each told her. Victor did, too. She'd say it's just "how Mair can be" and would leave it at that.

Tomas carried an issue of the *New England Journal of Medicine* in his carry-on. He crossed his legs and opened the journal to an article on myomectomies. He'd exchanged unplanned abandonment of his clinical duties with the obligation to present on the topic when he returned. He'd been given four days.

His mind drifted from the robotic-assisted procedure to the reason he was going to Baltimore. He wanted to support Summer as she faced her legal woes, sure. And he'd vowed to fight to have her love him. But he had hated Victor for years. Ever since he was a third-year medical student rotating on general surgery. He never understood why the oral surgeons in training had to work with the rest of the surgery team. Victor, as a resident physician, exacted and enforced the common culture on that rotation at the time: to treat male students as rivals and female students as pretty accessories.

Tomas had stood drowsy during the 3:00 A.M. repair of an acute compartment syndrome crisis, an overnight call with Mair and Victor. A Miamian had accidentally shot himself in his right calf. He'd been holding a loaded gun in his pocket. Pressure building in his leg threatened to strangulate and kill the muscle and the man. Tomas watched as Victor's smooth hands cut one long laceration from the patient's knee to his ankle. Muscle popped from the limb like opening a can of biscuits.

"Student Doctor Tornes," Victor said, addressing Tomas formally in front of the senior surgeons, "tell me five causes of compartment syndrome other than a gunshot wound."

Tomas's body wavered on the step stool at the bedside. He had been sleeping until he heard his name.

"Hello?" Victor continued. "Okay, you don't know that one. Let's try something else. Do you think a person with hypertension is more or less likely than a person without hypotension to tolerate rises in compartment pressures?"

Tomas blinked. "Uh… less likely?"

"Wrong. What compartment of the leg is most likely to develop acute compartment syndrome?"

"Anterior."

"Lucky. Name three late signs of compartment syndrome."

"Loss of sensation."

"Wrong."

"Weakness upon flexing the foot."

"You mean dorsiflexion? Wrong."

"Peroneal nerve… uh…" Tomas couldn't think of the word for dysfunction, "…uh, peroneal nerve not working correctly?"

"Is that what you're going to write in your patient's chart, Student Doctor Tornes? This patient's peroneal nerve isn't working? My ten-year-old niece could do better than that." Victor did not have a ten-year-old niece. "You're probably gonna fail this rotation. Just fair warning."

"Sounds like you already have," the most senior surgeon interjected.

Every call night, every few nights for a month, was like this. Tomas drank six coladas a day—enough Cuban caffeine to give him a semipermanent tremor and an ulcer—all so he could make it through the rotation. He'd passed only because of his stellar performance on his final oral exams and the fact they weighed more than Victor's horrible, horrible evaluation. He'd described him as having mediocre intelligence and a weak work ethic. Meanwhile, all the students hid the fact that Victor had conned the nursing staff into only paging him for his favorite types of cases. Mair did the scutwork to make him sparkle and shine, even when it wasn't her turn to be on call. And with this combination of circumstances, Victor had gained all the accolades a resident could, undeserved as they may have been.

As Tomas closed the journal, having read no further than the abstract, the memories of nighttime surgery call snapped safely back into his brain's box for medical-student trauma. The slight chill of September in Maryland was a respite. He could take a lung full of air. The sounds of Baltimore/Washington International Airport seemed muted when compared to the "*Bienvenido a Miami*" announcement blasting through the baggage claim carousels back home. There were no flashing-light palm trees. There was no suffocating humidity.

He folded his boarding pass as he stood on the curb under the "arrivals" sign waiting for Manny to pick him up. It was quiet until a lowered black Honda Civic sped by, distorting Fat Joe's voice on the song "Lean Back." Tomas counted four rounds of "lean back" before noticing Manny's maroon Escalade ten feet away. A half-dropped window created an open box around Manny's head. The blackness and illegality of the tints shocked Tomas. Manny nodded at Tomas when he entered the car, his lips folded on themselves, revealing dimples like tunnels in his cheeks. Tomas put his bag between his feet and focused so much on balancing his coffee between his knees that Dara's hand on his shoulder startled him.

"¡*Tia*! I didn't see you back there," he said, holding his dripping cup above his jeans. She handed him napkins, a smile, and a kiss on the cheek.

"Welcome to Baltimore! Here, let's put your drink over here." She'd reached through the seats to place his drink in the car's cup holder.

"Uncle Manny, how's everything?" Tomas read his lack of salutation as stress. His daughter, after all, was being held in a local jail. Manny didn't respond, so Tomas just looked out the window as they drove to the couple's sprawling Towson estate. It was his first time in Maryland. The thick and shiny leaves of the highway's purple trees reminded him of

Summer's hair. Being in the town where she was, even as an inmate, called memories to his mind's surface with ease. He loved her. He had always loved her.

Tomas looked around the home, touching the arched walls with their inlaid wood accents and bronzed lanterns. Two large, blue mosaic vases stood guard outside Manny's glass-doored wine cellar.

"*Bebo*," Dara said, smiling warmly as she watched him take in their home, "let me show you your room."

He followed her, noticing his fatigue for the first time. Ticket purchases and pleading for a short break from the hospital stole his sleep the night before. He sat down on the bed, just to remove his shoes, and woke up two hours later.

"Knock, knock." Dara leaned in with a tray. "Hungry?"

"Oh wow, *Tia*, my apologies." He sat upright and straightened his glasses.

"Don't apologize." She set the tray on the foot of the bed. "We've all had a lot on our minds lately, huh?" She gave a sideways smile. "It's so good of you to come up here. Summer has the most loving friends." Tomas decided not to tell her that Phoebe wouldn't be able to come. Dara kissed Tomas on the forehead as she did when his head barely reached her hip. She'd always cherished him, the one son born into the group of her very best colleagues. "Manny and I are going to head to bed. Tomorrow is a big day." She clasped her hands and looked down. "If you need anything at all during the night, just knock." Dara pointed out the TV remote and extra blankets before she left the room.

Within moments, Tomas heard the sound of a shower somewhere in the house, and he remembered his journal. He had to read and prepare for his presentation, even though the thought of Summer's arraignment caused a haunting, growing pit in his stomach. Tomas slid out of bed and walked out into the hallway, looking both ways as if preparing to cross a street. He walked back downstairs in hopes of finding Manny or the elderly woman cooking in the kitchen. The house's suede walls and low light gave a golden, warm glow. Leftover aromas of a dinner of cream and tomatoes called to Tomas's belly as he stood at the oversized kitchen island.

"Listen, we've already been over this." Tomas heard Manny's lowered voice coming from the walk-in pantry. He didn't move. "We agreed that you'd take care of them both, right? It's not that difficult to do. The deal was an exchange. You're supposed to make concessions for me." Tomas frowned, trying to imagine in what context asking for concessions would be good.

"Victor, we had an agreement. Take care of Summer." The acuity of Tomas's hearing grew sharp. "Take care of Summer. Play the game. Do what it takes to keep her happy. I don't care if I have to finance some of it." Tomas frowned and leaned forward to hear even better.

"And Mair. Take care of Mair. It shouldn't be too much to ask. What man wouldn't want this problem, Victor?!" Manny's voice rose and fell again. "Tell me a man who wouldn't love to be paid—*paid*—to sleep with two beautiful women!" Tomas's lips began to part. A pause was interrupted by a bang in the pantry. "Listen, I don't have to explain what I'm doing. Understand?" Another pause. Tomas crouched beside the island and waited.

"It's not a secret, Victor! It's business. You're not essential to that part of the business, so you don't need to know everything. Understand? But we've both got a lot to lose. I'm getting tired of this arrangement—not working out the way I'd hoped. Suddenly Summer's in jail. Just happens to get pulled over in your car. Do you think I'm an idiot? Huh, Vic?" Tomas pulled his legs into his chest. He hoped being smaller would make the impact of the words less awful.

"Keep trying me, and we'll see who's the idiot. Victor, why are police crawling all over my baby girl? Huh? I expect to see you at that arraignment tomorrow. And if asked, you're giving a statement of support to whoever's gonna listen." There was another silence.

"I don't know!" Manny's voice rose again. "Tell them whatever you want! But if I find out you have anything to do with why my kid's sitting in a holding cell tonight, I'll have you killed, Vic. And you know I will."

Tomas stayed under the lip of the island until his backside was numb. Manny's footsteps had trailed away hours before, right along with Tomas's understanding of the world and the uncle he thought he knew.

25

"THIS IS CASE 51325418, The State of Maryland versus Summer Clemens-Martinez. Ms. Clemens-Martinez, this complaint charges, in the town of Ellicott City, on August 27th, 2005, did commit murder in the second degree to Mr. Joseph Chae, contrary to Section 2-204 of the Criminal Code. Ms. Clemens-Martinez, how do you plea to this charge?" The court clerk was visible only from her low-hanging breasts and up. Her blue dress plunged at the cleavage line. Summer fought to keep her mind in the room and not get pulled into the orange one with mirrors where she had seen the first of life-changing blue dresses. *I thought they were just charging me with obstructing an investigation.*

"Ms. Clemens-Martinez?" the clerk repeated.

"That's Dr. Clemens-Martinez," Summer answered. Her lawyer, parents, Victor, and at the opposite end of the line, Tomas, looked at her, stunned. Her lawyer adjusted his tie.

"Excuse me?" the clerk asked.

Summer's lawyer leaned into her ear. She nodded.

"My apologies. Not guilty, your honor," Summer moved her eyes off the clerk's blue breasts. "I plead not guilty. Sorry."

The judge remained unmoved and looked as if he had not heard her. She reached for the microphone to enter her plea again. Her lawyer quickly covered it with his hand. "Dr. Clemens-Martinez, please stop. Just stand quietly," he whispered.

The disturbance on their side of the room cast her in a doubtful light. She appeared impulsive and strange, perfect starting characteristics for a murderer. Her lawyer poised himself in front of the microphone and broached an argument for bail to be set. Summer stood on his right, shackled and in orange, her hair in a crooked French braid. She looked at her parents behind her. They sat locked into each other like puzzle pieces. Manny's fingers wrapped around Dara's shoulder, pressing large prints into her turquoise blouse. Tomas sat beside Dara with his legs crossed. He held a coffee down at his side though it wasn't allowed in the courtroom. He winked at Summer when she turned around.

"I'm sorry," Summer mouthed to her parents, then turned quickly around as her lawyer pressed his elbow into her ribs. She watched him as he explained that Summer, whom he fully believed was innocent, had no previous criminal record of any sort outside one parking violation in Florida three years earlier. The prosecuting attorney, when asked if he had any special conditions he desired to be observed, requested Summer stay away, entirely, from the Chae family.

"The court will uphold that requested bail condition. Anything else?"

The judge continued to look down, writing as if transferring information from one logbook to another. As Summer's lawyer argued for bail to be set, the judge kept his face inches from the books. Eventually, he lifted his hand, interrupting the lawyer's appeal.

"Bail is set at five hundred thousand dollars, Dr. Clemens-Martinez. Should you be charged with another offense while this matter is open, you could be held without bail for ninety days. Understood?"

Summer nodded. The judge still hadn't looked up. Summer's lawyer responded, "Yes, your honor."

"Dr. Clemens-Martinez, I said, is that understood? By you?"

"Yes, your honor," she replied.

"Pretrial has been set for November first," the judge continued. "Anything else, folks?"

Though bail was normally set for at least ninety days after arraignment, Summer's legal counsel refrained from objecting to the six-week window he'd been given to prepare his case. The judge held no special sympathies for Summer or her father. In fact, her privileged presence threatened to irritate him. The lawyer didn't want to exacerbate things.

As the blue-chested clerk spoke again, Summer stood dazed behind her podium. "This case has been stayed until a date of November 1, 2006. Bail has been set at five hundred thousand dollars. Ms. Clemens-Martinez, excuse me, Dr. Clemens-Martinez, you should present to the probation department to sign the conditions of stay away and no contact with the family of the victim."

Summer looked at her lawyer's peeved face, which yielded no direction, and to her mother's, which was eased. "You can go," Dara mouthed to her confused daughter. Up until that moment, Summer had not seen Victor. But there he sat, beside her father, with his hands clasped together between his knees as if he needed to get to a bathroom. Summer turned quickly to a guard standing beside Tomas for direction and to be uncuffed.

"I knew you'd get out of here," Tomas whispered, leaning in and trying to kiss Summer's cheek.

"Sir," the guard rolled his eyes, "you can meet her at the probation department."

"I need to talk to you," she whispered back as she was shuffled down another linoleum hallway. She glimpsed Victor standing in the center aisle, near where he'd been sitting, watching them.

In the back seat of her father's Escalade, Summer sat closer to Tomas than was typical. She would normally be insecure about having not showered for days. He whispered in her ear, "What did you want to tell me?" She looked at him but didn't respond.

"Guys, I have to tell you something," Summer announced to the car. "Well, first, Tomas, thanks for calling Victor for me when I got arrested. He was already at the booking station when I got there." Tomas opened his mouth to speak, but Summer motioned that she wasn't finished. "Honestly, though, I think Victor is trying to set me up." Her voice wavered, and one tear spilled onto her left cheek.

Dara looked at Manny, and he looked in the rearview mirror.

"What do you mean, Summer?" His eyes stayed focused on her even though he was driving.

"Daddy, when I was in there, you know on the first day, the cops or detectives or whatever, they showed me the surveillance video. From when this kid was killed. Did you know they have a video showing someone switched his water bottle? They think he was overdosed with Halcion from drinking whatever was in there," Summer took a breath. "I mean, this kid had just been playing soccer all morning. There's no way he had been taking huge doses of sleeping medicine before his soccer matches were over!"

Dara turned her body to face Tomas and Summer huddled in the corner of the massive backseat.

"And anyway, when they showed me the video, I saw Victor's car pull up. A girl got out." Dara rolled her eyes and looked at Manny, "No, Mom, listen!" Summer urged. "A girl got out, carried a crate of water bottles to this kid's truck, and switched one of her bottles with the bottle that was in the kid's car."

"Well, if it's some other girl, why the hell were you the one arrested?" Manny demanded, his voice rumbling like thunder.

"That's what I was trying to say, Dad! The girl in the video is white with straight black hair. They're saying it's me, but clearly I'm not white and don't have hair like that. I think it's Victor dressed up in a disguise." Summer stopped and surprised herself with sobs. "I know this sounds stupid."

Tomas held her head to his chest, rubbing her back with his tan hand. "It's okay. We're going to get you out of this, Summer."

"I'm so sick of people having to get me out of things! My whole life feels like it's turning into one giant charity case!" She continued to sob but stopped once she realized she'd forgotten the most important parts of her story.

"When I got stopped, there was a Gatorade bottle in the car that had the name 'Joey' written on it."

"What?!" Dara exclaimed. Manny gripped the steering wheel tightly and pressed the gas pedal closer to the floor.

"And the outfit the person has on in the video? I had on the entire thing! Victor had just given it to me a few days before. The dress, the jewelry, everything." Summer looked at Tomas to see if he believed her words. "He actually gave me the same clothes he poisoned someone in!"

"Summer," Dara started, "if you saw a woman in the same outfit switching the bottles, why are you saying it was Victor who did it?"

"Because, Mom, at the very end of the video, well, the part they let me see, the person is standing there tapping their fingers on the car and biting their lip. Victor always, always, always does that when he's thinking. Always! Plus, why did he have the kid's water bottle in his car a whole year later?"

Dara sat back and looked out the windshield before her.

"It's true, Manny. That child's mother says that every time she's interviewed, that the water bottle found at the scene wasn't his 'cause his name wasn't on it. Remember? And murderers keep trophies of their kills. We know that." Manny's jaw clenched and nostrils flared. Dara placed her hand on his thigh.

"Don't get worked up, Manny," Dara said.

"Stop it, Dara!" he responded to her touch, "I'm fine. Summer, you listen to me. Not one single, solitary word of this to anyone outside this car. And do not speak to Victor again, at all!"

"Dad, what about my things at his house?"

"I'll take care of it. Don't worry. But you no longer have any reason at all to speak to him. Do you hear me, Summer?"

Summer squeezed Tomas, still wrapped into his chest.

"You're shaking," Tomas whispered to Summer.

"I'm going to kill Victor," Manny shouted.

Tomas pulled out a pack of cigarettes. "You can't smoke in the car,"

Summer whispered to Tomas. He nodded.

"Manny, calm down. She doesn't need this!" Dara scolded her spouse. "Don't be dramatic; you're not going to kill anybody."

"Call Victor! Get him on the phone, right now!" Manny boomed.

"I'm not! Stop it." Dara looked out her window.

"Tomas!" Manny had moved his attention back to the rearview. "Get him on the phone, now!"

Dara interjected. "Manny, you're being unreasonable. Stop this!"

"Dara, you calling me crazy again?! What type of psychiatrist goes around calling everyone crazy?" He looked at her with wild eyes and dry white patches at the corners of his mouth. "You do know it's everyone else that thinks shrinks are the crazy ones, right?"

Summer's head bounced from face to face like a perched bird.

"Dad! Relax, please!" Summer's voice was shaky. "Let's just let the police deal with it."

"Summer," her father responded, gripping his pulsing temples, "there are things going on that you have no idea about."

"Like what, Dad?" Summer looked at Tomas, sitting so close she could curl into his lap like a child. Tomas held her calmly. His heart, though, rattled in his young chest. The car ride was devolving—spiraling into an all-out screaming match. Tomas and Summer had never seen Dara raise her voice. Now her red hair was flying about her face like she'd become possessed.

"Manuel! That is enough! I mean it. If you can't calm down, pull over and let all of us out!" Dara demanded.

"Dara! Shut your mouth! I'm so sick of the sound of your voice!"

"*Tio* Manny!" Tomas finally interjected. He'd been trying to stay silent in this family quarrel.

"Stay out of it!" Manny blasted back.

"And this! Your temper, your arrogance, all your womanizing and putting me down—this is why my mother never liked you. Hated you, in fact."

"Bullshit!" Manny's voice shook the car's walls. "Your mother hated me because she's racist and miserable."

"Oh, well, now you just sound ridiculous, Manny," Dara scoffed. "You're white; what do you mean?"

Summer held her right hand over the side of her head.

"I'm not an Anglo, and you know exactly what I mean." Manny stared at her. "That bitch wouldn't even let her own grandchild in the house when we visited. And you just let it happen. Made your own kid ride her bike for hours until you had your fill of bigot biscuits and tea for the afternoon."

Dara disintegrated into tears.

"Summer, don't worry about this," Tomas whispered to her in Spanish. "I'm going to stay with you. I'm going to get this settled before I leave."

Summer lifted her head and looked at him. Her eyes had turned into question marks. "When are you leaving?" she whispered back.

"Wednesday afternoon. We have two days." Tomas kissed her at the natural parting of her hair, right at the center of her forehead.

BY THE TIME they reached their home driveway, Manny had been shouting to the point of hoarseness. Dara cried and jumped out at the edge of the driveway. She called her husband of twenty-eight years a "crazy SOB." Her thin legs scrambled to carry her into the house, bawling. Tomas and Summer slid out the backseat, hoping to go unnoticed by their raging chauffeur. Manny left the Escalade running, still shouting to himself as he got out. Summer and Tomas stood beside the truck, watching. He marched into the garage and reversed in his pearl Porsche 911, screeching backward, narrowly missing Tomas's left leg.

"Summer, I'm so sorry to tell you this right now," Tomas said, gripping her face, "but I heard your father and Victor talking last night. Your dad. *Dios mio*, I don't even know how to say this… He's somehow involved with Victor and you—and Mair?" Summer frowned and pulsed her head side to side, restricted from moving it in his grasp. She pulled his hands down from her face and threw them to his side. "Don't be mad, *Prieta*. I'm sorry."

"What did you hear?"

"*Tio* was telling Victor, basically, that one hand washes the other. I think he's doing favors for his career in exchange for you and Mair. Like *Tio* pays him to see you both. It doesn't make sense. I don't know, *mamita*, it's really confusing."

Summer looked over her shoulder at her father's disappearing car. The last time she'd seen Victor and her father together was at a brunch. They'd stepped outside to talk for what felt like hours.

"I think we should follow him. I bet anything he's going to Victor's," Tomas continued.

Summer tried to envision her father's betrayal in pictures rather than words. If she could see it, she could believe it. At least that's what she thought.

"Follow him to do what?!" Summer's head spun.

"I don't know. Confront them? At least confront Victor? He's seriously crazy; he's trying to have you spend your life in prison for no reason! Plus, I was thinking about this, *Prieta*, Victor knows you don't remember where you were last year. No one knows where you were at the end of August last year. You have absolutely no alibi at all!"

"Get in," Tomas continued as he jumped in the driver's seat of the still-running Escalade. He waited as Summer climbed up beside him. Tomas backed up, and they tore down the street.

"Slow down. I know where his house is," Summer warned Tomas. Adrenaline pulsed through his body. He could not slow down. He could not lift his foot from the gas.

The speed of the truck catapulted both Tomas and Summer into the backs of their own minds. Summer's head raced. How had she gone from trying to put back together a broken relationship to flying down the street in a convict's jumpsuit? How had she gone from an idyllic family life into what appeared to be the biggest unfolding betrayal she'd ever experienced? She looked over at Tomas. She still believed she could trust him, though he represented her last hope in men—and otherwise.

Tomas focused his eyes like an eagle. Victor, for years, had manipulated, shamed, and played the people Tomas cherished most. Now was the time to let him know his mind-bending boyish charm was a cracking façade everyone was beginning to see through.

"Where am I going, Summer?" Tomas looked at her, his hair hanging just over the top of his glasses.

"Get off at the next exit." Her thoughts were clearer than she'd imagined they would be. "Turn left at the light and left at the one after that."

Tomas's long, tan fingers whipped the car left, then left again.

"It's coming up, right down there." Summer leaned forward and pointed to her left. Instead of slowing to a residential pace, Tomas sped up. They heard a *bloop*. Summer looked in the passenger side mirror. Her skin went ashen. They were being pulled over by police.

"No way, bro. There's no possible way!" Tomas exclaimed. "Just be calm," he whispered. He pushed his glasses up into his hair and peered into the rearview. An officer stood with a hand on his gun holster, looking at something on his dash.

Finally, the officer walked to the driver's side window, lifting his face to meet Tomas. "Sir, do you know why I pulled you over?"

Tomas shook his head "no." Summer leaned forward to see the officer's face.

"Officer Montcliffe?" she asked.

"Martinez? Didn't you just get released today? Wow, sweetie, you're not off to a great start, I see." His tone had picked up new snark. She had not heard it before, with his good cop routine.

Tomas looked at her. "You know him?"

"He arrested me, unfortunately."

"Where are your clothes, Summer? I mean, really. A girl like you is way too cute to be seen in an orange jumpsuit, right?" Montcliffe turned his attention back at Tomas and winked. "Where are you two headed?"

"To see my boyfriend," Summer responded.

"The technical boyfriend? The one you think is trying to frame you for murder?" Montcliffe shook his head. "I'm not sure I can let you do that."

"Why not?"

"Why not?! 'Cause maybe you have a bone to pick with him. Maybe you could be headed there to try to kill him, too. That's why not." Officer Montcliffe leaned in closer to Tomas's window. "Listen, you two get out of here, and I won't write a ticket. I won't make a report. But if I see you over here again," he let out a rolling laugh, "I'll have to take care of it."

"Officer," Tomas interrupted, "I didn't catch your name."

"I'm Danny Montcliffe, buddy. You want my badge number, too?"

"No, Officer, thank you. We'll head out." Tomas nodded once and looked straight ahead. Summer had held her breath and her mouth open.

"Sounds good!" Montcliffe smirked and tapped the back window twice as he walked away. Summer's eyes followed his waltz back to his car. He turned his head to speak into his radio and scanned the neighborhood street. She tried to see if the other cop was with him.

"Seriously, *Bebo*!" Summer whispered. She pressed her nails into her thighs. "Are we really going to leave? We have to get to Victor's!"

Summer opened her mouth to continue, but Tomas put his forefinger as a latch over her lips. "Summer, I never called Victor."

"What?" she responded, disoriented from the day.

"I never called Victor to tell him you'd been arrested. I only called your parents."

"So then, how did he know?" She huffed. "My dad?!"

"Remember Victor's Super Bowl parties? The ones in his old condo on the beach?"

Summer looked annoyed. "Of course, why?"

"Remember some of Victor's friends would come down from Virginia and hang out with us for the weekends when you'd drag all of us to his place?"

"Tomas, what does this—" Summer stopped as he gestured for her to wait.

"Do you?!"

"Yes, oh my God, what? Why are you getting upset?"

"That guy used to be there. Danny Montcliffe. I know you're bad at faces, but remember? He'd cheer for the Steelers even though they were never playing. And Victor would be, like, 'Dude, the Ravens won in 2001,' and that prick Danny would keep shouting, 'Steelers, baby!' all night?

"'Hey, Summer,' he would shout, 'how do you deal with this guy? He's a total waste of space. But I love him. Do anything for this dude right here.'"

Summer's eyes glazed over. She had eaten chicken wings on Victor's gray couch. Danny had been trailing Victor around the house debating football stats. She did remember Danny Montcliffe.

Could he love Victor enough to help him frame me for murder? Summer knew the answer was undoubtedly "yes."

The officer drove past them, laughing as he threw them a sloppy salute.

"Tomas," Summer turned to her friend. "You've gotta help me find something that shows I had nothing to do with Joey Chae."

"They've got the car, the clothes, the water bottle. They've got basically all the evidence," Tomas replied. Summer nodded.

"But there's gotta be more. Maybe the wig, *Bebo*. We've got to find that wig."

26

DARKNESS AND THE SMELL OF RUBBING ALCOHOL enveloped Summer in Victor's closet. She pressed her body against the cold interior wall with both hands gripped around her mouth. Her dilated pupils blackened her eyes in the darkness. Navy scrubs, white coats, and a small dresser stacked with notebooks and pencils were organized right before her face. She tried to breathe silently, letting a small stream of air flow between her overlapped fingers.

A crashing, roaring sound outside the house lifted and fell.

"Mr. Victor," the housekeeper said with a strain of loud nervousness running through her voice, "we never see you anymore! How have you been?"

Summer inched farther behind the scrubs.

"Yep, well, I forgot something this morning. Wanted to swing by on my lunch break," Victor panted. "You ladies are here earlier than usual, aren't you?" Summer followed the bounce of his voice, wondering how far he was from her hiding place. "Don't you normally come here at twelve on Thursday, not Tuesday?"

"Yes, Mr. Victor, but your house is always clean. It's so easy. We added another house in the neighborhood today, so we decided to do both of them while we were here."

"Hmm," Victor replied, "you didn't tell me that."

"I'm so sorry, Mr. Victor. Is that okay with you?"

Should I get on the floor? Behind the dresser? Summer wondered.

"Uh, sure," Victor replied. Summer thought his answer sounded distracted. "Well, did you guys already do my bedroom?" He stood at the door threshold with both hands bracing the frame. He frowned and looked out the wall of windows, then over the cloud of white bedding, and finally the floor.

The housekeeper followed and stood behind him. "Yes, Mr. Victor," she replied as he walked heel-toe beside his nightstand and studied the carpet.

"Hmm," he said as he pointed to a trail of footprints that angled and stopped at the closet door.

Look at the light, Summer. She coached herself to focus on the tiny slit in the closet's door where she could see a sliver of Victor's face. She sunk her molars into the left side of her tongue to keep from making a sound. The crash outside happened again.

"What did you forget, Mr. Victor?" the housekeeper asked.

"My wallet," he barked his reply.

"Ah, yes, I saw it over here on the shelf beside the bed." The housekeeper began to walk to the shelves.

"No!" he shouted. "I like the carpet to have perfect lines." He pretended to joke. He peered forward to the closet, engrossed as if his eyes could hear.

Victor climbed on the bed and leaned to look at the empty bedside shelving. "It's not here." He looked over his shoulder at the housekeeper, who still stood as unanimated as a statue.

"I think I left it on the dresser, in the closet," he said as he slid to the end of the bed and dropped his toes on the carpeted floor. He drew back the closet door and glared inside. His eyes blackened. He waited. The scent of freesia lifted to his nostrils. Summer held her breath. She could feel his face floating two feet from hers. Victor reached into the closet between the third and fourth set of scrubs and gripped her curly top knot bun in his palm. Summer wondered if she should pretend she had slipped into another fugue state. She pushed back the scrubs and stepped forward between them.

The housekeeper gasped. Victor, however, stepped back. He smirked with just the left half of his mouth. "Oh, Heloise, you didn't tell me Summer was here." The housekeeper flushed red.

"Mr. Victor, please, we do good work."

"Don't be silly," Victor chuckled, glancing at his housekeeper. "I'm not going to let you go for letting her in the house."

"Yes, because I thought she lived here. I thought she was your girlfriend, no?"

Victor nodded. It was an image that he couldn't allow to fall—not with a dead kid and murder charges on the table.

"Oh my God, Victor!" Summer motioned to hug him from between the scrubs. "Babe! We haven't seen each other since that whole crazy situation! Thanks for coming to my hearing!" She leaned back and looked at his face. "Can you believe they arrested me?" She attempted a giggle. Summer's heart raced as she tried to reconcile his face with the water bottle of a dead boy she found in his car. She hoped, like most killers of his type, Victor would not harm her unless he'd calculated what to do. Having a housekeeping crew as witnesses in the home would not be part of his plan.

The crash happened once more, louder.

"Yes, I know, honey. I was going to call you tonight." Victor darted his eyes to the housekeeper. "But why are you in the closet?"

"Looking for something." Summer's eyes connected with the housekeeper's for a second. "I thought maybe it fell behind the dresser, here." She walked out and opened the closet to her left.

"I know I had," she pushed the clothes around, "a pretty purple fall coat here, didn't I?" She looked for confirmation from the housekeeper.

"Oh, I don't know, Ms. Summer. Did you?"

"Yes." She fingered more navy scrubs. "I remember I put it in one of these closets."

"Summer," Victor's voice oozed from his lips like oil, "I think it would probably be downstairs. In the mudroom."

"Yeah, that's what I thought, too, Vic." Summer pretended calmness. "But I couldn't find it down there." Victor and the housekeeper watched her as she closed each section's doors and walked to the final closet. "I don't think it was in this closet, was it Victor?"

Summer walked to the last closet door and opened it with a quick retraction of her arm. The table of accessories and glosses. Gone. The hooks of necklaces and wigs. Gone. The women's clothing was gone, too. The closet stood stark empty. Completely bare.

The crash grew louder as if it were directly outside the front door now.

"Oh, Mr. Victor," the housekeeper said, "what happened to all Ms. Summer's clothes that were there?"

"What are you talking about?" Victor spun to face the housekeeper.

The last loud crash spoke to Summer. *Trash pickup day*, she thought, and she sprinted past Victor and the cleaner. She ran down the stairs on the balls of her feet, landing on the tile before the kitchen with a painful shock through her right ankle. She looked over her shoulder to see Victor at the landing of stairs just above her. His eyes had become lasers.

She grabbed her ankle but released her grip as she heard his feet behind her. Summer turned to run left in front of the kitchen bar toward the front door. Victor followed close behind, close enough to reach and grab her hair. The cleaner dusting the dining room shrieked. Summer felt his fingers in her hair and leaned forward, now wishing she'd heeded Tomas's warning to only go back in Victor's house when a man was there to protect her.

Summer squinted. She looked ahead at the deadbolt lock on the front door, hoping the key was there. She stutter-stepped through the foyer to the doorway. But when she looked behind her again, he'd disappeared.

Outside, the garbage truck was at the house to their left. Victor's house was next. She dashed diagonally across the front yard to where the green-and-gold waste management bins were stationed near the garages. The garbage truck's driver looked at her running to the bins and began to slow down, motioning to her that she had time. Summer slowed her running right as her dampened shoes reached the paved driveway. She waved at the driver and mouthed the words "thank you" then drew a big breath. The driver pointed to the bins. Summer's eyes followed his finger and saw Victor standing with his hands on the back handle of the trash container, already pushing it to the street.

"No!" Summer shouted and slapped her thighs. She slid her hands down to her knees and rested there to catch her breath. The green bin and all its contents dumped smoothly into the truck. Victor waved to the truck driver and turned his body in one stiff motion to face her.

Something important must have been in that trash. Summer knew there could have been no other reason for him to try so hard to beat her to it.

She stood to face him as he walked toward her. She did not move but looked behind him, noticing that there was no sign of Tomas or her father's car they'd used to get there. She locked her eyes onto Victor's at first, then dropped them to his horizontal line of a mouth. Inches before her face, his protruding canines snarled in her face.

"What the hell do you think you're gonna do, Summer?"

"What do you mean, Vic?" she replied, with ice running through her words.

"You're obviously snooping around my house for a reason."

"Yeah, to find my fall coat," Summer replied. "I told you that, babe."

"Summer," Victor stepped closer to her face, "do you know how satisfying it was for me to know Joey Chae's body splattered on to US 29?" Victor laughed. "If I must, I'll find a discreet way to kill you, too. Nobody will know it was me. Nobody."

He stared at Summer, and she stared back.

"Really bad joke, Victor." Summer cocked her head to the side, feeling emboldened. "But I had no idea it would be a problem for me to come and get some of my things whenever I needed them," she lied. "You are my boyfriend, right? We're still okay, aren't we? Did you throw out my coat? Why are you being so weird? What's going on?"

Victor did not respond. He covered his right ear with his palm. Summer saw dread melt through his face and realized she'd just taken the upper hand.

"I'm just kidding, Summer." Victor reached for her face. She dodged his hand as she ducked to her left and began running again. She ran until shin splints tightened like braces at the fronts of her legs. Every few yards, she looked behind her, around her, anywhere she could for Tomas—and to be sure Victor wasn't there. Her final look over her shoulder spied a police car patrolling blocks behind her. She dashed between two houses.

She found Tomas in her father's car two blocks down.

"Jesus!" she exclaimed as she collapsed into the passenger's side. "Did you go far enough?"

"*Lo siento*," Tomas apologized. "But when I saw him pulling up in my rearview, I kind of panicked. I didn't want to get caught anywhere close by, after Danny. What happened in the house?"

"Nothing," Summer shook her head, "other than he confessed to murder and threatened to kill me. God, I wish I was recording. Now there's police patrolling around. Let's go to his office."

"Slow down. What? He confessed?!" Tomas looked at Summer, shaking his head. He scrambled in his pocket for a cigarette. "And now you want to go to his office when police are following us?!" Tomas worried Summer was breaking down again. He watched her try her best to figure out a plan to trap Victor and tried to distract her. "Did the housekeepers play along?"

"They said they had a new house to clean on Tuesdays in the neighborhood," Summer said, waiting for Tomas to start driving. "They didn't mention that I'd called them to come clean today. They totally covered for me."

"Did he buy it?"

"Tomas, c'mon. Stop stalling! I don't know where those cops went and if he called them on me or what. Drive to his office, 'cause by the time we get there, he'll be there, too."

"And then what?"

"I don't know. Listen, we've got to use what we already know about him to catch him. But please, drive!"

"He's an asshole," Tomas started, as he pulled out. "That's something we already know."

"Is that a clinical term?" Summer joked. "Okay, he's a jerk, but only to people he can't get things from."

"Okay, so he uses people."

"*Si*, and as part of that, he's super calculating," Summer added. "*Bebo*, what's the thing you hate about him most?"

Tomas didn't want to admit that it was that Victor had had the privilege of sleeping with her.

"Uh, he thinks he's smarter than everyone," he replied.

"That's right." Summer fell silent for a few seconds. "Which means the thing we need to connect him and this kid Joey is gonna probably be hidden in plain sight."

"You should have taken his laptop." Tomas thought out loud.

"True, I didn't even think of it in the moment." Summer said, ideas percolating through the notes of her voice. "But if we get to the office, I can tell one of the girls I'm planning a surprise for him and ask to see his schedule or something like that. I can see if he ever took care of that kid. He's gotta know him from somewhere."

"Maybe they'll give you his EMR password, and you can access it from anywhere," Tomas replied.

"Yes! You know what, let's not go there. Let's just call and tell them not to mention it." Summer looked at Tomas wide-eyed.

"Right, and then get the log-in info and go log in from your mom and dad's. ¡*Dale*! Let's go!"

Summer spoke aloud as she began to dial, "Four, four, three..." She stopped talking and held her ringing cell phone to her ear.

"Hello, you've reached Ellicott City Oral Surgery Center," a young, spritely voice answered. "This is Kelly; how may I help you?"

"Kelly! Hey! This is Summer—Dr. Jacobs's Summer," Summer whispered.

"Hey, Sum—"

"*Shh, shh, shh!* Don't say my name," Summer interrupted, "I'm trying to surprise Victor, okay, but I need you to do me a big, big favor."

Kelly whispered, too. "Okay, what's up?"

"Okay, don't tell him I called, okay?" Summer continued in a whisper.

"Alright."

"But I need a way to look at Victor's schedule for, like, the next four weeks or so."

"Uh sure," Kelly whispered.

"Okay, I know this is totally against HIPAA and everything, but I swear I'm only using it to try to plan something for him."

"I know, I know," Kelly responded.

"Can you give me his log-in information for your medical records?"

"The electronic medical record?"

"Yeah, the EMR. Which one do you guys use?"

"DentiTech," Kelly replied.

"Okay, what's his username?"

"Uh," Kelly began, then went silent. "Um, I can tell you his hours for the next four weeks. He's working pretty much until five every day."

"Kelly, it's okay, honestly. I promise I'm only logging in just to set up a surprise."

"Sorry, I just want to make sure I know who I'm talking to. Who did you say this was, again?"

"Summer. Dr. Jacobs's girlfriend." Summer grimaced at Tomas. She muted the phone and whispered, "She's freaking out a little. I don't know if she's going to give it to me." She unmuted the phone.

"You know what, Kelly? How about you give it to me and then change the password in like an hour. That way you don't have to worry about it being compromised or anything," Summer shrugged at Tomas. "What do you think?"

"Uh, okay." Kelly sighed heavily into the phone. "It's just his first initial and last name. VJacobs."

"Okay, and then his password?" Summer's mouth was dry with nervousness.

"I think it's his birthday. Uh, wait, hold on—I have to look it up. Can I put you on hold?"

Summer rolled her eyes, then looked at Tomas, who had been listening on speakerphone.

"Yeah, of course," Summer responded. Toto sang "Africa" on the hold line, and Summer tapped her feet anxiously on the floor of the car. The drums of the chorus amplified her anticipation. Finally, Kelly returned.

"Yep, I was right." Kelly laughed.

"What?"

"It's just his birthday, 11474."

"11474," Summer repeated. "You sure?"

"Yep, that's it!" Kelly replied.

"Thanks so much," Summer responded. "Give me one hour and you can reprogram it."

"Oh, Dr. Jacobs!" Kelly's voice wobbled. "I didn't see you come in. Is everything okay? Did you get what you needed from your house?"

Summer hung up, wondering how long he'd been lingering over his aide's shoulder.

"Got it." Summer smiled, looking at Tomas. "Come on, friend, we've got some research to do."

Tomas nodded and smiled, speeding up. "You're getting so comfortable breaking the law, Summer." He laughed, and Summer did, too, feeling hopeful for the first time since she'd returned to Baltimore.

"Oh, wow, look what I found!" Summer said. She smiled, looking into the bottom of her purse. "God is on my side. If all else fails, we've got this."

27

"HEY, COULD I HAVE AN ORDER OF CHEESE WONTONS and an orange chicken? Not the crab wontons. I'm allergic." Mair's eyes focused upward at the lighted black-and-white menu in Pei Wei. "Do I get a drink with that?"

"Yes, ma'am, you can get whatever fountain drink you want from over there." A petite blonde server turned over her right shoulder and pointed to the beverage machines in the back of the dark restaurant.

"Okay, thanks. So do I just go have a seat?"

"Yep, sit wherever you'd like and put this number on your table," the blonde handed Mair a round, red chip with white numbers, "and we'll bring it out to you!"

"Thanks," Mair responded, gripping her chip and her paper cup. "Do you guys have Thai iced tea?"

"No, sorry. Just regular Coke products."

"No problem." Mair smiled and walked along the red floor pathway. She filled her cup halfway with Sprite, then topped it with lemonade. She chose a table in the center of the dining room. Tapping the call log arrow on her phone with long graceful white fingers, she stared. *I wonder what he wants*, she thought, looking at Tomas's name in her call log and the number four in brackets beside it. She'd missed four calls from him. With intention. Looking at his name there, shining white light into her face, a heavy sadness sat on her chest and filled her with loneliness. She had not listened to the voicemail. She took a deep breath and held the phone to her ear.

"Mair, it's me again. I need to talk to you. So call me back when you can, okay? It's important."

She put the phone face down on the table, took another deep breath, and looked over at Pei Wei's open kitchen. Cooks in black tops and baseball caps swirled hands over woks. Mair picked up the phone and dialed. She waited through the ringing.

"Hello?"

"You're a hard man to surprise." Mair felt a flirt's smile stretching across her face.

"What do you mean?"

"Well, I stopped by your office this morning to surprise you. The girls told me you weren't there yet."

There was a long pause.

"Hello?" Mair checked if the call had dropped.

"Yeah, I'm still here. You came by my office today?" Mair confirmed and asked if he wanted to see her. She had called Victor instead of Tomas. Tomas represented the family, the group, all the friends. If she had to face him—or even talk to him—she had to face them all.

"What are you doing in town?"

"Oh, Victor, you never know the right thing to say, do you?" Mair responded. "Why don't you say, 'Oh! I'm happy to hear you're in town?'" But she knew the answer before she spoke. They both did. He wasn't happy to hear anything much about her, and he couldn't fake it.

"Yeah, I know. Listen, I've got a lot going on right now. Kinda have a headache, and I'm pretty busy at work. I'll call you when I get off if you want to go out or something."

Mair's food arrived at the table. A flat silver pan held two cheese wontons on semitransparent wax paper. Her orange chicken sat atop a hill of fluffy white rice. Looking at the food and smiling at the server as she held her red phone to her ear, she sipped her Sprite, swallowed, and said, "Okay," then added, "wait! Victor, have you talked to Summer recently?"

Another long pause separated them. "No," he lied. "I'll call you later." Victor hung up.

"I don't know why I keep coming back here," Mair said loud enough for a woman and her toddler two tables away to hear. "Sorry," Mair waved. "It's just one of those days." The woman nodded, then looked at her child and made an uh-oh face.

Mair placed a pointed corner of a wonton on the roof of her mouth and looked at the seat across from her. Its silverness, its emptiness. And the seat beside it. Empty, with a curved back, spacious enough that Phoebe would have folded her legs in it. Tomas and Carla would have fought over the last wonton, and Summer would have gone to the front to order another pan. Mair would have kept her legs crossed, reading a magazine. She would have looked up only long enough to tell Tomas and Carla they were uncivilized and Phoebe that it was unprofessional to sit with her feet in chairs in public places. They would have laughed and told her to shut up and that she was barely older than them and not their overseer. She would have rolled her eyes at Summer's assumption that there was always more to be had, to be bought. But belonging and warmth would have bounced in Mair's chest in the company of those four. Her family.

The tint on Pei Wei's window turned the outside world a bluish-gray that matched the emptiness of her aluminum table. Mair was beginning to think choosing Victor had been like spilling an entire tub of popcorn for one falling piece. And no one piece was so buttery, so perfectly salted, to make it worth the loss. Tearing a hole through Summer's engagement party had not been her idea. She would have never been strong enough to try it. But she'd been shifted and shuffled through bargains and plots for the entirety of her life, so she showed up when she was told to.

"Is it okay?" A server passing by noticed none of Mair's mound of chicken had been moved. "We can make you something else if you don't like it."

"Oh, no, sorry! I was just about to take my first bite." She shook her head and flipped her hand forward. "I was daydreaming." She forked up a round of fried, glazed chicken to prove it. Chewing the chicken, she gazed into her phone like it was a crystal ball. It was murky, though, and she couldn't see ahead into what land mine could be waiting when Tomas answered. Her food was not spicy, but Mair's eyes began to tear and her nose to run. The tears would not stay put and raced down her white cheeks to her chin. The toddler pointed and said, "Uh oh," to her mom.

I'll call him after I see Victor tonight. No matter what Tomas had to say, she knew nothing would make her feel lower than a night with the oral surgeon.

SUMMER SHOWERED LONGER than she'd intended to in the vaulted ceiling guest bathroom. Her fingers removed a line of dried, rolled blood hiding below the left curve of her behind. She stepped out of the shower and looked down to see if her legs were moving. The tremor was inside. It was in the womb of the bathroom that she finally released the fear of her ordeal. It went into the steam, lifting, swirling, then crashing to the floor.

My life is completely falling apart, she thought, hugging her nude body at the waist, still wondering how she could be shaking so much on the inside and not be seconds from death. She didn't want to cry. Tomas was in the next room on the laptop. He'd shouted, "I'm in!" at least ten minutes before. But no matter how she contorted her face or held her head in prayer up to the ceiling to press it down and in, a weep from behind her navel came barreling through her throat.

"Summer, you alright?" Tomas asked.

"Jesus, Mary, and Joseph, please don't let me get kicked out of residency for doing this," he whispered as he logged into the DentiTech EMR and entered '*Chae, Joseph*' in the clear bar that read 'Patient Name' in light gray font. His name appeared from a dropdown menu amongst two other Josephs of the same last name. Tomas blinked away an inkling of doubt and looked at the birth dates. The news could not stop reporting that Joseph was killed the weekend before he was supposed to begin college at Stanford. "He must be about eighteen, nineteen… maybe seventeen at the youngest?" Tomas said to himself.

He clicked on the Joseph Chae chart for the one born in 1987.

"Hmm, he was last seen in August 2005. Okay." Tomas clicked to another tab. "What did he come in for? What did you come in for Joseph Chae number one?" Tomas asked the screen. Insurance. Humana. Parents. Lisa and Derrick. "Derrick?" Tomas lifted his eyebrows. "Korean people have names like 'Derrick?'"

Summer stood at the bathroom door. "What are you whispering about Columbo?" she teased Tomas. Her hair had been pulled back into a neat high bun. Her oiled face and pristine white T-shirt made her back into the human Tomas had always known.

"You feel better?" he asked.

"So much," she replied. "I had a big cry, too."

"I heard. It's all good. You're strong. You're gonna get through this." Tomas wanted to distract himself from her breasts and glowing skin and the compassion he felt for her heartbreak. "So, are Koreans named 'Derrick?' Isn't that a black name?"

She shrugged and giggled. "I don't know. I think Derrick's a kinda universal name. You're silly." She giggled again. "Why?"

"'Cause there's two kids named Joseph Chae in here. Dates of birth are basically the same. Trying to figure out if this is the right one."

"And what's that got to do with the name Derrick?"

"It's the dad for the first Joseph," Tomas replied.

"Just search for the parents' names on Google."

"I don't think that's a good idea," Tomas responded. "Suppose someone looks at this computer and sees you've been looking up the kid's parents. You're not supposed to have any contact or anything. It's probably better to just leave it."

"True. Does this EMR chart have patient pictures?" Summer sat next to Tomas. "Scoot over," she said with the familiarity of a sister. Summer looked at the screen as Tomas moved out of the center of the bed. "Go back to the main patient screen."

"For all the patients, or this kid?"

"This kid," she replied. The page where the photo should have been added was filled with a cartoonish black head in a Polaroid-like frame. No one from the office had uploaded a patient picture. "When was this Joey Chae seen the last time?"

"Last August," Tomas answered, still clicking random tabs. "Oh look, it's his dad's driver's license, Summer."

She leaned in. "Oh, that's not the right kid."

"How do you know?" Tomas replied.

"That's not how our Joey Chae's dad looks. Plus, he's really tall."

Tomas read the height on the license. "Oh, okay, this guy's five foot eight."

"Okay, let's go to the other one." Tomas opened the other chart, and they immediately searched for his parents' information. The same license photo of Leslie Chae that Victor had selected to hunt and kill Joseph stared back at them. "This is the mom!" Summer leaned in even closer. "Yep, that's her."

"His last appointment was last August, too. Had his wisdom teeth out."

"Okay, cool," Summer responded. "So that's him."

"*Bueno*. Now what?" Tomas asked.

Summer looked at Tomas's eyes. "How is this going to prove anything?" he continued.

Victor had treated the kid. Just as his soccer coach had coached the kid. His schoolteachers taught the kid. Certainly having just had contact with him didn't implicate anyone in his poisoning.

"Um, the water bottle is super problematic," Summer finally responded. "Like, obviously a lot of people knew this kid, or had been around this kid, but how many of them had his water bottle?"

"Yeah, but we're looking for new evidence. Something creepy Danny Montcliffe hasn't already marked as proof against you at the police station! You were the one they found with it. Remember that."

Summer sat cross-legged on the bed. She tucked her fingertips in the gap between her thighs and sighed. Her eyes looked up, searching her brain for answers. They returned to their usual position empty-handed. She slid to the edge of the bed and jumped down. A hollow bellow echoed from the fireplace beside her.

"Where are you going?" Tomas asked. Summer walked across the room to where she'd placed her things.

"Hope he can help," she spoke, pulling the card she'd found from the bottom of her purse and holding it up for Tomas to see.

VICTOR WATCHED STREAMS of his blood mingle with the water flowing into the tub's drain. He inserted his left big toe into the faucet of scalding hot water and grimaced. He roared a scream and slapped his right hand eleven times into the healed cut over his right eye. That scar was from the worst of times. Tonight was close, though, because he hated every inch of his sinewy form.

Summer had to die. Not because she saw through his plot, but because she'd humiliated him. In his own front yard. She disarmed him with her act of cluelessness—so convincing he still couldn't be sure it wasn't true. And he hated himself for not being sure. He had to be smarter. He had to be certain. Of everything. She had to die. And he wouldn't wear yellow to comfort her parents like he'd done for the others. Like what had been done for him, and his dad, at his mother's funeral. He'd detach her freesia-scented head and maybe leave it at his mother's burial place. Then he would be free of them both.

His phone rang. It would be Mair. *Pathetic*, he thought. She was ground-scrubbing, low-hanging fruit. Too low to be a source of ego supply. So low he thought her only slightly less humiliating than poverty or a permanent sexually transmitted disease. He was saddled with her in the same way. It was incurable.

His toe throbbed as he stood. Blood flowed from behind his left testicle. He left the water running as he answered the phone.

"What?" he said.

"Hello?" Mair responded, confused.

"Yes. What?"

"I thought you were gonna call me tonight."

"Okay," Victor snarled.

"Okay, and it's like seven-thirty right now."

"Okay."

"Are you at home? It sounds like you're in the bathroom." Mair tried to divert his bubbling wrath. "Did you still want to hang out?"

"Does it sound like it?" Victor responded. "You're listening to sounds, right? Does it sound like I want to see you tonight?"

"Okay, Vic." Mair sighed. He ended the call with a quick click before she could begin her usual plea.

Victor walked, bleeding, through the bathroom. He smeared blood through his white billowed bedding and screamed, "Mom!" until his voice faded.

28

THE MOIST, DARK EARTH GREETED SUMMER with a scent reminiscent of her days in the high school band. The familiarity eased the fear of hiding in a park at night in bushes and spider webs. It helped even more that Tomas crouched behind her.

"What time is he supposed to meet us?" Tomas whispered. Summer turned around with her finger over her lips.

From where they sat, they could not see the walking path below, but if they were quiet, they could hear footsteps. A scurry through leaves rustled to their left. *Must've been a squirrel,* Summer thought as she looked back at Tomas and motioned to his watch. He held it up. 10:15 P.M. The park had been closed for over three hours. If they were found, they would be escorted out. Or locked up.

Tomas gave up protecting his pants and sat in the soil. He pulled Summer back and down to sit in front of him as they waited. With their shifting stopped, they heard a tap on the pathway below—every two or three seconds. *Tap. Tap.*

They heard a hiss from the walkway and looked at each other. They had followed directions and met in the cove in the park's walkway, directly behind the black iron bench. They did not think anyone had been there to see them.

"*Pssst!*" They heard the hiss again and stood. Tomas moved in front of

Summer and shielded branches from slapping back into her face as they descended the small hill in the chilly blackness. Summer kept hold of Tomas's hand.

"Agent Cline?" Summer whispered just feet from a clearing in the bushes.

They found him sitting on the bench in a black sweatsuit, his walking stick reclining at his side. He did not turn around to face them.

Summer motioned "do something" to Tomas as they stood behind the man.

"Sir?" Tomas asked.

"Come down," Marvin Cline responded, still not turning to reveal his face.

Summer's hand gripped around Tomas's, now pressing the flesh around her nailbeds nearly white. They stood at the man's side, eyeing the walking stick, and looking around for straggling parkgoers or teens.

"We meet again," Marvin smiled at Summer. "I've been waiting for this call."

"You have?" Summer asked, motioning for permission to sit beside him. He moved his stick to the other side and made room for her. She placed her bottom on the edge of the bench with her feet pressed together below her.

"Of course," Agent Cline responded. "That little boyfriend of yours is a liar."

"I know. But why do you say that?" Summer replied.

"You called me 'cause you've been framed for my neighbor's murder. Joey Chae. Isn't that right?"

"Your neighbor?" Tomas interjected. Marvin nodded.

"And your man-friend just happened to be driving around our neighborhood two days before Joey turned up dead. Twice in one day."

Summer's mouth dropped open as she looked at Tomas.

"What do you mean, sir?" Tomas asked. He moved beside Summer and sat with his legs wide enough to touch her. He leaned forward to look around her and clasped his hands.

"I was out for my first walk of the day. Neighborhood was still dark. Saw a silver Camry driving through the neighborhood. Slow. Strange. Only person ever driving through the neighborhood at that time is the paper lady and she flies through like a fugitive." Agent Cline seemed as if he were making a joke but did not laugh.

"A silver Camry?" Tomas asked, looking at Summer.

"He still has the one from Miami," Summer replied and turned back to the old man.

"And I told you," Agent Cline pushed his forefinger into Summer's thigh, "I notice every silver Camry I see now, after searching for you." Tomas frowned and looked at her but continued to listen.

"So, I stopped him. Said, 'Can I help you find something, son?' And he told me lie after lie about looking for a house for his wife. Said she wanted to live far away from Capitol Hill." He shook his head, "Goddamn liar."

Summer frowned now, too.

"Don't think too hard, honey. He's a snake, plain and simple. Funny thing is, he thought he could outsmart me." Agent Cline tucked his wrinkled hands under his armpits. "His type always does."

"So he was driving around your neighborhood in the dark doing what?" she asked.

"Stalking that Chae kid. Apparently."

"Uh, Agent Cline..." Tomas began.

"Call me Marvin, son."

"Ah, okay, uh, Marvin... uh, you said you saw him there twice?"

"Damn straight. He came back the same day. Dressed like a woman this time, in another car. Idiot."

"See! I told you guys!" Summer turned to Tomas. She lowered her voice. "How did you know it was him?"

"Didn't 'til you told me you got pulled over in his black Audi. Then it came back to me in a flash. Went to check the surveillance the HOA gives me access to 'cause I *am* the president after all. Saw him drive right behind the Chae kid's truck that afternoon. The same afternoon! Can you believe the balls on this guy?"

"You have video of all this?" Tomas asked. He stretched his eyes wide and squeezed Summer's knee. "Can we see it?"

"Of course, son, that's why we're here." Agent Cline pulled his cell phone out of his pocket. "Taped it right here on my phone."

Summer's stomach turned. She heard footsteps down the path and looked over her right shoulder. The men didn't notice.

"*Shhhh*," Summer whispered. "I think someone's here." She looked over her right shoulder again. Footsteps approached, growing closer and more rapid. Summer leaped to her feet and bolted. She ran up the beginning of the hill, losing her footing slightly. She corrected her body and kept running.

"Manny!" Marvin spoke again. "I was wondering if you were gonna make it."

Tomas stood and greeted him. "*Tio*, what are you doing here?"

"I guess I should be asking you the same," Manny joked. "But my good buddy here," he patted Marvin's shoulder, "called me out here to see if we can get Summer out of this mess."

"Where's *Tia*?" Tomas asked. He worried for Dara.

"She has no idea I'm here. Why?"

"No reason," he replied nervously. "Let me get Summer." Tomas turned behind him to see a space empty except for the wildlife. Summer had disappeared. He ran up the hill and out of sight, whispering her name.

"Manny," Marvin patted the empty seat beside him. He looked over his shoulder and made sure he couldn't see Tomas or Summer. "Have a seat, my friend. How are things? How's Dara?"

Manny didn't respond.

"How did you know we'd be here tonight?" Marvin leaned his elbows forward on his knees and tried to see cracks in the black asphalt between his feet.

Manny scoffed and refused to sit. Instead, he widened his stance and folded his arms.

"Marvin, you're a smart man," Manny began, "and we go back. Way, way back. I know you and Dara are friends. Heck, I thought you and I were friends, too."

"Right," Marvin responded. "Somehow, I feel like there's going to be a 'but' coming up soon."

Manny moved his hands down to his waist.

"I want you to enjoy your retirement, buddy. I really do. I want you to get lots of walks and visits with the grandkids." Manny stopped and pointed at Marvin. "You do have grandkids, right?" Marvin stared at Manny, face as plain as a wall.

Manny continued, "Okay, here comes the 'but.' *But* whatever you're up to with Summer and her friend, whatever you're trying to get them caught up in, whatever one of your paranoid plots you're trying to put in my kid's head…" he paused. "Stop it."

Marvin smiled. "I'll see what I can do, old friend." He stood and leaned over to pick up his walking stick. "And I want to give you a piece of advice, too."

"Save it," Manny interrupted.

"Nope." Marvin shook his head. "That's not fair. You're giving out advice tonight, right, son? Well, here's some for you." Marvin put the walking stick between his feet. The reflective stripe on his sweats did not shine. "I'll do my best to stay out of what's going on with Summer." He smiled. "And here's a 'but' for you, too. *But* keep in mind, when you live life with all these pesky secrets, you leave yourself kinda open to…" he paused and stroked his chin, "…whatever."

Marvin sauntered past Manny, patting him on the arm once as he walked by. His walking stick tapped the ground again. Manny flared his nostrils and clenched his jaw as he turned to watch him.

"YOU'RE GONNA HAVE TO RELAX, Summer, oh my God!"

"I can't Tomas!" Summer paced a flat ridge in the luscious ruby rug at the foot of the bed in the guest bedroom. "I'm about to freak out, seriously." Summer's arms wrapped around her chest and her red button-down sweater. She still wore dirt-covered jeans from the park.

"Call him again!" she prodded Tomas.

"Summer, c'mon. It's after midnight, and we've already called him five times." Tomas sat on the edge of the bed in his boxers and an undershirt. He gripped the bridge of his nose and rubbed his eyes as his glasses sat atop his head.

"So?"

"It's rude, Summer."

"Really? I'm going to end up going to prison for murder and you're worried about what's rude?!"

"I'm just saying there's gotta be another way we can figure this out," Tomas replied.

"How?!" Summer shouted before lowering her voice. "I don't even want to be in this house! I don't know what's going on. You're telling me my dad showed up at the park. How in the world did he know to be there?!"

Tomas repositioned his glasses and pressed redial for the sixth time. Summer stopped pacing to stand right in front of him, between his feet. At the third ring, he shook his head. "He's sleeping, Summer."

"Or dead. My dad probably killed him. Fine, just hang up."

"He said Marvin called him there to help." Tomas pushed both hands into his hair.

"Who?" she replied.

"Your father." Tomas squinted at her and shook his head.

Summer gripped her temples, trying to get more blood, and solutions, to her brain. She placed her hands on Tomas's shoulders and looked at the pupils of his eyes. "I am scared," she said with hard emphasis on each word. "You're leaving in twelve hours, and it's the middle of the night." She rolled her lips into her mouth. Glistening tears welled in her bottom lids. "I don't know what I'm going to do."

"Don't you want to ask your mom for some help?"

"She's got her own problems." Summer shook her head thinking of her father.

"I don't think your dad is a murderer, Summer. *Tio* may be acting crazy, but he's not *that* crazy."

"I don't even have time to worry about that sex trafficker right now," she said, laughing in fatigued disbelief. She slapped her thighs.

"That's extreme, don't exaggerate," Tomas replied.

"¡*Bebo*! He's paying Victor to sleep with me and Mair. Isn't that sex trafficking or something?!"

"I think it would be trafficking if Victor was paying *for* you and not the other way around." Tomas shrugged. His face had begun to regrow its beard hours ago. His eyes were injected with redness. The caffeine tremor he normally sported had worn off. He needed to sleep. "Summer, you know I love you, but…"

The phone began to ring. He slowly picked it up and Summer snatched it from his hand.

"Hello," she breathed into the receiver. "This is Summer." She raised her eyebrows and pointed to the phone nodding her head in quick bursts.

"Hey there, Summer. You left in a rush last time," Marvin Cline chuckled. Summer placed the call on speakerphone.

"Yeah, sorry about that. I've been trying really hard to avoid police, and I thought I heard someone coming."

"Ah, yeah, don't worry about that. It was just your ol' dad."

"I heard." She blew a short breath. "So can we meet tomorrow maybe, to see the video?" Summer asked, holding her hands in a prayer position between her breasts.

"Yes, indeed. How about 11:30 tomorrow morning? We'll be able to meet like regular people—in the daylight." Marvin chuckled again.

"Uh, are you free a little earlier? My friend, the guy who was with me tonight…"

"The Andy Garcia-lookin' fella?" Marvin joked.

Summer smiled. "Devastatingly handsome, isn't he?" she quipped back. "Um, he has a flight tomorrow at noon. I really want him to be there when I see the recordings."

"Certainly wish I could, darling, but I've got a commitment. It'll just take a second. I'll show it to you, and get you a copy, and you're all set. You'll beat that case with your eyes closed. So how about eleven-thirty? I've gotta stop by Home Depot on Broken Land. Meet me there?"

"Yes sir, okay," Summer responded, crestfallen. She pressed end on the call. Tomas had taken off his shirt and lay back on the bed with his eyes closed. His glasses sat sideways on his face. *Ah Bebo*, she thought, *I'm sorry. I've exhausted you.* Summer pulled the glasses away and set them on the nightstand. She looked at Tomas's tanned chest and felt a run of foreign nervousness tickle from her belly to her heart. She spoke into the room, although he slept.

"I'm going to take you to the airport, then meet him tomorrow at eleven-thirty." She looked over at her sleeping friend. "I love you, too, *Bebo*," she whispered, and kissed him on the cheek. As Summer crawled into bed beside him and drifted to sleep in three breaths, Dara stood outside the bedroom door, listening.

29

AT THE AIRPORT, Summer draped her fingers over a black, retractable belt barrier and squeezed it in her hands. "Okay, *mamita*," Tomas handed her the scribbled notes he'd taken on an envelope as they drove to the airport. They detailed her next steps.

"Ma'am, please don't disturb that," an AirTran agent shooed Summer's hand away. Summer rolled her eyes.

"Listen..." Tomas lightly gripped her face to refocus her, "you can do this, okay?"

"Should I call Phoebe and see if she can come? Maybe wait a few days and go with her?"

"Why? You don't need to do that. You got this. All you've got to do is watch the tape and ask him to email you a copy. If he can't do that, record it from his phone to yours. And if he can't do that..." Tomas left space for her to respond.

"Get him to mail it to you."

"Right, get him to mail it to me. Don't get anything delivered to your house, just in case. I'm going to come back as soon as I can. I promise." He kissed her forehead, and she held on to his elbows. She hugged him, then straightened the strap of his brown leather bag across his chest.

"I'm so glad you were here for all of this. Thank you."

He squeezed her shoulders. "I'll call you as soon as I land."

Summer stared as Tomas weaved his way through security with his boarding pass and ID in hand. He'd managed to keep his medical journal throughout the trip and now held it rolled under his arm. Once his head disappeared, Summer turned to face BWI's massive glass wall. She headed back to short-term parking. The sky was blue, but clouds threatened to roll in. Her phone made a sound. A text.

Only meet in a crowded place, ok?
Promise me?

> OMG, Bebo, why are you acting like
> an uncle? LOL. I will. Promise. <3

Cars whipped through the airport departures area. Summer trotted across the street in her rolled jeans and crinkled khaki coat made for early autumn. The air's bite chilled her skin. She couldn't decipher, though, if her goosebumps were from fall air or fear. Underneath the cover of the parking lot, she held her black purse close, as if she thought someone might take it. This would be the first time she'd get in a car and drive alone since her arrest. *I really hope no one is following me, and that this Agent Cline guy is legit*, she thought.

Summer drove in silence the twenty-five minutes it took her to get from the airport to the Home Depot in Columbia. *This is not exactly a crowded public place,* she thought as she pulled up beside an orange corral for shopping carts. It was 11:30 A.M. on a Wednesday. Only the retired or fired straggled back and forth from the store.

Sitting in her parents' Escalade, Summer scanned around her. Employees had parked their cars against a bush in an area far away from the store. Empty spaces surrounded her—except for an unoccupied gray pickup truck to her left. She looked at her car's clock. 11:34. Her body's nerves stood on end, though she couldn't pinpoint the locus of her worry. She tapped her feet, then pressed her head back into the car seat and inhaled a deep, deep breath. She looked at her hands and realized they were shaking.

"I'm Taja, and you're listening to Z104.3!" Summer slammed the radio off just as quickly as she'd pressed it on. The noise of the announcer's voice clashed like cymbals in her ears.

"I need to call someone," she said aloud. "I bet everyone's working, though." She looked through her phone's contact log, though she knew if she called anyone, it would be Phoebe, Carla, or her mom, all of whom had numbers she had memorized a decade ago.

"Hello?"

"Phoebe! I'm surprised you answered. What are you up to?"

"Hey, T!" She sounded out of breath. "I'm actually getting ready to go into Grand Rounds in like fifteen minutes. And I just got paged. Sorry!"

"Oh, okay, no problem, call me later," Summer responded. The call dropped before she could press "end." Her eyes peered at Phoebe's name in her phone. Her belly inflated with another deep breath. She and Phoebe hadn't talked in weeks, not about anything. Not about her getting her job back. Not about the stuff Tomas told her about her father. She worried she'd lost Phoebe in some way. Her eyes moved up and down the call log again.

"¡*Dime!*" Carla answered the phone in Spanish.

"¿*Que bola?*"

"*Chica*, I'm literally walking into a neuro consult at the ER. Let me call you back!"

"*Bueno*, I'll talk to you later. ¡*Besos!*" She'd gone from tapping her feet on the floor to tapping her knees together. *No one to talk to.* It was 11:38.

Should I call this guy? Summer wondered. *He seems like the punctual type. He did say he had something to do this morning. I'll wait. Maybe I should call, though. Maybe I'm not at the right store. I wonder if he realizes there isn't a Home Depot on Broken Land. It's really Snowden.* She turned her face to scan the parking lot and the streets beyond it. Only sun, air, and white lines filled the streets and surrounding parking lots. No one drove toward the store. *I'm gonna just call.*

Summer's right thumb grazed the green phone icon. She waited. Cold sweats tested her Dove deodorant.

"We're sorry, you have reached a number that has been disconnected or is no longer in service."

"What?" She looked at the contact number in her phone. She pressed the redial button.

"We're sorry, you have reached a number that has been…"

"Come on!" Summer's shaking hands rummaged to the bottom of her purse and found the white business card Marvin Cline had given her that day at Athena's. "Four, four, three. Seven, four, two. Five, two…" She looked at the card. *Same number.*

She dialed the number then plunged her forehead into her hands. Another disconnected message.

"No! I cannot believe this!" Her blank face and worried eyes gazed at the parking lot. "Okay, I'm gonna wait 'til twelve." Summer began to recline the driver's seat, holding her phone six inches from her face. She sent Agent Cline a text.

> Hey there. Just waiting for you at Home Depot. I'm in a maroon Escalade next to the place where you put your carts. See you soon!

Missed sleep reddened the rims of her eyelids. Coffee filled the car with its aroma. She looked in the drink console and realized Tomas had left some in a cup. Her fingers traced the top. Her eyelids slid down and flapped open every few seconds. She thought herself too nervous to fall asleep. But when she felt her body submerged from the neck down in warm water, she knew she'd descended into a dream.

Like the fins of a betta fish, Summer's arms and legs swirled underneath the water. The stench of neglected teeth breathed heavily in her face. He pulled her up and up. His hands were rough and marked instant bruises on every part of her

he gripped to safety. Her black dress wrapped tighter with each swirl of her limbs.
"Baby! Whatchu doin' in this water?!" He crouched down, round-backed like a
turtle. She looked over him. Her father embraced Mair in the shadows.

Bang! Bang! Bang!

"Hey, Summer!" Summer jumped from her sleep to find Victor standing at her window, pounding it with the closed fleshy side of his hand. She hadn't forgotten he worked nearby but figured he'd be occupied and she wouldn't run into him.

"Get away from my car before I run you over with it." Summer's tremoring left hand slid in the crevice beside the seat to let the back up. She powered on her car and reversed.

"Wait!" he shouted. "I just want to talk to you."

Summer's head snapped left, then right, as she looked around the seats of the car. *Was he in here while I was sleeping?* The taste of stale toothpaste clung to her tongue. She put Tomas's cold coffee to her lips and took a long sip. She sped to the first exit from the Home Depot parking lot.

At the first light, she waited in the turning lane to make a U-turn. Her phone began to ring. Victor. *Oh my God. What does he want?* Summer struggled to complete her turn in the Escalade and swerved out into the lane to her right. A loud beep startled her back into her place. A man sneered at her as he drove by, shaking his head. Inside Summer's abdomen, a rising sensation lifted from behind her navel and into her chest. When it dropped, it gave way to nausea. The rise and fall happened again, this time giving way to tears. And again, leaving her with more pronounced shaking. Then a raging hot flash. And finally, a suffocating inability to draw relaxed breath. She was panicking. It took her fifteen minutes to find her breath. It collapsed again once she realized her hopes of getting in touch with Agent Cline and proving Victor had been stalking the Chae kid were gone. So, too, was her last hope at creating a defense.

She screeched into her home's driveway. No cars were parked beside her mother's Volvo. That meant she didn't have a patient in her home office at the moment.

"Mom!" Summer ran into the house shouting, still shaking and weak from anxiety. She ran into the house, dropping her purse and keys at the front door. She could smell coffee on her own breath as she shouted. "Mom!" Summer ran to the last arch of the house, beyond which her mother had a home psychiatry office for certain patients. Patients she deemed safe. Or ones she'd known for decades. Summer approached the closed door, paneled with small squares throughout. She placed her head against it, and hearing no sound, flung it open. Nothing. No one.

"Mom!" She ran through the house to the back stairs, pounding up and attempting to skip steps. She tripped, scratching the flesh just above her foot on the edge of a stair she couldn't clear. She kept going. As she headed to her parents' room, a yellow sticky note on her bedroom door caught her eye. It was in her mother's handwriting.

"Got called up to Delaware. I'm so stressed. Gotta go through some charts. Not sure how long I'll be. Maybe a day or so. Call me if you need anything. Love you, baby girl!"

Summer's body bounced forward with rushing blood and a pounding heart. The blood bobbed her head, too. She brought both hands to her mouth as if to pray and wiped the corners of her lips, then rested her hands on her lower back and attempted to catch her breath.

Her eyes looked down and around her as her body began to slow itself. Her arrest. Menstrual blood. The arraignment. Every failed attempt to vindicate herself. Victor. Tomas. With every breath, an image of the past five days pulsed. Summer stooped to the floor, and, like a flash, the dream from the Home Depot parking lot came rushing toward her. *Was that a dream or did that really happen?*

She stood straight as a tack. A wave of dizziness pushed from her right temple. Her heart galloped in her chest, and for a moment, she thought she might vomit. She turned an about-face like an exhausted soldier. Back down the back stairs. Back across the perfect flooring. Back beyond the last arch. Back into her mother's office. The window opening to their gardens gave view to manicured bushes and fading annuals. Beside the windows stood dark bookshelves, filled from top to bottom with tales of psychiatry lore. Theories. Dream interpretations. Group therapy. Even a few on neurology.

Summer looked for the gray book. The gray book with a blue-ringed spine. The DSM-IV-TR: the book of diagnoses. The book that would tell you if the person sitting before you was sane or not. Properly developed or not. With a typical personality or not. *The Diagnostic and Statistical Manual of Mental Disorders, Fourth Edition, Text Revision.* A mouthful. An eyeful. A tiny book to explain all of humanity's oddities, toxicities, frailties. A psychiatrist's best friend. Summer knew. She'd carried one in her white coat pocket until she'd forgotten who she was.

She took her pointer finger down a journey of each bookshelf. Trailing and scanning. Trailing and scanning. The book was not there. She looked at her mother's pristine desk. A shining vase of peonies and a family photo framed in gold positioned themselves at one end. A box of Kleenex and a business card holder sat at the other. Summer stood behind her mother's desk. Guilt descended on her shoulders. Her mother had always been clear that her workspace was not only private but it was also sacred and protected by laws. No one could enter, or rummage through, or read files. The door should remain closed and locked. It was a vault of secrets.

Dara's confidence that her warnings would suffice had been misplaced. Because today, Summer sat behind the desk and opened every drawer until she found the gray-and-blue book and traced her same pointer finger over the words that diagnosed her.

Dissociative Fugue is characterized by sudden, unplanned trips from the home or workplace without the ability to remember some or all of the individual's past. Some of these patients take on new characteristics or aspects not related to their original identity.

"Yeah, like a doctor becoming a ballerina at twenty-six years old," she spoke out loud, doom filling her chest.

They tend to be running away from something of which they are unaware.

"Victor. Victor *and* Mair."

After a fugue episode resolves, patients are unable to remember the events of the state.

"Why?!" Summer shouted at the book.

Although moving occurs in other disorders, in fugue it is purposeful, and it is not enacted in a confused or dazed state. In a typical case, the fugue is brief, with purposeful travel, and limited contact with others. About 0.2% of the general population is afflicted with this type of dissociative disorder. (American Psychiatric Association, 2000)

"Zero-point-two percent of the population. Boy, aren't I special?" Summer's nose burned. Tears were generating out of frustration. And shame. Such deep shame. *How could I let a stupid boy make me go nuts?*

A large teardrop splattered on the tissue paper-like page, seeping through and revealing letters from the page behind it. She dabbed it with the sleeve of her khaki coat. She opened another drawer. And then another. They held pens and prescription pads. Gloves, a blood pressure cuff, and a stethoscope. And at the very bottom, files stacked on themselves—recorded in her mother's perfect handwriting.

Mr. Jefferson presents for continued treatment of generalized anxiety disorder. Patient reports medication adherence. No new side effects. Sleep, appetite, concentration are intact. No substance misuse or self-harm reported. Denies suicidal and homicidal ideations. Stressors include work and marriage. Patient contemplating divorce. Patient continues to struggle with worst-case scenario thinking. Remains in psychotherapy, completing CBT workbook. Patient is motivated for treatment. Intelligence and diligence are perceived as strengths. Recommend ongoing adherence to Sertraline 200 mg, weekly CBT, regular exercise, avoidance of alcohol and caffeine. Prognosis is good.

Summer moved to another chart.

Patient is a 27-year-old married white female. Complains of about 6 weeks of low mood, anhedonia, social withdrawal, undeserved guilt, fatigue, poor sleep, and thoughts of suicide. Says her one-year-old son, Ethan, is her deterrent to self-harm. Denies homicidal ideation. Denies manic, panic, and psychotic symptoms. Patient is future-oriented, contracts for safety.

And another.

Mr. Barker returns for continued treatment of Schizoaffective Disorder. Reports med adherence. Mother joins today and is main historian. Reports Mr. Barker has refused five of the last seven doses of his Risperidone. Reports patient is up in the middle of the night singing or loudly laughing to himself. Recently sent emails to over 150 people to announce his engagement to Mariah Carey, whom he believes to be working at his local CVS pharmacy. Patient has been asked not to return to CVS by management. Discussed again with Mr. Barker's mother, who serves as his guardian, the need for a long-acting injectable antipsychotic to improve med adherence and reduce active psychosis.

Summer's mother took ultimate pride in her reputation of being a caring and professional psychiatrist. She never betrayed a patient's trust or would allow their exposure. Summer battled with the wrongness of her choice. Her mother would be livid. But reading the charts made Summer feel less alone in her perceived craziness, in her brokenness. She picked up another chart and turned to the first page.

How am I married to a rapist? How have I lived in this mess for thirty years? How?

Summer closed the chart to the demographic information, looking for a name. There was no label. No insurance information. No identifying anything. She opened back to the same page and continued reading.

I can't get over it, 'cause I'd asked Libby to come out with me that night. She was visiting. And I couldn't ride to his house alone, even though it was for a class party and he was my boyfriend. Girls just didn't do that when I was young. We'd just finished our renal final. We were going to celebrate at Manny's house. Well, his uncle's house. The one with the banyans over in Coconut Grove. The Grove. It used to be one of my favorite places in the world. Now I can't stand the sight of it.

Summer sifted through the pages of the chart, frowning at the familiar handwriting starring familiar people. Her mother never wanted to go to the Grove when they were still living in Miami. She said it was boring and had nothing to see. She also never really wanted to see Summer's

Aunt Libby, either.

Summer leafed through further and saw her own name written on page after page. This medical chart, it seemed, was her mom's own way of processing the emotions she held so closely to her chest. The ones that remained secrets buried deep inside.

I feel like we were both dressed appropriately, party appropriate, but I know that has nothing to do with it. Libby's hair was flaming red and down below her butt. She wore a knit bra and jeans, but it was the times. And it was Miami. It was fine. I always loved that about her—her fun spirit. It made me a little jealous, too.

I remember that night how anxious I was to see Manny. He was so tall, and happy, and handsome. He picked me up and swung me around. I accidentally kicked a guy's drink out of his hand. We laughed and kissed, and it was perfect. Everyone commented that my hair was down. It was never down at school.

Summer's eyes went back to the top line of this apparent diary entry. *How am I married to a rapist?* She was afraid to keep reading. She closed the folder, and its plain manila back became the screen for a lifetime of memories with the man she believed was the most perfect father. The father who'd provided a beautiful life, and schooling, and trips, and clothes, and homes, and most of all, security. That kind of father. Over the past forty-eight, and with each passing few hours, though, he was being revealed as a sexual deviant. A monster. She couldn't reconcile the two faces of her father. She opened the chart again.

Libby said she was going to the bathroom. But she was gone too long, so I checked on her. When I walked in on Manny pumping his massive body over her open legs, I screamed and pounced on his bare ass. I hit him with my clogs. I don't even know if she yelled for me. The music was so loud. And she was so small.

Summer whispered into the pages. "What?!" and continued to read the last lines on the page.

Libby cried the entire way back to my house. I honestly feel bad writing this, but I couldn't tell if she was crying because she'd been saved or interrupted.

Summer slammed the file shut and threw it back in the drawer where she'd found it. She stacked the three patient charts back on top of it and pushed herself back. Her eyes caught the family photo on the desk. Her mother and father and her—they smiled under the bougainvillea in the backyard.

Her father's eyes in the frame seemed distant but somehow more familiar. Summer brought the photo closer to her face and focused on his features. She looked away, then back at the picture again. She realized she'd seen two sets of those eyes over the course of her lifetime—one on his face and the other on Mair's.

30

"I'M ALWAYS OVERDRESSED when I come here." Dara lifted her glasses and wiped sweat from the bridge of her nose. "Why is Florida still so hot in September?" she said aloud, laughing to herself. Dara looked around and behind herself. She sat on the large bench at the far end of the train platform. She placed her hand down, then lifted it. The humidity outside made the bench's green paint sticky. She looked at it, rubbing her fingers together and turning down the corners of her mouth.

"It's not really wet; it just feels like that," said a woman standing a few feet away. She held a black vacuum cleaner crevice nozzle under her arm and had a denim purse over her shoulder. She squeezed lotion into her palm and applied it heavily to her face, focusing on her eyebrows.

"Great to see you, sis!" Dara smiled and tentatively stood.

"Yeah, right," Libby responded. "Are you here to try to kidnap me again?"

"Come on, Libby, I'm never here to kidnap you," Dara replied, reaching for a hug.

"No, you come here to inject me with things," Libby shouted. Dara looked around. The student sitting next to her went to the other side of the platform.

"Well, that was part of the deal, wasn't it?" Dara asked.

"What deal?" Libby responded, now rubbing shea butter-based cream on her mouth.

"Your skin looks great." Dara attempted to change the subject.

"What deal, Dara?" Libby persisted. "Don't try that crap."

"Okay, the deal was," Dara sighed and adjusted her bag, "that you'd live where you want and do your thing, and I'd just come down once a month to make sure you were okay. Really, we should be doing the injections every two or three weeks."

"Oh, the injection deal? You mean the deal where you said if I don't let you shoot me up with drugs every month, you'd go to some judge and have my rights taken away?" Libby turned to face the oncoming train. "That deal?" she scoffed. "Thanks a lot. Thanks a whole hell of a lot, my generous big sister." She rolled her eyes, did a curtsy, then pushed between a couple waiting to board the train. Dara apologized to them as she passed.

Libby sat close to the door that separated one train car from the next, far from the others riding with them. Dara joined her. She sat next to her instead of across from her so they wouldn't be staring at each other's faces. Libby found that confrontational.

"So, how have you been?" Dara asked.

"You know. You follow me. You have people follow me."

"I really don't, Libby. What's happening to your hands?" she asked, looking at Libby's inflamed and peeling knuckles.

"Someone is attacking me in my sleep, thanks to you," Libby replied as if defeated.

"What do you mean?" Dara was familiar with her sister's paranoid imagination but still prodded her mind at times.

"I have signs," Libby responded. "You're constantly making things happen to me where I live."

"And where is that?" Dara asked, looking forward out the window at South Florida passing by.

"Ha! I'll die before I tell you. I'm here to keep up with this 'deal' so I can live my life and you can get the hell away from me." Libby held the vacuum cleaner piece up to Dara's face.

"Okay, and what's this, Libby?"

"Okay, and what's this, Libby?" Libby mimicked her sister with raging sarcasm. "What's it look like?"

"A part to clean crumbs out of a couch," Dara replied. "Are you staying somewhere with a couch?" Dara hoped her sister was no longer living at the park across from her old job, where she'd been a nursing assistant for twenty-five years.

"I'm never gonna tell you, Dr. Dara, so forget it."

"Elizabeth," Dara used her sister's full name, "why are you so antagonistic toward me? I'm only here to help. And that's 'cause I love you."

"You know who needs help? That lunatic daughter of yours. Where is she, by the way? Haven't seen her on the train in a few weeks. Every time I try to talk to her, she ignores me or says her name is 'Tuh-rez.'"

"She went back to Baltimore."

"Is she still batshit crazy?" Libby laughed with her head falling back. Dara didn't respond. Libby continued, "Look, don't get pissed at me because the stuff you do to people finally backfired."

"Where are we getting off?" Dara was ready to end the visit.

"Let's get off now." Libby stumbled into the train's forward motion and dragged her feet along the floor. She gripped a rail, standing inches from the door. Dara waited for the train to come to a stop and followed her little sister.

The two walked into the Panera at the bottom of the train station for lunch. It smelled of broccoli and cheddar soup in bread bowls. The kind Libby loved so much. She had plenty of money, but only ate at these places when Dara visited. Otherwise, someone from management would kick her out. She never understood why but figured Dara must have told them to.

After ordering their food, Dara and Libby walked to the bathroom, both washing their hands.

"Okay, which side this time?" Dara asked, frustration ruffling her voice.

"Right," Libby responded. "And let me see this box. What is this?"

"Risperdal Consta," Dara handed her the box her medicine came in, "the same thing as every month." Libby reviewed the words on the white-and-green carton, then handed it back to her sister. "I was a phlebotomist and nursing assistant, so I know about the medical field."

"I know," Dara replied as she removed the syringe from its packaging and began to mix the medicine. Libby hung her head and loosened her pants, moving the elastic of her panties down. Dara vigorously shook the medicine in the round glass vial from the box. She attached a covered needle, then passed an alcohol wipe over the skin of her sister's upper right buttock.

"Whoa!" Libby shouted. "Why's it so freakin' cold?"

"Libby, please, let's just get this over with and go eat," Dara replied.

"Yeah, right, Dara! When it's cold, it's gonna hurt for a whole week!"

"That's when the medicine is cold, which it's not this time." Dara sighed, trying to find her patience. She plunged the bare needle into Libby's flesh and pushed the medicine in. Libby uttered profanities under her breath for the full ten seconds that it took.

"Happy now?" Libby asked Dara once the injection was finished. She wiped tears away as she buttoned her jeans back up. She picked up her purse and nozzle and pulled a few paper towels from the holder to wipe her nose. Dara did not respond but slid the orange safety cap over the needle and placed all her materials in a red plastic bag to discard later. She held up a Band-Aid for Libby, but Libby declined. Dara opened the box of Band-Aids and slid the rejected one back into place. Her cell phone began buzzing beside the box.

"Hello?"

"Mom!" Summer was panting into the phone.

"What's the matter, Summer?"

Libby rolled her eyes and moved away from the door.

"Where are you? Can you talk?" Summer asked.

"Well, I'm at the workshop place, getting ready to start. What's the matter?" Libby held up her fingers in an "L" to signify to her sister she thought she was both a liar and a loser.

"Do you have something to tell me, Mom? Seriously. Don't lie."

"What do you mean?"

"Mom, don't play dumb. Have you been keeping a major secret from me? For a while now?"

"Summer…" Dara started.

"No, have you?"

"I have, sweetie. I couldn't find the right time," Dara responded. "But I was planning to talk to you really soon. So much has been going on."

"Really? Soon? Like when?" Summer demanded. "Hasn't it been long enough?"

"You're right, Summer. I didn't know how you would take it, though. I know how much you wanted to get back to work. I felt horrible when Uncle Mike told me they had to part ways with you because of the case, baby girl."

"What?!" Summer yelled.

"I know, it's so unfair 'cause you didn't do anything wrong, and you really wanted to get back to work." Libby was staring at her sister's mouth in awe. "But because of the murder trial, Mike said he had to let you go."

Summer was silent. "Baby girl?" Dara asked. "I'm so sorry. You know I was going to tell you! I wanted to be there when you found out."

"And do you have anything *else* you want to tell me, Mom?" Summer sounded winded. "Any *other* secret you might be keeping?" her voice wobbled as if she were about to cry.

"Of course not, Summer. I'm always one hundred percent honest with you. You know that."

Summer hung up.

Despite Dara's six attempts to redial her, Summer did not answer. Libby stood beside the hand dryer with her arms folded, laughing.

"Murder trial?! I told you she was crazy, Dara. She needs that shot more than I do."

"She's going through a hard time, Libby, but she's not paranoid. She's not mentally ill."

"Neither am I, Doc," Libby replied.

Dara walked to the exit and spread her fingers along the door to open it for her younger sister.

Libby began to speak, "But I have one question for you. Why don't you just tell her you're coming here to see me every month? Embarrassed of me?"

"I just don't, Libby," Dara nearly whispered. "Let's go."

31

THE SILK MAROON PILLOW COVER smelled of Tomas's hair. Summer planted her face in it to try to stop the next mounting anxiety attack, lifting and falling again from her navel to her chest. She couldn't catch her breath. She couldn't slow her heart. She couldn't stop crying, or shaking, for that matter. She lay diagonally across the bed Tomas had slept in while he visited. The scent of his shampoo soothed her until the moment was interrupted by two loud steps, then a hand at the back of her head.

"Summer? What's the problem?" Manny walked around the bed and sat beside her legs. He placed a hand on her right calf.

She froze. She'd succeeded in avoiding her father from the time he went racing out of their driveway two days before until this moment. She had been shielded by Tomas's visit. Without him, without Dara, she felt completely exposed to the dangers that lurked around her in Maryland.

She did not move. She did not respond. Her chest strained with captured breath.

"Summer? Are you okay?" Manny asked again. He controlled his voice.

"Not really, Dad," Summer responded, then waited.

"I hope you're not too worried about that case. There's no way your mother or I will let you get convicted. There's no way." Manny moved his hand from her leg. Whenever her father had offered reassurance in the past, Summer's worries would dissolve and lift away—in flight like butterflies. Not now.

"How do you know that, Dad?"

"I just do. This is Baltimore. There's absolutely no way they're going to let that happen to my daughter in my city." Manny's voice dropped. "I know way too many people."

"Dad, the children of prominent people go to jail all the time."

"Not really, Summer. But especially not in a situation like this."

"In a situation like what? What do you mean?" Summer flipped over. Her chest tightened. She tried to look into her father's eyes. Each time she did, though, the racing in her chest accelerated. She sat up and pulled her legs into her body. She placed the pillow over her lap.

"In a situation where you've basically been framed." Manny stood from the bed. "I never liked Victor. You know that. He's not right for you. And he's a sneak."

Tomas's warning about the paid dating arrangement rang through her head. Manny's mysterious appearance at the meeting returned to her memory. Her mother's diary notes describing her fun-loving and loud father as a rapist flashed in her eyes. His dimples no longer were charming; they were cunning. His eyes no longer conferred security; they suggested secrecy. Summer bowed her head and replied.

"Okay, Dad."

Manny's loud steps took him out of the room and down the hall. Summer's anxiety attack seemed to be giving way. But what lay behind it was worse. It was the despairing realization that her family life was shaping up into a massive lie. She had no idea where she fit in it. And there was loneliness. The deepest she had ever felt.

She wondered when the lie started. Maybe when she was nine and the family visited Sanibel Island for the summer. And she wore flamingo shirts and pink flip-flops with a bubble gum pink bow across her toes. Or it could have been at thirteen when Epiphany took all the eighth graders to Key West. Her mom was the most popular chaperone, and everyone called her Mama Martinez, which Dara loved. Tomas, Carla, and Phoebe hated it, though. It could have been around her sweet sixteen celebration at the Biltmore on Anastasia Avenue. It had been lush, over the top. It dripped with money and Miami's most prestigious doctors and their kids. It had been the first iteration of *My Super Sweet 16*-level birthday parties. Ridiculous. *Maybe they were overcompensating.*

Summer looked back over her life and felt confused. Nausea pushed up into the back of her throat, and she realized she hadn't eaten since the day before. Hunger could find no room in her body. Neither could sleep. And she really, really wanted to sleep. Her face throbbed. It was congested from crying. Her sinuses pulsed and even burned.

She leaped from the bed and ran into the bathroom. She vomited into the toilet, then squatted to the floor sobbing. She turned onto her hands and knees and crawled to open the cabinets beside her. Summer looked for a pill bottle, of anything, to take in handfuls so she could sleep. She found nothing but spa-folded white towels with the round edge facing out. Her fingers gripped the marble sink, and she lifted herself. She averted her eyes from the mirror and opened the small cabinets beside it. Empty, except for Q-tips and extra toothbrushes in their Oral-B packaging. She wondered if Victor had left those there during a visit and swallowed down another wave of vomit.

Benadryl.

She would take a few tablets of Benadryl. It would stop the nausea. Maybe it would stop the thinking, too. It would make her sleep, she hoped. She took three at once and lay across the bed again. She closed her eyes against her wakefulness. Each shutting eye replayed scenes from Miami weddings and masses and graduations and the charity events she'd attended, dressed the best and smiling in pictures. She saw the busyness of South Beach, the blueness of Bayside, and the windowed banquet rooms of the Rusty Pelican. And she wondered as these scenes worked themselves through her mind if she had been the laughingstock of her world, of her friends, and cousins, and community. The joke. The adopted girl who thought she had actually been loved.

THREE HOURS LATER, Summer ran to her car parked on the street beside her parents' driveway. She threw a navy bag of underwear and simple outfits in the backseat. Next to the rear passenger door, she made the sign of the cross. She had waited to make her exit at an hour when her father wouldn't notice. Now was the time. Now the night was black. Her tires spun on themselves as she looped her car in a tight U out of her parents' neighborhood. Intrusive recall of Dara's words flew into Summer's thoughts.

It's hard to admit the truth about the nature of Summer. The way she came to be ours. And Manny's reaction to it.

With another pointed finger, Summer had traced her mother's words in the chart. She'd pulled it out again, faced with the fact Dara was not going to tell her the truth about Mair's paternity. But this explained some things, like the memory of that night at the Harbor. Her dad and her nemesis in an embrace after her betrayal.

When Mair was born, Libby was just barely seventeen. She partied every weekend. She wasn't ready to be a mom. Me? I was, though. And I offered to care for her, the baby that is. I begged Manny for the four months we knew she was on her way. At every turn, he said "no," that he didn't want to adopt a baby. That "it" would have problems, thanks to Libby's "nature." He never once said anything about the fact that he had fathered the baby.

"Oh my God," Summer said aloud in Spanish, then covered her mouth. Mair was her sister and her father's daughter. More his daughter than she felt she could ever be. The entry continued:

Perhaps he questioned if she were his—until she was born with the exact same face. The only thing about her reminiscent of our Welsh ancestors was her name and her flaming red hair. Just like Libby's.

Summer waited until the middle of the night, and then drove her car to the Citgo three blocks from her parents' neighborhood. The fluorescent lights over the gas pumps interrupted the darkness in a harsh but necessary way. A lot like the gold-framed picture in her mother's office. A lot like the conversation Tomas overheard. Even like Summer's fugue the summer before—harsh but necessary interruptions to her life's deceptions. The weight of these painful intrusions dogged her head until Summer finally placed it on the steering wheel and began to weep. Had she known what she was going to discover in her mother's office, she would have begged Tomas to stay. She needed him now. She needed her parents, the ones she thought Manny and Dara were. She needed her friends. *But they don't need me and my drama*, she thought. She needed Victor's love. But Victor was incapable of and antagonistic to the very concept.

A man in a pea-green Plymouth Road Runner parked at the pump in front of her. He noticed her head on the steering wheel.

"Hey! You alright? Hellooooo?"

Her head popped up, tears streaming under her chin. She wiped her face on her shirt. The man moved closer and peered into her windshield, then tapped the hood of the car with two fingers. The same two holding his cigarette.

"What?" she asked.

"You're not dead, are ya?" The man's face lifted in folds as he smiled. One leg followed the other as he walked into the store.

The thought had occurred to her. To be dead. To end her life. It had occurred to her plenty of times when she miscarried—and again today. Sometimes the thought came and went, like a breeze. Sometimes the thought came and stayed, like a friend. Or a persistent foe. Telling her she wouldn't be a burden any longer, or missed too much, if she ended things. Telling her she'd be out of pain, and her people would move on eventually. Confusing her with thoughts about how she'd be found, and that being found wouldn't matter. That maybe she could have done it during her fugue, had she remembered she was unhappy.

But she had been a psychiatrist-in-training and psychiatrist-in-upbringing. She knew that the lies of suicidal thoughts were viciously convincing but were lies all the same. Tomas was the only person she'd ever told she sometimes considered suicide. The heartbreak in his eyes when she uttered those words was enough to let her know she could never do that to him, that she'd have to find another way to end her suffering.

Summer was still sitting with her chest leaning on the wheel when the man from the Plymouth returned, shoving a wad of cash into his front pocket. He wore dark jeans and a plaid shirt and had thick, brown hair parted and pushed to the side. He looked like he'd climbed out of thirty years ago. Summer got out of the car and looked at the pump instructions. She inserted her debit card and looked out of the corner of her eye at the man. He noticed.

"Hey there, sweetheart, you need me to pump your gas?" he asked.

A small laugh puffed through Summer's nose. "Uh, I think I got it. But thanks!"

"Oh, are you one of those women's lib types? You know," he continued, "women's lib and birth control ruined America. Turned it soft." He leaned his behind on the tail of his car and crossed one long jeaned leg over the other.

Summer nodded, wondering where this conversation was going.

"So, what were you crying for?" he asked.

"Nothing." Summer's eyes bounced, watching numbers spin on the gas pump dial.

"Yeah, you're women's lib. What on earth are you lying for, darling? I saw you crying your eyes out." He took a drag from his cigarette and blew smoke rings from his mouth, up toward the lights, "People don't do that for 'nothing.'"

"I just have a lot on my mind."

"Guess so if you're at a gas station at 2:00 A.M. You headed somewhere?"

Summer had no idea. Was she headed somewhere? Or would she end up just having to turn back around and go home?

The man stood from the car. The pump clicked against the full tank.

Forty-three dollars. She faced him as he approached, unsure what she would do if he decided to attack her. She looked up at the ceiling of the gas station for cameras. She shuffled backward as he took three steps toward her. He noticed.

"I'm not about to do anything to you!" He lifted his hands as if being accosted by police. "I just thought you could use some help. Geez. What is it with you women that you can't let a man help you?" He dropped his hands to his waist. "What the hell's that all about?"

"Appreciate the offer," she replied, "but I can take care of myself." She had never uttered those words. They made a curious sound in her ears.

He scoffed as Summer fumbled with the gas pump. A high-pitched clang polluted the night as she dropped the pump to the ground. With a struggle, she got it to sit sideways in its holder. "Looks like you can't."

Drops of gasoline had spilled onto Summer's hands. She smelled the backs of them, then looked around. She dipped her hands in the windshield wiper bucket and winced, then wiped her hands with paper towel.

"You said it yourself." Summer dried her hands and tossed the paper towel into the nearby can with the octagonal mouth. She put one foot back onto the gray, carpeted floor of her Camry. She was angered by the man's insult. "Giving women the rights to make their own choices ruined a nation, right?"

"That's right."

"That means women must be pretty powerful." Summer nodded her head. "And so must I."

"Guess if you believe that shit," he said as he shrugged and walked toward his car, "that's all that matters."

Summer listened to the Plymouth start up. The forceful second pulse of its engine startled her—scared her. *Relax, Summer, you're okay.* Her thoughts were convincing. They were calm.

"I'm going to Florida," she declared aloud to her silent car. "I'm going to go find my Aunt Libby."

32

THREE HOURS OF CIRCULATING BENADRYL AND ADRENALINE caught up with Summer. As the green car pulled away, her eyes followed a blurred trail of taillights. She realized her eyes were crossing. Drowsy. She rolled her Camry through the gas station parking lot, tapping her foot against the brake for no reason. The car's front tires came to sit aimlessly in the street. *What am I doing?* she thought. The corners of her eyes were dry and stinging. She turned right toward the highway. The streetlights in this part of town did nothing for the heavy, middle-of-the-night void. It was a darkness too black for her to notice Victor's silver Camry trailing behind her without its headlights on.

Summer looked at the buildings on the right side of the road for a place to pull over. Sitting back from the street was a hotel. The cursive red letters of the sign were dark as if to say they were sleeping. Summer wondered if she could get a room and start her trek to her aunt in the lighted hours. She pulled in.

The automatic doors remained shut when Summer approached with her purse and navy bag. She waved her hand under the sensor above her head.

"Hey! Can you see me?" Summer swayed in front of the door.

A woman in khaki pants leaned from behind the second set of doors and stared. She held a long black sweater around her round waist as if in her bathrobe. Summer chuckled to herself.

"Can I get a room?" she shouted.

The woman continued to stare and pushed her black glasses up on her nose. She turned in black, flat shoes and stepped out of sight. In seconds, both sets of automatic doors stood open. Summer watched them as if they were a Venus flytrap waiting to snap shut on her any instant. The woman in the khakis flagged her in.

"How can I help you, ma'am?"

"Thank you so much," Summer started. "I just need a room for tonight."

"Just tonight?" the woman questioned.

"Yep, what time is your check-out. Eleven?" Summer fumbled through her purse.

"Yes, ma'am. Check out is at 11:00 A.M. There's a complimentary continental breakfast from 6:50 to 9:30 A.M."

"How much for tonight?" Summer pulled out a debit card.

"One hundred and sixty-two dollars."

"A hundred and sixty-two dollars?! That's a lot." Summer complained.

"It includes tax, ma'am."

Summer laughed. "And the free breakfast, too, right?" She slid her card to the woman, who pecked the keyboard with one hand and bundled herself in the black sweater with the other.

"Are you cold?" Summer asked. The woman didn't respond. Instead, she reached her free hand down to the printer below the counter for the receipt. She slid the paper and a white pouch of two plastic key cards to Summer.

"You're in room 701. Elevators are to your left. Have a good evening."

Summer made her eyes wide and mouthed "Okay" to herself. She realized she may have been acting a little strange. She blamed a notoriously sensitive system and the Benadryl.

SOMEONE HAD BEEN SMOKING in Summer's non-smoking room. Her nose and throat confirmed it at the door. *Oh well, I'm not going to ask Ms. Friendly downstairs if I can move.* She sat her bags on the desk beside a burgundy room service menu and slumped onto the bed.

A suburban neighborhood street straightened itself before Summer's eyes. It was lined on both sides by tornadoes. They stood in place but spun like tops. Once she'd passed them all, they changed their configuration in the sky, rushing out of the line into a cluster. They followed Summer's car throughout the neighborhood, hovering whenever she was held up by a child crossing the street or a stop sign. Once she parked by the clinic, they lifted off. One by one.

"Attention! A fire has been detected in the building. A fire has been detected in the building. Please move to the nearest exit. Do not attempt to use the elevators." Blaring robotic warnings screamed through the hotel, jerking Summer from her dream. She tried to open her eyes. Her body ached. Her head fell back as she lifted herself from the starchy sheets.

"Attention! A fire has been detected in the building." The alarm looped the same announcement. Summer frowned and covered her eyes as if shielding them from the sun. Her head whipped to the side when the red light on her room phone began to flash.

"Hello?"

"Ms. Martinez," a woman's voice urgently spoke into the phone, "please take the stairs to come to the lobby. A fire has been detected in the building."

Summer began to respond but heard only a dial tone.

"Attention! A fire has been detected in the building."

Summer's head began to pound over her right temple. She slid to the foot of the bed, grabbed her bags and shoes, and stumbled to the door. In the dim hallway, couples in various iterations of dress roamed. They attempted to break from their slumber and confusion to put on coats and shoes with their pajamas or underwear. The alarm continued to shout. Summer looked for the red exit sign, leery of following the disoriented crowd.

A white metal door croaked open as she entered the stairwell. *Oh my God, I'm on the seventh floor!* Summer began galloping down the stairs. Grains of dirt and some flecks of peeling paint nestled themselves between the balls of her feet and the roundness of her toes. At the fourth floor, in came a lurching family of six. Two children shouted at their father that they were scared. The mother carried tow-headed twins. She wore a pink nightgown. The child in her left arm still slept.

Summer tilted her head back as her nose searched for the scent of smoke in the air. Her legs began to tingle with the fear that the fire waited below to incinerate her and the family.

"Sorry, excuse me." Summer squeezed passed them when they stopped to pick up one child's jacket that had fallen to the floor. She galloped again. The clamoring of the alarm left a high-pitched ringing in her ears. Small flecks of light flashed in her eyes. *God, please don't let me get a migraine.*

The khaki pants woman ushered guests from the lobby to far across the parking lot. Though hundreds of people filled the area, a blanket of quiet descended on the lot.

"Summer!" Victor shouted through the hushed crowd. She looked over her shoulder.

"Summer!" she turned around in a full circle, standing on her toes to see over the heads of women her height. She moved to the back of the crowd and saw him. In slacks and a pressed shirt, he resembled a toy soldier. Except for his right hand. It fanned fingers in a slow wave. The tingle in her legs returned. It settled behind her knees. She felt faint enough to fall to the ground, but she wouldn't allow herself.

Instead, she stared at him as he stared at her. The inclination to blink was too dangerous to consider. She thought as he watched. Intermittently waving. Intermittently smiling. Sometimes pulling his hands full of air in front of him, asking her to come near. She looked around the crowd and noticed that no one was noticing her or their exchange. No man was going to ask her if she was alright or threaten to beat Victor's face in.

Despite the disdain of her friends, Victor was the man she'd loved. He was also a criminal who poisoned a child. He had gone to great lengths to ruin her life. She knew he had every intention of killing her. And there she stood. Forty feet away. In a parking lot of sleepy zombies. And with a woman binding herself in a black sweater overseeing them all. Summer turned to find her.

"Excuse me," Summer whispered, pushing through small gaps in the crowd. "Sorry, can I get through? Excuse me," she muttered until she reached the very front where the woman kept watch over them like a camp counselor.

"Ma'am," she said as she saw Summer wriggle outside the front line of the crowd, "we haven't been given the all-clear."

"Okay." Summer realized there was no fire truck or men. There were no hats or hoses. "Is the fire department coming?"

"They're already here," she replied and pushed up her glasses, "in the back of the building."

"I don't see any lights, though," Summer pressed.

"Ma'am," the woman's sweater hung open and revealed a low-cut black shirt and a silver-maned horse tattoo peeking out from her left breast, "we'll let you know when we can go back in."

"I want to leave," Summer replied.

"Excuse me?" the woman responded.

"Yeah, I want to leave. I'm not going to be able to sleep now. I was going to leave at like six anyway. It's already close to four."

"Then why did you verify our check-out time?" The woman frowned.

"Just in case I overslept. Really, that's just check-in conversation." Summer stood wringing her fingers. She looked over her shoulder again, trying to spot Victor.

"Okay. Everything looks good." Summer turned back around to find a man in a navy uniform and heavy fluorescent jacket standing with his legs apart. "We didn't find anything except a pulled fire alarm in the back hallway. Second floor. Maybe a kid pulled it or something."

"That's why we've been keeping the doors locked after 11 every night. We've been having some trouble with kids coming in and messing with stuff." The woman wrapped herself in her sweater again. Summer watched the woman's face flush and realized she wasn't cold, she was scared. "Thank you for coming out. Can you tell them," she pointed her thumb backward over her shoulder into the crowd, "that it's safe to come back in?"

"Course."

The firefighter confidently strolled to his truck, which had been pulled to the back of the lot. He climbed up the side to get in the passenger's seat, unhooked the speaker from its latch overhead, and gave the all-clear. The crowd responded as if they'd planned to sleep in the parking lot—slowly, even annoyed. The truck pulled away, and as the crowd thinned in front of Summer's car, she realized Victor had disappeared.

"Ma'am!" the woman shouted to her. "Ma'am, do you still want to check out now?"

"Yes!" Summer shouted and moved her feet to the charging rhythm of her heart in her chest. She chipped nail polish from her big toes as she rushed across the cracked black asphalt. She knew he could be standing anywhere now, and if he planned to shoot her, she'd be less of a target in her car than in an emptying parking lot. She thought she felt a bullet strike her in the neck. She blinked her eyes to shake it off. She got to her car door and imagined she could feel his hands grip her ankles. She stooped to look under the car. Nothing. She opened the door and peered inside. Nothing. She kneeled in her seat and looked on the floor. Nothing. Even the trunk held no signs of him. She was not reassured, though. For all the years she'd wanted him, Summer had never been able to keep Victor. Now, even with the car empty, she realized that until one of them was dead, she'd never be able to lose him.

33

THE EMPTY HIGHWAY extended for long, dizzying stretches. On occasion, an eighteen-wheeler would whiz by. Summer grimaced and moved to another lane every time. Her hands throbbed around her steering wheel. Burning eyes and tight shoulders inspired excess blinks and deep breaths. She turned on the radio for companionship and wakefulness, but radio stations waned and died out into sizzling static every few hours. By 10:00 A.M., it started. The phone calls. Summer ignored them for the first couple of hours. They were from her father and Victor. They were from her mother and Phoebe. But then, when Tomas called, she answered.

"¡*Dime!*"

"Summer! ¿*Donde estas?* Your parents are blowing up my phone!" Tomas's voice reached a higher pitch than she'd ever heard from him.

She giggled, then fell silent.

"Honestly, it's not funny," Tomas continued. Voices and traffic noise blared behind him.

"You at Jackson?" She knew Tomas would be at the hospital. Maybe the time had come for him to do his presentation. Thursday morning. Back to work.

"Where are you?!" he demanded.

"I'm on my way to see you." Summer winked as if he could see her. "I just finished eating. It was just hash browns and ketchup 'cause the breakfast burrito was gross. I'm in Virginia Beach still, I think." She replied, then giggled again. "Surprise!" The chorus of James Blount's song "You're Beautiful" danced from her head onto her lips.

"Hey, Summer. C'mon, stop. What do you mean you're on your way to see me?" Strain tightened Tomas's voice.

"Literally, I'm driving down to you guys right now. I've been on the road six hours already!" Summer's mood swung from delirium to glee.

"Why didn't you tell anyone?"

"It's a surprise?" She squeezed her brows into a frown. "C'mon, don't be mad at me. I'm laughing now, but there is so much going on up here. Honestly, I'm just laughing so I don't go nuts again." She flapped her right hand at her eyes to quell the budding tears.

"But, Summer, you could have at least told *me* that you were getting on the road."

"I know. It wasn't planned. None of it was planned."

"So, what happened with the video?" Tomas tried to change the topic.

"Agent Cline never showed up. Victor did, though, and I freaked out."

"What?!" Tomas yelled, "What do you mean Victor showed up?!"

"Seriously!" Summer responded. "It's too much to even say over the phone. Victor is literally stalking me. All this stuff happened last night at this hotel."

"What hotel?" Tomas squinted.

"I'll tell you later. Anyway, I haven't seen him behind me since I got on the highway. But I'm scared out of my mind right now. I tried to take some Benadryl 'cause I was so anxious. But you know how medicines make me." Summer's eyes lifted to her rearview mirror and bounced from lane to lane behind her. No sign of Victor.

"And you're driving? Alone?!"

"I know. But what was I supposed to do?!"

"Did you get this approved, Summer?" Tomas's voice was loud again. "Are you even allowed to cross the state line?"

Summer's heart stopped in her chest. The acidic orange juice from her breakfast combo bubbled in her belly. It hadn't once occurred to her that she was out on bail. And not just any bail. Bail for murder. She didn't remember being told, but she was pretty sure leaving Maryland qualified her for another arrest if she got pulled over. She could not find her words.

"Summer?" Tomas spoke into the silence. "How far away are you?"

"Uh…" she gasped for air. "I don't know. I guess like another ten or so hours. Far."

"Are you going to stop and stay over somewhere?"

"I have to go." Summer replied abruptly. "Don't tell my parents you talked to me. I want them to be scared, both of them."

"What do you mean?" Tomas asked.

"Both. Just trust me. I'll see you soon."

"Summer, let me meet you somewhere. I'll drive up, and then we can drive the rest of the way down together."

"That's sweet, and I love you for the offer," she replied. "But I can do this myself."

"I know you can. But there's being strong, and then there's being stupid," Tomas sighed. "I'm gonna drive up to Daytona when I leave the hospital later, okay?"

"Okay." The realization that she might be a fugitive subdued her delirium and its giggles.

"*Bueno.* Go to Daytona and meet me there. You know that Friendly's right across from the Speedway on International?"

Summer knew. It's where they'd always gotten ice cream on their spring break trips to "The World's Greatest Beach."

"Of course, *Bebo.*"

"Okay, meet me there. Promise me, Summer."

"I promise," she responded. "But *Bebo!*" she shouted before he hung up. "I'm serious. Don't tell anyone we talked, okay? Promise me, too."

Tomas groaned.

"Just promise, *Bebo!*" Summer pleaded.

"Okay, I promise. See you."

"See you." Summer ended the call.

A highway sign read, "Welcome to North Carolina, STATE LINE, Surry County." *Now I've crossed two state lines, Bebo.* Summer counted in her shaking head.

"DR. TORNES, IS THERE A PROBLEM?" Tomas's attending physician stopped afternoon rounds. "What's so important on your phone? We'll wait."

"Uh, no, sorry." Tomas stuffed his phone back into his white coat between napkins and a blue-and-gold *Pocket Medicine* book. "I was just turning off the sound."

"Well, don't. Pay attention." The doctor turned to Tomas's classmate and nodded for her to continue.

I need to go, Tomas thought. *I don't even need to be here for this.* 3:54 P.M. Hardly late in a hospital workday. But he kept having visions of Summer half-asleep, rolling into a ditch to her death. He'd already managed to beg a classmate to wrap up his last hour of clinic. Patients would need labs repeated. Some would need a Kreyol or Farsi interpreter. There would be women eight weeks pregnant and miscarrying. They wouldn't understand that they weren't at the obstetrics clinic. They also wouldn't understand no one at *that* clinic would be able to save the pregnancy anyway. And then there would be women who would push themselves backward on the table at every attempt to examine them. "One more hour" in the general gynecology clinic could become three. Or four. Asking for coverage after four days of vacation might earn him enemies. He understood this.

From what he remembered of the patient census, afternoon rounds should have been quick. But there was always that classmate who had to add extra details to their report, maybe a journal study mention. Then they'd pontificate with the attending. Maybe they'd try to connect with the attending's native culture, using random words in Spanish or Portuguese whose meaning or context they didn't truly understand. But this was how some residents "gunned" for recommendation letters or a fellowship spot. This was as much a part of medical training as difficult classes and wearing a stethoscope. And all this had to happen at the end of an annoying and stressful day. A day when the team just wanted to sign out and avoid even looking at the on-call pager.

Tomas missed the opportunity to page himself out of rounds. He knew the attending would veto him going to respond to any other call in any other part of the hospital anyway. And one could never excuse themselves to the bathroom. Doctors-in-training do not go the bathroom. They ignore the urge and focus and pray they don't pee on themselves. Tomas looked at the time on the patient's room clock. 4:06.

After the attending laid a compassionate hand on his patient's forearm, reassuring her, the group migrated into the hall. Tomas's classmate still talked, giving a complete dissertation on her patient's urinalysis and her theories on its inconsistencies.

"Just culture it," Tomas said, not realizing the thought had not stayed in his head but tumbled from his mouth. As soon as he heard himself, he slowly blinked, then sighed.

His attending looked at him again. Directly in the eyes. A silent stare intentioned to kill. This attending, whose work ethic redefined the word "thorough," had no family to rush home to. He never admitted it, but the hospital was his life. His patients his children. The nurses his loves. And his residents his audience. Attempting to rush him out of his glory would result in punishment. Tomas knew it. He was going to "scut" him to death with tedious busy work. He'd never let him leave now.

6:47. Tomas had spent two and a half hours reviewing the team's labs, dressing wounds, and calling outpatient gynecologists—all tasks he could have done the following morning if he'd been able to keep his mouth closed.

252

"Dr. Tornes," the attending said as he stopped by the nursing station with his briefcase, "isn't your father Andres?"

"*Si*, I mean yes."

"Hmm," the attending said and turned to leave. Tomas had no idea how to read the *hmm*, but it felt ominous. He decided to wait until seven to leave.

"Summer! Bro, I'm so sorry. I literally just got out of rounds. Pissed off Dr. Driver." Tomas ran down the sidewalk that separated planters of tropical Miami blooms from the benches outside the Labor and Delivery entrance.

"Oh my God!" she responded. "It's gonna take you 'til, like, midnight to get here." Friendly's brimmed with senior citizens and school-aged children. The sun set behind the Speedway.

"I know. I'm so sorry."

"*Bebo*, honestly, I'll be fine. I'm not gonna wait and then drive in the middle of the night. Okay?"

"But we can leave your car, and I'll do all the driving."

"No, *Bebo*."

"Or we can stay over and drive down super early. I'm not on call to-morrow."

"*Bebo*, we'd have to leave by two in the morning so you could get back to rounds on time. It's okay, seriously."

"But at least you'd be able to sleep in the car."

"It's okay, *Bebo*."

"I'm really sorry, Summer." Tomas had stopped running. "I wanted to be there."

"You're always there for me," Summer replied. "No worries! I'll see you tomorrow. And since you're not on call, let's all meet up at Versailles tomorrow night." She couldn't remember the last time she sat with all her friends around a large table at the family-owned mecca of Miami's Cuban cuisine, but she needed it.

"Okay, I'll see you tomorrow. Be safe. Text me where you are, okay?"

"I will. Talk to you soon. Get out of there before Driver calls you back!" Summer said with a laugh.

Summer walked from her table at Friendly's back to her car. She wanted real food—not the ice cream store version of burgers. She drove down International Speedway Boulevard, passing the mall, an Olive Garden, and a string of fast-food restaurants across from a hospital and a high school. The school's name was in royal blue letters. She continued driving over the narrow and bumpy streets until she came to a park at the river-front.

"Ohhh, I smell shrimp!" she shouted and parked in the near-empty lot next to a tiny restaurant.

When Summer had driven into Florida about four hours before, and the palmetto trees lined the roads in a much more welcoming way than the tornadoes had in her last dream, she knew she was almost home.

The bell on the door announced her at Dot's Seafood. Jimmy still stood at the register. His blue Bic still nestled over his ear. Summer tapped her forefingers on the menu on the counter. The light caught her silver forefinger ring. Jimmy told her she was the most beautiful thing he'd seen all day. She ordered a shrimp basket and hush puppies. And they were in a red-and-white carton. They were hot and warmed her hand through the brown bag they were placed in. And nothing triggered a single memory of being there the year before. Not one single memory.

34

"WHERE THE HELL ARE YOU?" The bass of Manny's voice pounded into his phone. Victor sat clearing his throat on the other end of the line.

"Well, I, um…" Victor gulped against his tightening chest. His car sat behind a concrete pillar at the largest free parking deck in Boca Raton, just four rows behind Summer. He'd followed her as she crept by Veterans Memorial Park and around Sinai Ranches. She'd landed here. Victor didn't know why.

"I know you're not in town! Your receptionist told me." Manny shouted.

"Well, I drove down to Florida," Victor finally spat out his answer. He bit his bottom lip and tapped his fingertips on his steering wheel.

"For what?!" Manny demanded. "We have business up here right now."

"I won't be long. I j–just," Victor stuttered, "came down for a Grand Rounds at the med school. My buddy from FSU is giving one tomorrow." Victor's breath escaped in quick pulses. He tried to speak in short sentences.

He watched the rear windshield of Summer's car. She reclined her seat and turned off the engine.

"He thought I still lived here. He invited me. I didn't have anything to do. I thought it was okay," Victor almost whined.

"You didn't have anything to do, huh? You don't remember we agreed to do something about Cline?" He paused. "And do you think I believe you drove sixteen hours to hear a Grand Rounds presentation? You are not smarter than me, Vic. Believe me when I tell you. Is this about Summer? Do you know where she is?"

"I'm telling you the truth. I don't know where Summer is, but I thought I did what you asked."

"Stop lying. You know you didn't do what I asked. I told you to make sure he didn't come lurking around my house, asking my maid questions." Victor heard a loud boom and imagined Manny pounding his knuckles down into his kitchen countertop. "'Cause I want this handled and him gone before my wife gets back!"

"Where is she?" Victor inquired, hoping to sound innocent.

"I'd recommend you just worry about what I'm gonna do," Manny growled, "if you don't get your punk ass back to Baltimore tonight." The phone went dead. Victor didn't know what would happen if he didn't show. He decided not to call back to ask.

But Victor had the taste of other blood on his tongue. It consumed him and any thought of Marvin Cline. Instead, he salivated over the thought of killing Summer. He wanted to do it now, but there were cameras. Victor let a smug grin pull at the corners of his dusky pink lips, pleased that he'd gotten so close without her even noticing. Victor decided to leave the garage to pay one of Summer's old Boca-area friends a visit.

He looked down in his lap and rubbed the paper towel she'd dried her hands on at the Citgo back in Maryland. It would be the first of his trophies from her murder, he imagined.

MARVIN WRIGGLED HIS HEAD from side to side in the rounded wall of blackness. Gauze wrapped around his neck and through his parted lips. It smelled of his saliva and an antiseptic spray. He could not slip either wrist from the binding. Each pull against the rope tightened its grip and chafed away a layer of his wrinkled flesh. A dull, penetrating ache throbbed just inside each of his kneecaps. The same plagued the left shoulder he lay on. He could not see where he was but was intoxicated by the smell of fermented grapes and rum. He thought he heard thunder rolling. It was Manny's voice.

"I have one kid, Cline, and you know that." Manny knelt and placed his cheek on the empty barrel in his wine cellar. "And I asked you to stay away from her."

Marvin's eyes were wide and scanning back and forth.

"Now, 'cause you don't listen, we had to put you in here. Had to put you in my vintage Bordeaux barrel." Manny sucked his teeth. "A distillery back home sent this to me. I wanted to put rum in this, man." Marvin heard him tapping the barrel.

"Why are you so fixated on Dara? So loyal? You're not sleeping with my wife, are you, Cline?" He waited.

"Cline!" Manny continued. "Nah, you can't be. Aren't you gay? Hey, don't be sensitive," Manny shouted, as if Marvin had actually mounted a defense. "It's not my business. Doesn't matter to me. I'm just saying you better not be sleeping with my wife!" Silence.

"¡Holaaaaaa!" Marvin heard knocking on the barrel as Manny's laughter danced off hundreds of wine bottles, perched and pretty in their cases. "I'm really sorry we had to get in the way of your little meeting today with my daughter. What was that about anyway? Huh?!" Manny shouted and the notes of his voice became loosened, deranged.

"I warned you! I'm a good guy, Cline. Why did you have to try me? No one is going to look for you in my house. You know that."

Inside the blackness of the barrel, terror rattled through Marvin's chest. Tears were drawn into the rough gauze. His daughter's blonde hair rustled under his nose as his life's scenes filed through his mind. He wrapped her in his arms, and her giggles tickled his ear. He smiled, remembering her tiny four-year-old voice. Then, a brilliant flash hammered down. And he was gone.

"That smells smoky, but the silencer actually worked," Manny said, sliding his gun into a pine box on a corner shelf. "Good. Time to go catch the game." He nestled the barrel back into its place in the cellar.

THE DAY SHONE THROUGH the concrete slats and green gating in the D garage of Mizner Park. Summer's eyes met an overcast glare. The pulsing light of the sun shone bright white behind a straggling cloud and settled a pressure behind Summer's right eye.

Her stomach grumbled, but she decided to ignore it. Back in Boca, her mind reveled in every childhood memory she had of the place. And her Aunt Libby. Her lovely and favorite Aunt Libby. The one who lived in Horseshoe Acres. The one who worked in nursing for the fun, never the money. Summer's Aunt Elizabeth had been one of the major loves of her growing-up-in-Florida life. Aunt Libby could flash her perfect smile and dance and tell stories and chase and take you to the stables and brush horses. She could make you feel just like you were her very own daughter. Summer knew *that* Aunt Libby had given way to the homeless one who lived in the Veterans Memorial Park over on West Palmetto. She'd become the family's fragile tragedy, set on end by a fire that killed all her horses but one. That night, twelve-foot flames had engulfed the stables and a trailer on the property. Aunt Libby could do nothing but cry into the T-shirt she covered her face with at the scene. Firemen held her back from running into the blaze. They never determined the cause of the fire. In the months that followed, a spiraling mental breakdown made her forget her medical skills and fall into a pit of paranoia.

And after what my father did… Summer came back to her present-day thoughts, shaking her head. *Poor Aunt Libby.* Summer didn't remember her from the train or when she'd corrected her name to "Tuh-rez." Summer had last visited her Aunt Libby before the Match Ceremony in Spring of 2005, when Summer had learned where she'd go for her residency training. She had hoped it would be Baltimore—both for Victor and for a simpler life than Miami could provide. That day, Summer had found her Aunt Libby standing beside a bust of a veteran in the park. She was talking to him and tried to give him a piece of mango.

Today Summer drank in the ruffled gray and white clouds of a Boca Raton morning. She'd almost forgotten the wavy green leaves of mangroves and mixed tiny palmettos that lined the streets. Square buildings in peaches and yellows watched as she drove by. They held balconies and hopes and wealth. The Spanish-tiled roofs and arched breezeways marked higher sights. Summer set her eyes on them all. Though an hour north of where she grew up, the humidity still told her she was home.

"Aunt Libby..." Summer spoke to herself and her car, "...where are you?" She turned left into the park and scanned the space, especially to the right, where five dutiful statues flanked the flag. The benches beside them held no visitors or veterans. When three laps through the park didn't yield a sighting, Summer decided to pass by her aunt's old job. Back by the Sinai Ranches. But that became another fruitless search through a set of building loops.

Summer pulled into a Pollo Tropical. She needed to use the restroom. It was too early for rice and beans and chicken.

"¡Oye!" a worker at the register called out to her. "No public bathroom, mami! You have to order."

Summer nodded and waved. She would order chicken and plantains as soon as she peed.

"Uh, yes, can I have a quarter-chicken platter?" Summer fished around in her purse as a timid, smiling worker prepared her plate. Summer's cell phone rang. Carla.

"Summer! Oh my God, are you here?!" Her voice bounced with excitement.

"Bebo has a big mouth." Summer laughed. "Uh, white meat, sorry."

"Where are you?"

"Pollo."

"Pollo?! Why are you eating there?!"

"Shut up! You taking us to Versailles tonight?" Summer teased.

"Supposably!" The two laughed at the word's Miamian pronunciation.

"I better see you tonight! Let me call you back. I have to pay." Summer's cheek pressed "end" on her phone. She collected her change and the plastic bag decorated in green and yellow and palms. She looked down into her bag as she walked toward the condiments, glancing up just seconds before she slammed into a woman's side.

"Oh my gosh, sorry!" she said, stumbling backward. She stopped and frowned. Beside her mother stood her Aunt Libby, holding a quart of barbecue sauce.

"Summer?!" Dara chuckled and reached out to embrace her daughter's shoulders. Summer did not smile but instead squinted and looked to her aunt and the sauce.

"Mom, wait, I thought you were in Delaware!"

"And I thought you were in Baltimore!" Dara winked. Summer still did not smile.

"I told you, Dara," Libby laughed, "you should just tell her." Libby grinned at her niece. She had about sixteen teeth, all congregated at the right side of her mouth. Summer's stomach dropped. Instead of returning her mother's affection, she pushed her hands gently from her shoulders and reached for her aunt.

"Aunt Libby," Summer bent to hug her, "it's been so long. How are you?"

"Hasn't been that long, baby girl," Dara interjected. "Aunt Libby actually saw you on the train during your fugue. How long ago now, Libby? Maybe a month since she last saw you?"

Summer's tears returned.

"You were being so crazy," Libby laughed. "Told me your name was *Tuh-rez*." Libby began gyrating in front of the condiment station, singing "uh-huh, uh-huh" and "Tuh-rez, Tuh-rez." She looked into Summer's eyes, howling with laughter, but stopped when she saw the tears. "Oh God, why are you crying? I'm sorry, Summer, but you deserve this. You ignored me every day on the train, so tough!"

"Let us order something, Summer, and then we'll sit and have a talk. Seems like we could use a good one." Dara reached for her daughter's shoulder again. This time Summer didn't push her away. Instead, she wiped away tears.

The tables in Pollo Tropical sparkled with glistening epoxy resin. Summer picked a booth by the front window. Back at the counter, her Aunt Libby's raspy voice filled the empty restaurant with a rowdy rant and conspiracy theories. Her familiar voice wrapped in the violence of a psychotic thought process placed a stabbing ache in Summer's soul. This was the look of a woman broken by a life of more disappointment than is human to bear. Summer's heart fell again, then shattered. Memories of horses and playing with her aunt and beach sand between their carefree toes brought pain to the fore, seasoning her rice in tears.

Her eyes still burned when her breakfast companions joined her at the table.

"Summer, I know I have a lot of explaining to do." Dara emptied their trays and sat with her food before her. "Have a seat, Libby."

"Summer!" Libby interrupted, "did you know that your mom has people from her job making body doubles of me? Right off the 3-D printer."

Dara looked at her sister, wondering if her dosage was correct.

"Sorry to hear that, Aunt Libby," Summer said, sniffling. She took a bite of her chicken breast.

"Baby girl, you look like you're not feeling too well. Your eyes are red. Have you had a chance to wash up lately? What's in your hair? And what happened here?" Dara asked, pointing to the split in Summer's bottom lip.

"Mom," Summer looked up. "I'm too tired for a thousand questions and small talk right now. You lied and told me you were going to Delaware."

Libby held up the "L" fingers again. Dara shooed them down.

"And right now, I really need to know who in my family I can actually trust." She sniffed. "Victor probably followed me down here and is probably lurking around somewhere. And the reason I came down in the first place is because I read your diary. I'm sorry." Summer looked at her mother, who peered back at her over her glasses with kindness in her eyes.

"Victor is here?" Dara asked.

"I don't care, Mom. Can you please acknowledge what I just said?" Summer asked. Her face throbbed.

"I know and…"

"And what, Mom? It seems like what the diary says is that Mair is Aunt Libby's and Dad's daughter." Summer was surprised at the sudden nauseated gut punch that hit her. "Is that true?"

Aunt Libby looked down at the table.

"Are you guys saying my dad is a rapist and Mair is the…" she lifted her hands to the sky then down again, "…product of that?!"

Libby stared at Dara, then back at Summer, and at her barbecue sauce.

"It is true, baby girl," Dara started. "It is."

"And?!" Summer wanted more. A backstory. An explanation for how she'd played house with a monster for all this time.

"And that's it. And we handled it in the quietest, least damaging way we could, Summer. I'm so, so sorry you found out this way. It wasn't really my story to tell. Mair has known since you guys were in high school, though."

"Aunt Libby?!" Summer pleaded with her aunt. "Is that true?!"

"Summer," Libby replied, at once serious and sober, "when the Pentagon puts you on assignment, you don't turn them down."

Dara sighed, then took a sip of Mountain Dew. "Libby," she said, "I'm going to come back to do the shot in two weeks next time."

35

"VERSAILLES!" TOMAS SHOUTED in the parking lot. He'd come straight from the hospital and wore a fresh set of green scrubs he'd changed into. Summer descended from her car and wrapped her arms around her friend as if it had been years since they last met.

"I finally made it," she casually said as Tomas stooped to kiss both her cheeks. "Who's coming tonight?"

"¡*Todos!*" Tomas announced, excited that all their friends would join them for dinner.

"When are you on call again?" Summer tried to stay focused on his eyes. She didn't want Tomas to notice she was checking around her. A crowd of Cuban-American locals, and tourists, streamed into the parking lot. She felt both protected and vulnerable in the throngs of people. Victor could be anywhere.

"*Mañana*," he said, laughing. "But that's tomorrow. Tonight, I'm here with my friends, and I'm going to eat everything on the table, and it's gonna be delicious!" He laughed and poked her in the belly.

"How many coladas have you already had today?" Summer joked. Her friend seemed caffeinated and hyper.

"Not enough! Let's go to the *ventanita* while we wait for everyone. You know they'll be late."

"Ah, I know you think you're the stud of the coffee window, you poser!" Summer wore a black tank top and jeans. Even in September, Miami's humidity made her wish she'd worn a dress. She joked to try to feel light.

"The women at these windows love to make coffee for me, you hater!" Tomas said as they scurried across the lot.

Music from inside trickled out, entertaining the passersby on Calle Ocho. The smells and sounds of Miami shrouded Summer in memories—memories amplified in their importance since the fugue.

Tomas began to order from the window. Small women with their hair in updos spun through their tiny café, whipping sugar into foam. One elderly lady with ruby lipstick slid a Styrofoam cup of Cuban coffee across to Tomas. She stacked five tiny white cups on the lid. He'd pour coffee in each to share with his friends. The woman working the window asked if his wife wanted to order any pastries. He smiled.

"Oh, she's not my wife!" he replied in Spanish. "She's too bossy!"

"You look like you can handle it," the woman responded, laughing. "I think you're man enough for a bossy lady." The old woman winked at Summer. Tomas laughed and looked down at her. He noticed her skin didn't sparkle as usual, and neither did her eyes. He wrapped his right arm around her shoulder and pulled her to the side of the service window.

"You okay?" he whispered in her ear.

"Not really, *Bebo*."

"*No te preocupes.*" He held her to his scrubs. "Everything's fine. You don't need to worry."

"Oh my God! Why are you guys constantly touching each other?!" A familiar voice greeted them.

"Hey! Finally! Go get us a VIP table!" Tomas half joked. Carla had family connections at Versailles, and he knew she only used them for her most beloved friends. Tonight was special. Summer was back. Carla had called the restaurant hours earlier and asked one of her cousins to set them up for a grand time—a reunion dinner of sorts.

"We already roasted a pig for you, greedy!" she teased Tomas and kissed his cheeks.

Carla's dark brown hair hung below her shoulders. She wore a yellow sundress with a ruffle across the bust. Her skin looked milky in the dusk light. She smiled as wide as her entire face, and she, too, wore ruby-colored cream on her lips.

"¡*Que bella!*" Summer hugged and kissed her friend, holding her hand and taking in her beauty.

"You always look pretty, and I hate you for it," Carla teased. "Where's *la gringa?*" Carla meant Phoebe. "I don't expect any of the rest of you Cubans to show up on time."

Summer's stomach writhed in nervousness at the thought of seeing Phoebe. There had been no new indication something was wrong. Just a feeling.

Besides, Summer's worries riddled her mind. She was as troubled as tempest-plagued waters to know Mair was not only her former friend and sworn enemy—she was her sister, too.

Everyone began to mill in and kiss and compliment or lovingly tease about each other's looks. Finally, the group took a long table at the back of the restaurant near mirrors whose etched designs shone white light. The forest green and tan of Versailles rose to meet them like the royalty they felt they were in this place. Long tables held family-style food: spreads of fried yuca and plantain, black beans and white rice, pork, and beef in tomato sauce. And the restaurant moved with sound and conversation and salsa—the most alive and authentically Cuban restaurant in all of Miami.

"Did you guys know our parents used to hang out at Versailles all the time in med school? But then it was just a coffee shop." Phoebe had joined the group but sat on the opposite end, farthest from Summer. *Maybe it was too much seeing me lose my mind*, Summer thought as she scooped cilantro cream onto a piece of yuca.

"Why do you pronounce it like *Ver-sigh?*" Luca teased Phoebe.

"Uh, 'cause that's how it's pronounced," she replied.

"Americans!" he teased her. "*Ver-size!* Give it some flavor!" Everybody laughed at their only friend who was not of Latin descent.

"*Pobrecita*," Carla laughed. "Poor thing."

"Anyway…" Phoebe laughed and swatted at Carla. "…Summer's mom used to kind of run a little matchmaking thing."

"Really?" Luca inquired. He was friends with Tomas and only associates with the others. He was unfamiliar with their group stories.

"Yeah, she set up most of our dads with our moms. Actually, all our dads. You know, 'cause they were all in the same med school class."

"She told me she got tired of being one of only three women in their class," Carla jumped in, "so she set our dads up with the most beautiful women she knew from around town." Carla pointed to her own face to indicate she'd inherited her mother's looks. "I think she just wanted her own girlfriends. And to get *Tio* Manny serious enough to get married and make some babies!"

"And that's how we all got here," Tomas concluded.

"But who were the other women?" Luca inquired.

"In their class?" Phoebe asked. "Alejandra Kent. You know her. Mair's mom. And then some other woman. I think she's a dermatologist."

Carla laughed. "Only Dara could set up our entire lives through her shrink mind control."

The table laughed again.

"Psychiatrists are kinda creepy, bro," Luca added.

Phoebe rolled her eyes. "Luca, come on, you're a doctor. That's ridiculous."

"Dara's a good person," Phoebe kept talking around bites of plantain. "She's not like some psychiatrist who sleeps with her patients or is trying to analyze every conversation or whatever BS you see on TV."

"True!" Tomas chimed in. "But it is also true she kind of orchestrated our little social group. I find it disturbing I've been stuck with you losers my entire life." Tomas turned pink with laughter and pushed his hair back.

Summer had been occupied covering her *tostones* in salt and garlic.

"So, Summer…" Carla pulled her into the conversation, "…this better than eating at Pollo?!"

266

"Pollo's delicious!" Luca chimed in. "Okay, it's not Versailles, but, I mean, I like the rice."

Summer smiled. "I literally just went there to pee." She tried to giggle, but nothing happened. She decided to keep talking once she held the table's attention. "But you guys, I've got so much to tell you."

Phoebe shifted in her seat, then sipped her mojito. She commented on how delicious the *ropa vieja* tasted. Summer didn't see the change in her face, but Tomas did. He mouthed the words "What's wrong?" to Phoebe and watched her as Summer spoke.

"So, I—" Summer stopped, not knowing how to break into the story she wanted to share. "Guys, you're not going to believe this. I just found out Mair is my dad's kid," her chest heaved with a deep breath. Her eyes bounced to each face, worried they would think she was having another mental episode.

Everyone fell speechless except Carla, who shouted "¿Que?" and wiped her mouth. She looked at everyone at the table. "What are you talking about?!"

"It's a super long story." Summer sighed.

"Well, prepare to tell it, *chica*. We're not going anywhere!" Carla insisted.

"Ugh, I don't even know where to start." Summer sat back in her chair and smoothed up her bun with the condensation from her water glass. "My life is literally falling apart, you guys. Okay, my parents have been acting so weird lately. I found my mom's diary in one of the patient charts in her office."

"You were in her office?" Carla asked.

"Her home office," Summer responded.

"Reading her charts? And her diary?" Phoebe said.

"Listen, you guys… oh my God!" Summer interjected. "I was looking for a DSM, honestly, 'cause I was trying to read up on fugue states and dissociation. Long story, but I needed to read it. Anyway, I opened her desk drawer and found charts. I read one and realized it made me feel better to see someone else struggling. Made me feel less like a psycho. So, I kept going." She placed her hands on her cheeks. "I shouldn't have."

Phoebe looked down at the table and then searched for some food she wanted to try. "Can you pass me the *lechon asado*?" She tapped Luca, who had been sitting with his head tilted to the side, listening to Summer's story.

"Anyway," Summer continued, "I found this chart that really is a diary."

Carla opened her eyes as wide as they would let her, and her lips parted.

"And there was all this stuff where my mom's talking about this party they all went to. "

"Who?" Luca asked.

"My mom and dad and a bunch of other people from their class. Like when they were in med school. She took my aunt with her..." Summer paused, "...and my mom's, like, calling my dad a rapist in this thing she wrote."

"*¿Que?*" Carla repeated. She held her mouth open. A white ring where her lipstick had worn away created an "O" of her lips. "Hold on. This is really serious, Summer. *¿En serio?*"

"I know. I know." Summer held up her palm for Carla to stop, then frowned and leaned her elbows onto the table. Her black tank top revealed her cleavage, which had started to pale in the Maryland autumn.

"I actually ran into my mom here today. At Pollo of all places. And she was with my aunt."

"What aunt?" Phoebe asked.

"The one with the mental problems. Libby. The one I was just talking about. The homeless one." Summer shook her head. Phoebe knew that was her only aunt.

Phoebe and Tomas looked at each other.

"You randomly ran into them at Pollo?" Carla seemed to be reaching ascending levels of shock.

"*¡Si!* Anyway, the diary was saying my dad raped her."

"Raped who?!" Carla whispered.

"Libby!" Summer continued. "And she got pregnant with Mair. I actually called and tried to ask my mom about it yesterday, and she blatantly lied. So since I lost my job and have nothing else to do..."

"You lost your job?! As in you got fired from residency?!" Carla cupped her forehead just below her widow's peak. Summer was relieved Tomas hadn't told them about the murder charges.

"Long story. But I came down here to ask Libby myself—about the rape and Mair. Then I see my mom here. She's supposed to be in Delaware!" Summer's voice carried loud enough now to be heard over the bustle of the restaurant and the music. Tomas put a calming hand on her back.

"*Shhhh*." Tomas leaned in closer to her face. "You may not want your family business out like that. You know every ear in Miami is in here right now."

"I don't even care anymore," she lied. "I don't even know who my family is anyway."

"So you lost your job? Why? And you and Mair are, what, sisters now?!" Carla's mouth hung open. She sat back with folded arms. "Your mom must have some explanation."

"Not technically sisters," Phoebe interjected.

"What's that supposed to mean, 'not technically?'" Carla looked at her friend and frowned. Her eyebrows crinkled in the center of her face. She closed her lips and squared her jaw.

Phoebe didn't say more but kept eating.

"Summer, are you sure?" Tomas asked. He'd lowered his voice and was holding her around the ribs.

"*Bebo*, I literally asked my mom and Libby today." The garlic in her mouth made her thirsty. She sipped her water, "I'm sure."

A tense stillness sat on the table. Everyone stared at their plates and pushed food with their forks. They let the restaurant's music talk for them.

"Where are you staying while you're down here?" Luca finally asked.

"I didn't get a hotel or anything."

269

"Stay with us," Tomas jumped to invite her. She didn't resist. Everyone knew Tomas was so in love with Summer he couldn't stand himself.

"It's about time you guys got it on," Carla teased. "Go get a Cuban sandwich for the road, to tide you over for a lonnnng night." She winked, and the cloud over the table lifted a tad.

"Bathroom!" Carla announced, and all the girls at the table stood.

"I'll never get that." Luca chuckled at the group trip to the lavatory. "Wanna go to the bathroom with me, *Bebo*?" The men laughed. They didn't notice Summer frozen in place.

"*Chica. ¡Vamos!* Come on!" Carla called from the aisle leading to the restrooms.

Summer's nose was turning a deep pink, and a tear dropped from her left eye. She stared down at her phone. It dropped from her shaking hands and landed on the corner of a plate, sending the fork that sat there flying to the center of the table.

"What's the matter?" Tomas picked up the phone and looked at the screen. "Oh my God, Summer. We need to call the police!"

270

36

ST. AUGUSTINE GRASS CRUNCHED UNDER VICTOR'S FEET. Spanish moss hung from the oaks. The overcast sky in Boca shielded him and his tour guide from the harshest rays of sun. Sometimes, a breeze blew past his face or through his shirt. Marla's Acres was one of the most peaceful horse stables and farms near Boca.

An elderly man in gray overalls and a pink plaid shirt met Victor at the farm's front fence. "My wife typically does the tours," he said. "But we've got a calf being born as we speak. Come on this way."

The property at Marla's spread in all directions. Birds called and marked territory. Tiny purple moths flitted over damp areas. Roosters sometimes called to announce their presence, not the time.

"Beautiful place," Victor said. "How long have you had it?"

"This place?" The old man shook his head. "Well, this land has been in the family since long before the war."

"Civil War?"

"That's right. Belongs to my wife's people for generations. She's part Seminole." The man walked with his hands behind his hunched back. "Used to be an Indian camp right over there." He pointed. "Right on over by the lake. Lake Ida."

"How'd they keep it?" Victor asked, looking at the sky and wanting rain.

"Smarts and strategy." The history lesson continued. "Figured out a way to con Billy Linton out of buying up these acres." He waved his hands around. "And to keep that Flagler railway from busting up the property. Sometimes you've got to make people think they're getting over on you."

"What do you mean?"

"Ah, well, my wife's people figured they'd make a deal with some of the whites in the area. Even married a few. And when the time came to start talking about who was gonna get this and that, they were able to stake their claim. Mainly on account of being married to the right folks."

"I see." Victor nodded. "Marriage of convenience."

"Business agreements. It's what it came down to. Woulda done the same had I been there." The elderly man walked Victor to the door of their barn. Two large doors stood open on either end of the white-and-green structure. Horses poked their heads from their stalls, interested to see what would await them for the day. They neither neighed nor kicked. They just waited. And watched.

"Where do the horses come from?" Victor asked as he reached to stroke one's face.

"Approach like this," the old man said, indicating that Victor should approach from the side. "Don't want to spook her." He patted a black horse along her glossy neck. "Morning, Melba. You just get prettier every day, darling." He turned to Victor. "We get 'em from everywhere. Most folks just board here."

They roamed through the barn, swinging wide, slow steps. Victor placed his arms behind his back, too.

"For instance, my wife's oldest childhood friend boards ol' Freddy here." The man tapped his stall door. "And this one back here," he smiled and walked to the next one, "he was a rescue about ten years ago, I guess. Chip."

"For the color, huh?" Victor commented, smiling too.

"That's right. Name's really Chocolate Chip, but we cut it down a bit. Pretty, ain't he? Don't have any other one like him here. White. Brown spots." He patted his neck, too.

"Where'd you rescue him from?" Victor didn't move to the next stall but kept his eyes on Chip.

"Oh Lordy, years ago. Fire wiped out another stable not too far down the road." The man opened the stall door and began brushing the horse. "He was just a foal, somehow survived. They tell me they found him walking down 95 early on a Sunday."

"Wow!" Victor grinned. "Well, can I take him out?"

"Nah, son, my wife'll have my head. But you can come back later and talk to him. He likes talking. Loves it, in fact."

"I wouldn't take your head if somebody paid me to!" The man's wife, Marla, was beaming. Her green eyes set in crow's feet and round, pink cheeks shone like diamond light.

"Y'all done already?" her husband asked.

"Well, we didn't have to do the hard part, honey." Marla wiped her hands on her jeans and extended the right one to Victor. He shook it but clenched his jaw, imagining her hands plunged in cow afterbirth just minutes before.

"Hi!" Victor nodded. "I'm Vic. I was just telling your husband how gorgeous this place is."

"And he wanted to take Chip out." The old man straightened his back and lifted his overall straps with his thumbs. He winked at Victor.

"You pretty good with horses?" Marla looked Victor over. His loafered feet and fitted slacks and shirt signaled he was less country Florida and more flashy Florida. "Where you from?"

Victor smiled. "I wasn't planning on stopping by, or I'd be wearing jeans, too!" Marla giggled at her thoughts being exposed. "I'm from Maryland originally. But I did some training down at the medical school. Just drove down with my fiancée and decided to stop by this place while she's busy."

"Why?" the old man inquired.

"Looking to get one of these for her. I have a feeling she'd love Chip."

"Ah, he's not for sale. He's our boy." Marla smiled at the horse as if she'd borne him. "But you can take him out and talk to him. He loves talking." Her husband dropped his head to the side and pushed out both hands.

"Told ya."

Victor and Chip took the longest trail the two could find. The one where it seemed the cicadas sang more sweetly than anywhere else on the planet. And the trees made a canopy over fern-lined curves. Sunlight sprinkled down through the leaves to speckle the wooded floor. Every so often, light blue sky peeked through at them. Chip's brown eyes were large and soft and free.

And they did talk. Victor told him everything that led to their moment. Even about his father and the car. And even about the boy, Joey. Chip walked with a rhythmic bobbing head, as if he understood. That nodding head made Victor glad. He knew then it would be okay to slit Chip's throat and let him bleed out in the thick brush at the edge of the lake. He knew Chip would understand that, too. It wasn't that he hated the horse. How could he? He hated Summer, though, and knew she'd crumble seeing her tender Chocolate Chip, the lone horse survivor from her aunt's farm, slain in a heap at the back of the most perfect resting place anyone could hope to find.

So, when it was done, and the horse bucked and ran, then fell forward on his face into the coquina dust on the ground, Victor pulled out his camera and captured the two of them in a blood-soaked embrace. He'd become so enthralled in sending the photo to Summer and waiting for her response, he'd almost forgotten to think of a way off the farm that Marla and her man wouldn't notice. The one thing he was sure of, though, was that there were no human eyes watching him. And he figured there were probably no cameras in the trees.

"WE CAN'T CALL THE POLICE!" Summer's jeans swished as she rushed to the front door of the restaurant and out to her car. Tomas still held her phone. Carla stayed behind to thank the restaurant staff and prevent a scene from growing at the front door.

"Why the hell not?" Phoebe asked as they all gathered around Summer's car.

Summer peeked in the windows. She squatted to look around and under the car. Frantic. Just like how she felt at the hotel.

"What are you doing, T?" Phoebe continued. "Is there something wrong with the car?" Phoebe tapped it with her pink, square fingertips. "Why are you still talking to him anyway?"

Tomas's head snapped toward Phoebe. "Cut it out."

Phoebe placed her hands on her hips. "Yes, I know. You've got to defend your girlfriend." She shook her head. "T, I told you to stay the hell away from Victor. It's like you're begging for drama. I'm freaked out over this!"

"Phoebe, seriously." Tomas shook his head.

Phoebe leaned into his ear and whispered, "I love her just as much as you do, *Bebo*. She's my friend, too. I'm tired of playing games with this guy. He's already tried to ruin her life. Now what? Let him kill her?!"

"You guys, what's going on?" Carla approached the group, gathering her hair into her trademark low bun. Tomas held up the photo of Victor and the slain horse. She gasped, then read the accompanying text to the group:

This could be us, but you wanted to
go to Versailles tonight. I still love
you, baby, see you soon!

"¡Aye, *Dios mio*! He's crazy!" Carla spilled tears in a flash. "Did you know he was like this? Do your parents know what's going on?! He must've been here watching us!"

"It's so much worse than you guys know." Summer looked to Phoe-be, whose face had melted into a pool of compassion. "My parents know, but that's complicated. I think he's just trying to make me go into another fugue or scare me or whatever."

"I don't know," Luca said as he looked at the photo of Victor. The oral surgeon sat with his legs tucked under him, smiling broadly, like a five-year-old at his own birthday party. His eyes danced with excitement. "It looks like he's trying to do more than that. You need to be really care-ful, and you've got to go to the police."

Summer looked at Tomas. "Can I still stay with you tonight?"

Luca raised his eyebrows and slightly turned his head to say probably not.

"Of course," Tomas responded. "Let's go." He tossed his keys to Luca. "Can you guys figure out how to get my car to the house? I'm going to drive her car."

Phoebe reached to hug Summer before she sat in the passenger seat of her Camry.

"Guys, please call me with an update," Phoebe begged. Summer promised she would.

Summer and Tomas whipped through the tiny parking lot and onto the street. Tomas gripped the steering wheel and drummed it in quick pulses with the sides of his thumbs. Any time he came to a red light, he looked left, then right, and went.

"I'm sick of running from him," Summer shouted. "Let's go find him. I know exactly where that horse was boarded." She wanted to cry but refused.

"No, Summer!" Tomas exclaimed. "This is on a whole 'nother level now."

"So, what? Am I supposed to run from him for the rest of my life? Then wait for him to come slit my throat, too?"

Tomas didn't respond. Outside his condo, he pulled her out of the car, and they sprinted to the elevators. He pushed her inside and took a breath once the door to his place closed.

"Just 'cause we're here doesn't mean we're safe, now, *Bebo*."

"I know that, Summer, but I couldn't think outside with everybody standing there. At least I know you're okay right now. And we can breathe and figure out what to do."

"I wish I had a gun." Summer stood in front of the kitchen.

"Summer…" Tomas started.

"What?" she responded. "I have the right to defend myself."

"Yeah, defend yourself. But going to hunt someone down isn't self-defense."

"In this situation, I'd disagree."

"I don't think any judge would see it your way." Tomas came and stood inches from Summer's face.

"What are you doing, *Bebo*?" Summer replied. She was silenced by the deep stare and glint in his eye.

"I love you, Summer, and I'm not going to lose you."

She closed her eyes to try to slow her thoughts of self-defense. Of revenge. Summer pressed her fingers into her cheeks, took a deep breath, and focused on his face. In her mind, a flash of nighttime on a driveway exploded into view. Lavender lace. Peach tulips. Golden gravel. The sound of a saxophone and a singer. When she opened her eyes again, Tomas was still gazing down at her. She slid her fingertips to the nape of Tomas's neck. He pushed his glasses up into his hair, and she reached to kiss him. Surrendered to his embrace, Summer realized she had glimpsed their last night together. It was the only waking moment memory she had been able to access from her lost year in the fugue.

"I love you, too," she finally whispered. Tomas lifted her from the floor and carried her to his bedroom. He laid her across his bed.

"I'll be right back," he said and disappeared into his bathroom.

Summer strained to keep pulling more scenes from the last time she was in his bed. She remembered the valets at the Seaside 46 lobby door. She remembered lying in bed in purples and blues. And holding his hand… she remembered always holding Tomas's hand. She let a smile ease onto her lips and tears roll back into her hair. She'd always rejected his love because it was perfect, and she could never quite feel worthy of it. Victor's abuse and disdain and general indifference to her had felt deserved, and so she took it and made a nest of it. Lying in Tomas's bed, though, she carved a niche in her heart for his love—a treasure she finally felt deserving enough to hold. A vibration shook her out of her decision to coalesce.

"¡*Bebo*! Your phone's ringing."

"Answer it!" he called from the bathroom.

"Oh, it just went to voice mail." Summer could tell by the beep. She climbed to the nightstand and pushed the voicemail icon.

"Yeah, um, Tomas, it's Mair. Just returning your call. Sorry, it took me so long to get back to you. I hope you're okay. I miss you."

Tomas came to stand with one foot over the threshold of the bathroom door.

"No, no, no, no!" He began to yell. Every no was a prayer. But prayers of that sort were doomed before uttered. Summer swiped her keys and bags from the corner chair and ran out the front door.

37

MY PINK DRESS. My father. My man. My day. My dinner. My best friend. My one love. Take it all, Mair. You won't be happy until you take it all. The door to the stairs did not creak. It did not slam closed. The only sounds were of Summer's bare feet slapping down two flights of white stairs in Tomas's building and the thoughts in her head. When she reached the thirty-first floor, she turned into an open elevator and pressed her back against the mirrored wall.

There's no way, she thought. *There's absolutely no way Bebo would do something with Mair behind my back. I should go back upstairs.* As she began to lift herself off the wall, the door closed, and the elevator took her down, down, down.

"Great," Summer sighed and rolled her eyes on the ride downstairs. She turned her back to the door to look at herself in the mirror. "Geez, Summer," she said, "you look rough." She began picking white flecks of gel from the edges of her hairline. The elevator's bell dinged. She stepped closer to the floor selection buttons. If the floor was empty, she would press the buttons to go right back up to Tomas on the thirty-third floor. The doors opened to the empty lobby. Empty except for Victor.

Victor shoved Summer into the corner of the elevator, then pushed the "close" button behind him. Though she was too scared to scream, he held her mouth closed. The man at the desk was singing with his head leaning back. He had not seen them. Victor's finger pads pulled ashen stripes on Summer's arm. He thrust a thin needle into her supple brown skin. He injected a shot of the fast-acting sedative Versed to her shoulder. They heard another elevator ding and rumbling Spanish. It was Tomas. Victor kept his finger on the "close" button and signaled to Summer to keep quiet.

"You know he's going to look for me," Summer whispered to Victor when he dropped his hand from her mouth. Her voice shook. Her face shook—and she hated herself for it. "He's going to call my mom or friends or the police or someone, and they'll come look for me."

"You're right," Victor breathed the smell of ammonia into her face. "But where we're going, they won't think to look for you."

Tomas's voice faded. Then it returned. And the elevator went ding. They did not hear him again. *His car*, Summer remembered. *He doesn't have his car.* She kept silent. Victor let the elevator doors open. They briskly walked past the guard and valets outside in the parking lot. Her eyes crossed. *That injection is working already.* Terror gripped her chest.

"What did you give me?" Summer asked. Victor opened the back door of his car and pushed her in with both hands to her ribs. The valets noticed. The valets watched. But since there had been no tip given, the valets did nothing.

"Shut up, Summer." Victor's blood-soiled slacks sat spread-legged on his seat.

"What was it?!" she tried to demand. Her eyes crossed. *Don't lie down.*

"Where are we going?" she tried again.

"First, for sushi on Biscayne." Victor laughed. "Don't worry, just take out 'cause I'm not dressed for date night. It'll be quick."

One big, deep breath. Sleep. It was coming. *Look out the window. What do you see?* Blink. *Don't fall asleep. What do you see?*

Summer's shoulder inched closer to the seat until she was lying on top of a seatbelt buckle. It nestled into her collarbone. She couldn't wake to move. Victor turned on NPR. He pressed his forefinger to his lips and dropped his ear to one side. The topic was Charles Darwin and floating asparagus. Vegetables voyaging across the sea. Victor laughed as he pulled into Sushi Siam's parking lot. Three men stood closed in around a woman in a tank-style red-sequined dress. The back revealed two circles for the cheeks of her behind. Biscayne Boulevard. The sketchy part.

"Let's balance you out," Victor muttered. Summer mustered up all her strength, and yet her body lay limp. More Versed. To the other shoulder. "Just for good measure." Victor whispered, "Isn't it ironic, Summer? Tonight, when we're all done, maybe I'll make you a vegetable, too. Now you won't float. But it could be fun to be paralyzed while you're drowning. Blissful. I'm gonna get the sushi." He stuck one leg out of the car door but turned back. "Oh, babe, I didn't get you a roll. You're getting ready to die, though, so I hope you understand."

He took her purse from her lap to pull out her phone. "You didn't even try to call anyone?" Victor shook his head. "Wow! You're more pathetic than I thought." A black strap. From her black purse. He unlatched it and tied it around her hands. "We'll just use this for now as a little security. I'll make it a necklace for you later." Victor winked, then patted her on the head. No one seemed to notice him binding a girl in the back seat of his car. "Be right back!"

Summer's eyelids lay over her pupils. Her bottom incisors peeked in front of her top lip. Inside, her will pushed against her sedated body. But it was too heavy. It would not lift. It would not go.

The door opened. She did not move. It slammed closed. She could not move. Bumpy parking lot. Dusty gravel. Back onto some road. Her ringing phone sounded muddled in her sleepiness.

"Tommy boy, you're always a day late and a dollar short," Victor giggled into her phone, putting it on speaker.

"Put her on the phone," Tomas's voice growled. "I've already called the police."

"Yeah? And what they'd say? Let me guess. She's an adult and can go wherever she damn well pleases?" Victor taunted him.

"Don't worry about it. Let me talk to Summer," Tomas demanded.

"Nope," Victor said, laughing, and hung up.

Victor turned up NPR. "Summer, you really ought to listen to this. They have a whole segment on film. Well, you're into movies. You're not sophisticated enough for film. I don't know what it is with you. Well, maybe it's the adoption thing. I guess you can't outclass your gene pool."

Thirty minutes. Still driving, but then the car veered and stopped. There were horns blown. But it was Miami. Horns were always being blown. Summer opened her eyes, fighting heavy blinks.

"Summer, as long as I can keep you comfortable." Victor pulled out a prepared syringe and a shining silver needle. "That's all that matters. Comfortable, but not dead. I don't want you to stop breathing. We still have a ways to go before we get there. At least another hour." Victor was silent for several moments. Summer waited for another injection, but it did not come. She felt the car wobble over roadside gravel and debris. Back on the road, again.

Summer slept. Mental scenes passed. Silver skies and black branches. Singing birds. Dancers. A boy. Black hair. Pink lips. Dimples. White coats. Call rooms. Patients in seclusion. Patients in restraint. Like her. Like Summer restrained by chemicals and a purse strap in this backseat.

She dreamt.

Summer saw herself as a little girl in a neighborhood. It was shaded with lush trees. A wooden house, smaller than all the rest, sat on the corner. Robin Read Road sat in front of her. She stared at the stop sign. Summer wasn't sure how she ended up in the basement, but she knew it was odd for a Florida beach home to have one. She stood at the basement doors and saw an expanse of rooms unfolding before her. The home was full inside. A meeting. An angry one. Adults looked at her as she walked in. She was told to go and find her father. She climbed on her bike and tried to find her father. Street after street after street. Block after block. Endless roads of trying to find him. Finally, she came upon an old man, homeless. Urine-stained and black, crouched down, round-backed, like a turtle. She looked over him. Her father embraced Mair in the shadows. She heard a voice ask, "Why are you here?" She told it, "Watching them." Then there was nothing. And she floated in that nothingness, unsure if she was still alive.

"Summer!" Victor's voice abruptly danced with enthusiasm. "We're here!" She did not respond.

"Summer!" He repeated it. "Wake up! You're going to miss it. It's gonna be like fireworks. Kind of."

Victor crept beside a building. In the dark. Flagstone. Ivy. Three small stairs to rocking chairs. A glass kitchen wall. Victor pressed his fingers against the sliding door. It was the back door of 111 Crystal Cove.

38

"SUMMER!" A hushed rendition of her name wasn't enough to make her eyes open. "Are you okay?" Victor held his ear to her lips. He waited for a breath. Her cheek pressed against the car seat. Her mouth opened to a pool of saliva. The black tank top she wore twisted over her right breast. A small roll of flesh peeked from the waist of her jeans.

"You're okay," Victor hissed, wrapping his thumbs at the tops of her bare, dirt-speckled feet. He pressed his fingers in and leaned his weight back and down. Summer's body shifted to the right. The seatbelt buckle wedged itself deeper. Each tug shifted gravel pebbles from beneath his feet. Summer dropped onto the floor of the car, her left arm pinned above her head. The bang of her forehead into the door's panel pocket startled Victor but did not rouse her. Neither did rolling gravel spinning up and out from her limp body as he dragged her to the backyard. Nor did the three small collisions her occiput encountered on the way up the stairs. She did not flinch at the third one, the one that cut a two-and-a-half-inch laceration into the back of her head.

"I thought you were a dancer now," Victor chuckled. "You're heavy as hell." He dropped her heels from the height of his waist. They bounced against the floor. Victor noticed the streak of blood. It had smeared from the threshold of the door. He pressed her head to the left.

"Oh my God, Summer. So high maintenance. Now you have a scalp lac I need to sew up." Victor straddled Summer's chest, sitting up on his knees. He was covered in horse's blood. "Wake up!" he shrieked into her face, slapping it just over her cheek.

Victor pressed his behind into Summer's abdomen. He clamped four glistening teeth into his lip and drummed his fingers on the crest of his knees. After three seconds, he lifted himself and stood over her. With rapid, light footsteps he ran across the floor. Summer waited until she heard the glass door slide open. Her eyelashes snapped up as she opened her eyes. She had decided after the last dose of Versed outside the sushi restaurant to feign sleep. She knew another injection could be enough to kill her.

HIS CAR HELD A TORTURE KIT. He'd built it after his visit to Chip. Victor beamed a closed-mouth grin thinking of his cleverness. He'd brought Flumazenil, the antidote to reverse the effects of the sedative he had given her. Just in case. He planned horrors. He wanted her to be awake to experience them all. He also stashed razors, zip ties, dental elevators, and a chisel. They sat overlapped at the base of a plastic bag in a rolling cooler. The bag was tucked beside a large rope, garbage bags, a cinder block, and ankle weights. He pulled the cooler out from the front seat, cupped the black handle at the crease of his left palm and lurched forward. Before turning up the back porch, he looked out onto the night's settled black ocean. He inhaled until his chest crested like a bird, then released his breath. His face curved into a joyous smile.

It took two hands to lift the cooler onto the back porch. He arched his back and turned to the kitchen. Victor's bottom teeth protruded forward when his eyes fell on an empty kitchen floor.

"Summer!" he shouted into the house. "Stop your foolishness!"

Victor left the cooler sitting just in front of the glass door. Summer's silver ring glistened near the third kitchen island. In his hand, the ring sparkled as if mocking him. He searched the island, the back of the kitchen, and the living room by the niche. Nothing. He came back to the kitchen and opened each cabinet. Nothing. He stepped back to where she'd lain and looked for a blood trail but saw just a pool of it, that pointed into an amorphous blob where she'd painstakingly lifted her head.

He opened the closet door beside the stairs in the kitchen. Nothing. He slapped the top corner of the gold-framed Juan De Pareja portrait that adorned the hallway to the living room. The first painting of a Spanish-born African, his features mirrored Summer's. Except for the eyes. De Pareja did not have her green eyes.

Victor peeked into the living room. It waited in still and silent white. The shattered mirror had been removed. The whole debacle of Summer's emergence from Therese had been erased.

"Summer!" he said scowling, pressing his top teeth into his bottom ones. "I'm not going to play your little asinine games." He stopped. He waited. Shuffling. Back by the stairs. Behind the first curve of the spiral staircase, Summer was attempting to scramble through a three-foot utility door.

"Dammit!" Victor shouted. "I'm getting tired of having to grab your..." he reached down for Summer's left calf, "...dirty feet." With her free limbs, she clawed into the cabinet, then slapped the tile as he pulled her out. Her skin was moist enough to drag a high-pitched squeak across the floor.

"Victor!" she panted. "I don't know what I ever did to you."

"Nothing really," he panted back, grabbing for her moving body parts. "I did have to pretend to love you. I feel like that was a lot to ask. I mean, your real mom couldn't even do it."

His words cut deeper than the slice in the back of her head. "I'm going to get myself out of here," Summer protested. "And when I do, everyone's going to find out what you did to that kid."

"How?" Victor chuckled, stood upright, and stopped struggling. "From Agent Marvin Cline? And his fake-ass video?" Summer looked up

Victor's nostrils, then tried to flip onto her belly again. He pressed his foot between her breasts, pinning her to the floor. "Him?!" Victor demanded.

"You know, I was worried about him at first, too, Summer." Victor laughed. "But then your dad told me he's just one of your mom's patients. One that comes to her little office in the back of the house. He's not an investigator! He's completely psychotic." Victor's face turned pink, and he struggled to breathe through his snickering. "He got court-ordered to your mom years ago for acting out on delusions and stalking chicks around the city. He's not even really on the neighborhood watch. Never was." Victor knelt and pressed the tip of his nose into Summer's. She lay still and stared into Victor's eyes just inches from her face. "Did he give you one of those homemade business cards? They look so legit, right? I know. He got me, too. His name's John Barker, though. Lives with his rich, ninety-year-old mom, supposedly."

"You're a liar, Vic!" Summer shouted. "He found me when I went missing."

"Did you miss the part where I said he's a stalker? He can find anyone. Ask your dad. He'll tell you." Victor walked to the kitchen for something from his cooler. "It's a little surreal," he said when he returned. "Being buddies with your dad."

"Both of you are going to end up in prison."

"You want your dad to go to prison?! Hmm. For what?"

"Rape!" she shouted.

He lifted her to her feet and trotted her stumbling to the living room. The stiff cushions of the first love seat slammed into her neck as Victor pushed her into it. Her hand swatted the air as she tried to scratch his face.

"Do you want more Versed?!" Victor snarled.

"Victor," a voice spoke low and quiet from the open glass door. The heavy clunk of red wedge shoes on the kitchen floor froze him into place. To his left, Victor saw her. "That's enough." She stood with her feet apart. She removed her green trench coat. She wore a pleated calf-length yellow dress.

Summer attempted to push herself up and out at the sound of her mother's voice but collapsed one step from the seat's cushion. Dara stooped at Summer's side and swiped her hair over her right ear. Victor's jaw dropped as his eyes danced around the room. Sound stuttered and stopped from his hollow mouth. Cool air dried his palate as he sucked in shallow breaths in staccato. His hands trembled, and his bowels rumbled.

Dara clung to a slim, oversized square briefcase in her right hand. "Summer, stand up, slowly." Dara's tears spilled. She gathered her daughter's bloody hair in her hands as she helped lift her by the arm. "You're okay, baby girl. Walk to the door. Let's go." She braced Summer with each unsteady step she took.

Dara walked to the front door. Except for the sound of Dara's shoes, there was not a single sound in the home. Victor's chest rattled with uncoordinated breaths. He jumped down the three steps into the hallway and landed a foot shy of Dara's back. Air from his mouth blew her hair about her pale, wrinkled neck. "Keep walking, Summer," she said and closed her out on the front porch.

Spinning slowly on the balls of her feet, Dara turned face-to-face with Victor. The tap of her middle finger to his forehead sounded like a heavy thud in his ears.

"Victor, wake up," she said. His eyelashes fluttered. She took the silver ring from his hand and shoved the briefcase into his chest. He folded at his waist with a breath from the pit of his belly. He looked around himself, unable to recognize the home or even his own hands before his face. Dara gripped the door behind her and walked out, still staring into his dazed eyes.

39

"SUMMER, HURRY, SWEETIE, let's get in the car." Dara trotted down onto the ivy-covered porch and wrapped her hands around Summer's petite waist. She threaded her daughter into the passenger door and ran around to the driver's side, dropping Summer's ring into the cup holder beside her.

"Mom, are you okay?" Summer's eyes had widened. "Did he threaten you? He's really a psychopath, Mom!" she cried.

"He is, baby girl. Kind of…" Dara paused. "…and that's probably because of me."

Summer's sobs delayed the processing of her mother's words.

"What?" Summer finally responded, trying to catch her stuttered breath.

"No one just ends up like that, Summer. Something has to happen. To Victor, I'm that thing that happened." Dara's eyes appeared almost black in the night, except in the headlights of passing cars. Then they were ice blue and transparent. Her yellow dress billowed onto the steering wheel as she leaned forward.

"Mom, what do you mean?" Summer still struggled to settle her breath.

"I should have told her." Dara shook her head with vigor. Her red bob flew like feathers around her face. "Her name was Angie Jacobs. Victor's mother. She owned the cutest little bakery downtown. Sold me a croissant and coffee every morning of residency." Dara shook her head again.

"What do you mean, Victor's mother? Told her what?" Summer shifted her behind in her seat, trying to follow the story. She turned to face Dara.

"That I was too tired to take them home. But the bakery was right next to the hospital and not far from my place. Five minutes at the most." Dara's foot tapped the car's gas pedal.

Summer turned her body forward but left her eyes on Dara. A growing knot developed low in her belly. She waited.

"Vic was so cute as a little boy, Summer. And he was a gregarious little guy. He'd always have stories for me when I came into the bakery. And he'd want to tell me about his toy cars. He'd always say, 'Well, my mom says if I'm a good boy, I'm gonna get a new Hot Wheels.'"

Summer listened. "You've known Victor since he was little?!" she wanted to scream. She did not, though.

"You know how tired you are after being on an overnight call, Summer? Working over thirty hours straight?" Dara slapped the steering wheel. "We didn't even have hour limits when I was a resident. You got worked right into the ground at night, had to stay there to do morning rounds, then more scutwork all afternoon. Ridiculous."

"Yeah," Summer replied, the word creeping through her lips.

"That afternoon, Angie wanted to close the shop early. She wanted to get home to make a cake for Vic's birthday. 'Hey, Dr. D, can you give us a ride?' That's what she said. Victor climbed in the backseat, talking a mile a minute about his birthday cake, playing with a little car. Angie was in the front. And we were almost home. But I realized I had forgotten my pager at the hospital…" Dara paused as she gripped her forehead. "…just had to run right back for a second—a quick second. I tried to make a U-turn. But the streets were wet, and the car spun." She blew out a heavy breath. "I tried not to hit anyone, Summer! But we crashed into a wall. Over at Westminster cemetery. You know where I'm talking about?"

Summer nodded.

"Mom?" Summer's heart had been sinking, and she interrupted to make it stop. Dara ignored her. She turned the car around and drove back toward the house, still talking.

"And she died that afternoon. And he saw his mom dead in the car. Right in front of him. Because of me. And I just couldn't live with it. I'd lived with too much already with your father and his... his ways." Dara's voice began to crescendo.

Where are we going? Summer wondered as the same homes they'd just passed came back into view.

"You mean what Dad did to Aunt Libby?" Summer whispered. The pit in her belly was turning to a surge of panic.

"Manny never did anything to Libby," Dara snapped. "Your father wouldn't lay a finger on anyone unless they threatened his family. It's what he did to me. That he had slept with my sister behind my back for months and then ended up with this beautiful baby. I had already bragged to all of Miami that he was mine! How was I supposed to..." Dara's mouth caved into a deep C-shape as tears spilled onto her cheeks.

"Deal with it?" Summer offered.

"Right, Summer! How was I supposed to deal with it?! When she got pregnant, I lied to your grandmother. I told her he forced himself on Libby. She made Libby put Mair up for adoption... well, to give her to the Kents. Libby was devastated. At first, I didn't even care."

"But mom, the diary. It said—"

"Wow, you really bought that?!" Dara shook her head, exasperated. "I thought I raised you to be a little less gullible. I knew you would find it. I thought for sure you'd think it over, though. Aunt Libby and I don't have that much of an age gap, Summer. She couldn't have been sixteen or seventeen."

"What do you mean?" Summer shouted.

"It was obviously fake, Summer! C'mon. Do you really think I'd be married to a man who raped my sister?! I put that chart there and told you to read it so Daddy wouldn't be quite so perfect in your eyes—"

"I don't remember you telling me to read it," Summer interrupted.

"Of course you don't remember me telling you! That's how subliminal messages work. Do you remember finding a sticky note on your bedroom door two days ago that said—"

"It said you were going to Delaware," Summer interrupted again.

"Right, for what?"

"I don't know—I figured another workshop!"

"It said as plain as day, 'I'm so stressed. Gotta go read some charts,' right?" Dara scowled. "And what did you do, with your stressed little self, Summer? You went directly to my office, snooped around, and read charts. Baby girl, you've always been so suggestible." Dara sighed.

Summer's breathing was rapid. "But you and Aunt Libby told me it was true! What's going on?"

"What do you mean 'what's going on?' I'm telling you what happened. And you probably saw 'Agent Cline's' chart, too, but didn't realize it. I can understand how you'd miss that one. His real name's John Barker. Loyal patient," Dara chuckled. A wave of nausea lifted into Summer's throat. "He's helped me a ton," Dara said, still laughing.

Summer noticed her hand was bruised and pulsing as she brought it to cover her mouth. *Victor was telling the truth*, she thought.

"Anyway, I couldn't live with the mess I'd made out of Vic and Mair's lives." Dara looked again at Summer. "That's understandable, right?"

Summer could hear her breath passing through her nose.

"This is all Manny's fault, anyway. If he hadn't been messing around with Libby, there'd be no Mair. I would have stayed in Miami. And I would've never met Angie and Vic." Dara suddenly sobbed.

Summer's last tears dried, though, and the whites of her eyes cooled. Her mother's story and labile emotions put her attention on keen alert. "Did you do something to Victor, mom?"

"I did, honey. I did." Dara's speech raced. "I know it's not ethical to hypnotize a little kid. Not the way I did it. But he needed to forget."

Summer looked out the foggy, rain-spattered window and swiped her right forearm against it.

"What did you do?" Summer asked. The road was familiar and black. It ran in front of the wide, sparkling lake Summer loved.

"It wasn't meant to go as far as it did," Dara pleaded for understanding. "It was just supposed to help Vic forget the accident. And it was so easy that day. He was already stunned. His little yellow toy car and the sound of a fan were all it took to put him under. Fans work on everyone, though.

"After the accident, I started to realize I needed Victor. He could help me. I wondered if I left him hypnotized if he could help me make things right for myself. Turns out I could. That's how he's lived his whole life. Tranced. Well, up until a few minutes ago. Any cluster of symbols and sounds he was programmed to respond to, he did. He didn't even recognize me until he saw this dress today.

"I know it sounds bad," Dara continued, "but it was all to get justice. People like your dad, and anyone else who had used me, made me look stupid, they needed to get their karma. Like Leslie Chae, for instance. I knew the situation would eventually present itself for him to—"

"Leslie Chae?" Summer interrupted. "The mom of that kid? Why?"

"I'll tell you why, Summer!" Dara scoffed. "End of med school. She's in my class. I want to be a dermatologist. She wants to be a dermatologist. We both want to get into this program in Maryland." Dara looked at Summer. "We interview for the derm residency spot, and they give me the Golden Handshake. Tell me I'm definitely in the program." Dara pushed her hair behind her ear with her forefinger.

"But turns out I don't get the spot. Find out at Match Day Leslie stole it. She stole my residency spot, Summer! I thought women were supposed to look out for each other!" Dara put her forehead onto the steering wheel and sped up.

"Mom, sit up!" Summer lifted Dara back.

Dara continued, "No other derm program in the entire country had a spot for me. I didn't want to sit out a year and already had a place in

Baltimore, so I had to find another specialty. I had to settle for psychiatry. I never wanted to be a shrink!" Dara began crying again. "So, while she was living the life I should have had as a derm resident, I had to go to a program I had no interest in. Eventually, I had to see her bopping through the hospital whenever we needed a derm consult on the psych unit," Dara hissed.

"But the day I noticed she was pregnant was one of the best days of my life." Dara grinned and looked out her window. "I started working on Vic right away because I knew the time would one day come to, uh, get even. To balance things out. And it took a while, but it did—when I ran into her at the grocery store last year and she asked if I knew a good oral surgeon for her son."

Another wave of nausea washed over Summer.

"But, Summer, for the record..." silvery mucous drained from Dara's nose as she changed subjects, "...I tried to make things right where I could. I paid for Vic's education. I thought maybe I could get him and Mair together. She was so enamored with him after she met him at school. That's why I *had* to have her interrupt your engagement dinner party. I hope you understand."

"Mom..." Summer rubbed her head in disbelief. Her fingers found the blood in her hair. "...where are we going?" They looped back toward the lake again. Dara did not respond. She stared into the darkness. Summer rolled down her window, slid her fingers to the base of her seatbelt, and pulled it tight against her chest.

"Was there anyone else, Mom?" Summer kept up the conversation as she wondered how she could get out of the car. "Anyone else you thought made you look defective, like Leslie?"

"Of course! Victor's father, for one! Used me for sex after Angie died. I considered leaving your father for him, honestly. I mean, we were involved for a whole year. And that gave me access to Vic, which was a plus. But then out of the blue, poof, no calls, no visits." Dara began to sob until she coughed, and then a laugh erupted.

"But things are still falling into place. And Manny's finally going to get what he deserves for trying to ruin Vic and Mair's relationship. Imagine the nerve of him to try to replace her with you!" Dara laughed again. "How could he think I wouldn't find out what he was up to?"

"Where is Dad?" Summer shifted again in her seat. She looked down at her shaking hands. Her heart raced. She tried to appear calm. Questions swirled through her mind.

"He'll probably land at the Miami Airport any minute. I've already called him to say you've been killed in a car accident."

Summer's head snapped up. "Mom!"

Dara's foot slammed the gas pedal to the floor. "I never wanted to be a shrink, and I never wanted to be stuck with you!" she screamed. "Adopting you was just one more way for Manny to embarrass me. 'Oh, look at my barren wife!' Why, Summer?! Why does he always have to rub you in my face?! And give you every single thing you've ever wanted—including Victor?!" She slapped the steering wheel with both hands. "That bastard is always trying to undermine me!"

"Mom!" Summer shouted.

In the blackness of the night, the car went bounding over a cracked curb like a streak of lightning shot sideways. The two lifted and dropped over the unplowed earth of tall grasses and mounds of dirt. Dara veered toward the largest tree her headlights could find. Summer's hands waited until the strike seemed inevitable and then yanked the wheel hard to the right, sending the car flipping into the still lake waiting below them. Summer's head slammed into the window. With a splash, the two landed on the lake's surface. The car dropped lower moment by moment.

I knew it would sound like this. Under this water. I'm drowning. And I think I'm sleeping, too. My Havana abuela is dressed in fluorescent white. She's at the bottom of this lake smoking a cigar. She smells of prayers wrapped in Florida Water cologne. And she still wears her colorful, beaded necklaces for the spirits' protection. When I was three, before they took me and I never saw her again, I loved hugging her bosom like a pillow. She pointed to shells on a straw mat and told me my true mother was the water. I'm not so sure. Could I be drowning in my mother, with my mother? I've got to wake up and get myself out of here. My chest feels like it's going to explode.

Underwater, Summer opened her eyes. Dara's appeared stuck in a startled gaze. Her frantic waving arms slowed to a graceful dance, grabbing for Summer's help. Bubbles escaped her mouth one after the next. Summer still held her seatbelt with her right hand. She pressed the release with her thumb and fought the resistance of the water to float toward the surface of the lake. Her arms lifted over her head as she tilted herself out of the window, the water embracing and pulling her to air. Her right leg snagged and jerked her back into place. She looked down to see Dara's glaring pale fingers in a death grip around her ankle. Summer kicked and thrashed, blinking slowly, drowsily, between movements. Dara grimaced and gripped tighter, laughing.

Summer did not understand why she suddenly heard birdsong and violin, but she forced her feet together. Dara's hand slipped to the arch of her foot, then to her toe ring, as Summer rotated her legs like a corkscrew, spinning with the pointed toes Therese had used to dance Nikiya. She left her bloody toe ring in Dara's dying hand as she floated over the weight of the water, pulling herself to the ragged edge of the lake. Summer climbed over dirt to sit gasping in the grass. She wondered how she would make her way back to Tomas. But first, she would wait for Dara to drown—submerged in lake waters, revenge, and feigned love.

EPILOGUE
ONE YEAR LATER

THESE WOOD-PANELED WALLS and laminate-floored hallways feel different in some way, now. They're still ugly. I still catch the wafting stench of urine. My arm remembers being gripped and pressed. That left a bruise last time. Everything looks the same, but me. I know I look nicer. I'm showered. I'm wearing my own clothes. Tomas and I picked out a navy suit for me to wear today. A skirt suit, with three buttons down the top. Nothing that would reveal any cleavage. None, at all. In fact, it's plain except for the tiniest rhinestones beside the buttons on the cuff. I thought they matched my engagement ring well. Tomas thought they were small enough to be okay, not too flashy. We agreed I should wear pearls. Either earrings, a necklace, or both. 'Cause women who wear pearls to court always seem more believable for some reason. Tomas's mother said she'd hoped she'd be putting the pearls on me for my wedding, but that they could make an early debut for today. That made me smile. Made me feel a little less anxious. I know I look nicer this time, but that's not what's changed.

The courtroom buzzes. Four lawyers sit at tables shuffling papers and putting their reading glasses on and off. Two bailiffs precariously balance themselves on tiny folding chairs beside the door. They leave their radios turned up just high enough for an irritating, crackling static to be heard. It almost reminds me of the sound of a fly's wings.

And there are microphones on curved black stands. Everywhere. On every ugly wooden table, stenographer desk, and podium. There are two where the judge sits. And on the witness stand. It's empty right now, the witness stand. I sort of wish it would stay that way. That we could all say, "You know what, forget it. This is all a mistake. Unnecessary. Let's just go back home." Of course I know we can't. I can't. It's just a wish. My stomach rumbles as loud as a bowling alley in my ears. I hope I don't throw up.

There's a woman with feathered brown hair and too much eyeliner at the prosecution's table. Her figure has disappeared inside her black suit. All you notice are her maroon nails—and her downturned lips that settle into a squared jaw. I know everyone here suspects something of me. Looking at her, what I suspect is that her scowl is permanent. I've decided she's in charge over there, at that table. Regardless of her rank. I think at some point in this process, she's going to come after me.

"All rise!" Light shines off the bald head of the man to the right of the room. His desk name plate says something about being a marshal. I can't see it all from where I'm sitting. His face is calm, but his body sways behind hands folded in front of his waist. I wonder if he's like me—nervous. Chairs scuff the floor as the legal teams swiftly stand to greet the judge.

"Honestly, Summer, you don't have to testify." Manuel Martinez has been very much into giving me fatherly advice lately. I take it all with the largest grains of salt I can swallow. I still don't know the truth about him and his motives. Besides, his latest legal advice didn't quite line up with what the defense team hoped I would do. They admitted it might be a risk. That it was unusual for sure. But they wanted me on that stand, come hell or high water.

He's insisted on coming to any legal meetings I have. I don't balk at it, but I wish I could have my fiancé with me instead. I'm never angry at Tomas for not being here when he just can't. Doctors make sacrifices people never imagine. He has to work. He's setting up our future. My father, on the other hand, oddly seems to be setting up a future of sorts, too.

The team meetings had been going well. But this week there's been an issue. Another lawyer scuffle over admissible evidence. The same thing happened in my case. So many arguments over the lack of admissible evidence the whole thing was eventually dismissed. Even though I couldn't give account for myself on August 27th, 2005, the problem for the prosecution was neither could they. But this is not my case. This is another case entirely.

Her briefcase—well the things inside it, they've caused a problem. I've struggled to know what to call Dara Clemens since the night she tried to drive us into a tree. Often, I avoid referring to her at all. But that robs me of the right to talk about my memories. I did have some good ones, and neutral ones, and important memories, too. I can't let her steal them all.

One thing I do remember about her is that briefcase. It went wherever she did. She even had it that night. That night I thought she was coming to rescue me. It was always impossibly thin, and I never saw what was inside. But it seems whatever has been recovered from it is a jackpot for the defense. Well, that, and me. They need me to testify. So, while I can do little about my indifference to their predicament, and defendant, they snagged me with the promise.

"Summer, we promise," they said, "if you testify, we'll go over every single, solitary thing in the briefcase. No secrets, nothing off limits."

"When?" I asked them, just to be sure.

"During your testimony. We promise."

"The judge is going to allow that?"

"Yes," they nodded in their almost-matching gray suits, "once it's introduced into evidence, witnesses can interact with it in as much detail as they need to. Right up close."

My agreement to testify is not out of love, compulsion, guilt, or a magnanimous heart. It's simply curiosity. The desire to truly know Dara Clemens is what's calling me to the witness stand. Tomas and I have rehearsed what I should say once I'm up there. We've practiced in person, over the phone, and on Skype when we had to.

"*Please raise your right hand,*" he says, imitating a television lawyer, I assume. I do it. He tells me to state my name. And spell it, too.

"*Dr. Summer Clemens-Martinez,*" I say. I always refuse to spell it. I do promise to tell the truth, the whole truth, and nothing but the truth, though. And we sometimes stumble on the next part, but we've gotten it nailed for today—or whenever they call me to testify.

"*And how do you know the defendant?*" Tomas asks, part serious, part casual-confident.

"*Dr. Victor Jacobs used to be my boyfriend,*" I say, "*and later, under my mother's instruction, he tried to kill me.*" I'm not sure that's what the defense wants me to say. But I will anyway.

If Dara is what happened to Victor, I want to know what, or who, happened to her. Dara's secrets will all eventually tumble out from behind her locked doors, and bookshelves, and suspicious workshops. And when they do, I want to be there to hear them. Every last one.

Follow Natasha Jeneen Thomas

to keep up with new developments in the *Family Medicine* series.

Visit https://www.natashajeneenthomas.com or scan the QR code below for series updates and to enjoy free blog posts, poetry, and more.

Connect with Natasha on social media...

Instagram: @NatashaJeneenThomasAuthor

Facebook: @NatashaJeneenThomasAuthor

Twitter: @JeneenAuthor

CPSIA information can be obtained
at www.ICGtesting.com
Printed in the USA
BVHW071528091121
621183BV00009B/510/J